Caffeine

Snatched From Home

Graham Smith

Fiction aimed at the heart and
the head...

Published by Caffeine Nights Publishing 2015

CONDITIONS OF SALE

Published in Great Britain by

Caffeine Nights Publishing
4 Eton Close
Walderslade
Chatham
Kent
ME5 9AT

www.caffeine-nights.com
www.caffeinenightsbooks.com

British Library Cataloguing in Publication Data.
A CIP catalogue record for this book is available from the British Library

ISBN: 978-1-907565-90-8

Cover design by
Mark (Wills) Williams

Everything else by
Default, Luck and Accident

To Helen and Daniel. I could never have achieved this without your support.

Graham Smith is a joiner by trade who has built bridges, dug drains and worked on large construction sites before a career change saw him become the general manager of a busy hotel and wedding venue on the outskirts of Gretna Green. A crime fiction fan from the age of eight, he swaps the romance of weddings for the dark world of crime fiction whenever time allows.

He has been a reviewer for the well respected crime fiction site www.crimesquad.com for four years and has conducted face to face interviews with many stellar names, including Lee Child, David Baldacci, Dennis Lehane, Jeffrey Deaver, Peter James & Val McDermid.

Before turning his hand to novel writing, he was published in several Kindle anthologies including True Brit Grit, Off the Record 2: At the Movies, Action Pulse Pounding Tales: Vol 1 & 2 Graham has three collections of short stories out on Kindle. They are Eleven the Hardest Way (long-listed for a SpineTingler Award), Harry Charters Chronicles and Gutshots: Ten Blows to the Abdomen.

Away from work and crime fiction, Graham enjoys spending time with his wife and son, socialising and watching far too much football.

Recommendations for Graham Smith

Peter James – Author of the Roy Grace series
"...a talented story-teller."

Zoe Sharp –Author of the Charlie Fox novels
".....fast-paced and intriguing. It kept me turning the pages to the end."

Matt Hilton – Author of the Joe Hunter novels
"... Graham Smith is another talent to watch for..."
"... bloody good medicine for the mind."

Richard Godwin – Author of Apostle Rising, Mr Glamour and One Lost Summer
"Smith is a writer with a strong voice who catches the attention and holds it... sharp dialogue and tight plotting..."

Sheila Quigley - Author of The Seahills series and the Holy Island trilogy
"Graham Smith is not just a rising star, but a shooting star."

Joseph Finder - New York Times bestseller
*"Smith's anti-hero, Detective Inspector Evans, is the kind of cop we don't see any more, a man more interested in justice than the law. If my children were kidnapped, he's the man I'd want on my side. Surely **SNATCHED FROM HOME** won't be his last case."*

Acknowledgements

Without delivering an Oscar style speech, there are an awful lot of people who have helped me to get to this point. From the early writing classes I've attended, the friends I've made both online and in person, the whole community of crime fiction writers have been supportive and have welcomed me into their ranks. Special mentions of course must include Darren Laws of Caffeine Nights who has shown great faith in me, the team behind him, Chris Simmons at Crimesquad.com and Matt Hilton, Michael Malone, Sheila Quigley, Col Bury, David Barber and the whole Crime and Publishment gang for their friendship, advice and unconditional support. My sincerest thanks to you all, I just wish I could find the right words to say how deep my gratitude is.

Graham Smith 2015

Snatched from Home

To Carissa

thanks for your
support

[signature]

'When I come home late at night, don't ask me where I've been. Just count your stars I'm home again.'

Guns N' Roses

Chapter 1

Good Friday

Victoria Foulkes's head snapped up when she heard the crunch of her husband's nose being broken. The next sound to assault her ears was him crashing to the floor. Heavy thumps followed, as a large man wearing black clothing and a latex Tony Blair mask dragged Nicholas into the lounge. He was followed by an even bigger man wearing an Elvis mask and carrying a holdall.

Victoria rose to her feet and squared up to the masked intruders fear somersaulting her stomach. 'What's going on? What the hell do you think you're doing?'

Elvis was about to speak when screaming and shouting pierced the house. A series of thuds on the stairs preceded the Foulkeses' children being ushered into the lounge by two men sporting masks of Barack Obama and Hannibal Lector.

Seventeen-year-old Samantha was clutching a strappy top in one hand while covering her bra with the other. Victoria guessed Samantha had been trying on various outfits in preparation for the date she had tomorrow night.

Her brother, Kyle, clung limpet-like to her back, his Mario Kart T-shirt belying his tender age.

Victoria pushed her children to the far side of the room and asked the men what they wanted.

Elvis answered, his accent holding a deep Lancastrian twang. 'We've come to collect our money from Nicky Boy here. He owes us ninety-five grand.'

'Don't be silly. He doesn't owe you or anyone else anything of the kind.' Victoria turned to her husband who sat on the floor nursing his shattered nose. 'Tell them, Nicholas. Tell them they've made a mistake. Tell them that you don't owe any money.' Victoria's eyes searched her husband's face looking for any sign that this was all a terrible mistake.

The way his chin dropped onto his chest made something inside her sink.

This can't be true. There was no way he's amassed such a debt without me finding out. It's not possible.

Nicholas didn't lift his eyes high enough to make contact with his wife's. His body language shouted defeat. His head dropped to his chest and his shoulders began to shake as sobs wracked his body.

Victoria fell to her knees and with a tenderness she didn't feel, lifted his head and forced eye contact.

'Is it true, Nicholas?'

Unable to speak, he nodded his head, tossing droplets of blood from his nose onto her knee.

Victoria slumped beside her husband soaking up his aura of despair as his blood stained her tights. Her mind raced with thoughts of denial.

This can't be happening. It must be a nightmare. I'll wake up any second. Nicholas will start laughing and tell me it's all just a joke.

Nicholas found his voice. 'I thought my debt was eighty-five, not ninety-five grand?'

'There's an extra ten grand for operational costs.'

Victoria's brow furrowed 'Why do you owe them so much money? What is the debt for?'

Nicholas didn't answer so Victoria flicked her eyes towards Elvis.

'He's been playing cards with grown-ups. Unlimited games of poker is where the debt is from.'

Pushing disbelief and panic down with a determined gulp, Victoria looked up at Elvis. His rubber mask was undeniable. A part of her brain told her this was not a nightmare or a joke. It was real, and it was happening right here in her home. Swallowing hard and working her tongue around her mouth, she forced herself to speak. 'We can't pay that amount to you today. We'll need time to re-mortgage the house. To get a loan. To raise the money.'

'It's not that simple. Nicky Boy has been stalling us for months now, and it's time he paid up. What we're gonna do is this, we're gonna take something very dear to him with us, so that he gets us our money.'

Elvis clicked his fingers, prompting Obama and Lector to brush Victoria aside. They grabbed Kyle and Samantha, then made for the door, dragging the struggling children behind them.

Blair took a large knife from the holdall he was carrying and held it against Victoria's throat.

'Hey, kids.' Samantha and Kyle stopped trying to escape their captors long enough to look at him. 'Be quiet, or else Mummy here gets a new necklace.'

Victoria felt tears filling her eyes as she begged Elvis not to take her children, but her pleas were ignored as she watched them being loaded into their van.

Elvis pushed Victoria across the room before pulling a lance-like implement shaped like a putter from the holdall and displayed it to Victoria and her weeping husband. 'D'you know what this is?'

Nicholas was too absorbed by his own private hell to answer. Victoria shook her head wondering what the strange tool had to do with their children being taken. Her tears were blinked away as she sat stony-faced and broken-hearted. Her opaline eyes flickered between the lance and Elvis.

There were two pipes, which made up the shaft, and at the end they were fitted into a nozzle that stood out at ninety degrees from the lance.

'It's an oxyacetylene torch, used for cutting metal. It can slice through steel, so imagine what it will do to your children if you don't pay up on time.' Elvis gave them a minute to digest the threat, then putting the oxyacetylene torch back in the bag he asked Victoria for her mobile number.

'No. Don't hurt my kids. They've done nothing wrong.'

'Make sure you and your husband get us the fucking money then. Now give me your mobile number.'

Victoria recited her number to Elvis with defeat weighing heavy in her voice and heart. She rose to her full height and, with arctic fury, tried one last tactic. Her arm extended until a mauve fingernail pointed at Nicholas. 'Take him. He's the one who owes you money. Hurt him, not my babies.'

'Believe me, I would love to take him. But I doubt you'd pay us a penny to get him back after what he's done. All I want is the ninety-five grand by midnight next Friday. 'Sides, you'll likely need his help, or at least his signature to raise the money in time.'

Victoria felt her composure shatter and she rounded on her husband with a bitter rage fuelling her actions, kicking at him where he lay on the floor.

'What have you done, you stupid bastard?' A kick landed in his midriff doubling him into a foetal position.

'If anything happens to my babies, I'll bloody well kill you!' The next kick hit his raised legs.

'How could you run up such a debt and not tell me? How could you be so stupid? What the hell got into you?' Victoria took careful aim and scored a direct hit on Nicholas's balls, causing him to scream in agony. As much as she wanted to punish him, she knew she could never inflict upon him the level of pain she felt. Her heart had been pierced by a frozen stiletto. Her brain turned into mush as disbelief and denial battled the memory of her children being led out of the door.

Elvis caught Victoria by the shoulder. 'Stoppit.'

Seeing he had her full attention he laid down his terms. 'If you call the police, your children will lose a limb each. If you fail to pay us on time, they'll lose an arm *and* a leg.'

'But that's only a week. We'll need more time than that to get that much money.'

'Sorry, lady. Your husband has been stalling us for six months. You should be grateful the boss isn't charging him interest as well as costs.'

Elvis turned on his heel and strode out of the room with a final warning not to contact the police.

Victoria dashed to the window and watched Elvis climb into a van parked in front of their house. The van turned out of Park End Road onto the A66 towards Cockermouth and Penrith.

Grabbing a pen and paper, she wrote down the van's registration number although she knew she didn't dare call the police. The consequences of a botched rescue attempt were unimaginable.

Her stomach roiled like a stormy ocean, as her body succumbed to the numbing effects of the nightmarish situation. Her legs threatened to give way, forcing her to sit on the armrest of the sofa.

Surely this can't be happening? My children have just been kidnapped from under my nose, taken as collateral against my husband's debts. This is Workington, for God's sake. A sleepy town on the edge of the Lake District. This kind of thing only happens in places like New York or Las Vegas.

She turned to face Nicholas, feeling nothing but contempt for him, for the tears of self-pity staining his cheeks. 'Get up, you useless lump. You've got some explaining to do and then we've got to work out a way to pay them, so we can get Samantha and Kyle back unhurt. So help me God, if anything happens to them, I'll... I'll—' Nicholas's protested apologies cut off her threat, but she slapped his face. Anger fuelled her every word but Elvis had been right. She would need his help raise the money.

Chapter 2

The van reversed up to the house, Samantha and Kyle were herded through the door, upstairs and into a bedroom. The door slammed behind them. On the floor was a dirty mattress and TV with a games console.

Seeing Kyle in floods of tears, Samantha wrapped her arms around him and fought back her own sobs. She would do her crying later, when Kyle was asleep. Just now he needed her to be strong. In a soft voice she consoled him until sobs became sniffles and sniffles became snores.

The nine years that separated them meant they were closer than many siblings with less of an age gap. Kyle had been her walking, talking doll, her half-size shadow. Their bond was concrete and when terrors assaulted his dreams, it was Samantha whose comfort he sought, not their parents.

Slipping his embrace, she pulled the thin sheet over him and set about inspecting the room for ways to escape. The door was solid wood and was as old as the house in which they were kept. It was closed tight and as they'd been led into the room by Obama and Blair she had seen sturdy bolts fixed top and bottom. There was no way they'd get through the door without alerting their captors. The bedroom walls were coated with a dirty off-white paint. The lone window had been bricked up in a haphazard fashion. The ceiling was at least ten feet high, preventing her from finding a way into the attic.

A second door led to a tiny, windowless bathroom. She climbed on the toilet and looked out through the grill of the ventilator fan. Through the narrow opening she could see starlight. There were no landmarks visible. No defining characteristics to be seen; only the dark shapes of hills outlined against the starry sky.

She had tried to count time in her head while in the back of the van. Her calculations were not exact, but she was confident the van had not been driven for more than an hour. That meant they would still be somewhere in Cumbria. Judging from the number of sharp turns and potholes the van had encountered she reckoned that they were in a rural area, probably somewhere remote. The guessed knowledge of their location gave her no comfort whatsoever, but at least she'd know what to expect if they got a chance to escape.

Samantha had expected to be looking after Kyle this week, as neither of her parents had been able to get time off work. She just hadn't expected to be looking after him in these circumstances. In silence with head bowed and hands clasped, she vowed to do whatever she could to protect her little brother.

*   *   *

Downstairs the four kidnappers were sitting around a table littered with beer cans, takeaway containers and overflowing ashtrays. The leader of the gang – Thomas Marshall, who had worn the Elvis mask – was arguing with the men who had worn the Obama and Hannibal masks.

'I know you didn't sign up for kidnapping but it wasn't my decision to make. I only got the message a couple of days ago meself.'

Len Williams threw his Obama mask onto the table before giving his opinion. 'It was bad enough when I thought we were gonna be kidnapping the wife. Whose idea was it to take the kids?'

'Shut the fuck up and remember who we're working for. If he says jump, we ask how high.'

Billy Alker put his beer can down beside the Blair mask he'd worn and reached for his cigarettes, ignoring the others as they argued back and forth. His thoughts were on finding a way to get some time alone with the girl. Since they'd moved up here last month there had been no female contact whatsoever. All he'd done was work all day, then spend the evenings drinking tins of beer and bullshitting with the others, before repeating the cycle the next day.

Marshall pulled him from his scheming by asking what was ready to go.

'The two tractors, four quads and all of the power tools are ready. We'll have the other tractor sorted by dinner time and the two ride on lawnmowers by tomorrow night.'

'Good. The boss just sent me a message to say there'll be a delivery tomorrow morning and he wants to collect whatever we've got.'

'Fair enough. But I'm not getting up in the middle of the bastard night again to load his wagon.' Alker waved his hand at Williams and Pete Johnstone, whose Hannibal mask hung at his side. 'They can do it this time. I'm stayin' in me bed.'

Chapter 3

Victoria wiped her eyes and pushed the tissue under the sleeve of the lilac blouse she was wearing. Crying would not help her babies now. Action would save them. Not despair. Not recriminations, however tempted she may be to throw them at Nicholas.

To think of how she'd loved him. The sacrifices she'd made for him, only for him to bring this ridiculous situation to their door. Her children kidnapped as collateral against *his* gambling debts. The thought of him filled her with revulsion, but deep down she knew she would need him to get Samantha and Kyle back.

Victoria quashed down the nagging doubt that a good wife should know a husband's debts. Should have known he was gambling. Should have recognised the stress and worry he must have been carrying. She was not going to allow herself to shoulder any blame for this. It was his doing, not hers.

With the kettle filled, she switched it on and resisted the temptation to half fill her mug with brandy before adding the coffee. Retrieving her briefcase, she prepared her things while the kettle boiled. A pad, pen and calculator were aligned on the kitchen table beside her laptop, which she powered up.

Her beloved kitchen, the heart of their home, would now become her operations centre. The heat and ambience of the room had left with Samantha and Kyle. Until the laughter of her children again burbled in her ears, it would be the cold functional place it was when they bought the house some twenty years earlier.

'Nicholas. Get your sorry arse in here.'

A sheepish Nicholas entered. 'I'm sorry, Victoria. So very sorry.'

'Sit down and shut up. If anything happens to Sam and Kyle then you'll be a damn sight sorrier. Believe me, I'll make sure of it.' Victoria was not ready for his apologies and she didn't care about the hurt in his eyes when she spoke to him.

Fighting the panic that threatened to overtake her, Victoria focused her mind on working out their finances. This whole mess was about money and until she knew if they had enough for the ransom, she didn't dare to think of the consequences.

'Get your laptop,' she said as she picked up her pen and opened the pad.

While he got his laptop, she drew a series of columns on the pad, titled 'Accounts', 'Cars', 'Loans', 'Jewellery', 'Shop' and 'Miscellaneous'.

Using the laptop to establish totals for their joint account and her personal one, she noted down the figures. Next she went onto the *AutoTrader* website to get approximate values for her car and the van Nicholas used for his shop. Taking a guess at the worth of her jewellery, she wrote down £2,000. Another £2,500 was added under the miscellaneous column for household items like the TVs, laptops, etc., which she planned to sell online.

As Nicholas plugged in his laptop and switched it on she started questioning him about his finances.

'What do you expect to take this week?'

'Anywhere between twelve and fifteen hundred.'

'Does anyone owe you for outstanding bills?'

'Joe Hilton owes me six hundred and forty something pounds and there's the Laingson account. They pay monthly, and their bill is always around a grand.'

'Anyone else?'

'A dozen or so small builders have accounts. But they would be less than a hundred quid apiece.'

'That's still almost a grand.' Victoria scratched her nose as she thought. 'Right. Here's what you're going to do. You're going to contact all of them tomorrow morning offering a special rate for preferred customers. If they pay you cash by Thursday night then they only have to pay seventy-five per cent of the bill.'

'Tomorrow's Easter Saturday. I don't know if they'll be in their offices then.'

'I know it's Easter Saturday tomorrow, but if we don't get the money by next Friday my children will be mutilated.'

'Sorry.'

'Stop saying bloody sorry and start telling me what money is in your accounts.'

'There's five thousand, three hundred and twenty five in the business account.'

'What about your personal account?'

Nicholas couldn't bring himself to look at his wife as he told her the account was overdrawn.

Victoria glared at him until he met her eye. 'That's hardly a surprise to me after everything else I've learned tonight.'

'How much have we got?'

'If we sell my car, your van, my jewellery, the tellies, the kid's laptops and scrape every penny from our accounts and the shop then we'll have just over forty-two thousand pounds. We're short by fifty-three grand.'

'Christ Almighty. What are we going to do to get the rest of the money?'

'For a start you are going to get on the phone to your parents and every friend we've ever had.'

'What am I going to say?'

'Whatever the hell you like as long as it's not the truth. You're a salesman. Sell yourself. Do whatever the hell it takes. Just borrow as much money as you can. Tell whatever lies you need to.'

You've become good at lying lately, the unspoken words echoed in her head.

'We'll never raise enough to pay them back.'

'Sod paying them back. That problem can wait until my kids are home. If we'd known about this months ago we could have remortgaged the house or the shop. We haven't even time to take out a loan.

Nicholas poured himself a glass of water and went through to the living room to start making calls.

There weren't many people he could ask for a loan. They were both only children and while his parents were alive they too had no siblings. Victoria was estranged from her family and hadn't spoken to any of them since her mother's funeral sixteen years ago.

While her husband was on the phone, Victoria retrieved the packet of menthol cigarettes she kept hidden behind the baked beans and stepped out into the garden. Sheltering in the lee of the conservatory, she sparked the lighter and drew the minty smoke into her lungs.

As she smoked an idea pushed its way to the front of her thoughts. It was not something she wanted to do. It was not a course of action she wanted to take. It went against all of her principles and values, but she would take it, if Nicholas couldn't beg enough money to pay the ransom. It held risks and dangers, but there was more than enough at stake for her to take any risk necessary.

Filling her cup with more coffee, Victoria sat down at her place and started scribbling a new list onto her pad. She knew there was no way Nicholas would be able to raise enough money from friends and family. She was now working out the details of her plan. Planning, plotting and scheming were the emotional crutches she now relied on.

Victoria's hand strayed across to her mobile for the twentieth time and once again she pulled it back lest she call the police. The consequences for her children were far too great for her to risk. Yet every instinct of her middle-class lifestyle screamed at her to make the call. She picked up the mobile and dropped it into her bag.

Out of sight, out of mind.

A sheet of paper was laid down on top of her notes. In Nicholas's neat cursive script was a list of names and pledged amounts. The total at the bottom amounted to £15,000.

After checking the total, Victoria read down the list of names and saw Nicholas had spoken to everyone who may be in a position to help them.

'What did you say to them?' Victoria didn't care, but knew she'd better know in case she had to speak to one of them.

'I told them I'd been offered a lease on larger premises, but I had to pay cash upfront. I also told them we'd pay them back their money with a five per cent increase within a month.'

'Why did you say that?' Victoria was gobsmacked at her husband's stupidity. Here they were in danger of losing everything to save their children and he was offering interest on loans they couldn't afford to repay.

'To give them some reassurance.'

As the sense of his words sank in she nodded. 'Was there no way you could get any more? We're still thirty-eight grand short.'

'I'm sorry but no. I think that they all gave as much as they were prepared to.

'Right then, I've been thinking. Here are the options we have left. One, we take out every payday loan we can and pay the ransom to release Samantha and Kyle. We also remortgage the house and shop so that we can pay them back first. Friends and family can wait. Hopefully we can avoid bankruptcy, but if it happens then so be it. It'll be a small price to pay.'

Nicholas's shame-faced grimace told the tale of his feelings for option one. 'What other options have you thought of?'

When Victoria told him of her plan, he shook his head. 'We can't do that. We'd never be able to do that.'

'I agree. So it's option one.'

'There is something I have to tell you, Victoria.' Nicholas's face was downcast as he explained in a bland tone that he'd already remortgaged the house and shop two months ago to pay off other gambling debts.

'Why the bloody hell didn't you tell me? What else haven't you told me, you useless bastard? Our kids have been kidnapped because of your fucking idiotic behaviour and our only chance of getting the money will see us out on the bloody street.'

'I'm sorry, Vicks.' Fat tears rolled down Nicholas's face as he swore there were no more nasty surprises to come. Taking a deep breath he steadied himself. 'I'll do whatever it takes to get them back.'

'Don't you fucking "Vicks" me.' The steely venom in Victoria's voice cut through Nicholas's self-pity making his head snap up. 'Go get some sleep. We start with my plan tomorrow.'

Her husband's use of her pet name had struck a blow deep into her heart. Even if the kids were rescued unharmed she knew her marriage was now dead. A chasm had opened up between her and the man she'd married. No bridge could ever span this ravine. Nothing he could say or do would repair the damage caused by his lies.

Chapter 4

Saturday

Detective Inspector John Campbell lifted the stack of newspapers and offered up a silent prayer today would be the day he'd meet the protection racketeers. He had been playing the part of a shopkeeper for four days and the newsagent's was bang in the centre of town.

When the shop had become available the police had taken on the lease and installed Campbell as the new shopkeeper. While the shop was being refitted, hidden cameras had been installed along with recording equipment. All he had to do was provoke the thugs into some violent act or get them to ask for protection money on tape, then they would have grounds for arrest and evidence for conviction. The shop was one of many in a row with the usual smattering of independent shops mixed with national chains and charity shops; the same as any other city centre. The white sandstone of the buildings weathered grey black from decades of smog and exhaust fumes.

He was bored rigid by the tedium of playing the part. The harsh accent of Cumbrians sat uneasy on his ears. He struggled to make sense of the local slang, to the point where he wrote down the words he didn't understand and asked Sarah to translate when he got home. He would be a lot happier when this was over and he could take up the new post he'd got with his transfer.

Carlisle had a lot of history, once a Roman fort, a medieval outpost and an integral part of the border wars between Scotland and England. He'd looked up his new workplace on Google and was astounded and more than a little proud to learn that for a nineteen-year period in the twelfth century the city had been ruled by the Scots.

There was no excitement for him in running a newsagent's. The only amusement he'd had was a well-dressed man hiding a copy of Good Time Guys inside PC Business, when a bunch of schoolgirls came in as he was waiting in the queue. The rest of his time had been spent restocking shelves, taking payment from customers and trying to keep an eye on the multitude of kids who tried to shoplift the various chocolates bars on sale.

Four men wearing construction worker's fluorescent jackets walked in. The lead guy was few inches shorter than Campbell, but much broader across the shoulders. A trim waist gave him the appearance of either a serious bodybuilder or a competitive swimmer. Campbell's money was on bodybuilder though, as the veins in the man's arms stood out like ivy growing on a tree – a common occurrence in bodybuilders after steroid abuse. One of the others wore a blue Carlisle United bobble hat while the other two wore no hats but one of the two was completely bald.

'Can I have twenty Lambert and two hundred and fifty quid from the till?' It was Ivy Arms who spoke.

'What do you mean?'

'I'm your new insurer mate. Me and the lads will be in to collect our premium every Saturday morning. When you insure with us, then you are safe from vandals, thieves and accidental damage.'

Campbell put the packet of cigarettes on the counter and held his hand out, palm upright. 'Six eighty-nine, please. I already have insurance. I don't need your policy, thank you.' He shifted his feet ready for any attack that may come.

'Big mistake pal.' Ivy Arms sidestepped around the counter.

'Wreck it, lads.' A vicious uppercut was aimed towards Campbell, who leaned back and helped his assailant's right arm travel upwards as the punch missed his chin. This manoeuvre left a wide open space between belt and ribs into which Campbell threw two solid blows before using his already raised right hand to deliver a stinging backhand punch.

This was almost enough to finish Ivy Arms, but he was rescued by one of his bare-headed compatriots who pulled him away from Campbell's next flurry of punches.

Being keyed up for this moment for almost a week caused Campbell's body to dump an overdose of adrenaline into his system.

As the guy with hair squared up to him, Campbell caught sight of a fifth man entering the shop. Quickly he shot a left through the hands held in front of his attacker's face, hitting him on the forehead with a jab, knocking his head back, giving a sweet target for the uppercut which was launched as soon as the jab landed.

The fifth man just stood in the doorway, his hands in his pockets, watching as Ivy Arms and his two remaining cohorts tried to decide what to do next. An amused smile labelled the craggy face as he watched the ruckus.

'You're fucking mine.' Ivy Arms turned towards Campbell his composure returning after his earlier defeat.

Campbell seized the advantage of the distraction created by the fifth man and punched the bald guy in the gut doubling him over. A quick combination of blows left Carlisle Hat on his knees with any vestiges of a fight long gone from him.

The fifth man pushed himself from the door frame as Ivy Arms ran towards him, intent only on making his escape. Ivy Arms reached out a muscled arm to brush aside the fifth man.

The fifth man shrugged his way inside the arm to deliver a stunning head butt, sending Ivy Arms crashing to the floor with a reverberating thump.

'He-Man one, fuckwit nil.' The fifth man raised his arms like a boxer after a winning bout and did a little Ali shuffle.

He then pulled his left hand from his coat pocket, showing a warrant card to Campbell, identifying himself as DI Harry Evans.

Evans was the man Campbell would be replacing now that this case was dealt with.

A bunch of PCs charged in the shop. 'How many are there, guv?'

'Four. They're here, here and here. Oh yeah, there's one here as well, Sergeant,' Evans indicated each of the gang to the policemen who were charging into the shop, with a hard kick timed to match each call of 'here'.

Chapter 5

Sitting alone in his flat, Evans laid down his glasses and the faded letter he was reading. He'd read it a thousand times before. With each reading it made perfect sense, yet at the same time it made no sense at all.

The letter was from the love of his life. The one he'd forsaken all others for. She'd made him the happiest man alive the day he'd married her. They'd been married for just two years when she'd written the letter.

When Janet had told him she was expecting, he thought his heart would burst from his chest and wrap its arms around her such was the love he felt. The child he hadn't known he wanted was due to make an appearance, but he'd never meet his son or daughter.

Janet was twelve years his junior and before he'd met her, he'd given up any hope of marriage and children. Like almost every copper he knew, he'd had a series of failed relationships. The job had seen to that. Few women would tolerate the string of broken dates, the endless uneaten meals and telephone calls at all hours of the night.

Janet had. She had embraced it, knowing it was what made him the man he was. Her father had been an inspector, her upbringing conditioning her to the vagaries of life with a dedicated copper.

Yet here he was alone. Single. Empty. Reading and rereading the last note she had written him.

His detective's mind had analysed her words and cross-examined her motives countless times. Every time he read it, he understood why she had chosen to leave him, but he could never understand why she actually had.

Five months had passed since she'd written that damned letter and still he couldn't accept she was gone from his life. That he'd never see his child grow up. At his age, he'd long ago given up on finding love and starting a family. Janet was his last and only chance.

His fifty-first birthday was charging over the horizon at him and he knew that once again his life would change forever. After thirty years of service, detective inspectors like him were retired from front-line policing. Of course, they didn't call it retired any more and had some fancy management term for it. But that didn't change anything in his mind. A sack of shit would always be a sack of shit, despite some desk-bound fuckwit calling it a manure-transfer system.

Most of the coppers he'd known over the years had been only too glad to reach retirement, many of them taking it after reaching their thirty years. Those who didn't want to retire stayed on in an office-based role supporting the front-line troops.

He couldn't envision a worse fate. He would sooner retire than be tied to a desk, reading other people's reports. A people person at heart, he would find life as a desk jockey akin to imprisonment.

DI Harry Evans knew countless hundreds of people around his native Cumbria and they all knew him. They knew he was hard but fair. An old-school copper who would still dish out a clip round the ear where it was needed. A blind eye where appropriate. Yet when necessary he would bring down the full weight of the law. No career criminal in the county had escaped his attention.

Yet all this was about to be taken away from him. Like Janet. Like his last chance of fatherhood.

He had options of course. Local security firms were falling over each other to offer him consultancy roles. G4S had offered him a full-time position managing their Carlisle office, but like the police role he would be desk-bound.

A high-street retailer wanted him to manage store security across their north of England shops. While it was the best offer he'd had, he was more familiar with catching murderers, rapists and drug dealers than shoplifters. It was a step down and he wasn't ready to step down yet.

A wet tongue slithered its way across his left hand, jolting himself out of his melancholy. Evans petted the aged Labrador who was never more than six feet away from him, whenever he was at home.

'Good boy. Wanna walk?'

Seeing the Labrador caper around on its three legs, Evans eased his slender frame from the wing back chair, wandered into the hall and shucked on his jacket to brave the chill evening one last time.

'C'mon, Tripod, walkies.'

Chapter 6

After her fruitless search, Samantha had cuddled into Kyle's back and pulled the thin sheet over herself. Sleep hadn't come easy to her as she fretted and worried about their fate.

She was more worried about her brother than herself. He hated being away from home. He was uncomfortable visiting friends and he even got homesick when they went on holiday. If they had to stay in this room for any length of time, she knew he would suffer greatly. Without a window and with no watch between them, there was no way to measure time and when they awoke they had no idea whether it was early or late morning.

'Can we have Coco Pops for breakfast?'

Samantha smiled in spite of herself. Kyle was treating their imprisonment as a holiday. 'We'll have to wait and see what they bring us.'

'Why don't we bang on the door and shout to them? Tell them we're hungry?'

'I don't know what time it is. It might be the middle of the night. I don't think it will be a very good idea to make the men cross.'

'But I'm hungry and I want to see Mummy.'

Samantha faked a smile and admonished him with a wagging finger. 'You're always hungry. You eat more than I do.'

A metallic clatter interrupted them and they shrank back, hugging each other tight. Samantha identified the sounds as bolts being drawn back and a key rotating the tumblers inside a lock.

The bedroom door opened to reveal the man in the Elvis mask. He was holding a tray bearing a carton of orange juice, two plastic glasses and a pile of buttered toast.

Making sure he kept himself between them and the door he set the tray on the floor and then faced them. 'You are going to be here for a few days at most. If you're good, then we won't harm you. If you're not good, then we will punish you. Do you understand?'

Samantha nodded and held a crying Kyle closer to her body.

'Come with me for a minute, lass.'

When Samantha didn't move, he crooked his finger at her. 'You're not exactly being good, are you? I'm not gonna hurt you. I've just got something you need to see.'

'You make a start on the toast, Kyle. I'll be back in a minute.' Samantha tried to reassure her brother, but she was petrified of being raped by the masked man.

Surely that was what he wanted her for. The one wearing the Blair mask was a definite perv. She'd felt his hands grabbing her backside and boobs when he led them from the van last night.

'Don't even think of trying to escape, 'cause we've still got the boy.' Elvis locked the door and pocketed the key.

This is it. They're going to rape me now.

Trudging down the stairs in front of her captor, Samantha tried to push her plight to the back of her mind. She was no virgin and only a few months ago had allowed a drunken boyfriend to make love to her when she was afraid to say no. If she didn't fight with the men then perhaps it wouldn't be much worse than that ordeal.

The house had a decayed feel to it, as if it had been neglected by its owner for many years. Mould adorned the top of skirting boards, the wallpaper was decades out of date and there was a damp fusty smell in every room.

Samantha tried to look out of the windows to see if she could spot a local landmark but all the curtains were pulled to. Elvis was hot on her heels, uttering one-word directions until they were in a small downstairs room.

The room held one chair and a desk with a laptop. Sprouting from the side of the laptop was a mouse and what she recognised as a dongle to connect the laptop to the Internet.

At Elvis's command, she sat in front of the laptop and clicked play to activate the video on the screen.

'Pay attention. This is what will happen to you if you don't do as we say.'

The blood drained from Samantha's face as she watched the forty-five second video.

'Oh my God, no.' Samantha propelled herself back from the laptop until she was tight against the wall. 'Please no, I'll do anything you want, don't do that to us. I beg you. Please. Anything you say, I'll do.'

'Now that I've got your attention I want you to listen very carefully. If you try to escape, you'll star in the next video. If you don't do as we say, you'll star in the next video. You hold the power of decision.' He paused and stared at Samantha.

'We'll be good. I promise. You won't hear a peep from us. We'll do whatever you say.'

'Good. Now that we're on the same page you can go back upstairs. There are a few games up there for the PS2 to keep you amused; the telly is already tuned to the right channel. We don't mean you any harm so long as you do as you're told.'

Returning back to her prison, Samantha found Kyle curled up in a ball with silent tears running from his one visible eye. When she called his name he leapt up and ran to her flinging his arms around her waist and squeezing her tight.

'I was scared, Sam. I thought those nasty men were going to do something to you. I didn't know if you were coming back.'

Swallowing back an honest answer, Samantha pried her brother loose and offered him a piece of toast.

'Don't be silly. They are looking after us for a few days and if we're good we can play video games all day.' A smile was forced onto her lips. 'Now, who said they were hungry?'

* * *

Once the girl was locked back in the bedroom, Marshall pulled off the Elvis mask and hung it on the door handle.

Lighting a cigarette, he walked through the front door, admiring the sight of Skiddaw bathed in morning sunlight. Sheep munching at the tough hill grass dotted its flanks.

Not keen on hill-walking or hiking, he still enjoyed looking at scenery and had spent many a weekend in the lakes with his ex-wife. The only blots on the landscape he could see other than the farm buildings were the dry stone dykes on the lower hills and the TV mast at Caldbeck.

A short saunter across the yard and he pulled back the shed door to find Alker on his back underneath a small tractor. Sparks were flying in an orange arc as he ground away serial numbers. Williams and Johnstone were at work replacing the tin tags on small power tools with ones they had fabricated themselves.

'How you getting on?'

'Like he said last night, we'll finish this lot today. When they drop off tonight's load they can take this lot away with them.'

'Make sure that you get them done and ready to load then. We don't want them here any longer than they need to be.'

As Marshall left to return to the house, Johnstone turned to Williams. 'He doesn't want them here any length of time yet we have to unload all the stolen stuff. We work our arses off while he spends all day on that laptop. He's in the warm drinking coffee and we're covering stolen goods with our fingerprints.'

'Quit moaning, will you? You knew what the deal was when you signed up. He's the one who knows where the stuff is available and how to get it. Without him we'd be wasting our time trying to rob places which have nowt worth taking.'

Chapter 7

The pair of thieves sneaked in through the back door, entering the required code into the panel beside the door before the alarm announced their presence. They made their way through the building to the manager's office, the leader guiding the way using familiarity instead of light.

The leader opened a desk drawer and pulled out a key that opened the safe cabinet and then bent down and entered a code into the digital lock on the internal strongbox.

The three lights flashed red as the code was entered and then turned green as the last digit was pressed. Turning the handle, the leader opened the strongbox and removed all the cash and stuffed it into a cloth money bag, which was then secreted into a poacher's pocket of the accomplice's wax jacket.

Closing the strongbox and locking the safe cabinet, the leader took the accomplice's arm and guided him out the way they had came, only pausing to reset the building's alarm before exiting and locking the door behind them.

Each breathed a sigh of relief before a noise startled them both. Shrinking into the shadows on either side of the door, they held their breath expecting a police torch to shine into their eyes at any moment and a stern voice to speak. All they heard was the sound of a zip being pulled down and the sounds of running water as a man relieved himself, his contented sigh interspersed by hiccups. The smell of alcohol as strong as the caustic tang of ammonia.

The accomplice pointed in the opposite direction to the man. They walked away from him, taking care to make as little noise as possible. They were in luck, the man was so wasted, they could have been leading a brass band and still he would have been unaware of their presence.

Chapter 8

Easter Monday

Campbell was in the first official day in at his new station and already he was having doubts about his transfer. The new police station at Durranhill was located in the middle of an industrial estate and the building looked like the back end of a grandstand. He believed police stations should be cold unedifying buildings, steeped in history. Their imposing structures ought to strike fear into criminals, not have them admiring the architecture. Modernity was always going to win out when the new station was built as a replacement for the old one, which had been submerged along with large sections of the city, in the January floods of 2005.

Monday mornings were never his favourite and this would be his first real meeting with the officers who would be in his new team. Plus, he had the outgoing DI showing him the area he would be covering, giving him a rundown on where the local stations were all located.

He'd begun the morning with an extra long shower, followed by three cups of coffee. His stomach had been too knotted with tension to allow him the luxury of breakfast, and he'd nicked himself twice with the razor. Hardly the first impression he wanted to give his new team. All cut up and rumbling guts.

'Good morning all.' DCI Peter Grantham entered the room with Campbell trailing behind him.

Grantham waited a moment until all the eyes in the room were on him. 'I'd like you all to welcome DI Campbell here who has just joined us from Strathclyde force. He's the person who helped catch the muscle behind the protection gang that has been plaguing small shops and businesses. You may not know this yet, but we managed to roll one of them and he's given us solid leads on the gang behind a lot of protection rackets in the county. So well done to him.'

A smattering of applause rang round the room, but as there were only five people to clap, the noise was more embarrassing than deafening. Campbell raised his hand in acknowledgment and said that he looked forward to working with a new team.

Nodding at Evans, Grantham held up a sheaf of papers. 'I'll let you make all the formal introductions later, Harry; I have some cases for you. Firstly, there have been three break-ins into licensed premises in the last two days which appear to be inside jobs, with a total of just over thirteen thousand pounds stolen. So either a crime syndicate is forcing people to help them or there's a common factor between the pubs and nightspots that've been burgled.'

'Who's been done over?' Evans was slumped in a chair opposite his standing DCI, his disrespect obvious.

'Jumpers in Silloth, the Black Horse in Bowness-on-Windermere and Beenies in Carlisle. Plod and local CID have been round, but I think they are all connected and I want you to look into it.'

'You mentioned cases, sir?'

Campbell looked across at the new speaker. As she was the only female in the room he didn't need to be a detective to work out that she must be DC Lauren Phillips.

He'd been given a full briefing on the team he would lead. The mandate simple, he was to bring order to the chaos of Evans's reign, to end their renegade ways.

It was Lauren who puzzled him most. According to the files he'd read, she was a brazen exhibitionist. Shameless in her dress sense, she used her femininity as a weapon of mass distraction. In his experience, most female officers dressed to hide their curves not emphasise them. Their biggest enemy, speculation as to whose bed they were sharing.

Her pretty face and wavy blonde hair didn't fill him with confidence. The cleavage she was showing would be a distraction. She'd be nice to have around in a decorative way, but would she be any use to him?

Tuning back into the meeting, he listened to Grantham's report.

'Farm vehicles such as quad bikes, tractors and the like have been going walkabout from all over the county again. Lots of hand-held power tools are also being taken at the same time.'

'So much for the SmartWater campaign.'

'That's enough thank you, DC Phillips.' DCI Grantham struggled to look at her face as he snapped at her. 'Not one of the farms affected has the SmartWater technology.'

'Any other cases, sir?' This from the obese man wedged in front of two computers. Again Campbell knew his name without being told. This would be DS Neil Chisholm; the file Campbell had read on his team stated Chisholm was a computer genius who researched details and did all the cross checks necessary to compile evidence.

'Yes, we've had ten complaints of a man and woman conning car dealers out of money while actually paying them. They count out the cash to them in fifty-pound notes and the dealers agree to the value, yet when they cash up at the end of the day, they've all been short by two thousand pounds.'

Campbell saw the remaining member of his team raise a hand, the too-big suit jacket rucking at his elbow. 'I'd like to look into that, sir.'

'Thank you, DC Bhaki. DI Evans will allocate you tasks as he sees fit.'

Evans scowled at Grantham. 'Are there any decent cases, sir? All we have so far are thefts and a few second-hand car dealers getting ripped off. It's hardly a call for the specialist team we have here.'

'I trust you are not hoping a murder or kidnap investigation comes our way, Quasi?'

'Of course not, *sir*, but I was hoping for something juicier than other peoples cast offs. I was hoping for one last big case before… you know?'

'The more mundane the better if you ask me; now get cracking and stop complaining that we do not have any serious crimes to investigate.' Grantham walked towards the door and then turned with a final comment. 'Quasi, try not to piss the locals off too much. I don't want you riding roughshod over everybody and getting their collective backs up just for the hell of it.'

'Yes, sir, no, sir, three bags full, sir.'

When Grantham left, Evans glared at the team, 'If I hear any of you lot calling me Quasi, I'll use your guts for a skipping rope.' Receiving muted replies he got a pen from the tray below the whiteboard on the tiny room's back wall and wrote up the three case headings: 'Pubs', 'Farms' and 'Cash Con'.

Under the headings Pubs and Farms he wrote DS Chisholm, DC Phillip's name went under 'Farms' and he added DC Bhaki to the third category of 'Cash Con'.

'Chisholm, I want you to contact the guys in the CCTV control rooms. We need any footage that covers the properties that have been robbed. Bhaki, go over all the statements from the robberies and get me the gist of each one. Me and Campbell are gonna visit them. I don't want to be asking questions plod has already got the answers to and making myself look like a twat. When you've done that, you can crack on with the garages. Lauren, find out what's been stolen from the various farms. Also speak with crime prevention or whatever it's called this week and find out if the farms who've been done over had been offered SmartWater, and if not, why not. Bhaki, you find out if there's a pattern with these garages that've allegedly been ripped off.' Evans looked around the room. 'Questions?'

Campbell watched with interest as the team reacted to their orders. He needed to see them working to assess their capabilities.

'Is there any connection with the ownership of the garages?' Bhaki was the first to lead the questioning.

'None as far as I know, but check it out anyway.'

'Same question for the pubs and clubs, sir.'

'The last I heard Jeremy Cussiter owned Jumpers at Silloth and Pete Mitchers owns Beenies.

'What about the Black Horse?'

'That's where me and DI Jock McJock are going. It's owned by the Leightons now. Fat Larry runs it for them.'

Evans looked around the room waiting for more questions. Receiving none he reached for his jacket. 'I'll call in about lunchtime, so have some answers for me.'

As Campbell followed Evans, he was already working out what changes he would make to the team. Evans seemed to rule the roost with a combination of threats and disregard for his superiors.

'We'll hit Beenies first, mara; they do a breakfast which'll set us up for the day.'

When they left the station, Evans led the way to his car – a BMW M3, which he claimed to have inherited from Traffic. The back was littered with case files, jackets and a pair of pizza boxes, while the front seemed to have had a bucket of ash sprinkled on any surface not buried beneath empty cigarette packets. The smell of stale tar and decaying food spurred Campbell's already knotted stomach to new levels of disquiet.

Parking in a public car park and neglecting to pay for a ticket, Evans started walking up Botchergate to where Beenies was located. The sun was shining, although a cool wind surged between the sandstone buildings.

A council worker pushed a handcart along the street picking up the detritus from the previous evening's revelry. Even a Sunday night down Botchergate was raucous and most mornings there was a sea of chip papers, half-eaten kebabs and pizza littering the pavements or swirling in the wind that always blew down from the Crescent.

It seemed to Campbell every third person they met on the short walk to the disco-pub knew Evans, as he was greeted with a cheery good morning or Evans would make an enquiry after a family member of the people he passed.

When they walked into Beenies, his amazement was compounded further as Evans walked right up to the counter, engaged the barmaid in a conversation about her boyfriend's mother and then asked for two full English, two pints and a meeting with Helen Salter, who Campbell presumed was either the manager or a CHIS – confidential human intelligence source – who worked there.

'Oh, and, Pam.'

Hearing Evans call after her, the barmaid turned and threw him a questioning look.

'Do us three breakfast rolls to go as well, would you?'

Pam punched their order into a till and after contacting Helen Salter via an internal phone turned to face Evans. 'I'm afraid I can't serve the pints, It's only half nine and there are coppers in.'

As they waited on the breakfasts coming, having spent little time in each other's company since they had collared the gang extorting money for protection, the new colleagues started in on small talk and a natural assessment of each other.

Beenies was the kind of place where most of the clientele are on the pull or just want to be seen in the trendy place. A cafe-bar through the day it morphed into a cool hip place in the evening, with a clever use of different lighting systems. The decor was ultra-modern with retro touches such as the mosaic of a seventies' hippy wearing a beanie hat. There were two or three tables occupied with people having breakfast and coffees, but it was still too early in the day for any of the lunchtime crowd.

Campbell guessed Evans was an alcoholic ordering drinks so early in the day, and while he obviously had no time for his superiors, they must have had a great deal of faith in him to let him run this team. He made a mental note to find out why the DCI called him Quasi.

A woman in her mid-thirties came over carrying two breakfasts. Her admonishment was delivered before the plates. 'You should know better, Harry, asking staff for a pint outside licensing hours.' She then went and poured the drinks herself, setting them down in front of Evans and Campbell.

'DI Campbell, Helen Salter.' Evans made the introductions while reaching into his jacket pocket and producing a small bottle of Tabasco sauce. Spreading a liberal splash over his breakfast, he picked up his knife and fork to begin his assault on the food.

Evans questioned Helen Salter as he ate, half-masticated food visible in his mouth as he made his enquiries. 'Where the money was taken from?'

'The main safe cabinet.'

'Who had keys?'

'Only me.'

'How much money was taken?'

'Over six grand. Six thousand and twenty-three pounds and fifty pence, to be exact.'

'Why was so much in the safe?'

'It was the weekend's takings.'

Slowly they went over who had keys to the building, when the theft was discovered and by whom, whether there any obvious signs of how the thieves had got into the building and what, if anything, had been taken from the safe other than money. Helen answered each question with tightly-suppressed irritation.

'Why didn't you read the notes the detective took when he questioned me yesterday?' she asked when they were finished.

'If I ask questions myself, I remember the answers better.' Evans paused for a moment. 'Do you remember the name of the investigating DC?'

'Patterson. DC Patterson.'

Evans put down his knife and fork for a moment and looked at Helen. 'He's an imbecile who couldn't find a pane of glass in a greenhouse.'

She nodded. 'He didn't seem like the brightest spark in the fire to me.'

Campbell was trying to write down her answers but couldn't keep pace. Evans made no attempt to commit anything to paper, trusting his memory.

As he listened to Evans's questioning, Campbell revised his opinion of the man's ability. While his approach was unorthodox, there was nothing haphazard about it. Evans was asking all the right questions. Every question he thought of, Evans included in his debrief of the woman.

Her answers were short and to the point. Not the usual rambling answers witnesses gave. None of the usual evasion or tentative guesses, just the information asked for in a brief statement.

Upon finishing his breakfast, Evans downed his pint and, without announcing his intentions, stalked off towards the door marked 'Private', through which Helen had entered.

Helen and Campbell tagged along behind him and Helen showed them where the cabinet safe was.

The cabinet safe was roughly six feet tall by four wide and two feet deep. It sported a secure lock on the outside and shelving with files and backup computer CDs stacked neatly throughout. At the bottom there was a safe with a key code lock from which the money had been taken.

Evans asked for a list of employees for the last two years and a list of all suppliers, reps and repairmen who may have been in the office over the same period. Handing Helen a card with his contact details on, he asked for the list to be emailed to the address on the card as soon as possible, then he led Campbell out, stopping only to drain Campbell's untouched lager and collect three tinfoil parcels from Pam.

As they walked to the car Campbell rounded on Evans, asking why they had not paid for breakfast, why he was drinking before ten in the morning and why Helen Salter was not under suspicion, as she was the only person who had keys for the cabinet, the building and knew the internal safe code.

'Helen Salter used to be Job. She left after she blew the whistle on some bent coppers who were taking kickbacks. That's how I know she isn't the thief. Plus the fact we've had three of these types of burglaries in one night across the whole fucking county.' Pausing only to draw breath he resumed. 'Maybe in Glasgow there could be a coincidence like that, but three across Cumbria in one night just doesn't happen.'

'OK, I was wrong to miss that, but it seems too hard for anyone else to rob it that neatly. Typical burglars of licensed premises smash a way in and leg it with as much cash, booze and fags as they can carry.'

Evans scratched his backside without any attempt at discretion. 'That's what we've got then. A burglary committed by an atypical offender. It's not a bunch of scrotes or petty criminals who are little more than smash and grab merchants. They'd have left a trail a mile wide. What we're looking for is a thief who has a reason to be there if challenged and every cause to be concerned about leaving signs of their crime as they are trying to shift the blame onto those in possession of the keys or safe codes.'

Campbell didn't back down when Evans stood toe to toe with him. 'I don't yet know how much of a copper you are, sonny, but if you had been paying attention you would've seen me drop a twenty spot on our table as I finished the drink you left untouched. The breakfasts were three quid each and the pints two quid apiece. The rolls were nine quid in total, which leaves a pound tip. As for the pints I only drink when I need to think, and based on your current form, I can see I'm gonna have to do all the fucking thinking.'

Campbell cursed himself for not seeing Evans leave the money. Some new start he was making. One unorthodox character and he was distracted beyond belief.

Evans disappeared into an alley behind Beenies. Chasing after him Campbell half expected to find Evans relieving himself, instead he found him distributing the tinfoil parcels to a trio of homeless men.

The two men walked back to the car park, each wrapped up in their own thoughts and climbed into the BMW. Evans jumped into the driver's seat, despite Campbell's protestations that he better drive as he hadn't drunk two pints in the last hour.

Evans's response was typically uncompromising. 'Shut the fuck up, if I want nagged I'll bring the chief super along.'

Campbell was glad that he'd only be working with Evans for a week. He promised himself he'd make sure he insisted on using his own car tomorrow.

Chapter 9

Victoria's mobile beeped just once. Snatching it she tapped the screen until she could read the text message. It was from an unknown number and contained just two words.

Visit watchmykids.com

She reached for her laptop and while it booted up, summoned Nicholas to join her in the kitchen. Every second that passed was an eternity for her frayed nerves and unsettled stomach. The pretence of hiding her cigarettes had long gone and she now smoked in front of Nicholas as she plotted their next move. Nicholas's comment on her habit had earned him a face-full of second-hand smoke and a curt dismissal.

As soon as the laptop gave out the four tone chime of Windows loading, she went to the website which had a picture of her daughter holding that day's Daily Mail while Kyle held up the Sun.

Stifling back a sob, she thanked God they were unharmed. As they stared at the screen, the image of their children disappeared and was replaced with a video of Samantha walking around in a ridiculous French Maid costume serving food and drink to three of the four masked men who had abducted her. The camera seemed to find every opportunity to show what the maid's outfit was designed to cover and one lingering shot appeared to be taken from the floor and the cameraman zoomed in whenever Samantha bent forward. Both were struck dumb as they watched the perverted video of their daughter.

'Your kids are fine. Make sure you get us the money and they'll stay that way.' Elvis's voice sounded tinny coming from the computer. 'Watch the next video and you'll see what will happen to them if we don't get paid, or if you call the police. On this website is a contact form. Use that to let us know when you have the money. Remember no police. We have friends who'll tell us if you call them.'

The picture faded out and was replaced by a naked man tied to a wooden chair. From the right-hand side of the screen, a blowtorch of the type Elvis had shown them when he took their kids entered the shot, and moved towards the man's right knee.

A short blue flame blazed from the end of the nozzle and when a thumb depressed the long lever on the side, it changed as oxygen forced its way through the nozzle and fanned the flame into an intense silver blue.

A whooshing sound could be heard as the flame was applied to the man's leg. They watched agog as the heat blistered the skin until it blackened as the flame got ever closer. Nicholas turned and vomited into the sink until he was incapable of vomiting any more.

Victoria sat transfixed, ignoring the acidic smell of Nicholas's sick. Her eyes never leaving the screen, as she watched the torch burn its way through the man's knee. Once the torch had passed through the knee, the man's lower leg fell away, only prevented from hitting the floor by the duct tape binding his ankle.

The camera then shifted and zoomed in on the blackened and cauterised stump of the man's leg. The victim had passed out from the pain but his screams would haunt her forever.

'We've got to get the rest of the money together.' Victoria's voice cracked as she spoke. Tears formed silent rivers as they poured from her eyes.

The last three days had felt like purgatory. Every waking moment had been spent crushing down mental images of her children in peril at the hands of their kidnappers.

She had alternated between Kyle and Samantha's beds as she beckoned sleep to take her from the waking nightmare. Plots, schemes and plans ran through her mind as she tried every avenue she could think of to find the money needed to save her children.

Calls from Samantha's friends had become regular occurrences. They didn't believe Victoria's lie that she was ill. Samantha's missed date on Saturday coupled with her Facebook silence worried them. It took all Victoria's self-control not to scream at them to leave her alone. That Samantha was gone and may never come back.

She had toyed with the idea of using Samantha's Facebook profile herself. Making a few token comments and likes to quieten the friends, but she didn't fancy her chances of impersonating Samantha without fuelling suspicion. Kids these days had a language of their own and she'd be found out in no time.

If one of Samantha's friends was suspicious enough, they might call the police with some crazy idea fixed in their young mind. The last thing Victoria wanted was the police showing up at her door. If the kidnappers were watching them as they'd said they would, they'd know straightaway and her precious children would bear the brunt of their wrath.

To compound her situation, Victoria was forced to stay and work with Nicholas. He was the architect of her children's plight. Every word, gesture or mannerism assaulted her sensibilities. She could not bear to think of him, finding herself filled with disgust and self-loathing at the way she had been deceived by his lies.

Snatching her mobile from the table, she tried dialling the number with the intention of begging for her children to be released. All she got was a network message saying the number could not be connected.

She'd rather have been working than stuck at home with nothing to do. At work she could glean information to help her efforts in obtaining the ransom money. All she could do today was think dark thoughts.

The Easter eggs Kyle had so carefully arranged on the mantelpiece taunted her, mocking in their sentinel presence.

Helplessness and self-pity were her greatest enemies. Action was her friend, but until she was back at work, she couldn't get the data she needed to continue with her plan.

Instead she filled her day listing every saleable item in the house on eBay. Set to finish in three days' time, she made sure that every listing was also set to receive payment via PayPal or cash on collection. Cheques and postal orders were no use to their cause, so she blocked these methods of payment.

Chapter 10

Upon leaving Carlisle, Evans joined the motorway and went south before cutting across the fells and heading towards Bowness-on-Windermere. The majority of the journey was travelled far above the speed limit, with any hold up causing a stream of invective and politically incorrect abuse to spring from Evans's mouth.

Campbell having worked in the sectarian world of Glasgow was no stranger to bawdiness and black humour, but he couldn't stop himself from laughing when Evans berated one women driver – who looked younger than he did – for taking an age to turn a corner. 'For fuck's sake, Jock, look at that dithering old cow. I bet she's got the seat so far forward her lipstick will be rubbing off onto the windscreen and she daren't turn the wheel too quick in case her droopy old tits get tangled in it.'

As they'd barrelled down the M6, Campbell had queried Evans's choice of Bowness-on-Windermere as the first destination when Silloth was nearer to Carlisle.

'Silloth CID are far better than Bowness's, I trained most of them myself. The guys at Bowness are so shite that if you gave them a perfectly good fanny they'd only go and fuck it. We can trust the Silloth boys to have done the job right, so there's no immediate panic to get there, as I doubt we'll learn owt that'll not be in the report.'

Evans supplied a running commentary on the local history as he drove, only changing the subject whenever they neared a town with a police presence. Then he would inform his replacement of the various officers and detectives at each location. When Campbell asked for descriptions of any of the people Evans named, there would be a one-line description of their physical characteristics.

Campbell made furious notes of all the information he could and questioned Evans about the team he'd be taking over. He wasn't too bothered about their abilities; he wanted to make his own judgements on that. What he wanted to know was the background details that could take months to find out. He quizzed Evans on the team's work relationships, traumas they may have been through and family life.

As Evans navigated his way through the holiday traffic, Campbell looked at the quaint town with a visitor's eye. A riot of colour assaulted his eyes. Each shop, pub or cafe was painted in a different primary colour to the ones adjacent.

The pavements were filled with tourists dressed in shorts and T-shirts, the various cafes, restaurants and souvenir shops advertised their wares via window displays and sandwich boards. The road was filled with cars negotiating the streets with a newcomer's unfamiliarity. Sudden braking and un-indicated turns were the norm as drivers tried to find their way to their destinations.

From the outside, the Black Horse was a traditional small town hotel with whitewashed walls and black-painted window frames.

Evans marched round the back of the hotel and walked through a door, which led into the kitchens. Campbell followed Evans through the building, until they came entered the main public bar. A barman was restocking shelves in preparation for opening time.

Evans flashed his warrant card. 'Go and find that fat imbecile Larry.'

When the barman scuttled off to find the hotel manager, Evans set about pouring two pints of Stella, one of which he handed to Campbell. 'Drink it, there's no room for lightweights on my team.'

The hotel bar ran true to Campbell's expectations – a low ceiling with exposed wooden floor joists, a smattering of brass ornaments and a fireplace which, though not yet lit, was set ready with coal and kindling piled atop balled newspaper. A battered dartboard adorned one wall with the legend 'John was ere' chalked onto the scoreboard. Off to one side was a lounge bar-cum-restaurant where hotel residents and tourists would be served meals.

Campbell listened with interest as Evans filled him in on Fat Larry's history.

'Larry is the best hotelier in Cumbria. He spent his life savings putting his daughter Emily through rehab and then the poor bugger had to take a job working for the Leightons to pay off the money she snorted. He hates it, but he's a man of honour and will pay her debts off if it kills him.'

By the time Larry came into the bar, Evans was onto his second pint while Campbell had drank less than a mouthful. Larry was a dishevelled man in his fifties, whose girth caused him to wheeze with every step he took.

'Morning, Harry.' Larry poured a pint for himself and then sat down with the two DIs and lit a cigarette. Evans got up, retrieved an ashtray from behind the bar and helped himself to Larry's cigarettes, oblivious of the smoking ban.

Campbell introduced himself. 'We're here about last night's robbery.'

Larry looked at Evans, his face a portrait of misery. 'What do you need to know, Harry?'

Evans fired off the same list of questions he had bombarded Helen Salter with earlier. When he was finished answering the questions, Larry heaved his huge frame off his seat – which Campbell could have sworn gave a sigh of relief – to show them where the safe was kept. It was an old-fashioned style of safe, the kind you would expect to see in any John Wayne western. Standing three feet high and two wide it would weigh in excess of six hundred pounds, but it was opened with a single key.

'Who has keys for the safe?'

'There only is one.'

'And who has that key?'

'Me, of course.'

'Who else, Larry? If you'd stolen the money then you wouldn't still be here, you'd have fucked off away from the reach of the Leightons.'

'There's just one key and I keep it on me at all times.'

'Don't lie to me, Larry. If you have the key, someone must have picked the lock twice to steal the money.'

'Twice?'

'Of course twice, you imbecile.' Evans fixed Larry with a stare. 'You said a minute ago the safe was locked and when you opened it you discovered the money was missing. So either you stole the money, which we've already established didn't happen. Or the thief picked the lock to open it, stole the money and then picked the lock closed again. So tell me where the fucking key is kept.'

Larry's shoulders drooped as Evans shouted his last sentence. 'It's kept here.' He opened a door leading into a storage cupboard with a nail hanging from it.

'We made sure the staff knew who they were working for so that they wouldn't dare steal.'

'Someone dared, didn't they?'

As they made to leave Evans turned to Larry. 'What have you told the Leighton brothers?'

Larry's face was filled with self-pity. 'The truth, for what good it done me. They have added the missing money onto my debt but are charging twenty per-cent interest on it.'

'They can't do that to you, can they?' Campbell's mouth hung open.

'It was that or a one-way boat trip to the middle of Lake Windermere. Please, Harry, you've gotta find the thief and get the money back, or I'll never be out of debt to them.' Larry's eyes began to moisten.

'Then you better tell me the truth about everything and stop lying if you want us to catch this fucker.'

'OK, OK.' Larry took a long pull of his cigarette before continuing. 'The alarm is bust and has been for three months. The Leightons believe their reputation will keep the locals away and make me keep the safe key there so that they can come and get a few grand whenever they please. I called them yesterday to ask how much they took as they have always left a note in the past and I thought they had just forgotten.'

'Are you sure they aren't just tying you tighter to them with this apparent theft? You have this place booming most days and the profits must be good as they're hardly likely to have any mortgage to pay.'

'No, they've always been seen and usually have a drink in the bar before going to the safe. Besides I have been paying Emily's debt off religiously. They've even been sending the managers of their other hotels here to learn from me. I've got cancer, Harry, and they want me to teach their other hotel managers before I kick the bucket. The doc has given me eighteen months. I would've been free from them in six months. I planned to spend the time with my Emily before the cancer gets me. We've missed too much of each other's lives with me working all the hours God sent and her being off her face.

'Anything else to tell me?'

'Is that not enough?'

'Probably too much. You let me know if you think of owt else.'

While Evans took the A591 towards Keswick, Campbell put a call through to Chisholm. As he updated the DS, Campbell watched Lake Windermere flash past on his left. There were secluded marinas among the various hotels that bordered the lake. Out on the lake itself, boats of all different sizes powered or sailed their way forward. A steamer packed with waving tourists was rocking smaller boats with its wash.

When he'd finished his task, Campbell asked Evans who the Leighton brothers were.

'They're the ones who run most of the serious crime in Cumbria. I've got a file on them six inches thick but I've never managed to convict them. They're a right pair of bastards. They'd kill for fun, but their elder sister is the brains behind the operation. They're nothing more than the front that the criminal element knows about.'

As they were skirting Ambleside, a call from Lauren came through. Evans punched the button to answer the call through the car's hands-free system.

'Guv, we have four suppliers in common. They are Bandits' Express, Euston Vintners, Cumbria Food Service and Peters, Waugh and Beckett who are the accountants for each of the affected businesses.'

'Arrange a meeting with their head honchos for later today or first thing tomorrow, an' let me know who I'm meeting along with where and when.' He paused the conversation to berate a driver, who had the temerity to slow him down by driving at the speed limit.

'Put Bhaji Boy on the line.'

'You're on speaker, guv.' Bhaki's voice was easy to identify against the harsh Cumbrian accents of the other team members.

'Why didn't she tell me that from the start? I could have been using profane language or being politically incorrect about one of my team. Tell the stupid splitarse never to fuck me over like that again.'

'Enough with the bullshit, Quasi! Get to the bloody point!' DCI Grantham's roar almost deafened Campbell and Evans.

'Hello, sir. Could I please inquire of DC Bhaki as to which garages have been conned and if there is any pattern?' Evans's voice was sweetness and light as he winked at Campbell.

Campbell could picture Grantham's apoplexy and had to bite his lip when the slamming of a door came through the speaker.

Bhaki filled the silence echoing down the line. 'Sir, there's been seven garages complaining of the con over the last six days.'

'We're halfway between Ambleside and Keswick, are there any near us?'

'Duncan's in Silloth and the Gateway Garage in Cockermouth are the nearest. Do you want directions?'

'No, I know where they are. How much did they each have missing?'

'Duncan's were down by two thousand exactly; so was the Gateway Garage. Both sold a car for five grand.'

'Did any of them have CCTV?' Campbell joined the conversation.

'No, they didn't, but Duncan's sold their car to a woman and the Gateway Garage sold theirs to a man.'

'What about the other garages, did they all have a two grand deficit on a five grand motor?'

'Yes, and they all said the customers walked into the showroom and done the deal there and then. In each case, they drove the car away. Sometimes they bartered down the price to five grand and sometimes they paid the asking price of four nine nine five. All of the garages sold a car to a person who gave their address as fifty-one News Street, Wigton. DS

Chisholm looked the address up on Google StreetView and it's the police station.'

'Get onto them all and get descriptions of the people who ripped them off and compare them. Lauren, what have you found out about the farm robberies?'

'I'm still working on it and compiling lists for cross-referencing, but from what I can gather about a dozen places have been affected in the last week alone.'

'Send it through to us and let me know as soon as it's been sent.' Evans hung up.

'I've seen this kind of thing before, and think I know how they are doing it.'

'How?' Evans fumbled in his pockets for a lighter and lit his cigarette as they rounded a sharp bend.

'By jumping up numbers when counting. This is done by distracting the seller with questions. When we get to a shop I'll get some playing cards and show you. It's easier than explaining.'

They arrived at the Gateway Garage in Cockermouth and found the salesman who had made the sale. Campbell took the lead with questioning him, asking for details of the car and its number plate and vehicle identification number.

He also asked if the V5C paperwork had been sent off to the DVLA yet to register the car with its new owners.

'Yes, of course it has.' The salesman took Campbell across the forecourt and through the tired showroom with dirty windows in desperate need of a clean to a small office.

Campbell pulled out the two packs of playing cards he had bought on the way to the garage. He handed them to the salesman and told him to count out one hundred cards.

'Why?'

Campbell noted a marked difference between the salesman's accent and the harsher more guttural sound of East Cumbrians like Evans and Lauren. The salesman possessed a softer, more drawn-out accent. His words were stretched, rather than the abbreviated slang common to quick-speaking Carlislers.

'I'm gonna show you a trick. Harry, come and see this.' Evans had wandered around the forecourt and was paying more attention to a second-hand M5 than he was to Campbell.

Campbell got Evans to re-count the cards the salesman had counted and they both agreed there were one hundred playing cards in the pile.

Picking up the stack of cards, Campbell sat down at a desk and motioned for the salesman to sit on the opposite side. Once the man was seated, he started counting the cards onto the desk.

'One.'

'Two.'

'Three.'

'Four.'

'How many cars have you for sale today?'

The salesman took a moment to calculate the number before he answered Campbell. 'Twenty-three.'

Campbell laid a card down. 'Twenty-four.'

'Twenty-five.'

'Twenty-six.'

'How old are you? You look near retirement age?

'I'm only fifty-four, so a few years yet.' The salesman pulled a face at Campbell's question, irritation creeping into his voice.

'Fifty-five.'

'Fifty-six.'

'Fifty-seven.'

'Fifty-eight.'

'Sorry about that. I'm twenty years younger than you. I was born in December seventy-nine.'

'It's OK.' The salesman nodded at Campbell's apology.

'Eighty.'

'Eighty-one.'

'Eighty-two.'

'Eighty-three.'

'I've heard the temperature is to hit ninety-eight this weekend.' Campbell laid down another card as he spoke.

'Really, ninety-eight?'

'Ninety-nine, one hundred.' Campbell crossed his hands on the table.

'Please, can you count the cards I have given you?'

'Again? They been counted three times now: first, I counted them and then he counted them and then you counted them in front of us both.'

'Just count them for me please.'

'This is where you learn how you've been tricked, you imbecile.' Evans made no attempt to hide his disdain of the salesman.

The salesman counted the cards that Campbell had laid on the table, and looked up in amazement when he finished. There were only twenty-one cards in his hands.

'Are you looking for these?' Campbell lifted his hands to reveal the other seventy-nine cards.

'How the hell did you do that?'

'I distracted you by asking you questions which had numbers as the answer or were about different numbers. When I started counting again I carried on from the number which had just been spoken.'

'Well, fuck me sideways with a pickaxe.'

'Was that familiar?' Campbell ignored Evans's outburst, and directed his question at the salesman.

'Yeah. That's just what it was like.' A hand rubbed the salesman's reddening face. 'Mebbe the jumps in numbers weren't as big, but that's just how it was when he counted the money out.

Campbell was elated at discovering the method used to con the garages. As they drove out of the forecourt he explained the methodology to Evans. 'It's a simple enough scam if you have the confidence to pull it off and if you use the same questions at each garage you get the same amount of money. The key is the questions. The ones I chose were designed to annoy or interest him, which gives the bigger distraction. Also I overcooked it for effect. He would never have missed the jumps in numbers if I had given him notes instead of playing cards.'

'So these folk are walking in with three grand and driving away with a car worth five? That has to be one of the best cons I've ever heard of. When we catch them we should give them a medal for services to motorists.'

'Is it even illegal?'

'If both parties agree to the amount of money that changes hands, I think it'd be very hard to prove otherwise in court.'

'That's what I was thinking. Say we do catch the folk who're doing this, what then? We know how they're doing it, but it'll be a nightmare to prove without CCTV footage. Any halfway competent solicitor will get them off the hook in a few minutes.'

Evans gave a twisted smile. 'I'll think of something. There's no way we can let people get ripped off like this.

While Evans rocketed the BMW to Silloth with his usual disregard for traffic laws and other road users, Campbell used the time to call Bhaki, instructing him to get onto the DVLA and flag up the cars on their system. With luck they could trace the new owners and find out who was behind the scam.

When they reached Silloth, Evans declined Campbell's suggestion of a visit to the garage, instead pulling into the sprawling caravan site that housed Jumpers Entertainment Centre. A disco-pub, family-style restaurant and games machines were all housed in one shed-like building.

There were rows of static caravans running perpendicular to the Solway Firth, most had cars parked in front of them. People wandered back and forth in holiday clothes despite the cool sea breeze carried from the nearby shore.

Pulling into a disabled parking space, Evans switched off the engine, pulled out his mobile and sent off a short text which Campbell did not get to see.

A groundskeeper approached them and pointing out they'd parked in a disabled space. Evans fixed the man with an icy stare. 'I've got Tourette's. Fuck off.'

'You can't speak to members of the public like that.' Campbell struggled to keep his face straight while getting the right amount of condemnation into his voice, as the bemused groundskeeper walked away shaking his head. Despite being shocked by Evans's cavalier attitude to public relations, he couldn't help but laugh at his terminology.

'Jobsworths get right on my tit end. Why is this place not open yet? Don't they want to get back on track? Or are they having a coupla days' mourning for the missing wonga?'

'There's somebody in there.' Campbell had ignored Evans's latest diatribe and was peering through the window. He banged on the glass and the person who came across to the door was in charge of something or other, if the flashy suit and expensive haircut were any indication.

This guy has to be a wanker; he's dressed like he's managing the Waldorf Astoria, when in reality he's in charge of a shitty little caravan site in a godforsaken, weather-beaten hellhole.

'DIs Campbell and Evans.' Campbell made the introductions to the man who identified himself as George Davis, the manager. 'All we need to trouble you for is a look at where the safe is, our colleagues have got most of the details we require.'

'Just follow me and I'll show you where it is.' Davis led them through the building into the back of house area. An emergency exit and the door to the public areas were the only means of accessing the area.

'Is this door alarmed?' Evans peered at the back door looking for wires or contact sensors.

'No, it's not, unfortunately. I've asked the proprietor to have the alarm system added to it, but he was reluctant to spend the money.'

'He'll mebbe have more of an incentive now.' Evans turned to Campbell. 'Right, mara, take a look at this safe then tell me what the code number is.'

Evans scribbled on a piece of paper he retrieved from his pocket, while Campbell scrutinised the safe.

Campbell studied the safe for a moment and when he felt confident he straightened up and faced Evans. '0898A.'

Evans unfolded the scrap of paper he'd written on. '0898A.'

'How the hell do you both know that?' Davis was now questioning the validity of these policemen who had waltzed in and cracked the safe code in less than two minutes.

'The numbers eight, nine and zero are practically worn away, while all the others are virtually factory fresh, as is the letter B while A is again very much worn. By the look of the safe it dates back to the early nineties at most. This was a time when the number oh eight nine eight preceded all the phone sex lines, so it would be a good mnemonic.'

Campbell was enjoying the look of dismay washing over the pretentious Davis.

'Bloody hell, it's obvious when you explain it like that.'

They made their way out with Evans pausing to look at a scenic calendar that hung in the manager's office.

Campbell got a text from Lauren informing him that they had a meeting with Bandits Express's owner at 3 p.m., Cumbria Food Service's manager at 4 p.m. at their respective offices in Carlisle. Euston Vintners was a national company whose head office was in London, but she had arranged for their area manager to meet Evans and Campbell at Carlton Hall – the regional HQ – the next day at 10 a.m. Peters, Waugh and Beckett were Kendal based and the managing partner had rearranged his schedule to see them at noon the next day.

Campbell relayed the information to Evans who checked his watch.

'Right, let's get some brain stimulus. We've got an hour before we meet with Bandits Express.'

Evans was a good as his word and he pulled into the car park of the Coach and Horses at Wigton just off the A596 – the main artery from Carlisle to West Cumbria.

'Two pints of Jennings, please, Mike.' Evans again ordered the drinks without asking what Campbell wanted.

As they made their way over to a vacant table in the busy roadside pub, Campbell steeled himself as they sat down on opposite sides of the table 'With all due respect, do you realize you are a real-life, walking, talking cliché?'

'What do you mean, like?'

'Well, I've made your acquaintance twice now and worked with you for half a day. In that time, you've assaulted a suspect, driven under the influence of alcohol, smoked on public premises, been less politically correct than Bernard Manning and taken freebies from a member of the public, who we are supposed to protect from gangsters. You are like every seventies TV cop who ever walked the beat. It's the twenty-first century now and that kind of behaviour is no longer acceptable.'

'Don't start to idolize me until you know the full score.' Evans's face twisted into a scowl. 'I was the original and they are just copying what we did back then. Mebbes I can sue the telly companies for plagiarism, if you're right with your assessment of me.'

Campbell wasn't prepared to let Evans dodge his accusations. 'That's no answer and you know it.'

Evans ignored him and pulled out his mobile, scrolling through the different screens, he found the one he was looking for and showed Campbell the text he'd sent earlier.

Maureen, Larry is innocent on this one. Harry

'So who the hell is Maureen then?'

'Let's just say her surname is Leighton and leave it there.'

'Then why have you got her number in your mobile? Are you bent or what?' Campbell tried to appear calm, but inside he was furious with this throwback from the seventies.

'No, I'm not bent. The longer you are by my side the more you will learn. I may not have been some protégée who set the world alight in the Big Smoke, but I'm the best known copper in Cumbria for two reasons. One, I catch the buggers that no fucker else can, and two, I make sure that the criminals in this area get what's coming to them, whether by my own methods or through the courts.' He paused to gulp down a mouthful of the hoppy beer. 'Anybody I've ever brought in has been bang to rights and not one of the fuckers has escaped prosecution. The Cumbrian people either love or fear me, but they all know who I am and what I stand for.'

'Jesus Christ, man, you can't behave like this way in today's world. You've got every chav in the land with a mobile phone, videoing every move you make and word you say.'

'It ain't happened yet and I'm not worried about it.'

'Well, you bloody well should be. It's no wonder they are not offering to keep you on as an active DI. You must get more complaints than a dozen officers.'

'I'll admit I've been in the rubber-heeler's office from time to time, but I don't let that shite stop me from doing my job, which, in case you've forgotten, is protecting the public and locking up criminals. The public want to feel safe in their beds, and they all want a return to the days when coppers caught bad guys, and locked them up for a long time.'

'That's no reason to go running round like you're Gene Hunt. There are set procedures and we are supposed to inspire confidence in the public, not insult and offend them.'

'I don't give a shite about political correctness and diversity. I have a job to do and I do it. Ask any person on the street if they've heard of DI Harry Evans and you'll get an answer that'll tell you if they are a criminal or not. The law-abiding applaud me and the scallies do everything they can to keep out of my way.'

'Just don't expect me to condone or defend your behaviour. I'm not risking my career just to give you a last week of uncontrolled mayhem.'

'Don't worry, mate. I don't want you or anybody else covering my back. You can piss about being polite and diverse. I'll do what needs done and catch the buggers.'

The barman came across with the burgers Evans had ordered and asked them to keep their voices down. Both men reddened as neither had been aware their voices had risen during the argument.

They used the interruption to cool down and attacked their meals, with Evans again dispensing Tabasco sauce from the bottle in his jacket pocket.

Campbell recognised the fact he needed Evans's help. Swallowing his pride he offered an olive branch. 'Look, Harry, we've got to work together for the next week and I need you to show me round Cumbria and make the introductions to key people so I can carry on when you retire. I won't grass you up or cause you any bother if you give me the best possible chance of succeeding in my new role.'

'Keep your sermons to yourself and I'll do it. Mind, I'm doing it for the good people of Cumbria. No bugger else.'

Chapter 11

A memory plucked at Victoria's subconscious, causing her to leap from her seat and race upstairs. Crashing into the master bedroom she crossed to her chest of drawers and sank to her knees, dreading what she may not find. After a deep breath and a mental crossing of fingers, she had drawn enough courage to open the drawer.

Pulling out the expensive lingerie piece by piece, she rooted through her 'naughty-knicker drawer' until she found what she wanted and didn't want to find.

With white knuckled fingers she removed the maid's costume she had worn as a treat for Nicholas's last birthday. Rising to her feet, she strode across the bedroom, lips thinning with every step.

She found Nicholas in the kitchen washing his face at the sink, while cleaning up the mess from his vomiting.

'Do you remember me wearing this?'

Nicholas's head snapped round at her accusatory tone. He'd had many a deserved barrage from her over these last couple of days, but now there was a different edge to her voice. She'd crossed the line from anger into fury and carried on into the zone where red mists enshrouded reasoned thought.

Victoria held the French Maid costume in front of Nicholas's eyes. 'Answer me, damnit. Do you remember me wearing this?' She poked him in the chest to punctuate every word.

'Of course I do. You wore it for one of my birthdays. As soon as I saw Samantha in that video I remembered it. That's when I started to throw up. I remembered what we did that night.'

'Well, that's exactly what those men will be doing to Samantha. And it's all your fault.' Nicholas backed against the worktop but Victoria still jabbed at his ribs with a well-manicured forefinger. 'I wish it was me they had taken, not Samantha and Kyle. I would sooner die than let anything happen to them. And then look what happens. They get kidnapped and the kidnappers make Samantha parade around like some cheap prostitute for their pleasure.'

'I know, Victoria, I know. Why do you think I was sick?' Nicholas put his arms around his wife and held her tight, both to calm her down and as a means of self-defence.

'Get your hands off me.' Victoria fought her way free and delivered a vicious slap to his cheek. 'If *any* harm comes to my babies, then I'll bloody well kill you.'

Nicholas stood without moving, waiting for calmness to wash over his wife.

Taking control of her emotions, Victoria backed away from her husband. 'Get your act together, you wimp. We've got a busy night ahead of us.'

'D'you think I don't fucking know that, woman?'

The sneer in his voice was alien to Victoria's ears. Taken aback she retreated from this different side of Nicholas.

'The rotten bastards.' His foot bounced off a cupboard door. He repeated the kick. 'Twats. Motherfucking twatting bastards.'

More kicks followed as hatred and despair flew from his mouth in a series of swear words Victoria had never known him to use before.

When he was spent he flopped onto the floor panting.

'You finished?'

A nod.

Victoria stood over him and pointed at the ruined cupboard door. 'You're a joke, Nicholas Foulkes. You attack a door that can't fight back, yet you sat on your arse while your children were stolen from under your nose. I hope that you feel proud of yourself. The one time you do show some balls, you damage something of ours. Run up another expense. I hope your self-loathing eats you alive.'

Chapter 12

'Do you think tomorrow will be as bad then?' Campbell was at home with his wife, Sarah. They had been married just under a year and she was excited at his transfer out of Glasgow to the safer parishes of Cumbria.

Their semi-detached home was on a new estate bordering Gretna. Sarah had been a wedding planner at one of the Gretna Green wedding venues when Campbell had been his brother's best man. They had started a romance that had soon become very intense. Six months after that first meeting they'd announced their engagement.

'Every day will be like that with him.' Campbell wrapped his arms around her legs and kissed her swollen stomach as she stood over him. 'I didn't say it was bad, just over the top. It's as if he's stuck in the seventies.'

'You haven't talked about anything else since you got home. I thought it was bothering you.'

'Maybe it is bothering me a bit, but not in a bad way. I've spent my career as a Glasgow copper where almost everyone you meet is a stranger. He seems to know everybody wherever we go. Cumbria might be much bigger than Glasgow but there's less people.'

'You did expect it to be different to Glasgow.'

'I know, and it is different. Just different-different if you know what I mean.' Seeing her nod, he carried on. 'The rural areas may well be very old-fashioned in their views on policing, but I'm used to a low profile and he is as subtle as a punch in the nose. It's just a way of policing I thought had died out with flares and kipper ties.'

'Well, what are the rest of the team like then?' Sarah wanted to get her husband talking about the team he'd be working with. Not the man he was replacing. 'What are they like as people? Do you think you'll get on with them?'

It was a good question, which Campbell answered after a moment's thought. 'They seem decent enough. Getting on with them depends very much on the way Evans has worked with them. If they are all as unconventional as him, it'll be tough to get them policing properly.'

'How many are in your team?'

'There's a DS and two DCs in the team. The DS is a big fat guy who does nothing but sit in front of a computer all day. One of the DCs is an Asian guy and according to Evans he's a shit-hot detective.'

'What does the DS do all day at a desk?'

'He fills all the reports in and does the team's paperwork, but he mainly deals with cyber crimes and runs searches through databases, that kind of thing.'

'And the other DC?

Campbell hesitated before telling his wife about Lauren Phillips. Pregnancy had left a trail of destruction across his wife's body as well as adding a glow of contentment. The nubile Lauren had been wearing a skirt suit which had risen to flash generous amounts of stocking clad thigh. 'Evans reckons she's a top-class interviewer who can break people quicker than the Gestapo.' What he didn't add was that Evans had also told him Lauren was a nymphomaniac who kept a string of lovers.

'She's not competition for me, is she?' Sarah was only half joking. A previous boyfriend's serial infidelity had shattered her ability to trust. Campbell had proved himself time and time again, but doubts were never far from her mind.

'Of course not. You're the only woman I'm interested in.' Campbell was lying though.

Recalling Evans's earlier description of a Penrith DI, Campbell almost told his wife that Lauren Philips had a face like a gargoyle licking piss off a nettle, but he managed to stop before telling the lie.

'Glad to hear it.' A smile caressed her lips. 'Although I did have another woman knocking at my door asking for your services.'

'Who?'

'Rachel. She was round to ask a favour of you.'

Campbell sighed wondering what Rachel wanted. Her boyfriend had been killed by a roadside bomb in Helmand two years ago. Grief had made Rachel pile on the pounds as she sought comfort in junk food. Left alone with a young son and no family members nearby, Rachel had leaned on him and Sarah since they'd moved into their home. There had been a constant request for favours and help. A blocked drain, a sticking door and advice on her car were just some of the worries she'd come calling with.

Being full of sympathy for his neighbour and her situation, he'd been happy to help whenever he could. However, the last couple of times he'd done a favour, he'd noticed her giving him the glad-eye. Reluctant to tell Sarah of Rachel's flirting lest she upset herself about something that would never happen, he'd resolved to scale down the speed of his responses in the hope she'd find someone else to be the man about her house.

'What's she want done this time?'

'John.' From Sarah's lips his name became an admonishment. 'Don't be like that. She called round to ask if you could teach Kyle to ride the bike she got him for his birthday.'

Campbell saw the opportunity to practice his parenting skills as well as score a barrow-load of brownie points with Sarah. Kyle was a good kid who lacked a male influence in his life. Teaching him to ride a bike would be a fun task for them both.

'Tell her I'll be happy to teach him.'

Sarah patted her pregnant stomach. 'Good. Now if you have anything about you, you'll take me upstairs and give me a right gentle seeing to. That may just get Junior here to make an appearance. If that doesn't work then you can take me for an Indian tomorrow. I know he's not due until next week, but I don't know if I can wait that long to meet him.'

'I say we give the sex another week.'

Sarah laughed as she took her husband's hand.

Chapter 13

Emerging from her fourth shower of the day, Samantha attempted to dry her body but the sodden towel was worse than useless. Her skin glowed bright crimson where she had repeatedly scrubbed herself with the rough flannel.

The captor wearing the Tony Blair mask had made her dress up in a sex costume and parade about while he'd filmed her. Try as she might, she couldn't cleanse the revulsion from her body. His every look a perverted caress. Her skin crawled and twitched. She knew that before long, she'd be back in the shower.

Kyle had been terrified when she'd been taken out of the room for a second time. He'd tried to fight the men off, but Blair had given him a firm push that landed him on the mattress. She'd had to cuddle him for an age upon her return.

Wrestling a still damp body into her clothes, she attempted once again to erase the memory of his eyes looking down the top of her costume or up the skirt. He'd made a point of having her bend over so she was at her most exposed. One more than one occasion he'd had her hold a pose while he'd zoomed in.

'What's wrong, Sam? Why do you keep having showers?'

'I feel sweaty. That's all.'

She hated lying to her brother, but he was too young to understand. Samantha well remembered the conversation her mother had had with her some years ago about sex. It wasn't a conversation she wanted to have with Kyle. She knew that if she explained to him what had happened downstairs, he'd be terrified for her.

'Sam.'

Kyle was looking at her face. She could see in his eyes that he knew she was holding back on him. Such was the strength of their bond they both knew he would accept her lie.

Wise beyond his years, Kyle knew when to press matters and when to let them go.

'What game are you playing?' The question was designed to change the subject and it worked. Kyle bounded across the room and showed her the box.

'It's an eighteen.' Looking at the box in detail she recognised the title as one of the most popular video gaming franchises.

'It's brilliant. You drive around in different cars. You can even get guns to kill people.'

Samantha felt she ought to persuade him to play something more suitable, but in their current situation his playing an eighteen-rated video game was the least of their worries.

As the game was for one player, Samantha sat on the mattress watching him while thoughts of Blair's predatory eyes ran through her mind.

Kyle paused his game and went to the bathroom only to return a few seconds later.

'Why is your new dress in the bin?'

Samantha fought the urge to snatch the costume from his hands. 'It doesn't fit very well. Put it back in the bin.'

With him seated in front of the TV, shooting the characters he didn't run over, she focused her mind on trying to combat her revulsion.

She recalled the holiday she'd enjoyed last autumn. Seven days of Mediterranean sun with her best friend. Six nights of clubbing in micro-skirts that she hadn't dared bring home lest her mother see them. Their days spent by the pool or lying on the beach, they'd revelled in wearing bikinis that had less material than the underwear she now wore. Remembering the way they had courted gazes from the lads they saw gave her strength, but didn't change one simple fact.

Back on Ibiza, she was in control. She could cover up, walk away, or as she had on one occasion, allow things to progress further. In this house, she had no control. The men held all the cards. She was at their mercy.

Assessing the threats, she knew Blair was the one to worry about. The others had done the typical male thing of having sly looks. Blair, on the other hand, was blatant with his lecherous behaviour.

'Sam, look.' Kyle held a small white tooth in his hand. 'Do you think the tooth fairy will come here if I put it under the mattress?'

Samantha mentally searched her pockets before answering. Realising she didn't have any money on her, she gave a little shrug. 'I don't think the tooth fairy comes unless you put it under your own pillow.'

Kyle's chin wobbled as he fought back tears. 'Are you sure? Jamie was at his granny's house and he got two pounds instead of one.'

Samantha lifted a corner of the mattress. 'We can try. But if the tooth fairy doesn't come here then I'm sure she'll leave the money under your pillow at home.'

Chapter 14
Tuesday

'Right then. What we have on the robberies is as follows. Firstly, they have all been done without damage to property or environs. Secondly, there are no obvious suspects yet. We've had word back on the dabs and they are all accounted for. None of the staff have a record except for Fat Larry who was done for assault when he foiled a break-in fifteen years ago. Thirdly, whoever is behind these crimes is fucking with us: all of the safes were left in the closed position. This does not take much time but does point the finger at people who either had the keys or codes to the safes. My hunch is that the thief is trying to deflect the blame elsewhere. Fourthly, some of these buildings weren't alarmed; the thief may have known this. There were many others they could have hit for a larger payday, but these were chosen. There must be a connection between them that we've yet to find. The bosses from Bandits Express and Cumbria Food Service we met yesterday are going to fax us their delivery logs for the last year. We can find out from them if there are any common denominators among their delivery men.'

Lauren updated the whiteboard as Evans spoke.

Evans took the marker from her. 'OK, now we'll hear what Totty Tits has to say about the thefts from the farms.'

Throwing Evans an indulgent smile, Lauren gave her debrief. 'Me and DS Chisholm spent yesterday afternoon compiling a complete list of everything that has been reported stolen from farms on our patch. Let me tell you, the list is a long one. There have been twenty-eight quad bikes, seven normal motor bikes, five ride-on lawn-mowers, three tractors which strangely had no cabs, over seventy hand-held power tools like chainsaws and hedge cutters. They were all stolen in the last five weeks with only odd thefts before then. Incidentally almost half of the power tools were stolen from one farm at Stonethwaite where the farmer had a sideline in repairs.

'Was it James Johnson's place?'

'Yes, guv. How did you know that?'

'He's well known for repairing small tools in that area. His workshop is always full of them as he cannot keep on top of the repairs, what wi' running the farm as well. Besides he's got a drink problem and is unconscious most nights.' Seeing Campbell failing to conceal a wide smile, he turned to face him. 'What the hell is wrong with you?'

Campbell scowled the smile from his face. 'Nothing.' He was amazed when he heard Evans say someone else had a drink problem. The man was a walking, talking hypocrite.

He'd sat quietly through the briefing, making notes on changes he wanted to implement to the way the team was run. Top of his list was to change the way they spoke to each other. A DI calling a DC 'Totty Tits' was unacceptable. Although he possessed enough self-awareness to admit to himself that if he wasn't married he'd love to get to grips with Lauren's tits.

'Sorry. Lauren, did you say the three tractors had no cabs on?'

'Yes, sir. We had a run of similar thefts last year which lasted a couple of months and then stopped dead. The general thinking is it's gangs coming from elsewhere and robbing a few places a night. We even suspected they were following delivery wagons to find out where new bikes and so on were being sold. One farmer surprised them last year and was put in hospital after confronting them. He'd said he couldn't count them all, but there seemed to be about a dozen of them.'

Evans parked his heels on a desk. 'What did Eddie at Crime Prevention have to say about the SmartWater aspect then?'

'He said, and I quote, "Tell that CID clown that I'm one man covering one of the most rural counties in the country. And if he thinks he can do any better then he's welcome to try."'

'So the budgetary cuts have reached Crime Prevention as well. There used to be five of the buggers and now it's just Eddie. No wonder there are still farms without SmartWater when he's got to do it all himsel'. Farmers can be stubborn bastards at times; most of them live in the past. They never lock their doors or take keys out of tractors and seck like.'

Campbell stood up to address the team. His management training told him it was best to be in a dominant position and also one where he could establish eye contact with whomever he was speaking to. 'What height and width were the tractors, Lauren?'

'I don't know, sir, but I have the make and model numbers if that helps.'

The disparity in respect levels from Lauren might be blatant, but it was to be expected. Evans would always get 'guv', whereas he would be just another 'sir' until he earned the team's approval and respect. He'd been the same himself with new bosses.

When the team honoured him with the term 'guv', he'd know he'd been accepted into their ranks. Until then he was just another boss.

'Can you get me that info from the web, please, Chisholm?' Using good manners was yet another edict he'd learned from the DI course. 'I think that what they are doing is bringing a cattle wagon from wherever they belong and filling it with any vehicles or tools that can fit into it. They will have a separate car or two filled with bodies to help them load up. They'll get maybe eight or ten quads a night into the wagon along with any small tools they can lay their hands on. What looks more at home in the country than a cattle wagon?'

'Makes sense to me, Jock. Lauren, get onto traffic and have them pull every cattle wagon they see on the motorway south of Penrith and on any country road after ten at night. Bhaki, did you get owt back from Swansea about the cars?'

'Not yet. They are supposed to be getting back to me before lunchtime, but you know what they are like.'

'Idle buggers are slower than treacle running uphill on a frosty morning. If you've heard nothing by dinner-time call again, say you are me and hurry the lazy sods along. Chisholm, find out from the licensing boards across the county the name and address of every licensed premises and send them a letter warning them about the break-ins and to increase their security. Also do the same for all of the garages that buy

71

and sell cars. Eddie at Crime Prevention cannot possibly do that as well as trying to educate every farmer in the county, but at least let him know what I've asked you to do and liaise with him about the content of the letters.'

'OK, sir. By the way I've just googled the tractors that have been stolen and the largest is six foot high by seven foot wide. They would easily fit into a cattle wagon.'

'Good, now find out how many dealers in Cumbria sell quad bikes and the average cost of a new one.'

Chapter 15

'Sir, have you got a minute?' Evans walked into Grantham's office without knocking and took a seat opposite his boss.

'What do you want, Quasi?'

'We have a few leads on each of our cases and I want to set up a sting on the farm robberies as they are the largest crime so far.'

'What do you have in mind, Harry?'

'I want to place orders for three or four quad bikes from each of the main dealers and have GPS bugs planted on them. They will have to be sold to a farm that does not have SmartWater technology. Then we wait for them to be stolen and track them down and nick the buggers in the act. Signed, sealed and delivered.'

'And just how much will this cost?'

'With a bit of luck and some careful finessing, nothing; but without, three and a half grand for each bike, plus VAT, plus whatever the homing device costs. After that it's just manpower and the costs associated with that.'

'What exactly do you mean by careful finessing, Harry? Because there is no way I can condone spending anything like three and a half grand, plus VAT, times however many bikes you want to put out there with GPS systems hidden in them.'

'I think a call from a high-ranking officer such as the assistant or deputy chief constable to one of the leading manufacturers such as Honda, Suzuki, or Polaris asking for some quads to be loaned to us would drastically reduce the cost. If they refused, then we'd inform them of how their competitors had happily complied with our request. And that when the story broke after the operation we would praise the efforts of the companies who had aided us, and imply through the farming press that the companies who had refused to help us were delighted with the thefts as it meant sales figures were up.'

'Bloody hell, Quasi! That's blackmail. We can't be seen to blackmail people; we're the police for God's sake.'

'With all due respect, sir, you are missing the point entirely. It is merely a question of whether they choose to help the police, and receive praise for their assistance in helping their customers fight crime. I reckon magazines such as the Farmers Guardian would jump at the story of how companies teamed up with the police. The refusing companies' omission would be damning.'

'That's still blackmail you're talking about.'

Evans shook his head with a wry smile on his lips. 'It's honesty. Taking into consideration farmer's typically cynical and mistrustful nature, all we would have to do is thank the companies who took part and let it be known that other major manufacturers did not answer our call. I know I could talk them into it, if I had the seniority of rank.'

'Don't even think about it, Harry. I know for a fact you have passed yourself off as every rank imaginable to get what you want, but enough is enough.'

'Not an issue. There'll be photo ops with this one. Even I can't get away with that. On the other hand, we could always buy the quad bikes ourselves and sell them on after the op.'

'I'll speak to the ACC and see what he says, but believe me, if we get the green light, we better get a conviction from this, Harry, or I'll have your balls on a plate.'

'You'll need a platter.'

Recognising his luck was pushed to the edge of a precipice, Evans made his way out of Grantham's office and back to the cubbyhole he and his team inhabited.

Chisholm greeted him with a sheet of paper. 'There's been another break-in, guv.'

'Where at?'

'The Vaults.'

'How much did they get this time?'

'Just over four and a half grand.'

'From a Monday night. We're in the wrong game.'

'Apparently they had a birthday party last night.'

'From a Monday. Does nobody care about being sober at work anymore?'

Coffee flew from Campbell's mouth and covered the PC monitor in front of him.

'Problem, Jock?'

Seeing Campbell shake his head, he turned back to Chisholm.

'It was for a traveller, guv.'

'Hah! All those dodgy notes they'll have taken last night have been stolen from them. Save them the hassle of trying to bank them or pass them on.'

Evans checked his watch and dropped his feet back to the floor. 'Right, Jock, you and I are going there to see what we can find out before the CSI boys get their arses parked. We've got enough time for a preliminary visit before we have to be in Penrith.'

Evans was impatient to get going. 'Come on, hurry up, we have to get to the Dogs before the CSI team. They never let me near enough to learn owt useful.'

Confused by the name change, Campbell queried Evans. 'I thought it was called the Vaults?'

'It is, but it's known as the Dogs 'cause it's bollocks in there.'

Parking in the loading bay of a shop, Evans hustled Campbell into the Vaults. The street-level entrance was open despite the club being closed. Evans hadn't been inside for years, but he remembered the layout. The Vaults was built astride one of the city's former walls. It was ground level at one side but descended down four levels as it trailed the outer skin of the city wall.

His nose crinkled at the overpowering odour of stale beer and sweaty bodies. The cigarette ban had done a lot of good things, but the one area where it failed was the way that you could now smell what pubs were really like.

Never a fan of the club scene, he was grateful that the place was closed. Packed with bodies this place would be sauna hot, the stench unbearable. In his mind, he could picture the customers. Girls with their muffin tops wedged into boob tubes and short shorts two sizes too small. Their hair scraped back into a ponytail with such venom it gave their faces no room for expression. Apart from the ever sullen pout. The lads were no better. Kitted out in Matalan's finest, they would be drunk, stoned or both. Eye contact would be an invitation to fight. Speaking to a girl they knew would precipitate a broken glass attack. The aim of the evening a union neither party would want or be able to remember.

Finding the staircase, he went up a level and found the manager's office. The manager was dressed in casual clothes and sat at a desk, a telephone pressed against his ear.

The half of the conversation Evans could hear sounded cloying and apologetic. Surmising the manager was advising the proprietor of the robbery, Evans allowed him to finish his call.

As soon as the call was ended the manager fired questions at Evans and Campbell. 'Who are you? Why are you here?'

'We're the police.' Evans flashed his warrant card. 'And, we're the police.'

Listening to the manager's account, Evans took in the position of the old Milner safe from which the money had been taken.

Evans examined the door where the manager suspected the thief had entered. Beside the door was an alarm keypad with the cover hanging down over it. Lifting the cover with a pencil he had purloined from the manager's desk, Evans shook his head in disbelief. 'Is your code number for this alarm six seven nine five.'

'How do you know that?'

'Because some imbecile has written it on the back of the cover, that's how.'

Evans shook his head and walked away from the alarm panel. 'You might as well hang a sign on the door saying "Please rob us", you are so stupid about security. Get me a list of everyone who has been in this room in the last two months, their purpose for being in this room and who they work for. I also want names, addresses and National Insurance numbers for all employees and ex-employees for the last six months to be on the list and that includes the Polish polisher mopping the floor out there.' He tossed the dumbstruck manager a card. 'We expect this information to be with us by three o'clock today.'

'I'll do it straightaway.'

Evans left the office and went to speak to the crime scene manager who had just arrived.

As the man wrestled his way into a Tyvek suit, Evans listed the areas where there may be some trace evidence worth collecting.

'You've got to be joking. These places have hundreds if not thousands of folk through them, I don't fancy our chances of picking the doer up from all the samples we get.'

'Me neither.' Evans scratched the back of his hand and pointed at the CSM's Tyvek suit. 'Wish I'd had one of them to wear before I went in.'

Picking up on Evans's theme, Campbell added his thoughts, 'No wonder that place is called the Dogs. I wanted to wipe my feet when we got out of there'

The CSM chuckled. 'It is also an apt description of the women who frequent the place. You should see it of a Thursday. It's grab-a-granny night and no mistake. Mate of mine pulled a bird in there one Thursday. Friday morning he was at the doctor with a terrible dose of arthritis.'

As the two men reached the M3 there was a loud crump as a Golf GTI rear-ended a stationary van. Campbell started towards the collision to see if anyone needed help, but stopped when the GTI driver climbed out of his car with blood pouring from a gash to his cheek .

Evans knew the driver, so he decided to deal with the matter himself. Grabbing him by the jacket collar, he spun the luckless man around and banged his head off the already dented bonnet.

'Ian Dawson, you have hereby been tried, convicted and punished for driving like a muppet. Give the van driver your insurance details and go home to your wife and kids.'

'Yes, DI Evans, sir.'

Dawson was fighting the concussive effects of the crash which had been amplified by Evans's antiquated brand of justice.

Campbell rounded on Evans with amazement all over his face. 'I bet you are on first name terms with the IPCC and all of the rubber-heelers from Professional Standards.'

Evans wasn't concerned by Campbell's ire. 'They can't handle me.'

*   *   *

They arrived at Carleton Hall Police Headquarters in Penrith a scant twenty minutes later thanks to Evans driving as if the hounds of hell were after him. When Campbell suggested he call ahead and get somebody to let the area manager of Euston Vintners know they were running late, Evans told him not to bother as the longer people waited for an interview with the police the more they divulged.

'That's bull and you know it. This guy is innocent and he's helping us with our enquires. If you believe that making people wait is better, why are you driving so fast?'

'This isn't fast. I'm only doing a ton five.'

'That's fine then. For a moment I was worried we might be speeding'

Evans couldn't resist crowing to the younger man. 'I've got immunity from speeding because of my role as DI for Major Crimes. I made sure it was written into the contract I signed when I agreed to head up this task force. My number plates have an anti-flash coating which works like a mirror when speed cameras take a photo of my car.'

'How the hell did you talk them into that?'

'I explained that in my new position as the head of coordinated police response to interlinked crimes, I would need to travel around the county very fast or most of my time would be wasted driving. I told them the car had to be unmarked as I didn't want the few people in Cumbria who don't already know me, to know when I was in their area.'

'And they swallowed that bullshit?'

'Hook, line and laxative-coated sinker. I did suggest a helicopter, but they told me to bugger off and sent me on an advanced driving course instead. I had one chance to get a hundred per cent pass rate to get my own way.'

'You jammy sod. I'd love a go at that.'

'The driver training was one of the best weeks of my life. One hour of theory per day with the rest of the time spent putting the car through its paces until I had a perfect understanding of its limits.'

Upon entering Carleton Hall, Evans greeted the receptionist with a question about her daughter's forthcoming wedding. After hearing the latest news, he asked where his interviewee was.

'Your man is interview room two and is not looking the happiest chappie I've seen today.'

'Then let me go and ruin the rest of his day.

'Good morning, Mr Drewitt, thank you for taking the time to meet with us.'

Drewitt rose from his chair upon seeing the two detectives. 'I demand that you show me some respect, instead of treating me like a common criminal and locking me in an interrogation chamber for no good reason.

'I think you'll find that if you were being treated like a common criminal, then waiting for twenty minutes in an unlocked room with overworked police support staff bringing you tea and biscuits would seem like a week at the Waldorf Astoria.'

Evans was less than impressed with Drewitt's manner. Carleton Hall was the headquarters of Cumbria constabulary, not some tea room.

The old building had been the manor house for the Carleton family until 1707. Several different families owned the manor house and surrounding lands throughout the eighteenth, nineteenth and twentieth centuries until it fell into the hands of the public sector. Now the grand old building held the top brass of Cumbria constabulary, training facilities and a lot of the administration offices and social services that went hand in hand with modern policing.

Its frontage was tired and many areas were in need of repainting, some of the twelve paned windows showed signs of decay and the whole building with its high ceilings, servants' passages and poor insulation was an impractical choice as the home of a modern, forward-thinking police force.

Yet Evans loved this building and all that it stood for. Its grandeur gave a sense of stability. Like him, it had seen better days, but it still remained standing, weathering the elements, surviving winter storms and summer heatwaves. A sense of affinity washed over him whenever he walked into Carleton Hall.

A subdued Drewitt returned to his seat. Pulling a comb from his pocket he straightened his already straight comb-over. The action reinforced the truism that only balding men with comb-overs carry a comb.

Evans set to with his questions and had the poor Mr Drewitt sweating in a matter of minutes, as he peppered him with questions about travelling salesmen, draymen and any other Euston Vintners employees such as himself or repairmen who visited the affected premises.

Campbell observed in silence as the questions and answers flew across the Formica-topped table. Drewitt's comb-over slipped forward every few time his head moved. At one point when he was too flustered to replace it, Evans reached across the table and relocated the errant hairs, forcing spluttered thanks from the now shaking Drewitt.

'Thank your time, sir. Your answers have been most helpful.' Evans ended the meeting by rising from his chair and exiting the room without a farewell.

Just as Evans had expected, the interview with Drewitt had produced no solid leads, but it narrowed their options further, as none of the employees from the company had worked with either of the two other suppliers they had already talked to.

When they were back in the M3 and heading towards Kendal, they discussed the interview they'd just done. Both men agreed Euston Vintners employees would top their suspect list. The Vaults got their beer from a different supplier and their draymen had been regulars on the run for years.

Evans turned down the police radio and switched on the CD player. Singing along with more enthusiasm than ability to most of the tracks, he skipped backwards and forwards between his favourites.

Campbell busied himself looking through the CD collection in the tiny glove box. When the track finished he reached over and turned the volume down to a background level.

'Have you not got any music that was recorded after '95? Everything in here is ancient. Have you never heard of Snow Patrol, Muse or Biffy Clyro?'

'You can't beat hair rock. Every one of those bands lived the full rock and roll dream and they have the sound to prove it. You know when a band has the right rock and roll ethos when one of them dies a proper rock and roll death.'

'What do you mean?'

'Name any band there.'

'Why?'

'Just do it.'

'Sweet then.

'Brian Connolly, died of liver failure due to drinking himself to death.'

'INXS?'

'Michael Hutchence, died of suspected auto-erotic asphyxiation while shagging someone who has never been named. Next.'

'The Who?'

'John Entwhistle, a cocaine-induced heart attack on top of a prostitute in Vegas. That must be the ultimate rock and roll death. Keith Moon died after overdosing on pills to combat alcoholism.'

'Guns N' Roses.'

'Slash was unresponsive to paramedic's efforts to bring him back to life for seven minutes after a heroin overdose. Steven Tyler, the original drummer, was little more than a vegetable for years because all the drugs he took. Next.'

'The Stones.'

'Brian Jones, found face down in his swimming pool.'

'Hang on then, why is there a Beatles CD in here? Are you gonna try and tell me that McCartney realised what was missing and had Lennon shot?'

'Don't be an imbecile. McCartney would never have done that. Lennon made him and he knew it. That's why he kept trying to re-unite the partnership. It was Ringo who paid Mark Chapman. He never forgave Lennon for the drummers comment.'

'What drummers comment?'

'Lennon was asked in an interview, if there were better drummers in the world than Ringo. His answer was "There are better drummers in the Beatles".'

Campbell could not contain his laughter. 'I bet you believe in Roswell, the sniper on the grassy knoll, the moon landings being a propaganda hoax and Prince Philip being behind the death of Princess Di.'

Chapter 16

The rows of numbers had never made less sense to Victoria. Normally they spoke to her, told her of inconsistencies, highlighting errors as they informed her of mistakes, omissions and misdemeanours.

Now all they did was mock her. Rows and columns of figures staring back at her. Mute, yet insistent: 'How are you going to save them? Do you really believe you'll get the money in time? If you don't raise the money, how are you ever going to look Samantha and Kyle in the eye again?'

Tears filled bloodshot eyes without seeking escape. Another night had been spent tossing and turning. Restless, she had wandered between Samantha's and Kyle's bedrooms. Held their toys. Deep breaths had drawn their scent from crumpled pillows into eager nostrils.

Only when she held her children in her arms unharmed would Victoria be able to relax enough to rest properly.

A blonde head poked round the scuffed door. 'D'you want a cuppa?'

Forcing her voice to sound as normal as possible, Victoria asked for a cup of tea. The interruption distracted her from her woes long enough to allow Victoria to pull herself into a vague semblance of her normal businesslike self.

Focusing her eyes back on the columns, she could here tiny murmurs from the numbers. She hadn't wanted to work today but knew she had to. Every penny mattered and if she didn't work, she didn't get paid. There was also the fact she needed information from work. Without it she couldn't progress her scheme to raise the ransom money to the next level.

'There you go.' Sally put the cup down and took a look at Victoria. 'Are you OK? You look terrible, if you don't mind me saying.'

A lie fell from Victoria's lips without her even thinking of it. 'I didn't get much sleep last night; my tummy was off. I'm feeling better today, though. If I get a good night's sleep tonight, I'll be fine tomorrow.'

Victoria turned her back on Sally, trying to drive thoughts of her children from her mind. She needed to rush through the mundane daily tasks so that she could do the more important research later. What she learned today could complete or destroy her plans altogether.

Chapter 17

Campbell and Evans reached the offices of Peters, Waugh and Beckett which overlooked the river Kent. As they were twenty minutes early for their appointment, Evans headed for the nearest pub – the Ring O' Chimes, a dilapidated dive with scratched tables and bench seating that was moulting upholstery – and ordered them each a quick pint and a brandy as it was cold outside. Campbell ignored his comment, as it was another warm spring day. He found them a table which appeared to have last been wiped sometime around the Queen's coronation.

Campbell sipped at his pint and, when Evans went to the toilet, fed his brandy to a potted plant. The tired plant looked more desperate for a drink than any alcoholic he'd ever met.

Evans returned from the gents and set about persuading the barman to spill the beans on a few of the shady deals which took place in the pub and who was doing them. He ordered another round and dropped a £50 note onto the bar telling the barman to keep the change.

As they walked round the corner to the offices of the accountants, Evans was whistling a tuneless riff.

Ending the tune, he passed Campbell a piece of paper with a name and telephone number on it. 'That's another snout on our books. I suggest you become a regular in there. You've done undercover work before.'

'I moved here to get away from that stuff.' Campbell cursed himself for admitting his undercover past.

'I've read your file. You were undercover for years in Glasgow. All you have to do here is drop in a few times over the next week or two, have a few pints and keep your ear to the ground.'

'No way. It's not gonna happen. And how the hell did you read my file? It's confidential information.'

'Chisholm got it for me.' Upon hearing the computer geek's name, Campbell realised Evans could get whatever he wanted.

Processing this information, he acknowledged to himself the team were as cavalier in their attitude to rules as Evans, who conducted their behaviour like an errant ringmaster.

'With my accent they'll never take to me. It's a non-starter.'

'I'll get Mikey to introduce you as his wife's cousin. He'll be able to get you into the crowd who are pushing most of the drugs in Kendal.'

'Why's he doing that? Surely a few quid from the CHIS fund is not gonna make him take the risk of grassing up a drug dealer. You know what happens to grasses; if he introduces me, then he is putting himself right in the firing line.'

'He's pissed off at the way he is being treated in there. The main dealer has a share in the pub and treats it like his own fiefdom. All he wants is a few hundred quid so he can piss off back to London. You're supposed to be the undercover hotshot, so it will be up to you to get the dirt on the dealer so we can nick the bastard.'

'You are going to set up a whole undercover op based on what a guy has told you in the pub?'

'No, of course not. Don't be a dickhead. You are going in for a few beers a coupla times a week and Mikey will tell the dealer you want some charlie. You buy some a couple of times, and then you'll say that the quality is good and you want to buy bulk so you can sell it on in Glasgow if the price is right. Your main supplier has been taken out by rival firms and this has created a space you can fill. He'll want the trade and the profit that goes with it. You will seem safe 'cause he thinks he owns the barman.'

'No way. My wife is due to give birth any day now, and I don't want to be sixty miles away half-cut, doing drug deals.'

'Don't give me that shite; you only left the undercover squad 'cause your card was seriously marked. You're forgetting I've read your file and know everything about what happened.'

'Leave it. It's a long story and one I'm not proud of, needless to say that what's in the file is only the tip of the iceberg.'

'Sounds about right.'

'Since then I've had to work my arse off to get myself back up to DI. Ten years' worth of promotions were wiped out because of one error of judgement.'

Evans considered what the younger man was saying and worked out that while Campbell had made a mistake, there was probably a senior officer equally culpable who had covered his own misdeeds by blaming Campbell. Shit always rolled downhill in hierarchal organisations.

'How the hell did you get this gig then?'

'Hard work and some good results. My HR file says I'll never rise above DI, but as DI jobs go this is a good one, as you well know.'

'That it is, lad. That it is.' Evans drained his glass and met Campbell's eye. 'So after all your sanctimonious preaching yesterday, you're telling me that you're just as liberal with the rules as I am?'

Campbell shook his head. 'No way. I don't treat the law or the public the way you do. I made one mistake and was hung out to dry, while my DCI wriggled off the hook.'

'Aye, but you're not lily-white either, so stop preaching to me and let me do things my way until they get rid of me and then you can do whatever the hell you like.'

Before Evans could probe further into his past, Campbell made a suggestion: 'C'mon, let's go visit this Peters guy, see what he has to say for himself.'

They walked along Highgate towards the accountant's offices without speaking. Once again Campbell was amazed at the number of people who greeted Evans, or were on the receiving end of a comment from him about their welfare or that of a family member. What should have been a five-minute walk took closer to twenty due to the number of people he spoke to.

Campbell spent the time waiting for Evans assessing the area. Driving in, he'd seen signs for Kendal College, which accounted for the high number of obvious students walking back and forth from the town centre. The shops lining Highgate were an eclectic mix of local services, tourist traps and student Meccas. A newsagent was wedged between a clairvoyant's and a trophy shop.

A series of gate-style doors were located at various points along the terrace, one was open giving him a glimpse of an alleyway leading to a row of houses. Judging by the proximity of the doors, these houses would be tiny student dwellings.

Across the street a pub was boarded up, fine steel mesh protecting the windows. Scaffolding adorned a section of pavement where a building was being renovated.

The river Kent flowed past, its banks edged with retaining walls built from blue Lakeland stone.

The office of Peters, Waugh and Beckett was located above an antiques shop overlooking the river Kent. A brass plaque bearing the company name adorned the wall beside an open door leading to a narrow staircase.

Campbell went first and at the top of the stairs was met by a chest-high reception desk on the first floor. While the decor was fresh, the space was without any vestiges of a personal touch. A functional area clean and tidy in appearance, but cold and unwelcoming in atmosphere. A vase of golden daffodils adorned the counter, testimony to someone's attempt to imbue blandness with a little character.

'We are here to see Mr Peters.' Evans leaned over the desk to get a better look at the ample cleavage on display as he flashed his warrant card to the young receptionist.

'He was expecting you half an hour ago.' There was no warmth in her voice as she spoke. Campbell wondered if she'd been trained as a doctor's receptionist.

'Police business, love. Now give him a bell to tell him we're here and tell us which room he's in.'

'He said to send you straight through when you got here. His room is the one at the bottom of the corridor with Mr Peters on the door.' She picked a well-thumbed magazine off the desk and used it block Evans's gaze.

'Thank you. You have been most kind and may I say that that blouse really suits you.' Evans's sudden charm lowered the girl's defences making his parting shot easier to aim. 'It draws the eye from the face.'

Campbell only just managed to keep his face straight as the girl looked to him for support, but he looked away, unwilling to challenge Evans in front of her.

Peters's door was open and he was busy with a large account ledger under a framed picture of Ullswater. Campbell judged the painting to be an original, although the signature in the bottom corner was illegible, he guessed it would belong to a local artist.

'Good morning, officers, can I get you anything to drink?' Peters rose from his desk to greet them.

Peters had the bookish air of one who spends most of his time indoors poring over documents of one kind or another. His frizzy hair was only evident at the sides of his head and was overdue a trim by at least six months. He wore no jacket and his shirtsleeves were held in place by an expensive pair of cufflinks, his top button behind the red, spotted bow tie was fastened, despite the room's high temperature.

Lined along the back wall with military precision was a series of certificates. Every other wall space held filing cabinets, bundles of invoices, statements and general office accounts. The aged desk was strewn with paperwork; a laptop was perched on one side, with the ubiquitous family photo balancing precariously on the other.

'I'll have a whisky, please, and DI Campbell here will have a coffee, thank you very much.'

Campbell said nothing, as a coffee was exactly what he needed. The two pints he'd laid onto an empty stomach were affecting him rather more than they should. He couldn't begin to guess as to the effect Evans was feeling as he'd had two brandies as well.

Peters picked up his phone and asked someone called Michelle to fetch some coffee. He rose from his chair and poured a small measure of whisky for Evans and a larger one for himself.

'What we need to know is whether you or any your staff have visited certain licensed premises over the last three months. In a professional capacity that is.' Campbell started the interview, hoping the Michelle who was asked to bring coffee wasn't the receptionist Evans had insulted.

'That should be easy to find out from our records.' Peters reached for his computer. 'Which premises are we talking about?'

After Evans listed the premises, Peters admitted that he took care of the Black Horse and Beenies personally and a colleague did the accounts for Jumpers.

'What about the Vaults in Carlisle?' Campbell wanted to know if the firm also represented the latest victim.

'Not one of ours, I'm afraid.'

'Do you regularly visit your clients?'

'It's preferable when collecting accounts as there's always something they forget, but I haven't personally collected accounts since some of your colleagues relieved me of my license a couple of years ago. I prefer customers to come to me anyway.'

'Why's that?'

'Because most people try and hide things from their accountant, which we inevitably find. This often leads to confrontation and I prefer having the home advantage. Also it means that if a member of staff has been stealing from them, they have a cooling off period before they confront the staff member. This can save unnecessary violence.'

Throwing a look towards Evans that he was ready to go, Campbell stood, thanking Peters for his time and information.

Evans was nursing his whisky with an uncommon slowness, but he got the message, drained his glass and hauled himself out of the chair. When Campbell opened the door, Michelle was walking their way with a tray of coffee and biscuits, wearing a self-satisfied smile on her less-than-pretty face.

'You're too late, lass.' Michelle's smile dropped when she saw them leaving the office.

Evans didn't give her a chance to respond. 'Your skirt helps the blouse, but you need to lose a coupla pounds from those hips or the weight will spread like wildfire to your already rounded backside.'

Fearing the tray was about to be thrown, Campbell held the door open and suggested that she give the coffee to Mr Peters and before she had time to make a choice he shepherded her into the office.

Campbell couldn't contain his dislike at Evans's treatment of the girl. 'Why are you such as bastard to some people?'

'No silly little girl is gonna tell me I'm late.'

'We were late.'

'That's not the point and you fucking well know it.'

'Why the hell do you do it, Harry?' Campbell spun to face Evans as he questioned him. 'One minute you're chatting to every Tom, Dick and Harry on the street and the next you're abusing that receptionist like there's no tomorrow.'

'I've know them folks for years. Now stop your bleating and come on.'

They climbed back into the car and Evans set off into Kendal's bewildering one-way system with the assured confidence of a local.

'Where are we going now?'

'I want to check in with an old acquaintance in Windermere before we go back to the station. Do us a favour and call Lauren to get us an update.'

Campbell made the call and asked her to fill them in on any developments, taking care to inform her she was on speaker. She reported there had been a breakthrough on the car cons as one of the first cars to be sold had been resold to a man from Preston. 'He bought it from a garage in Lancaster. The salesman told the buyer the car was part of a trade-in deal he had just done and sold it for fifty-five hundred.'

Evans's reaction to this news was typically profane. 'Two and a half grand, made on one second-hand car in less than a week. Well, roger me with a pool cue until my eyes bleed. If the guy wasn't a car dealer then I could start to like him.'

Ignoring Evans, Campbell took over the conversation. 'Is there any word from CSI about the theft from the Vaults?'

'Nothing worth reporting yet, sir. They've lifted some prints and had a good nose about, but they're saying it's such a public place that they can't draw anything conclusive without a mass canvass and fingerprinting of all staff members.'

'Then that's what they'll have to do.'

A loud sigh came through the speaker as the line disconnected.

They pulled into Windermere, where Evans dispensed with any parking etiquette by bumping his nearside wheels onto the kerb, almost crushing a traffic warden's toes in the process. Campbell winced in anticipation of the forthcoming battle, but made sure he was out of the car in time to enjoy the full spectacle.

'Do you realize, sir, that you almost crippled an officer of the Crown?' The traffic warden approached Evans waving his arms and gesticulating at the double yellow lines.

'Of course I do, you imbecile. I made it into the police force, unlike you.'

'Who do you think you're speaking to?' The traffic warden started to write out a ticket. His white knuckled hand making bold strokes across the ticket pad.

'A trained monkey who likes to bully motorists for no good reason other than the erection it gives him.'

'I'll have you know I'm an officer of the Queen.'

'Do you answer to Chief Constable Fuck Off?'

'Who?'

'*Fuck off.*' The words left Evans's mouth at a volume capable of splintering rock. All around them tourists and locals stopped to look at the commotion. 'You are the kind of parasite who gives the police and law enforcement officers a bad name. I have been a copper in Cumbria for almost thirty years now and have never come across a jumped-up fuckwit like you before. I am parking here whether you, the Queen or Mary-bastard-Poppins approves. When I get back to my car I do not expect to find a ticket. If I do find a ticket on my car, I will hunt you down stuff it up your arse and set fire to it. Understood?'

Striding off, he left the speechless man behind.

Campbell ran after Evans as he walked into a pub called Peter Rabbit's Warren, in honour of the character created by local author Beatrix Potter. When he caught up with Evans at the bar, he was in time to hear him order two pints of Guinness and a pint for Baconlugs.

Baconlugs turned out to be an elderly man. His face spoke of harsh winters and hot summers, coupled with a lifelong addiction to a drop of the hard stuff. His cheeks were crisscrossed with fine red lines, deposited by weather and whisky. One look at the man's ears explained his nickname.

'What you got for me today?' Evans put the Guinness in front of the old man and sat opposite him.

'Nothing much, Harry.' The old man raised his new pint in silent thanks. 'Those kids down the road from me have a lot of comings and goings, but nowt I can put my finger on. Oh and that girl I was telling you about last week is definitely on the game or something. She gets picked up twice a day by different blokes and she's always dressed up sexy like, but with different clothes for each guy. I've been watching her for two months now and she has meetings twice a day for three weeks then a week off then another three weeks of meetings.'

'What's her name and address?' Campbell took a sip of his pint his eyes bust darting around the room.

Baconlugs was beaten to the answer by Evans. 'Jennifer Mills, 24 Coniston Crescent. She's been at it for years, but she calls it escorting and declares tax on her earnings so it's all legal.'

'Aye, that's her. How do you know her?'

Evans ignored the question. 'Anything else going down or any other crack I should know about?'

'I s'pose you've heard about Big Billy?'

'No. Who's he dropped now?'

'No one yet, but his wife sold her car for five grand, watched the guy count the money out and agreed it was five grand. Yet when she went to bank it, it was two grand short. He's out for proper blood this time, Harry, I wouldn't like to be in the shoes of whoever did this to him.'

Campbell understood the glance Evans threw him and kept quiet.

Instead of informing Baconlugs it was a common trick, he changed the subject by asking Evans a question. 'Who's Big Billy?'

'A builder and a local hardman, he's been lifted numerous times for fighting.'

'Not a man to con then.'

'Not if you don't fancy eating hospital food.' Evans took a healthy slug from his pint. 'C'mon, I want to pay Big Billy a visit before we head back.'

Instead of returning to the car, Evans led Campbell through a couple of small alleyways onto a main street. Walking along the street he turned into a cul-de-sac. There was a builder's yard halfway along; timber, bricks and slates were stacked on pallets for easy transportation. At the back of the yard a worker was transferring tools from an old shipping container into a van.

Trailing two paces behind the older detective, Campbell watched with interest as Evans marched into the office sitting himself down opposite a huge man. If this wasn't Big Billy, he didn't want to meet the man who was.

The man across the desk from Evans was at least six foot six, his body a mass of knotted muscle. He didn't have the sculpted muscle sported by gym attendees, his body was conditioned by years of hard graft, making him look as though he'd been hewn from the nearest of the Cumbrian fells.

His chiselled face was handsome until he saw Evans. When recognition set in, it transformed into a grotesque mask.

'What the fuck do you want, Evans?'

'Just to talk, Billy. That's all.'

'I ain't got time to talk to no fucking coppers.'

Campbell slipped a hand into his pocket and slid his fingers around the collapsible baton. If Billy decided he was coming across the desk at Evans, he wanted a weapon to help take him down.

'Not even if I can tell you a story about the man who bought your wife's car? And how the payment was two grand short despite her watching him count the money?'

'Who told you about that? How much do you know?'

'My paperboy and everything.'

Big Billy stood up, fingertips curling toward palms. 'Don't fuck with me, Evans. You were lucky last time.'

'Anytime you want a rematch here's my number.' Evans threw a card onto Billy's desk. 'I know you got conned, which is wrong, but all I'm here for is a quick photo.'

Before Billy could reply, Evans pulled out his mobile and took a quick snap of Billy, making sure to include the filing cabinet he was dwarfing.

Campbell could see that although Big Billy had almost a foot in height and a twenty-year advantage on Evans, he was afraid of the older man. There was nothing obvious, just a sense that his big talk was all bluster. He never actually confronted Evans or stood within striking distance. He eyed Evans the way a rattlesnake watches a mongoose.

'I doubt you'll get your money back, but if you do it will be thanks to me. Next time we meet, I expect you to be a little more polite to someone who's trying to help you, or you'll become my pet project for a little bit of police harassment.'

'Just tell me who the bastard is and I'll get my own money back.'

'No can do, Billy. Leave it to the He-Man.' Evans turned around, leaving the office and a frustrated Billy behind him.

'We need to call this in, Harry.'

'Wait until we get back to the car and I'll explain my plan to you.' Evans had a twinkle in his eye and a mischievous grin on his face.

They walked to the car in silence, with Campbell wondering what diabolical plan Evans was concocting now, and how many laws it would break. Upon reaching the car, Campbell half expected to find it ticketed or even clamped, but it was untouched, the traffic warden favouring discretion over valour.

Campbell waited until they were back in the car and heading back towards the motorway. 'So what's the plan then?'

'Tomorrow morning we're gonna go and visit that car dealer. I'll show him the picture of Big Billy standing beside the filing cabinet. Then I'll show him Billy's arrest sheet and suggest that he tells me all about his little con, in case I let it slip to Billy, where he lives.'

'That ought to make him confess there and then. By the way what was that all about with Billy and you offering him a rematch?'

'He got out of hand one night when someone spilled his pint. I let the plods handle it for a while, but when the eighth one went down, I decided I better lend a hand. I had to take a hard line before he succumbed to my charms. He was out of hospital sooner than any of the plods he hit that night, so he's little cause for complaint.'

'You took him on?' Campbell was incredulous, he didn't fancy tackling Big Billy with anything less than a howitzer.

'No, I didn't take him on. I kicked his arse and he knows it. The rematch is all about him trying to saving face.'

Campbell changed the subject before he heard any further incriminating confessions. 'How many times do you think the couple have pulled this stroke on dealers and people selling cars privately?'

'Hundreds probably. As long as they're clever about it and get away before the seller counts the money again, they're home and dry. If he doesn't do it on his doorstep, then he'll get away with it for years until he gets caught out. I think we've only found out about him because he got greedy, and done some dealers as well. Most people wouldn't bother the police with this as it only makes them look stupid, but dealers know what the score is; plus, they hate someone outsmarting them.'

Chapter 18

Time dragged long and heavy for Samantha. With nothing to entertain them beyond video games she was bored. Without Facebook, her mobile or a magazine to read she was without any familiar stimulus.

Kyle, however, was fully occupied with his new favourite game. He'd discovered there were missions to do and he was so entranced, the fact they were prisoners had slipped from his memory. His eight-year-old brain was delighted to have nothing to do but play a game he knew his mother wouldn't let him play. He even had his sister's blessing.

His only upset of the day had come from finding his tooth still under the mattress. She'd agonised long into the night about the best course of action to take. Whether to tell him the truth, to take the tooth and flush it down the toilet then tell him the money would be at home. In the end she'd decided to do nothing and stick to her earlier insistence that the tooth fairy would only retrieve his tooth from under his pillow at home.

Samantha was pleased for her brother's sake their plight was not at the forefront of his thoughts and emotions. She was just tired of the endless squealing of tyres and the gunshots coming from the TV. Even at its lowest volume she heard every sound.

Plus, there were the constant updates from Kyle about his progress. As much as she loved him, she just wanted him to be quiet for two minutes. Ever since being locked in the room, she'd sought ways to escape. Every inch of wall had been examined. The door had been tested every time the men had brought food.

She had tried to make sense of events.

To rationalise what was happening.

Elvis had said they were kidnapped as collateral against their father's debts. Surely he couldn't have debts that bad. Plus the men always wore their masks. That had to be good, didn't it? She dared to hope they planned on letting her and Kyle go and they didn't want her doing those photo-fit thingies with the police. If they weren't wearing those masks she'd be far more frightened.

She hadn't been able to place their accents beyond a Lancastrian twang similar to her friend Beth's stepdad. Try as she might, she couldn't remember the exact place he was from. It could be Bolton, Blackburn or any of the surrounding towns and cities.

'Look, Sam. I've got the car on two wheels.' Again Kyle interrupted her thoughts.

'Well done.' The reply fell from her mouth unbidden.

A rattle of locks announced the end of her boredom. Before the door had swung open she longed for a return to the nothingness of the morning.

'Aww. He shot me.'

Ignoring the opening door, Samantha reassured her brother. 'Just start again. You'll manage it next time, Kyle.'

The man wearing the Tony Blair mask stood in the doorway. A carrier bag was thrown to her. 'Put these on. I'll be back in five minutes.'

'Why?'

''Cause it's time to make another video.'

A look in the carrier bag made Samantha's heart plummet.

Chapter 19

'Everybody, follow me.' Evans bulldozed his way out of the tiny office and led the assembled group to DCI Grantham's office, where there was a large table for meetings at one end. 'Sorry, sir, but our office is too small for all five of us at once and we need to have a meeting to plan our next moves.'

As the team invaded the DCI's office, Evans took up station at the head of the conference table and began the meeting, ignoring DCI Grantham, who joined the group, taking a seat halfway along the table. 'Where have you got to with the crime prevention letters, Chisholm?'

'I have both proofed and OK'd by Sergeant Edwards and the press officer. The ones for the licensed premises are printing as we speak. Sergeant Edwards is still going round the farms and he told me that any help would be gratefully received.'

Evans looked at Grantham. 'Can I get a PC to fold and envelope these letters to save the valuable time of my team?'

'Speak to Sergeant Anderson, see if he has anyone he wants punished.'

'Thanks. Bhaki, have you got an address for the car dealer from Lancaster? And what have you learned about his finances?'

Bhaki passed across a slip of paper with the address of the dealership, the names of the proprietors and the company name, Pentwortham Prestige Motors. 'His finances are in order, although he didn't show a great deal of profit on the accounts he submitted last year.'

Evans glanced at the paper. 'If a five grand motor is prestige, then what the fuck is a decent car known as? That tosser wants nicked for crimes against English, or fraudulent representation at the very least. I'm not surprised his official accounts don't show much profit. I bet he only declares a fraction of the cash he handles.'

Campbell joined in with the questioning, fully aware his new DCI was observing him to see how he behaved in comparison with Evans. 'Amir, have you compiled a list of descriptions of the buyers from all the people who were caught out by this pair?'

'Yes, sir, the general consensus seems to be that he is mid-fifties with salt and pepper hair and of average build and height. The woman is of roughly the same age and all the people I spoke to said she wears a hell of a lot of jewellery. She's approximately one point six metres tall.'

Campbell bit back the Mrs T. wisecrack before he said it, but it was a close thing. Luckily for him, Evans's impatience with Bhaki dominated the conversation. 'For God's sake man, what's that in real money?'

'About five foot four, guv, give or take an inch. The men I spoke to described her as having long red hair and a, erm…' Bhaki's cheeks were darkening.

'C'mon, spit it out.'

'A large chest, sir. She always wore clothing that allowed them to look down her top when she leaned over the desk to count the money. She never sat down at the desk preferring to lean over.' The nervous recounting from the young man led Campbell to speculate to himself about Bhaki's lack of experience with the opposite sex.

'A classic distraction. I do that all the time. I'll bet she wore a short skirt as well.'

'That's enough thank you, Lauren.' Grantham gave up all pretence of silent observation and fully engaged in the discussion.

'Long skirts are for fat lasses, I've used exactly the same tricks many a time in the interview room.'

'I said that's enough, DC Phillips!'

Grantham was trying to sound authoritative, but it was clear Lauren was a weakness of his. Grantham was sneaking what he thought were furtive glances at her, but Campbell could see that she knew what the DCI was doing, and was playing him the way an angler plays a prize catch.

'Coming back to the point: they have tricked at least a dozen people we know of, and probably as many again that we don't. We need to do something about them and stop them before they rip any bugger else off.'

Chisholm spoke up for the first time at the meeting. 'I took the liberty of speaking to a friend at the CPS, she told me that as long as both parties agreed on the amount of money, there was nothing they can do by way of prosecution.'

Evans turned to face Chisholm. 'I want full search on him and his business, accounts, trading contraventions, reputation, credit ratings and anything else you can dig up on him. And I want it on my desk when I come in tomorrow morning.'

'As you don't have a desk, sir, where shall I put the report, under your windscreen wiper?'

'Don't be smart, it doesn't suit you.' Evans glared at Chisholm before continuing. 'Maybe I should give Big Billy his address and call the Preston station with a tip off about a major drug deal at the other side of town.'

'Quasi! Nothing like that will happen and if it does I'll have your badge. Vigilante action is *not* the answer…'

'Just a thought, sir. Did you manage to speak with the ACC at all?' Evans knew when to change the subject and the tracking devices on quad bikes was as good a distraction as any.

'He's mulling it over and will get back to me later today.'

'OK, then, does anyone have any bright ideas about the robberies from the licensed premises? I've heard from the CCTV monitoring posts and there's no cameras overlooking the back entrances of any of the premises.'

Lauren's eyes flashed. 'That's bloomin' typical. CCTV cameras all over the bloomin' place watching people's every move, yet when we need one, there isn't one there.'

Campbell was convinced there must be a common link between each of the venues that had been so meticulously burgled. He also wanted Grantham to see him make a worthwhile contribution to the discussion. 'Is it possible there is a common supplier who we have missed from some of the premises?'

'We have gone over every possible avenue and have found no common link between all four properties other than Bandits Express and they always visit in daytime opening hours and never go beyond the public areas.'

'I still think that's how they are getting access and knowledge.'

'Anybody else got any ideas? No, well what about the farm robberies? Come on! Someone give me a wild guess or something. We're supposed to be a crack team and you're all sitting on your arses like a bunch of old women.' When he was greeted with silence, Evans adjourned the meeting and stomped off.

Left behind in the office, Campbell gathered his own thoughts while filling out his daily report. As far as he could see the con with the counting was pretty much solved, all he had to do was prevent Evans from bringing the couple to the wrong form of justice. The burglaries from licensed premises were another matter, although the team had investigated each one on an individual and collective basis, he could not find the common denominator he was sure existed and was the key to the robberies. He knew the main clue was locked somewhere deep in the evidence swirling around his brain, but he couldn't bring it to the forefront in a recognisable form. The robberies from the farms were the latest of a cyclic pattern, occurring every year or nine months, depending on how often the criminal gangs targeted the area. They would be solved either by luck or by the implementation of the tracking devices.

Chapter 20

Clutching the bag, Samantha went into the bathroom to change. She wanted to cry but couldn't. The bag contained a red dress that was made of nothing but lace. A matching pair of heels was also inside the bag. As she pulled out the dress a note fell to the floor.

Six damning words confirmed her worst fears about the outfit.

WEAR NOTHING BUT THESE OR ELSE

The words were scrawled in a childlike hand but that didn't matter to Samantha. Nor did the lack of punctuation. What mattered was the message.

'Wear nothing but these.' She would be exposed by the thin pattern. Her body revealed to the hungry lecherous eyes of the men. Especially that creep Blair. He was the one who would drink in her curves, leer at her body as they filmed her. She would bet her last penny that he chose the dress.

'Or else.' The two-word reminder of the fate awaiting her and Kyle, if she did not do as bidden.

Screwing up every last ounce of her courage, Samantha took her clothes off and pulled the dress over her head.

Pulled down it reached mid thigh, but when she straightened after pulling it down, it rose two inches. Looking in the tiny mirror from a distance of three feet she could see her skin through the lace, although mercifully the designer had saw fit to increase the pattern in the lower half of the dress.

Grateful her downstairs bits were better covered than her boobs, she pushed her feet into the shoes which were at least a size too small. Tottering on the heels that were higher than she was used to, Samantha practised walking back and forth in the bathroom. No way was she going to fall over and expose herself even further!

Determination was creeping into her mind. Scaring away the nerves, the worries. Hadn't Amy worn something like this that night in Carlisle? Sure she'd worn a bra and hot pants underneath the dress, but she'd worn it round the pubs and clubs. If Amy could choose to dress like that for the world to see, then she could for a private audience to save herself and her brother.

A gruff voice interrupted her thought processes. 'C'mon then. We 'aven't got all bloody day.'

Opening the bathroom door she saw Blair's head poking into the bedroom. Kyle dropped his controller and pressed himself into the furthest corner.

'C'mon!'

'I'm coming.'

Seeing Kyle's worried face, she reassured him on her way across the room. 'It's all right. I won't be long. You try and finish that level before I get back.'

Samantha's bravado almost deserted her before she left the room. Blair had a way of breaching any defences she created. His probing eyes covered her body like a second skin.

Her instincts told her he would be the captor who'd instigate raping her. It would be his hands she'd feel grabbing at her.

Feeling like a lamb being taken to the slaughter, she halted in front of Blair, awaiting his next order.

'Go downstairs. The boys are there with the video.'

Blair stood to one side in the doorway, his low hanging gut forming a barrier which Samantha would have to squeeze past.

It was a toss-up which option would be worse, facing him, and giving the close up view he wanted, or turning her back and risking him grabbing her boobs as she brushed past him.

His eyes made the decision for her as they locked themselves on her chest. With skin crawling at the thought of his sweaty body touching hers, she barged her way through the gap with her back to him.

The pained grunt as her back thumped into his bloated gut was satisfying to Samantha's ear, although her back twitched with an involuntary spasm where contact had been made.

As Blair slammed the door behind her, she used the small victory as a way of boosting her resolution to face what lay ahead.

Fearful of his grabbing hands, she hurried down the stairs as fast as the towering heels would allow her. Her hands slid down the banisters on each side of the staircase, caking her palms and fingers with a layer of grime.

Heavy boots followed her down the stairs, but she could sense him keeping enough distance between them to afford him the best possible view of her bottom.

Reaching the living room she found the man in the Elvis mask, sitting by himself. The table and chairs had all been pushed to one side of the room. Beside Elvis was a video camera; a laptop was perched on his legs.

'Over there.' Elvis pointed to the clear area of the floor as Blair followed her into the room.

Samantha waited for the next instruction. Her nose crinkling from the stench of days' old curry and nicotine.

Elvis stood up and pulled an iPod from his pocket, which he then placed in a docking station. 'Right, love. Here's what you're gonna do. I'm gonna play three songs and you're gonna dance to them. Properly with all the right moves. And don't try and fool us 'cause I've just watched the videos on YouTube so I know exactly what you should be doing.'

As Elvis had been informing Samantha of what to do, Blair busied himself in opening the windows as far as possible. A chill wind blew the curtains back, raising goosebumps on Samantha's exposed skin.

'The fuck you doing? It's bloody freezing in here.'

Blair pointed at Samantha who was standing with one arm covering her chest and the other hand over her crotch. 'If she's cold, her nips'll stand out better.'

Shaking his head, Elvis turned to Samantha. 'He's got a point. Just be glad you're doing the dances I chose, and not the lap dance he wanted you to do.'

OMG, that Blair is so pervy!

Something in Elvis's voice told Samantha that he wasn't getting the same perverted kick from her torment as his friend. Although he wasn't stopping Blair, he was acting as some kind of restraint. Keen to acknowledge his different behaviour, she nodded her head once and quietly thanked him.

The one positive about the open windows was the breeze taking away the worst of the fetid smell.

Blair picked up the video camera and after spending a minute fiddling with settings told Elvis that he was ready.

'Right. When the music starts, you do the dances in full. No turning away from us, no adjusting your clothing. Just dancing. Do them right first time and it's pizza tonight. If you don't you'll be dancing naked until you get them right.'

Samantha could have sworn that Elvis winked at her behind his mask as he issued his instructions. While she wasn't foolish enough to believe he was on her side, she felt he was trying to encourage her to get the dances right the first time. Whatever it cost her in terms of dignity would be a small price to pay compared with the penalty for failure.

Steeling her nerves as she prepared to move her hands from their covering positions, she heard the first rhythmic beats of 'Cha-Cha Slide'. With her courage fighting to thaw the ball of ice in her stomach, Samantha began to move in time to the beat.

In her mind she was picturing herself and Amy practising the routine in their bedrooms. Those had been good times. Innocent times when two pre-teen girls had danced routines, giggling about boys they would never admit to fancying.

Closing her mind to the lecherous eyes of Blair, she danced to the music in the most sedate way she dared. Her ears strained above the music waiting for a command or word that would condemn her further.

Samantha's closed eyes raised her other senses, she could feel her hemline creeping up her legs. The lacier top of the dress rubbed coarse against her jiggling boobs as they moved unbidden with her moves.

As the music faded out she risked a look at her captors. Elvis was leaning against the wall, arms folded. Blair however was directly in front of her with one hand pressing the video camera to an eye while the other hand was massaging his groin. The temptation to pull down the hemline felt irresistible, but Elvis's warning remained front and centre in her thoughts.

The next song began and with a sinking heart, Samantha recognised the pumping dance track from Los Del Rio. Throwing her mind back to dancing with Amy once again, she launched herself into a three-quarter-hearted rendition of the

Macarena. Distraught as Samantha was, she was still trying to balance what she must do with what she could get away with not doing.

With each move she cursed the two men for subjecting her to this ordeal. Blair with his wandering eyes and oily hands, rubbing himself as she danced; Elvis with his threats and false shows of support. Elvis could stop this any minute he chose to, yet he allowed her degradation to continue.

The hip-swaying, pelvic-thrusting dance ground to an end and Samantha breathed a sigh of relief. The urge to pull her hemline down was now unbearable but again she fought it back, afraid of the consequences the action may bring.

Her only consolation was so far the dances had not made her raise her arms above her head, lifting the skimpy dress further up her body.

A glance at Blair, gave her a look at eyes shining with desire. Lust poured out from the mask's eye holes, filling the room with the heavy scent of testosterone. His left hand still massaged his groin, irrespective of her and Elvis's presence.

Licking her lips as she always did when nervous, Samantha waited with trepidation for the final song.

Samantha gagged when she heard the trumpeting intro of 'YMCA'. Her arms would have to go above her head in this dance. Their view of her boobs would be unobstructed while she mapped out the letters, but Samantha was more concerned about how far the hem would raise before the dance ended.

Swallowing the bile in her throat, she threw a pleading glance towards Elvis. He unfolded his arms and moved one hand in front of him. With fingers extended he rotated his hand at the wrist, signalling her to carry on.

She knew better than to even try to sending any appeal Blair's way.

Then out of the corner of her eye a shape moved beyond the window.

It can't be!

It is!

We're gonna be saved!

Samantha moved her right foot back and with a sudden thrust flung herself towards to the window. A scream erupted

107

from her mouth as she charged forward. To freedom. Towards the police car pulling into the farmyard.

Chapter 21

Evans was ordering a second pint when his mobile rang. 'Quasi, DCI Tyler would enjoy your company for a brief chat.'

'I'll see him tomorrow, I'm off shift now.'

'Now. It's not a request.'

'Oh goody, I'll enjoy talking to him.' The sneer in Evans's voice told of a renegade's hatred for those who sought to bring order and conformity to their world.

There was always someone willing to stab a knife into his back, undoing his efforts to make the streets and alleyways of Cumbria safer. Why couldn't they just leave him alone to get on with his job?

Evans made his way back to the station, and stalked through the pastel corridors, grumbling about desk-bound fuckwits who'd never slapped a pair of handcuffs on in their life.

Reaching the office of DCI Richard Tyler, the head of Cumbria's Professional Standards Department., he crashed through the door, almost knocking over the young PC being reprimanded.

Evans tapped the unfortunate man on the shoulder. 'Run along and play nice, else next time I'll be the one to deliver the bollocking.'

'Yes, sir, thank you, sir.' The PC who wasn't sure whether he was being saved or threatened, but he had the good sense to escape before either of the senior officers could shout at him any more.

'Hello, Dickie.' Evans relaxed into a chair without invitation, putting his feet onto Tyler's desk. 'Before you get started, can I just say that I overheard PC Pot using racist language when referring to PC Kettle?'

'Who the blazes do you think you are? Coming into my office, taking over a disciplinary matter, making bad taste jokes and disrespecting a senior officer?'

'I'm Cumbria constabulary's leading copper. I'm the man who is running three different cases. Young Miles there was in trouble for being overheard by an offender's family, saying he thought the guy had received a light sentence. He was off duty and talking to friends. That's bollocks and you know it as well as I do.'

'Coppers like you are the reason the public has little faith in the police force.'

'Bullshit.' Evans's voice was calm while Tyler's was rising in anger at the disrespect shown to him and his position as the moral authority. 'It's lazy bastard rubber heelers like you who are keeping good coppers from doing their job. The amount of paperwork we're supposed to file is mind-numbing and it's all driven by desk jockeys and paper-pushers. We're losing more good coppers than we're gaining recruits. Sometimes you have to fight fire with fire. If we stopped fucking about shuffling paper and got you and your mates back on the streets, that would restore public faith far quicker than curbing the odd sweary word or unfortunate comment.'

'That's enough, DI Evans.' Tyler fought to regain supremacy and retreated behind his superior rank to do so. 'I've had it up to my back teeth with your insubordination and blatant disregard for procedure. It seems like hardly a day goes by without some tale of you upsetting a colleague, intimidating a suspect or witness, using violence as a means of self-gratification. I know that you know all about procedure. I know that at least three times a week, you give DS Chisholm a list of procedural errors in whichever crime novel you've just read, so that he can email the authors. For goodness' sake, Evans, the IPCC have my number on speed dial because of you.'

'Well, you'll have to go ex-directory then, 'cause my methods aren't gonna change just because some interfering bastard wants a game of pin-the-tail-on-the-good-guys. Now, tell me today's problem so I can ignore it, you and the fucker who's wasting valuable police time.'

Sighing, as he knew battling with Evans was a waste of time, Tyler outlined the complaint an unnamed traffic warden had brought against Evans, which had in turn landed on his desk via the Independent Police Complaints Commission.

'Fair enough. I'll make sure he doesn't have the same issue next time we meet.'

'I hope so, Harry, I hope so.'

'Don't worry, Dickie. Next time I'll park on top of the bugger and stop the hassle at source. Now if you'll excuse me, I have to go and catch some criminals.'

As he reached the door he turned back to Tyler. 'Bullshit apart, Richard. You've been in the force as long as me, and you know I'm right. If you do your job and run interference for me, then I'll fill the jails while you shuffle the paper. Just cover for me these last few days. Warn me of what bollockings I'm supposed to have had and I'll agree I've had them. Otherwise you might want to rearrange your office so I have my own desk; we're short of space in our office and I'll be here more than there anyway.'

Evans knew he was almost untouchable by Professional Standards – all they could threaten him with was the loss of his pension, and at this stage of his career he knew they daren't take that away from him, his arrest record alone would make it a PR disaster.

Rather than wait for the negative reply he knew Tyler would have to give, Evans left the office and headed back into the maze of pale green corridors linking the various departments within the station.

Knowing what he had to do next was one thing; doing it was another. The long empty nights he endured on his own were bad enough. The thought of not having a purpose or a day job terrified him. He was self-aware enough to recognise the fact that while he was a people person and craved company, he also needed periods of solitude. Time to reflect upon losing the wife he still loved with every fibre of his body.

Janet's departure had wounded him to such an extent that he couldn't begin to think of being with another woman.

When his natural urges began to drive him to distraction, he knew what he would do to have his itch scratched. Money would change hands, safe sex would be practised and the itch would vanish for a while. It would be a transaction, nothing more.

As he reached his destination, Evans paused to collect his thoughts. He slipped a mint into his mouth and gave three sharp raps on the door.

'Come.' The word carried authority.

Swallowing his nerves, Evans opened the door and walked into the office. This was his last chance to stave off enforced retirement. To fill his days with a worthwhile purpose, instead of trading on former glories to secure a job he didn't want.

'Hello, Harry, have a seat.' Warmth had replaced the stern tone in the voice of the assistant chief constable. 'I'll order some coffee.'

Evans took the seat offered and waited while ACC Greg Hadley put the request to his assistant.

'Greg.' Evans swallowed again, pride instead of nerves troubled him. 'I need your help.'

'I must confess, I've been expecting you to come and see me.'

'So you know then?'

'That you're due to retire. That you've spent the last six months trying to persuade anyone who'll listen to extend your license to roam Cumbria as a one-man crime-fighter. I got you the team you have now to show you that modern policing is about science and evidence, not gut instinct or hunches.'

'Has my arrest rate suffered with the new team?'

'You know fine well that your team has far and away the best arrest record in the county.'

Both men fell silent as the civilian secretary brought in a tray of coffee. When she had padded her way out the door, Evans picked up the conversation while Hadley added sugar and cream to the two coffees.

'I have local knowledge. That's what gets me my results. I know everyone worth knowing and I know where they live. This Campbell that you've got to replace me seems basically all right, but he's far too regimental. He hasn't got the same instinct we have. Remember how you and I cracked cases based on hunches and guesses?'

It was a low blow from Evans to remind Hadley of the time they'd worked together. Twenty-five years ago Greg Hadley had been an eager DC, intent on climbing his way up the greasy pole called promotion. For two years they had worked side by side out of Kendal Station.

'That was a long time ago, Harry. Even then your methods were becoming old hat. Hunches don't have a place in modern policing. We used to do it all ourselves without help from the lab. Think about the support your team give you now. Without them' – Hadley raised a hand to cut off Evans's objection – 'without them, your arrest rate would be much lower and you know it. They do all the boring stuff while you run around playing Superman. The days of kicking down doors and beating confessions out of suspects are long gone.'

'You used to do it with me.'

'I know I did. But times changed and I changed with them. You haven't, Harry, and that's the problem. It's not just about arrest rates anymore. It's also about the number of complaints against us, public confidence, accountability, transparency and a hundred other things.'

'That's all just management bullshit—' Evans bit off the rest of his sentence. Hadley was a friend. Antagonising him wouldn't help his cause.

'Perhaps it is. But that's the way the police force is run these days.'

'So I'm a dinosaur waiting for the meteorite to land. Is that it?'

'I'm afraid so.'

'There's got to be a decent opening somewhere in the force for me.'

'Have you tried applying for a Traffic Statement position?' Hadley was referring to the role offered to retired officers. They would be called out to assist with taking statements at major road incidents.

Evans pulled a creased envelope from his jacket and tossed it across the desk. The action grieved him: Janet had been the only person he'd ever allowed to read his mail. However, he didn't trust himself to tell Hadley about it without losing his temper.

When Hadley finished reading the letter he reached inside his desk and pulled out a bottle of whisky and two glasses.

'They turned you down then.' A simple but damning statement. Every one of the five words painful to hear.

Evans took a swig of the whisky, savouring the peaty tang as the secondary flavours washed down his throat. Hadley had always liked Islay malts and this one was smokier than a seventies tap room.

'The least shitty stick in my pile doesn't want me. That wasn't even a job I wanted, but at least it would have kept me in the force.' Evans saw the scowl and corrected himself. 'After a fashion, that is.'

'I don't mean to kick you when you're down, Harry, but have you never considered that years of erratic behaviour and rule-breaking would catch up with you?'

'My arrest record speaks for itself.' Evans wanted to kick himself for the pleading tone that had crept into his voice.

'So do the files the IPCC and PSD have on you. All that comes into account, you know.'

'So what am I supposed to do? Get a hobby? Go fishing, gardening? Can you picture me standing in a freezing river or fucking about in an allotment?'

Smiling at the image, Hadley shook his head. 'No, I can't imagine you doing either of those.'

Hating himself for almost begging the man who'd once called him 'sir', Evans changed tack. 'Surely there must be something you can sort out for me. A cold-case division or something like that would be perfect. I could work cases myself, with occasional backup from the current team.'

'I'll try, Harry, but I seriously doubt the chief constable will sanction it. Budgets are tight enough without creating new positions.'

'Thank you. I appreciate your help.'

'If it doesn't work, there'll be nothing else I can do. I'll be in touch when I've spoken to him.' Hadley steepled his fingers before changing tack. 'What do you plan to do once the trial is over?'

'If I can't stay on in the job, I suppose I'll take one of the jobs the security firms have offered me.'

'Perhaps a change of pace will be good for you... with the trial and everything.'

Evans fought to keep the scowl off his face.

The trial of Janet's rapist was due to begin next week. Scheduled for the whole week, the trial would span the anniversary of his thirtieth year as a policeman.

Compassion lined Hadley's face. 'How you coping?'

'I'm fine. Or at least I will be when that bastard is behind bars.' Evans didn't believe in the touchy-feely modern way men shared their feelings. His lip was always stiff while in public. Only in the privacy of his flat would he allow it to wobble, Tripod his sole confidant as he poured his heart out.

'The case against him is solid. I've talked to the CPS and they said that Yates's solicitor has been trying to get him to cut a deal.'

'No fucking way. I want that bastard to go down forever. Janet was his second count, remember?'

'It's OK, the CPS aren't budging on this. I've made sure of that.'

'Thanks.'

Hadley opened his mouth to speak but hesitated.

'What is it?'

'Have you... er... taken any of the counselling offered?'

A rueful smile crossed Evans's lips as he raised his glass high. 'What do you think?'

Chapter 22

Elsewhere in the station, Campbell was sitting at a desk going through the lists of suppliers for each of the burglarised premises. As he always did, he arranged the information in front of him into a timeline and tried to find a pattern between events.

Lauren was busy on the phone, double checking with the various license holders about the service providers who were on the lists of premises other than theirs. It was a menial task, but important, in case someone had missed a supplier off their list when questioned. Her flirtatious tone told him she was speaking to a man.

Chisholm was tapping away at his keyboard. The printer beside him spitting occasional documents out with a clattering whirr.

'I've spoken to them all, sir. Apart from the guy at Jumpers. He's gone on holiday for a fortnight.'

'Holiday? After the place he runs has just been turned over. Did you get the details of where he's going?'

'Of course I did.' Lauren bristled at Campbell's unspoken accusation. 'He's gone to Tenerife for a fortnight. Apparently he booked the time off months ago. It was a relief manager I spoke to. He wasn't happy about having to pick up the reins after the place had been robbed. "Pissed off" would be the words I'd use to describe him.'

'Are there any other members of staff worth speaking to?'

'They are all temporary staff. Mostly Eastern Europeans from what I could gather.'

'What about the parent company then? Someone there will know which suppliers they have.'

'I've got an email address for their accounts department. I'm gonna send a request off for a full list of suppliers before I go.'

'Go?' A look at his watch made Campbell realise he'd lost track of time as he'd read and reread the lists on his desk.

'Yes, I've got a date tonight.'

'OK then. Do that and get yourself away.'

Campbell wanted to get back to his wife, but the urge to beat Evans to the solution, thus proving his ability to manage this oddball group, made him stay at his desk.

When Lauren got up to leave, Chisholm grunted a goodbye without bothering to take his eyes off the screen in front of him. That, coupled with the fact Bhaki had not returned from his visits yet, told him that the team were dedicated to their jobs and weren't the clock-watchers he was used to. Something told him that he would make allowances for Lauren and that nobody would complain. She'd been wearing a mini-dress that had given him flashes of stocking tops whenever she crossed or uncrossed her legs, actions she did on a regular basis.

A text message came in from Sarah asking what time he'd be home. Checking his watch, he tapped out a reply telling her he'd be home by seven. He knew she wouldn't be happy, but he'd explained the importance of him to make a good impression on both his team and his new superiors.

Returning his attention to the papers on his desk, he tried to clear his mind of the details already ingrained in the hope of gaining a fresh perspective.

The new tactic was starting to frustrate him when his mobile shrilled. Sarah's name and a picture of her bump decorated the screen.

As soon as he thumbed the phone, he started to speak, intending to head her complaints off before they reached the pass. 'Hi, I'll be home by seven. I promise.'

'John. The baby's coming—'

'I'm on my way. I'll be there as soon as I can.' Campbell was halfway across the office before she finished the sentence.

Running through the station, he made it outside in record time. Fumbling keys from his pocket, he pressed the blipper to unlock the doors of his Mondeo before he even reached it.

As he twisted the keys in the ignition, the enormity of the situation hit him a devastating broadside. He was going to be a father. His son would soon be born. No longer would he and Sarah be a couple. Instead they would be parents. Tutors in life. Guardians of morality and well being.

Holding his breath deep, he exhaled to calm himself. His hands shook as he released the handbrake and engaged first gear.

Chapter 23

Throwing herself forward, Samantha ran towards the open window intent on diving through it. Towards the police car which had driven into the farmyard. Towards rescue. Towards freedom. A scream burst from her mouth as she tried to attract the attention of the car's passengers.

She was six feet from the when she felt a muscled arm coil around her body, slowing her momentum. A second arm joined the first as Blair tackled her to the ground. Her face colliding with a pair of boots left beside the couch.

His weight pinned her down, a hand clamped itself over her mouth. His stinking fingers polluted her nose as she tried to wriggle free. Trapped by his fat body, face down on the disgusting carpet, she struggled to get enough air into her lungs as his fingers half blocked her nostrils.

'Stay quiet, you little bitch.' His free hand found a pressure point on her upper arm, causing a wave of agony to shoot through her whole left side.

Samantha thrashed about beneath him until she realised the futility of her action. He was too strong for her. With him lying on top of her, there was no way she could get enough purchase to attack him or let out another scream.

As she lay squashed beneath his body, her defeat became obvious to him and he started to gloat.

'Thought you was gonna escape, did you? Thought you was gonna leave without giving me my goodbye fuck, did you?'

Urghh, God. No.

Hearing his foul intentions renewed Samantha's determination to escape his grasp, yet try as she might she couldn't break his grip. Her exposed skin rubbed against the carpet, raising angry red burns as she fought her captor.

'Don't you like the idea of fucking me? 'Cause I love the idea of fucking you.'

Samantha did her best to ignore Blair's perverted words, to close her mind to the whispering in her ear about how he planned to take her any and every way he desired. Reacting to his fantasies would drive him on and her crazy. As time dragged on, his words became ever-more depraved until his lips spewed nothing but filth. Samantha knew it was only a matter of time before he realised the police weren't going to rescue her.

When that penny dropped into the cesspool of his mind, she expected his hands to start wandering to the more intimate areas of her body.

A door bumped shut and Elvis's boots appeared in her eyeline. 'You can let her up now. Plod's away.'

Feeling Blair lift his weight of her back, Samantha grabbed for the hem of her dress. Pulling it down as far as she could, she climbed to her feet trying to preserve as much dignity as possible. Her arms became shields against Blair's leering gaze.

Looking to Elvis she awaited his instruction.

'Back upstairs, you. And don't even think about doing that again. Right?'

Samantha nodded to satisfy him although the gesture was a lie. Given half a chance to escape or instigate a rescue she'd always try to get away.

She trooped up the stairs, fighting the multitude of emotions coursing through her body. She had been so close to escaping only for it to be snatched away. Yet Elvis hadn't carried through on his earlier threats about trying to escape.

Does that mean they're bluffing?

Then she remembered the video. The threats were no bluff. These men would take that torch to her.

A hard push from Elvis propelled her into the bedroom.

Kyle watched as she picked herself up, concern written all over his face. 'Are you OK?'

'I'm fine. I just tripped and fell. Nothing to worry about.'

'What happened, Sam?'

'I told you. I fell over. That's all.' She put a tone of annoyance into her reply as she needed him to stop asking the same question.

'I don't believe you.'

Samantha wasn't surprised he wasn't accepting her lie. She'd walked out of the room in one piece and had returned with torn clothing and a gash on her forehead that covered one side of her face with blood.

How could she tell him the truth? He wouldn't understand why the men had made her dance. If she tried to explain it to him, she'd be faced with having to explain about sex, territory he wasn't ready to explore.

Could she tell him about a police car coming into the yard? Could she really tell him how close they had been to being rescued? What would that do to his young mind? Wasn't their imprisonment bad enough as it was without telling him how close they had come to being free?

*   *   *

Turning her back on Kyle, Samantha rubbed at her hair with the damp towel. Once again she'd had numerous showers. Only this time she was trying to wash the stench and the touch of the loathsome Blair from her body, rather than cleansing herself of his gaze.

When she turned round Kyle was sitting on the mattress watching her, the video game forgotten. The lacy dress held tight between his slender fingers.

'I could see your boobies through this. Why did you wear it for the nasty men?'

'Because they made me. They made a video which they're gonna send to Mum and Dad.'

'Why?'

'So that they'll get the money quicker.'

Samantha explained the basics of kidnapping to Kyle without telling him anything about the threats, or what would happen if their parents didn't raise the ransom.

Those details she kept to herself along with the fear Blair had instilled when he was whispering his perversions into her ear. Now more than ever, she was convinced he intended to rape her before they were either released or mutilated.

His foot stamped down. 'I want to go home. I want Mum and Dad to give the bad men their money so we can go home.'

'Me too.' Samantha pulled him close, so he couldn't see the tears filling her eyes.

Chapter 24

The door opened as soon as he pulled into the drive. Sarah waddled out carrying her hospital bag. She threw a smile his way as she turned to lock the house up.

Calmness overtook him when he saw her. Now that he was with her, he felt he had a measure of control over matters, even though he was wise enough to know it was an illusion.

'It's OK, honey.' He held the passenger door open for her and took her bag. 'Let's get you into the car and you can tell me all about it on the way to the hospital.'

He reversed the car out of the drive and drove carefully out of Gretna and joined the A75 heading west towards Dumfries and the Cresswell maternity wing of Dumfries and Galloway Royal Infirmary.

Once he was onto the A75, he increased speed until Sarah told him to slow down. 'I'd rather give birth in the car than not reach the hospital.'

He eased back on the throttle a little, but the road was quiet and he made good time along the dark road.

Campbell gabbled away to his wife. The imminent birth of their son filled them with a sense of elation and excitement.

'What's that noise?' Her voice sharp, laced with worry.

'Shush a second and let me hear.' Campbell could feel the steering pulling to the left. A puncture. After a few seconds he announced this to Sarah who took the news with a stoicism he wished he could share.

'Should I call an ambulance?'

'No don't bother, there's a side road up here, pull in and change the wheel there.'

'OK, but are you sure you'll be all right?'

'I'll be fine. The contractions are still quite far apart.'

Campbell pulled the car off the A75 into a single-track road, leading to a farm. Leaping out of the car he opened the boot. Sarah's bag was pushed forward onto the back seat as he prayed the spare was inflated.

It was. Grabbing the jack and wheel-brace, he wheeled the spare to the side of the car and dropped to his hands and knees. Working by touch alone, he managed to change the wheel in a few short minutes. Throwing the flat tyre into the boot along with the jack, he made a mental note to buy a head torch to join them. There was no way he ever wanted to change a wheel in darkness again.

'I'm going to let the car down again now.'

Sarah sat in the car throughout the wheel change, despite being tilted over when the jack raised the car.

Climbing back into the car, he rubbed his dirty hands on his shirt, turned the car around in a gateway and rejoined the artery connecting Gretna with Stranraer.

'Let's go meet Junior.'

Reaching the hospital, Campbell dropped his wife at the door and raced off to find a parking space.

He caught up with Sarah as a kindly nurse was escorting her to an examination room. After about five minutes a midwife came and joined them. She asked Sarah when her waters broke, what contractions she had felt, their timing and other such questions.

The midwife rose from her chair, asking them to follow her to one of the birthing suites.

'Is everything in order?' Sarah was the one who voiced their concerns.

'I think so, but I want a doctor to listen to the baby's heartbeat... it's just routine.'

The way the midwife had tagged those last three words onto the sentence informed Campbell it was far from routine. Hiding his fears behind what he hoped was an impassive face, he assisted his wife through the door of the birthing suite.

Sarah had barely settled on the bed when a doctor walked in without knocking, introducing himself as Dr Prior.

He wasted no time feeling Sarah's distended stomach, using a foetal Doppler to enable him to listen to Junior's heartbeat. He listened for less than a minute, and then sat down on the examination stool at the foot of the bed.

'What is it, doctor?' Campbell squeezed his wife's hand as he asked the question.

'The baby's heartbeat keeps slowing down and then returning to normal. It sounds to me as though the umbilical cord may be around baby's neck.'

'Oh my God.' Sarah was fighting back tears, in the hope that by keeping her emotions together she could somehow help her unborn child.

'What can you do, doctor?' Campbell's face was grave as the nightmare enveloped him.

'We can either perform an emergency caesarean section or induce labour. If we induce labour, then we'll monitor baby's heartbeat; if there's any complications, you may have to have an emergency section anyway.'

'When would the section take place?'

'In the next twenty minutes. There is no time to waste. I'll give you a quick minute to decide and then we'll have to start treatment.'

When he left the room, Campbell and Sarah sat together, holding hands as they contemplated their options.

Campbell hoped Sarah would choose the caesarean section, as he did not want any risk to his unborn child or his wife, yet instinct told him it was her choice and he was ready to support her, whichever path she chose. He looked up from the floor, which had become the focus of his unseeing gaze, and held her eye. He knew without speaking which course of treatment she wanted to take.

'Caesarean?'

She nodded. He kissed her hand as he rose to go and look for the doctor. Before he could exit the room, the door was opened by Dr Prior trailed by a couple of midwives and a third person dressed in scrubs.

'I want to have a caesarean.' Sarah answered the question before it was asked.

Dr Prior took their decision in his stride. 'A wise choice.' Pointing at the man in scrubs, he made an introduction. 'This is Dr Wilson, our anaesthesiologist. He will give you an epidural which will numb you from the chest down.'

'If you'd like to come with me, Dad.' A midwife laid a gentle hand on Campbell's arm. 'We'll get you a set of scrubs and you can meet up with your wife in the operating theatre before we start the section.'

Campbell kissed Sarah's sweat-coated forehead. 'I'll be there, baby, I promise.'

'You always said you'd take me to the theatre.'

Relief coursed through Campbell's body. She was now in the doctor's hands. The way the nurses and midwife moved around her with practiced movements and a calm manner was subduing his fears, although nothing except Junior's first cry would lay them to rest.

Chapter 25

Victoria's mobile beeped once. The clear, insistent sound told her she had a text. Snatching up the mobile, she tapped the screen until the message was displayed.

Her heart fell as she read it. Just like the first one from the kidnappers, it told her to visit watchmykids.com for an update. Running through to the kitchen, she grabbed her laptop from its case and began the task of plugging it in and booting it up.

Conflicted between dread and a natural desire to see if her children were OK, she prayed to a god she'd never believed in. Bile threatened to erupt from her throat, but she swallowed it back down. The taste in her mouth would have repulsed her in less trying circumstances; now she used it to focus her mind on what she was about to see.

Victoria told herself that there was little need to worry too much. The deadline was still three days away. Despite this knowledge, she knew that what she was about to see would not give her any pleasure, other than potentially seeing her children were unhurt.

She had tormented and reassured herself at least five times a day by watching the first video of her children. While they looked fit and healthy, watching Samantha parade around in the sexy costume sickened her every time she watched it.

As the laptop prepared itself for use she yelled to Nicholas to come and join her. Bringing up the home page she went straight to the site using a shortcut she had saved to her desktop.

This time when she got to the site there was a different video link, clicking on it she could Samantha was standing in front of a wall wearing a red dress. The video had been shot from a distance and she couldn't make out many details.

Thank God. She's got a dress on. They haven't made her strip.

As she peered at the screen trying to see if her daughter was injured in any way, music sounded out and Samantha started to dance. It was the most half-hearted, lacklustre dance she'd ever seen her daughter do.

The focus of the video was adjusted, until it was zoomed in on Samantha's face. Victoria examined her daughter's face looking for any sign of mistreatment. Finding none she sank back in her chair, exhaling the breath she hadn't known she was holding.

With an inexorable slowness the camera panned down until Samantha's breasts filled the screen. Her nipples visible through the thin material of the dress.

Unable to watch any more, Nicholas turned his eyes away, but Victoria grabbed his head and pointed his face back at the screen.

'I can't watch this, Victoria. It's not right. No father should ever watch his daughter in a video like that.'

'It's your fault she's in that bloody video. Not watching it isn't an option for you.'

Victoria's eyes never left the screen as she spat the words at her husband.

The music changed and Samantha began a new dance routine as the camera kept creeping down her body.

With her eyes locked onto Samantha's lace-clad body, Victoria searched for any sign of a pair of knickers. It was bad enough that Samantha's breasts were exposed through the sheer material without her groin being displayed in the same way.

Thicker lace came into view causing Samantha's skin to be less defined. Blurrier. Still the camera descended, the hem of the dress coming into view. Halting, the camera went out of focus for a second. When it adjusted itself, Victoria could see tufts of hair through the thin material.

Lingering on the scene for an age the cameraman zoomed out just enough to show Samantha's body from the knees up.

Looking on aghast, Victoria and Nicholas could see Samantha's dress climbing her legs as she danced. Each bounce of her breasts tugged the thin fabric ever higher. Soon the hem would no longer cover Samantha's most intimate areas.

'They're sick. How can they do that? Why are they degrading her like that?'

'Don't be such a dickhead. They are doing that to give us extra incentive to get the money. To keep us off-balance and compliant to their demands.'

Victoria was still admonishing her husband when the video stopped with a suddenness that surprised them both. A still of Kyle sitting cross-legged, a games controller in his hands, lasted a few seconds before fading out.

A jolting memory caused Victoria to leap from her seat. Her footsteps thudded up stairs as she charged toward the master bedroom, propelled by a sense of dread.

Entering her bedroom, she fell to her knees and grabbed the rough wooden handles which adorned her naughty-knicker drawer, then pulled the drawer right out from its socket. Lifting it above the bed, she turned it upside down, emptying the contents onto the crisp, white duvet.

Tossing the empty drawer aside, she grabbed at anything red she saw.

A bra was discarded first, two pairs of knickers followed. A flimsy red basque was grabbed in hope, before it joined the other rejected items.

Dispersing the pile across the full expanse of the bed, she looked in vain for the lacy red dress she'd worn for Nicholas.

She went down on her knees snaking her arm into the gaping maw left by the missing drawer. Groping around she felt carpet and then her fingers touched lace. Pulling her hand out, she identified the lace as a pair of briefs.

Trying again, she found nothing more than balls of lint and a biro that had rolled underneath the chest of drawers.

Everything she feared regarding the red dress Samantha had worn was true. It was hers. She'd bought it last year as a birthday treat for Nicholas. The man whose reckless actions had precipitated the whole sequence of events, transforming their respectable middle-class lives into a waking nightmare.

Revulsion at the kidnapper's twisted imagination, spurred Victoria towards the bathroom where she vomited until nothing else would come out.

A thought pierced her brain and heart like a dagger. Hollering downstairs, she demanded Nicholas come up to join her.

'What's up?' Concern at the way she had summoned him showed on his ashen face.

'We need to go through these.'

'Just bung them back in the drawer. We have more important things to do.'

Victoria had to fight back another bout of nausea before she could speak again.

'You don't understand. That dress Samantha was wearing. It's the one I wore for your birthday.'

'Shit. I thought it looked familiar.'

Victoria shook her head, trying to clear it before explaining, 'My dress is missing. The dress Samantha's wearing in the video is identical to the one I wore for you.'

Waving away his protestations that she must be mistaken, Victoria began sorting her lingerie into matching sets.

'We've got to check all of this and work out if anything else is missing.' As she spoke Victoria was trying to recall if she owned any underwear that was more revealing than the missing dress. Every outfit she remembered morphed into the red lacy number she'd seen her daughter wearing.

She needed Nicholas's help to recall the details. He'd always liked her in sexy underwear and since the early days of the Internet he'd even bought her some bits and pieces. Unlike a lot of other men buying their wives underwear, he'd shown good taste and had purchased quality garments that made her feel sexy rather than slutty. It was she who'd bought the sluttier items.

Nicholas started to help. Together they paired bras and knickers, laying the various chemises and babydolls out flat so they were easier to identify.

Set by set, they ticked each item off their mental lists, sometimes questioning each other about the occasion something was worn.

Victoria made neat rows for birthdays, wedding anniversaries and other occasions. One gap glared at them. Nicholas's last birthday.

When Victoria was sure that she could recall nothing more, she set about questioning Nicholas, probing him for details about other outfits he'd liked to see her wearing, in case they missed a set that the kidnappers had stolen. Any he could remember were ones she was positive she'd thrown out.

Dumping the outfits back into the drawer, she grabbed the pairs of stockings and started tossing them into the drawer when her fingers noticed something amiss. The familiar waxen feel of her fishnets was absent. Victoria thought hard and a memory of putting them back into the drawer after she'd last worn them surfaced, but a frantic search through the pile did not uncover them. They were gone.

They've taken them too. Oh my poor girl, what will they make you do next?

Chapter 26

Evans needed food but he didn't know what he wanted to eat. Bored with takeaways he fancied something more nutritious than chips, pizza or Chinese food. A curry was an option, but he'd eaten two vindaloos and a phaal in the last week.

Instead he decided to try the Mexican restaurant on the Crescent. He'd always wanted to dine there, but Janet had preferred to eat at Italian restaurants or find a country pub with low beams and a traditional menu.

Evans followed the waiter who seated him at a small table in a back corner of the restaurant. He didn't care about being given the worst table in the room. As a single diner he knew he couldn't expect anything better and the seat allowed him to watch the whole room.

As the waiter had deposited a beer on the table and taken away his order, he'd noticed three familiar faces walk through the door.

The woman in the velour tracksuit was the first to spot him but as she strode forward, her brothers' faces darkened with barely supressed anger when they recognised him.

Standing up, he greeted Maureen Leighton and exchanged scowls with Tony and Dennis.

'You here on your own, Harry?' Maureen's accent was pure Carlisle. 'Because if you are, I'd like you to join us.'

'I'm not eating with him.'

'Suit yourself.' Maureen turned to her other brother. 'What about you, Dennis?'

He shrugged. 'I don't give a fuck who's at the table so long as I get something to eat soon.

'It's all right, Maureen. I'm just in for a quick bite and then I'm heading home.'

'Nonsense. I won't have a man in your position eating alone. Besides, I need to talk to you.'

Evans stood up with reluctance. While he was glad of the opportunity to talk to Maureen, a detective inspector shouldn't be seen dining with the people behind organised crime. On the other hand, he was curious to know why Maureen wanted to talk to him.

Evans was ushered by a nervous-looking waiter to a large round table, where he made sure he sat next to Maureen but opposite Tony. He could handle any confrontation the man threw at him, but he'd prefer to have a calm discussion than a shouting match.

'It's the trial next week, isn't it?'

'Yeah.' Evans hoped this wasn't what Maureen wanted to discuss. The trial of Derek Yates wasn't something he was looking forward to although it was dominating most of his thoughts. Maureen's lined face held a sympathy Evans found disconcerting. 'I hope you get the right result. The bastard deserves to go down for a long time for what he did.'

'Thanks.' Evans decided to change the subject to a safer ground where he could be more assured of his footing. 'There's a lot of stuff coming to my attention these days. I do hope you're not involved in any of it.'

If the Leightons weren't behind the crimes, there was a good chance they'd know who was. Failing that, they'd be determined to discover who was operating in their territory. While the crimes weren't in their usual sphere, there was no telling what they were involved in.

'You mean the robberies and those garages getting ripped off?' Maureen's eyes narrowed as she watched his face.

'Just the robberies. I know who's behind the garages.'

'That's nothing to do with anyone we know. Who's at it with the garages?'

Evans smiled. 'I see no need for you to know that name. I'll deal with them.' He took a slug of his beer and eyed her. 'Would you tell me if the boot was on the other foot?'

'Of course I would. You know I always do my very best to help the police with their enquires.' Maureen's reply drew a smirk from Tony.

'Touché.'

When their meals arrived, Evans was amused to see Tony had also ordered fajitas. As he pulled out his bottle of Tabasco sauce he saw Tony's watchful glare and decided to have some fun. 'I like to add a little kick to my meals. Do you want some?'

'Too right. Gies it here.'

Evans passed the bottle across once he'd added a liberal amount to his meal. Tony's eyes were full of challenge as he splashed Tabasco sauce all over his plate. The table was silent as they ate their meals. Evans could see Tony was struggling with the heat. His hand would reach towards his beer only to recoil as he realised taking a drink would be seen as a sign of weakness. Evans had no such fears and kept sipping at his beer between mouthfuls, so his mouth was treated to a cool–hot cycle which retained the fire in every bite.

When the meal was finished, he stood up and dropped enough money on the table to cover his share. Before leaving he couldn't resist firing a parting shot at Tony, 'A wee word of advice, Tony. You may want to put the toilet roll in the fridge ready for the morning.'

He left with a Maureen's chuckles in his ears and a picture of Tony's stricken face imprinted into his mind.

Chapter 27

Elvis and Blair were relaxing with a couple of beers. Foil trays littered the table and the air was filled with the scent of Chinese food battling against stale cigarette smoke.

'That copper was telling me about their new technology for identifying stolen property. It's called SmartWater. The basic idea is that you buy a fifty-mil vial of this SmartWater from the police and swab your stuff with it. A little swab on any area – say the steering wheel of a tractor – would identify the tractor as belonging to a particular farm thanks to a unique code, which is specific to each vial. All you have to do is record what you swabbed and where you'd swabbed it. If anything is stolen you show the cops your records. The SmartWater shows up under a particular frequency of UV light. Apparently all recovered stolen goods are now scanned as a matter of routine.'

'Fuck, that's clever.'

'It was first used in Derbyshire about eight months ago. According to the copper it cut down the number of farm robberies by sixty-five per cent.'

Blair gave a snorted laugh. 'That's fucking hilarious. Eight months ago we left Derbyshire to go to Wales. That's why the number of robberies dropped.'

'That'll have a lot to do it.' Elvis was smiling, although the whole episode had scared him. They had been a whisker away from being caught and he didn't want to repeat the experience any time soon. He was too old to go to jail again.

'What did you tell him when he tried to get you to buy some?'

'I told him it was a good idea and agreed to buy some.'

'What the fuck did you do that for?'

'It would have been odd if I hadn't. Today was close enough as it was. I don't want him coming back trying to sell me it again. Thirty-five quid is a small price to pay to make sure that we don't get bothered by him again.'

'Fair point.' Blair drained his can as he acknowledged Elvis's logic.

'It's also good to know what the police are up to. When you sign up for this stuff you get a sign for your gate saying you've got it.'

'So we can tell which farms have it and which don't. That's handy but it won't tell the coppers much unless they catch us with the stuff. I'm not worried about it. Are you?

''Course I am. How many crimes do you think that stuff would tie us too if they looked in the barn or stopped one of the wagons?'

A tinny crackling sound filled the room as Blair opened another beer can. 'We run that risk now. As far as I'm concerned it's nowt to worry about. It's for them to trace stuff rather than catching thieves.'

'What concerns me is they're working to prevent the thefts as well. Plus, what about the guys we sell to? They won't want any gear with this stuff on, will they? You ask me, this stuff is poison. We need to make sure we don't nick anything from anywhere that's got this stuff.'

'I still say it's nowt to worry about.'

'I'll let the boss make the decision on that one. He's smarter than both of us.'

Chapter 28

Campbell was seated on a stool beside his wife's head, dressed in hospital scrubs. A curtain was erected over her chest. Neither of them could see what was happening as the doctors performed the emergency section.

They held hands, each squeezing the other for reassurance, then relaxing their grip so as not to inflict pain. The doctors were talking to each other throughout the operation.

Listening to the voices, Campbell realised the doctors were discussing a television show aired the night before. Interspersed through their conversation were calm requests for various surgical instruments.

Through speakers in the ceiling a radio was playing a local station. The usual mix of adverts and forced wackiness separated the songs regular listeners would be subjected to several times a day.

The realisation that the people on the other side of the curtain were just having another day at work did little to anaesthetise Campbell's nerves. He wanted their total concentration. A complete focus on the task at hand.

The hidden radio was playing 'Hotel California' by the Eagles when a tentative wail was followed by a louder more indignant cry as Junior protested at being evicted from his mother's comfortable womb.

Sarah and Campbell looked at each other, relief washing over them. Baby was OK. In the background a voice could be heard noting the time of birth.

A head appeared round the curtain and a smiling nurse congratulated them on the birth of their son.

Unable to contain himself, Campbell rose to his feet in time to see a midwife carry his son to a digital scale, where she began the ritual of weighing the baby and checking that all fingers and toes were present and accounted for.

Feeling a sharp tug on his sleeve, he sat back down and told Sarah what he had seen. After what felt like an eternity, Junior was brought over by the midwife who handed him over to Campbell.

Having kept a tight grip on his emotions during the evening, Campbell shed a few tears as he held his son for the first time. Junior was swaddled in blankets and retained a coating of amniotic fluid over his body, but this did not prevent Campbell from kissing his son and then offering him to Sarah so she could do the same.

'He's beautiful.' Fat tears of joy rolled down her cheeks.

'Isn't he?'

'I'll just take him for a little clean up, while you are taken through to the recovery room and then you can give him his first feed.' The midwife held out her arms for Campbell to give Junior to her.

'Just a moment.' A look at Sarah. 'Alan Geoffrey?'

'Definitely, though he'll be called Alan.'

'Here you are.' Campbell returned Alan to the midwife after planting another kiss on his messy forehead.

* * *

Two hours later Campbell kissed a sleeping Alan and drowsy Sarah goodbye and returned to his car. Pulling his mobile from his pocket, he began calling the family members on the list Sarah had dictated to him earlier.

He greeted each family member with their new status of Grandma or Auntie as he worked his way through the list, sharing the good news.

Filled with exultant joy, he talked and laughed his way through the many conversations, until he'd spoken to every name on Sarah's list. Checking his phone he saw a text from Evans:

Chisholm told me you ran out the office like a scalded cat. Guessing baby on way. Hope everything OK. Let me know.

Seeing the phone battery was about to fail, he sent Evans a quick text rather than calling him.

The drive back to Gretna was the first time Campbell was alone with his thoughts. He could not believe the emotions coursing through him. Tonight was the greatest night of his life. Far better than the night he'd spent fumbling around with Georgina Urquhart until they'd both managed to lose their virginities. Better than the night he'd met Sarah. Better than when she'd agreed to be his wife. It even topped the day they'd said 'I do' to each other.

Using the controls on the steering wheel, he selected CD five from the auto-changer. Selecting track two, he pressed his right foot to the floor as he waited for the iconic riff to begin.

The speedometer crept round the dial until it entered three-figure territory. Campbell was driving on automatic pilot, duetting with Axel Rose as 'Sweet Child o' Mine' blared out from the speakers.

Tonight he was invincible. Ten feet tall. The deserted road was his alone as he sped home, replaying the song every time it finished. By the fifth rendition his singing had lost none of its gusto, although tone and pitch had been abandoned somewhere near Annan.

Chapter 29

Evans drew on the last fraction of his cigarette before flicking the butt over a hedge into someone's garden. Fingering the scented nappy bags in his pocket he looked for the dog he'd got from Wetheral Animal Refuge.

He'd chosen the one nobody else would take – an unnamed Labrador puppy that had been savaged by an Alsatian. Missing half an ear and the lower part of his right foreleg had not affected the puppy's enthusiasm for life. Shining eyes and a doggy smile had been the clinching factors. Evans had been smitten by the pup as soon as it hobbled over to him and licked at his outstretched hand.

Janet had fallen in love with Tripod as soon as she'd met him, although she refused point-blank to use his name in public. When she moved into Evans's flat she made sure that Tripod was no longer allowed to sleep on the bed. It was one of the few things Evans had rowed about with her.

Tripod rooted around underneath the hedge, following some scent or other. Losing interest, he squatted down to do his business.

Depositing a bulging nappy bag into a nearby bin, Evans clipped Tripod's lead onto his collar and returned to the flat.

Unplugging his mobile phone from the charger, he checked it for missed calls or messages. The lone missed call from his sister he deleted. She'd call back if it was important.

Tapping at the screen he brought up the text from Campbell.

Reading the two-line text filled him with a heartfelt delight for the younger man's good fortune.

It also triggered bitter pangs of jealousy.

There was nothing personal about his envy. He now envied all new fathers. They possessed something he'd had snatched away.

Campbell now had the thing he desired most of all.

Someone to call him 'Dad'. A son. An heir. A carrier of the family name.

As he did upon hearing of a new child entering the world, he picked up Janet's letter and told her all about it.

They had been so close to starting a family themselves when fate intervened. Janet was ten weeks' pregnant when she had been raped. She had born the burden of her ordeal alone for a week. Unable to tell him she carried the secret until an infection set in, causing her to miscarry their child.

While he understood why she hadn't told him, he couldn't help but feel betrayed by her silence. She hadn't told him about the rape until after losing their precious baby. The twin hammer blows, instilled a numbness he still felt.

A botched dilation and curettage after her miscarriage had left her needing a hysterectomy. Janet's body healed, but her mind never got to grips with the experience. She tortured herself about her inability to give him the family they'd planned and blamed herself for being nice to the man who'd knocked on their door pretending to be some kind of salesman.

Evans's numbness had increased as he sat by her hospital bed contemplating the news. He'd worn a brave face and talked to her of adoption and fostering. Returning home between visits he'd washed the bravery from his face and dealt with his grief alone.

The rapist had stolen the life they'd planned together. He'd stolen their unborn baby and the others they'd talked of. Never would they have children or grandchildren bouncing on their knees. He'd taken all that away from them with his selfish needs.

Base instincts coupled with a desire for revenge had murdered the soul of his wife. The unborn foetus inside, a secondary victim, as were the others intended to follow the firstborn.

Many times he had tried to comprehend the torment of her thoughts. His own were terrible in their intensity, yet insignificant compared to her suffering. He still couldn't bear to think of the pain she must have felt when writing the letter he so cherished. Grief did powerful things to the mind. He'd long forgiven her for leaving him, taking solace in the knowledge that she was now at peace.

Derek Yates, however, could never be forgiven. Five months after Janet filled her stomach with pills and vodka, Evans's hatred of Yates remained as fierce as it was the day she'd told him of the rape.

When Yates was brought in, he'd begged for five minutes alone in the cell with him but had been refused. Grantham had dealt with the case in conjunction with a different team. Rumour had it that Yates had fallen down the stairs a minimum of eight times the night he was brought in. Rumour wasn't enough for Evans; he'd wanted to tear Yates limb from limb.

He'd gone to the custody suite intent on meting out his own justice only to end up wrestling with three PCs.

It was Grantham who'd stopped him, who had talked to him until the fire in his gut was manageable.

Evans still wasn't sure if he was pleased he hadn't got his time with Yates or not. His career would have ended then, but it was about to end now anyway. He was honest enough with himself to know that if he'd got into that cell: he would have tried to kill Yates. He knew it was wrong. But in the days after Janet's death – he still couldn't call it suicide – he would have killed Yates without a second's thought.

Chapter 30

Samantha lay on the grubby mattress with Kyle cuddled into her side. His soft snores the only noise she could hear. The day's events played a slideshow in her mind, a burning sense of failure dominating her thoughts. She had failed to dive through the open window. She hadn't screamed loud enough for the police to hear. Not only had she failed herself, she'd let Kyle down as well.

A different sound assaulted her ears as heavy footsteps thudded along the corridor outside their prison.

The creak of hinges was followed by noisy splashes as the man relieved himself. When the flow ended there were no sounds of tap water.

Blair, Samantha guessed. *Typical of him not to wash his hands.*

There were more heavy thuds as he returned. But not enough!

Samantha sat bolt upright.

No! What's he doing?

The sound of footsteps resumed, but quieter now, as if he was tiptoeing.

Oh, thank God. He's gone back to bed.

Relaxing back onto the mattress, Samantha could feel the relief flood through her body.

Is that him coming back?

Straining her ears, she sat upright once more.

It was. Shit. He's coming back. He's going to rape me.

The sound of a bolt being slid back was much quieter than normal.

First one. Then the other.

Paralysed by fear, Samantha was rooted to the mattress. Terrified of Blair's intentions when he came through the door. She'd learned earlier that she wasn't strong enough to break free of his grip.

What can I do? How can I stop him?

A key was placed into the lock with far more care than usual.

He doesn't want to be heard! He doesn't want the others to wake up and stop him. Remembering the way Elvis dominated the room, Samantha realised Blair was scared of him. The knowledge gave her a strength and bravery she'd never experienced before.

A plan came into her head. It was simple, yet it should work. Kyle would be afraid for a minute or two but there was nothing she could do about that.

Taking up station by the door she dropped to her knees, pulling in deep breaths, filling her lungs as she awaited the door opening.

Blair's face appeared in the crack, the mask backlit as he made his way into the room.

Samantha emptied her lungs in a high-pitched scream designed to wake the whole house.

Blair recoiled. 'Bitch.'

Kyle woke up and started crying. From along the landing, panicked curses filled the air.

Blair slammed the door shut and fired home the bolts. The need for stealth gone as Samantha's scream died out.

Samantha could hear Elvis's raised voice as he caught Blair coming back from their room. Blair made the mistake of trying to defend his actions, but Elvis would have none of it. Both men were shouting at full volume, when the sound of knuckles colliding with flesh ended the debate.

The door opened a tiny fraction and Elvis's voice carried across the darkness. 'You all right?'

'Yes. Thank you.'

Chapter 31

Jonny Green was trying to work out why he'd allowed himself to be talked into this. Steve had been insistent it would be easy money. He should have stuck to his guns and refused to come along.

Both he and Steve were dressed in dark clothes, gloves on their hands.

Darkness enshrouded them as they parked in the lay-by. Climbing over a gate they followed a short farm track which led them past the back of the Drover's Inn.

A half-rotted timber gate offered them passage through the blackthorn hedge that separated the track from the grounds of the hotel.

Hefting a crowbar in his hands, Steve levered the hooked end into a window and applied a firm but steady pressure, intending to pop sash from frame.

Inexperience foiled him. He'd made the mistake of not levering the frame next to the catch. The rotten wood of the window gave way and the glass shattered.

'Let's get out of here.'

'Don't be soft. You know what an old drunk Armstrong is. He'll be too pissed to hear anything.' Regardless of his bravado, Steve held an ear by the smashed window listening for sounds of discovery.

Jonny hid in a bush, watching the upstairs window for signs of Armstrong.

Both lads were familiar with the layout of the small hotel. Attracted by the opportunity for a spot of underage drinking and a pretty barmaid, they had become frequent visitors to the public bar attached to the property.

Placated by the lack of imminent discovery, Steve removed as much glass as he could from the frame and climbed through after putting on his balaclava. Following his friend's lead, Jonny readied himself then went through the window. They made their way to a storage room, head torches throwing illumination wherever they looked.

Crossing to the wooden cabinet where Armstrong stored bottles of spirits, and more importantly left the tills overnight. Steve again went to work with his crowbar. Inside the small room, the sound of wood splintering was deafening to Jonny. Lifting a hand to silence Steve, he listened but heard nothing.

Steve emptied all the notes from the tills into the backpack he'd been wearing, while Jonny was pulling out a case of vodka from the bottom shelf. Various bottles of spirits which lined the shelves followed the cash into the backpack.

Laying the full case of vodka beside the window, Jonny was about to climb through when a light blazed into the room. He and Steve whirled round to see Armstrong standing in the doorway, a cricket bat in one hand. His bowling-ball gut overhanging the one item of clothing he wore: faded pyjama bottoms.

Armstrong's eyes were unfocused, but his jaw was set with determination. His fingers tightened around the cricket bat as he prepared to defend his property.

Unsure what to do, Jonny froze. His heart said run and his head agreed, but there was no way they could both get through the window before Armstrong caught up with them.

Armstrong's tales of his life in the army flooded back to Jonny's panic-stricken mind. The boxing medals were in a display case above the bar.

Armstrong advanced on them. His voice an adrenaline-tinged slur. 'Ya bastards. Thought you were gonna rob me, did you?'

Steve lifted his crowbar and held it in front of him as if it was a sword. Armstrong swung at him with the cricket bat, but Steve deflected the blow.

The fight between Steve and Armstrong motivated Jonny into action. Bursting open the vodka case, Jonny lifted a bottle in each hand and threw them at Armstrong.

The first bottle missed as Armstrong ducked beneath it, but the second landed on the side of Armstrong's head before smashing as it made contact with the floor.

Steve wasted none of the advantage gained from Jonny's missiles. Stepping forward he swung his crowbar catching Armstrong just above his left ear. Even as Armstrong was falling, he was heading to the window, pushing Jonny through first.

Running down the track, Jonny was aware of his body dumping the adrenaline that had entered his system during the brief fight. His legs were unsteady and a cold sweat was enveloping his body. Ahead of him, Steve was stumbling as he ran. He too would be experiencing the same problems.

As they got into the car another concern hit Jonny.

'D'you think old Armstrong will be all right?'

'Yeah. I didn't hit him that hard. Just enough to stun him.'

'I bloody hope so.' Jonny's mind turned to worry over Armstrong. He hoped the old guy was OK. It was bad enough hitting the old pisshead with a crowbar. He didn't want him to suffer any permanent damage.

'We did it, though. We got the money.'

Jonny didn't answer his friend. He was too busy looking at the blood on his glove.

Chapter 32

Wednesday

Evans addressed the team. 'We're all gonna be uncles and aunties to our new colleague's son, Alan Geoffrey Campbell. The proud father is having a small head-wetting get-together tonight. We will all be there. No excuses will be accepted, except death, and then only if a written letter is received one week prior. Understood?'

As well as a good piss-up, tonight Evans wanted to give Campbell the chance to get to know the team away from work. He hated the idea of team-building sessions, but experience had taught him a night in the pub was always good for morale.

'Lauren, get your profiling head on: I want to discuss these break-ins on our journey south.'

'Why, where are we going?'

'To see a man about a car.'

'I thought that was all cleared up?'

'Not to my satisfaction it isn't.'

A desk phone shrilled out its chime. Lauren picked up. 'Yes, ah-ha, I see, thanks for letting us know, Yvonne; we'll look into it right away.'

'What's the crack?'

'That was control, there's been a break-in at the Drover's Inn at Melmerby last night and three different farms in the Silloth area have been turned over as well. They are sending all the details to Chisholm now but gave us a call in case he wasn't at his computer.'

'They have obviously never met him then. Jabba, get all the details printed so Bhaki can compare them against known robberies from other licensed premises. Then I want you to tap into the power grid companies and start looking for any residential or small commercial property that has an unusually large electricity usage. When you have the list, the Nymph and Bhaji Boy can do a few visits to check out the premises.'

'It would be hacking not tapping, sir; and fat people have feelings, too.'

'Potayto, patahto, I'm not interested in what it's called, just write the fucking programme, get me my answer and stop your bloody whining.'

'Sir, did you get a reply from DCI Grantham about planting homing signals on some quad bikes?' Bhaki changed the subject in the hope of preventing one of Evans's legendary rants about how you could no longer call a spade a spade.

'No. He's probably not in yet, I'll call him later.'

As Evans left with Lauren to go about his daily terror regime, he stopped off at the duty officer's front desk and made a murmured request. When he saw the smile on the sergeant's face he knew he had got his own way. Pushing his luck to the limit, he dashed out to his car and came back with a pair of rolled up posters, which he gave to the desk sergeant along with specific instructions on where he wanted them hung.

As they headed south on the M6, Lauren took a call from Chisholm. Listening to one side of the conversation, Evans could tell something was wrong.

'Well?'

'That was DS Chisholm, the email came through about the Drover's Inn robbery.'

'And?'

'The cleaner found the manager lying on the floor covered in blood when she went in this morning. He's in an ambulance on his way to Cumberland Infirmary.'

'Poor bugger. Is he gonna be OK?'

'Chisholm didn't have that information.'

'I hope the old bugger's all right. He's a good man. He's hit the drink hard since his wife died a few years back.' Evans realised what he'd said and reflected that most people would say the same of him.

Lauren kept her eyes down as she related the rest of the information to Evans. Apart from the injury to the hotelier, there were signs of damage to the property this time.

'A CSI team from Penrith are en-route and the responding DC is staying on until we get there.'

'Best hurry then.' Evans added another twenty miles an hour to the already illegal speed he was driving at.

Evans parked behind the CSI chief's car. He figured he would be leaving before the CSI team, and this way if they wanted to leave sooner they couldn't without speaking to him.

Deep in the recesses of his mind lurked a significant clue as to the identity of one of the thieves, but he couldn't coax it to the fore. Past encounters with this surety had taught him to embrace the feeling without haste; the connection would come sooner if it weren't pursued.

Dragging his mind back to the present, Evans started after Lauren who was marching towards the entrance of the Drover's Inn. He caught up with her just as she entered the main bar area. As they went in, both were stopped by the crime scene manager, who was taping off the area.

Evans leaned his head in and surveyed the area. A pool of blood was soaking the carpet over by the bar. One of the CSI technicians was photographing everything, while another was taking swabs.

This was a massive development in the case, as the thieves hadn't encountered any resistance on their other jobs. With luck the owner would recover and be able to give them a description of the thieves.

Evans said nothing, preferring to stand and absorb the feel of the crime scene. He took in every detail: the cloying smell, the broken window allowing a cool airflow into the room, the regular splat of water dripping onto stainless steel coming from behind the bar. Mingled with the landlord's blood was broken glass, a section of it held together by a Smirnoff label.

When something piqued Evans's interest he used his mobile to take a picture.

What really got his attention was the broken window. The bench seats below were coated with glass fragments indicating the window had been smashed from the outside.

'What d'you reckon, guv?'

'Either the crew we're after are getting desperate or it's someone else.'

Evans went through the building. In the main office he found files but no safe, or a space where one had been. On his way back to the bar he found a cupboard hanging open with a few bottles of spirits inside it. A cash drawer containing only small coins rested on one of the shelves. The door had been levered open.

The obvious deduction was the cupboard had been used for storing bottles of spirits. It was just bad management the cash drawer from the till was left in there as well.

Evans was in the process of looking for the first responder when he was approached by a young DC who introduced himself as Ben Thompson.

'What is it, lad?'

'I've just had word from the hospital, sir. Mr Armstrong died a few minutes ago. DC Garrett who went down with him said there was massive internal bleeding through a skull fracture.'

'Thanks for letting me know, son. Now I want you to go through his things and try and identify his next of kin. When you have a name, speak to your sergeant or DI and arrange for someone to deliver the death message.'

Turning round he waved Lauren across. 'I want you to get on to DI Hughes at Penrith and let him know what's happened here. We now have a murder inquiry to deal with. I'm going to use DC Thompson as my contact until I get a report from CSI, who will now have to give this a proper going over, instead of the quick glance they give for thefts.'

'Sir, I've identified the next of kin. It's his daughter. She lives in Southampton.'

Evans produced a card with the numbers of all of his team and handed it to Thompson. 'Here, call DS Chisholm. Tell him what you know about the daughter and he'll do the rest. When you've done that, find out what you can about the staff here, so that you can call one of them in to lock the place up again when CSI have left. You'll also need to call out a glazier. DI Hughes will be informed that as of now you are under my command so get cracking with that lot and then call me. Understood?'

Heedless of the answer he went in search of the CSI chief to inform her it was now a murder case.

She was busy taking samples and lamenting the fact that so much of the crime scene had been contaminated by paramedics. Evans looked at the CSI chief, amazed at how CSI attracted so many good-looking women, all of whom must have a ghoulish streak to want to tackle such a macabre task.

Collecting Lauren, Evans left the CSI chief to her job after getting her promise to provide a report as soon as possible.

'Surely we're not leaving, sir? We've got the murder case you've been after.'

'Of course we're leaving. You don't really think I'm gonna waste all day fucking about here when we could be making ourselves useful elsewhere. We've seen the scene. We're now going to have a discussion on the way to our next call. If we have any further queries, DC Thompson is on the ground for us.'

Lauren fell silent as Evans hurtled back towards Penrith. Evans wasn't talking as he contemplated the new turn the case had taken. At any minute he expected a call from Penrith CID demanding they handle the case. By involving Thompson he hoped to placate them long enough to solve the murder himself. Melmerby was without doubt on their patch. Located halfway between Alston and Penrith on the twisting A686, the small village was a farming community through and through. As far as he could figure, this was a different kind of robbery from the other ones. Entry had been forced, there was no safe to steal from, no alarm. The empty cash drawers spoke of a lower level of sophistication altogether.

He took his phone back from Lauren who had been forwarding the pictures to Chisholm and called his sister. After a brief conversation about family matters, he asked her about last night's local news. A regular watcher of the news, she was the one person he could rely on to have seen it.

He got the information he wanted and ended the call as soon as he could.

'Sir?' Lauren was looking at him as if awaiting a divine pronouncement.

'You first, lass. What do you reckon?'

'Well. I'm not sure, sir.' A pause as she considered her words. 'But I don't think it's connected. There was an amateurish feel to this one. All the others were clinically done, whereas this one was haphazard. My best guess is that it's someone else.'

Evans smiled to himself, proud she'd reached the same conclusion as he had.

'According to my sister there was a piece on the news last night warning publicans and hoteliers of the robberies we've been investigating.'

'On Border Crack and Deeks Aboot?'

'Aye.' Lauren's use of the nickname for the now replaced Border News and Lookaround amused him. 'I bet it's some chancers who saw the news and decided robbing pubs was a good idea.'

As Evans was pulling off the M6 at Lancaster, a call came in from an unknown number.

A press on the screen. 'DI Evans.'

'Sir, it's DC Thompson. I just thought you should know, one of the CSI team has found blood on a piece of broken glass still in the smashed window.'

'Good work, lad. Get them to have the lab rush it through. I want to know who that blood belongs to by this time tomorrow.'

'I've already made the request, sir.'

'Keep me posted.'

As he ended the call, Evans made a mental note that Thompson was a bright lad who would be an asset to his team. Then realisation hit him. He wouldn't be a copper in a few days, let alone have a team to manage. He'd be on the scrapheap. Sure he could take any of the jobs he'd been offered, but he despised the idea of being a glorified security guard instead of a detective. He couldn't bring himself to play deputy to someone else's sheriff.

Chapter 33

The lines of numbers on Victoria's laptop mocked her as she tried to make sense of them. Close focus on a particular line or column was fine, but when she leaned back to take an overview then the numbers blended together into a digital mosaic.

Whenever they did this, the numbers formed different versions of the same two images. Kyle and Samantha's faces. Sometimes they were smiling, sometimes grim, sometimes as they had looked as babies. The images that haunted her were the ones that came at her own lowest point. These were conjured from her deepest fears, produced by betraying eyes, which manipulated a spreadsheet into grotesque likenesses.

In these images Kyle and Samantha were screaming in pain or fear. Yet she must endure the torment of the numerical visions. She needed to work to gain the information necessary to continue on the crime spree.

Turning away from the screen she told herself she must be strong, determined. The memory of last night's haul buoyed her. She and Nicholas had burgled Maryport Golf Club. As a committee member, Nicholas had known the location of the bandit keys and the alarm code. He'd picked the lock with ease and they'd emptied the safe and bandit to add to their ransom fund. The fact the club steward was on holiday, coupled with a wedding at the weekend and annual membership payments, meant that there was far more money in the safe than usual. They had managed to get another £3,700 towards the ransom from the safe, plus another £653 from the bandits in the hall.

So far they were on target to reach the £42,000 of their own contribution. The £15,000 from friends and family members had already reached Nicholas's business account. Their burglarious activities had netted them a total of almost £28,000 so far, but they were still £10,000 short with just two days to go.

Nicholas's van was due to be sold today and they had managed to get three hundred more than expected for it. Her car would be passed over to a local garage on Friday morning, although they'd had to agree to two hundred less than they wanted for a cash purchase. All of the saleable electrical goods had been sold on eBay and they were all packaged up for either posting or collection.

They planned to use Nicholas's business account for the transfer as the sudden deposit of many thousands of pounds into a personal account may raise a lot of red flags at the bank and the police could be called. Nicholas had put on his best suit and visited the bank to forewarn the manager he was going to be making some large cash deposits during the week, and would then be making a single transfer on Friday night. He'd hinted a once-in-a-lifetime deal had come his way and the bank manger, a golfing buddy, had been happy to help. He'd even gone so far as to warn Nicholas he'd need to make the final deposits by midday on Friday.

On her way to work this morning, Victoria had changed over a hundred pounds' worth of coins into notes at a couple of different banks, and she planned to change more during her lunch break. Now she must focus on work for a few hours. Get through the drudge of the day. Keep her eyes open and learn what she needed to know for tonight's job. The last targets could possibly be the most lucrative yet, but she must do all she could to simplify the robberies. Two tonight and one tomorrow night. Bank the money on Friday morning. Pay the ransom and then wait to see if her children were handed back unharmed.

Please God let us get enough from these last three places to complete the ransom.

Sometimes she believed the kidnappers would honour the deal, releasing Samantha and Kyle once they had their money. At other times her fears got the better of her and she doubted she'd ever see them alive again.

One belief held a dream she daren't hope for, the other was too horrific to contemplate. The thought of harm coming to her precious children was too much for her to bear; her knees weakened and she felt an actual pain in her chest at the thought of them suffering. During the first two days of their captivity, she'd tortured herself, imagining their fear, the possibilities they'd been harmed, that Samantha had been raped by the men.

Victoria knew that worrying about events she couldn't influence would hinder her efforts to free them, so she had conditioned herself to banish the darker thoughts and concentrate on raising the ransom money. She didn't always succeed in banishing the darkest thoughts, but she achieved enough success to afford her the level of functionality required to keep fighting.

Nicholas, on the other hand, was falling apart in front of her. The weight of guilt had sloped his shoulders, sunken his cheeks and dulled the sparkle in his eyes. Her once-buoyant husband now bore the appearance of someone in the final stages of a terminal disease.

She felt no pity for him. Yes she'd loved him for many years. They'd built a life and a family together. But his selfish actions had threatened their finest achievements. Victoria guessed most people who had loved ones kidnapped could share their torment with their partners or spouses. No such luxury was afforded to her. If she turned to him for comfort then she may grant him some in return. The thought abhorred her. He was the architect of their destruction and she wanted him to suffer as much as possible. If that meant that she had to face this ordeal alone, then so be it. It would be worse for him, he had guilt and shame to deal with as well as worry.

Let him suffer. She wanted him out of her life at the first opportunity. His betrayal was too great to bear. Why couldn't he have taken a mistress instead? She could have left him without too much disruption to the children's lives. Sure they'd have acted up for a while, but it would have been a million times better than what they were going through now.

Chapter 34

Evans scoured White Lund Industrial Estate looking for Pentwortham Prestige Motors. The industrial estate was home to the usual mix of garages, trade counters, builder's merchants and haulage firms.

Pentwortham Prestige Motors was located beside a greasy spoon cafe. Evans swung the BMW in, screeching to a halt between a Mondeo and a Peugeot 307.

'Guv, please don't do anything silly. There are cameras all over the place.'

'Oh, ye of little faith. Now just follow me and look pretty.'

Walking around the cars in the forecourt Evans picked out a used Alfa, which he then spent time circling. After a few moments inspecting the bodywork, he tried the door handle and was surprised when the door opened. He climbed into the passenger seat and gestured for Lauren to sit behind the wheel. She climbed in, reinforcing Evans's charade as a prospective buyer.

As they exited the car, a salesman was on his way over from the Portakabin which acted as an office. The salesman was in his early twenties and launched into his spiel before he was within ten feet of Evans and Lauren.

'Go and get your boss.' Evans ignored the proffered hand. 'I want to speak to the organ grinder not the monkey.'

Evans had no time for the rehearsed patter of a salesman at the best of times. The young man with his cheap suit and oily hair set his teeth on edge just by being alive. There was no way he was going to waste time or energy dealing with him.

The salesman looked to Lauren for support, but she shifted her eyes towards the Portakabin, suggesting he do as bidden. Finding no alternative course of action, the young man turned and walked back to the Portakabin in search of his boss. The stiffness of his back showed his disappointment and anger at being dismissed.

Evans followed the salesman into the office and overheard him giving an assessment of his character to a middle-aged secretary whose blouse displayed a large amount of blue-veined cleavage. Blushing, the salesman retreated to a desk and hunkered down behind a computer screen.

The manager, Mike Pentwortham, took control of the situation with practiced charm. Inviting Evans and Lauren into his office, Pentwortham asked the secretary to bring some coffees.

'Jason tells me you were looking at the Alfa 156 we have out there. It's a two-point-four-litre diesel with fifty-two thousand miles on the clock, a full-service history, CD interchanger with iPod connectivity, five spoke alloys, ABS, airbags, cruise control and a full leather interior. We also give a three-month warranty on any car we sell. I'm asking five thousand, four hundred for it, but I'll take five three for it if you agree to a deal today.'

The secretary brought in a tray laden with cups of coffee. Bending over to lay the tray on Pentwortham's desk, she gave Evans a generous look down her top. A flick of his eyes told Evans that Lauren had reached the same conclusion. The secretary fit Bhaki's description of the woman who'd bought some of the cars.

Pentwortham stood up to serve the coffees. 'How do you like your coffee, sir?'

'Irish. And I'll give you four eight for the Alfa.'

Pentwortham reached into a drawer and produced a half-finished bottle of Bushmills.

'I can certainly do the Irish, but I'll struggle to do four eight, how does a straight five sound.'

'Five with a full tank and the obligatory bouquet of flowers for the lady.'

'You drive a hard bargain, sir.' Penwortham paused to consider Evans's offer 'It's a deal. Do you require any finance options on the car or will you be buying it outright?'

'I'll pay cash today.'

'When would you like to collect the car?'

'My daughter here is going to drive it away when we leave today.'

Evans flashed a warning look at Lauren when she almost squirted a mouthful of coffee across the office.

'I'll get Jason to go fill the tank and buy the bouquet while we sort the paperwork.' Reaching into his wallet he pulled a pair of fifties out and went to the outer office to give Jason his instructions.

'Did you see all the fifties in his wallet, guv?'

Evans nodded as he replenished his cup with the bottle of Bushmills.

When Pentwortham returned, Evans pulled out the thousand pounds worth of fifty-pound notes he'd withdrawn from the bank that morning. He dropped the money on the desk. 'OK then, let's get the money sorted out so I can finish that bottle of yours.'

'Sound like a plan to me.'

Evans gathered his bundle of notes in his left hand and started counting.

'One.'

'Two.'

'Three. How many cars do you have for sale here?'

'We have thirty-seven at the moment, sir. Are you interested in another car?'

'Perhaps. Thirty-seven eh?'

'Thirty-eight.'

'Thirty-nine.'

'Forty.' Evans was not even looking at the money, instead focusing on boring his gaze into Pentwortham's eyes. 'Was it eighty-seven you were born, Lauren?'

'Eighty-eight.'

'My mistake. Seems like bloody yesterday. Now where were we? Ah yes, eighty-nine.'

'Ninety. Shall we stop for an ice cream on the way home?

'I'd love a ninety-nine, Dad.' Evans caught the mischievous tone in her voice as she played her part.

'A ninety-nine it is then. One hundred.' He proffered the pile of bank notes to Pentwortham whose eyes had gone from incomprehension to acceptance via fear and hatred.

Evans could tell that Pentwortham knew his scheme had been rumbled. The question was what he would choose do about it.

'That seems to be in order, sir. Jason will be back soon with your car.'

'You know, Lauren. All those dealers we spoke to in Cumbria were right. This is a very cheap place to buy cars. I think I'll tell all my workmates to come here when they need a new motor.' Turning to Pentwortham he added, 'That'll be good for your business, won't it?'

Pentwortham's jaw wobbled, but his voice was confident when he spoke. 'I think that your deal will be a one-off, sir.'

'In that case, they'll be visiting you professionally.' Evans placed his warrant card on the desk.

'The other option you have is to reimburse every dealer and private seller you have tricked. I don't care how you do it, so long as it's done by the end of the week.'

Few things gave Evans the rush he got from dispensing justice. Either his own unique brand or through the legal system if it was a more serious crime.

Evans dropped a card on the desk. 'My number is on that card. I want you to make sure everyone you return money to calls me to confirm they have the cash. I have a long list of people you have conned and if I find you've missed one, then I'll do two things. First, I will have every police force in the country descend upon you as prime suspect for every unsolved crime since Cain murdered Abel. Second, I will tell Big Billy that you live at twenty-three Gardner Road.'

'Who's Big Billy?' Pentwortham was rattled, but he wanted to know who might come crashing through his door.

'A man whose wife you tricked.' Evans showed him his mobile. 'Here have a look at him.'

The picture of Big Billy dwarfing his filing cabinet ended Pentwortham's attempts at bravado.

'OK, I'll do it. I'll square everyone up.'

'You'd better. Billy won't be satisfied with money, he wants blood. I'd hate to get drunk and tell him where you live. Now, give me back my money before I call your wife, and tell her about the affair you're having with Little Miss Typist out there.'

Stuffing his money back into his wallet, Evans warned Pentwortham he had three days to make the necessary payments or he would return with Big Billy and half the local constabulary.

As Evans went through to the main office, he noticed Jason's desk was littered with a half-eaten baguette and other dinner-time detritus. Seeing an opportunity too good to waste, he used careful enunciation to tell the secretary that she was needed in her boss's office for some dictation. When she left the room giggling, he opened the half-chewed baguette and sprinkled the filling with his bottle of Tabasco sauce. Closing the baguette, he made his way to the door and walked outside with Lauren.

Just then the Alfa returned with Jason at the helm and screeched to a stop. He pulled an enormous bouquet of flowers from the boot.

'Hey, fuckwit.'

A bemused Jason turned around, offering his face to Evans in time to receive the next broadside.

'What the *fuck* do you think you're up to screeching about in *my* new car? I've just paid five grand for that and you treat it like your own personal rally car. And where do you think you are off to with those flowers? Are they not for the lady?' Evans glared at the dumbstruck Jason. 'Don't just stand there, man. Give them to her with a smile and wish her happy motoring.'

Fixing the now terrified Jason with one eye he held his hand out and demanded Pentwortham's change as compensation for his shredded tyres.

Jason duly delivered a twenty-pound note and some shrapnel and then gave Lauren the flowers with a smile that was more of a rictus grin than an expression of pleasure.

A smiling Lauren accepted the flowers from the luckless salesman. 'I hope you get time to finish your lunch. I understand you and your boss are gonna have a busy few days ahead of you.'

Evans could have kissed her for that statement. As usual, Lauren's sharp wit had pierced the matter at hand with precision of a scalpel-wielding surgeon. In all likelihood, the first thing Jason would do as soon as he entered the office would be to take a huge bite of his baguette.

As they left the forecourt in the M3, Lauren struggled to stop giggling long enough to ask how Evans had known that Pentwortham was sleeping with his secretary.

'Bloody obvious really: his desk had twice the paperwork hers did, she's glammed up like Claudia Schiffer to work in a Portakabin on an industrial estate, her nails were far too long to be a typist's, therefore she had to be shagging someone who worked there. It can't have been that spotty dickhead Jason or she would have been fired and replaced with somebody who could do the work, ergo she was exchanging a shag or a blow job for a regular wage.'

'Please, Lord, don't let me ever get as cynical as DI Evans.' Lauren gave a mock prayer with hands clasped together and eyes skyward. 'D'you think he'll ever repay the money?'

'Fifty-fifty really. Can't say I'm too bothered either way. As long as he stops ripping people off I'll be happy.'

Upon leaving Lancaster, Evans fell silent, not even bothering to swear at other drivers.

'You're quiet, guv, what's on your mind?'

'Just thinking about the robberies. There's a connection between them and I know I've seen the same thing at every site, but I just can't put my finger on what it is.'

As they discussed the robberies, Chisholm called to inform Evans that Maryport Golf Club was the latest place to be robbed. The thieves had got away with over three and a half grand, plus whatever had been in the fruit machines.

Evans asked Chisholm to learn all he could, from the investigating officers and let him know as soon as possible.

Chapter 35

Jonny was sitting on the couch biting his nails when Steve came into the room. His friend looked calm, but Jonny wasn't fooled. He could see the tick which only surfaced when Steve was stressed out.

They were in their rented cottage on the outskirts of Alston, high on the edge of the Westmorland Hills. The two-bedroom cottage was dilapidated and possessed by a dank smell, but it was all they could afford on their meagre incomes. Besides, the smell could always be hidden with a scoosh of deodorant on the rare occasions either of them brought a girl back.

He'd known Steve for sixteen years. They had begun school together and Jonny had long ago learned to monitor his friend's left eye. It was the projector of all emotions. When still and calm his friend was at ease and planning something, be it tickling fish from the banks of a river or shoplifting sweets. Yet when Steve's eye twitched, he was nervous or insecure. The trait at its most common when Steve was around a girl he fancied. Despite being the class clown, Steve had never had Jonny's confidence or easy manner with girls.

Today his left eye was jerking the way it had when they'd been summoned to the headmaster's office along with their parents. An experience neither wanted to remember. They'd been expelled by the head before being taken home and punished by their respective parents.

'Have you heard the news, Steve?'

'Don't worry, we were in and out clean, like. They'll never connect it to us.'

'You killed a man. Don't you feel bad about that? I feel like shit. His blood was on my trainers.'

'No, I don't feel bad. What do you think he was gonna do with that cricket bat? Knight us? He was gonna crown us with it. We coulda been lying dead instead of him. It was survival of the fittest.'

'Fuck, man, I don't know. All I'm sure of is that we'll get caught for this.' Jonny was terrified of being sent down for murder. What should have been easy money was turning into a nightmare.

Try as he might, he still couldn't work out how he'd let Steve talk him into this latest escapade. All his life he'd followed his friend from one disaster to another. Enough was enough. If they got away with this one, he'd never let Steve drag him into another hare-brained scheme.

'Don't be soft, they'll never trace it to us. We'll take a run out on the moors tonight and burn the clothes we had on. Then what proof'll they have?'

'Proof? I cut my hand there and even I don't remember where I did it. If they find my blood and discover it isn't Armstrong's, it's only a matter of time before they come knocking on our door.'

'They haven't got your DNA, have they, dickhead?'

'Just how fuckin' stupid are you? Remember when Tracy Scott was raped and they took samples from us to eliminate us from their enquiries?'

'They said the samples would be destroyed once they had cleared us. I bet they haven't kept the records.'

'Are you prepared to bet a murder charge? 'Cause that's what's at stake.' The twitch moved into overdrive. Jonny could see his friend was now experiencing the same panic he'd felt since hearing of Armstrong's death.

'Shit. Fuck. Fuck.'

Steve started dashing about the small flat they shared, grabbing at any clothes they had been wearing and stuffing them into the holdall they'd had with them. Trainers, coats, gloves and even socks were stuffed into the bag.

Now that Steve's mind was infected with his friend's panic he could barely focus on the task at hand. Jonny's mind was clearer as he'd had more time to come to terms with the enormity of the situation they were now in. He made sure that every scrap of clothing worn to the robbery went in the holdall.

'Right we need to go up into the Dales and find a place where we can burn these clothes and hide the cash we took last night. No way can we account for that much money if plod come knocking.'

'What we gonna do with it?'

Jonny thought for a moment. 'Get a Tupperware box from the cupboard. Put the cash in it, then wrap it to death with cling film. Wear your gloves while you do it. I'll borrow a spade from my folks. We'll bury it this afternoon when we burn our clothes.'

'Isn't it better to wait until night-time?'

Surprised at his now clear head, Jonny was almost relishing the way he was taking charge of the situation. If it wasn't for the fact he was on the point of shitting bricks, he'd have enjoyed the role reversal he and Steve had just experienced.

From now on he'd lead with logic and common sense instead of following with faith and naivety.

'How long does it take to trace DNA?'

Steve scratched his head. 'Dunno.'

'No, neither do I. That's why we should do it as soon as possible.'

Jonny managed to get Steve, the stolen money and all the stuff they planned to burn into Steve's car and heading along the A689 towards Durham in less than five minutes.

'Steve, will you slow down, for fuck's sake.'

'I want that shit out of the car and on fire as soon as possible.'

'So do I. But if you crash before we get there, then we're practically handing oursel's over to the cops.'

Jonny was amazed at the logic that had overtaken him. He'd never expected to be calm in a crisis, yet here he was plotting and scheming ways to give them the best possible chance of getting away with a crime they'd never intended to commit.

Reaching the town of Stanhope, Steve turned right down a narrow road and followed it as it wound its way south towards Barnard Castle with snow poles marking the roadside every fifty metres. The countryside here was rugged and inhospitable. The North Pennines rose around them. Scrub grass and heather covered the hills. Patches of white-tipped reeds indicated marshes. Finding an old track, they hid the car behind some dense gorse and trekked over the brow of a small hill so that they could build their fire away from the road.

Steve's eye twitched like a beheaded snake as they reached the bottom of a valley. Jonny scanned the horizon looking for shepherds or gamekeepers who might be wandering the hills. Finding neither, he squatted down on a pebbled area beside a burbling stream and started emptying their clothes from the holdall until they were piled in front of him.

Pulling a bottle of brandy from the backpack, Jonny drenched the pile of clothes with half the bottle before lighting a cigarette and dropping it onto a brandy-soaked T-shirt. Flames billowed out from the pile. The fire sizzled and twisted as the man-made fibres melted and burned. A foul stench hung in the smoke from the fire. Jonny blamed Steve's trainers for the smell and told him so. Steve just stared at the fire, oblivious to the insult.

As the fire died down, they used the shovel to push the charred remains together until there were no longer any visible flames. The small pile that remained bore witness to a few scraps of burnt clothing and a twisted mess of plastic from their trainers. Jonny emptied the rest of the brandy onto the pile and relit the fire using another cigarette.

While the last of the evidence against them was burning, he turned his mind to finding a plausible reason for his blood being at a murder scene. Not knowing if the cops were going to knock on his door was terrifying, but it still wasn't as scary as the thought of the cops knocking on his door asking questions he didn't have answers for.

Steve picked up the spade and the Tupperware box of money. Between them, they found a place they could identify at a later date and buried the money.

Returning to the now extinguished fire, Jonny dug a hole into which he put the final embers of the fire. With all the evidence either buried or burned they returned to the car. As Steve drove back towards Alston, Jonny filled him in on the lies he'd concocted to explain the presence of his blood at the hotel.

Jonny knew he should blame Steve for getting him into this predicament. Yet his sense of loyalty prevented him from blaming Steve. Instead he blamed himself for being fool enough to listen to Steve.

If they got away with this, he'd make sure he never made the same mistake again. Today's power shift in their relationship would prevent Steve dragging them into future trouble. From now on he was going to resist his friend's wild adventures, the madcap schemes, the challenging dares.

Chapter 36

Samantha rolled the shoe over and over in her hand. Her fingers brushing the smooth plastic as a plan began to germinate. The shoe had stayed on her foot as she'd been pinned down by Blair. The other lost in the struggle.

This was the fifth day of their kidnapping and she was worried by the lack of signs pointing to their release. The day after tomorrow they'd either be released or would have to face the burner. Blair's lechery was getting worse by the day and his attempt to get into their room was uppermost in her mind. Elvis had been quick to stop him, but she expected Blair to try again.

Doubt flooded her mind as she wrestled with the plan taking shape in her head. It would involve an act of aggression that could see them receive a dire punishment if it failed. On the other hand, if she judged it right, they would have a chance to get away. To escape their captors.

She weighed the consequences against the thought of a successful escape. If she'd been alone, she'd accept the risk and go ahead with her plan without a second thought. She had Kyle to consider, though. He was fast for his age, but she knew he wasn't as quick on his feet as she was. He would slow her down and if they failed to get away he too might face the kidnapper's wrath.

She had to protect her brother and any failed escape attempt would endanger him. It didn't take much imagination to guess the punishment Blair would suggest, but what of Elvis?

He was not as perverted as Blair, but he possessed coldness in his demeanour. Aloof and uncaring, he'd appraised her with a clinical eye rather than lust. She might beg and plead that she alone should face the music, but Elvis was the kind of person who would leave her untouched, choosing instead to hurt Kyle as a better way of punishing her.

Samantha couldn't bring herself to take the gamble yet, but she knew that unless things changed then she would have no choice. Their best hope of escaping would be tomorrow, she decided, and so she began refining the finer details of her plan.

When to carry it out?

Night would be good, as they could hide in the shadows once they got outside. However, all four men were usually in the house by nightfall and there'd be less chance of getting passed four than one. Early morning would be the same. Lunchtime seemed best as there was always less noise carrying up from downstairs around noon than at other times. Plus, lunchtime was one of the three times of day when the door was opened. A new tray was brought in and the old one taken out by either Elvis or Blair.

How far to go with the distraction?

All the way would give the greatest return, but it may backfire if it was Blair who brought their lunch. Halfway would carry as much initial impact but may not buy them enough time for her plan to work. Fully committing to the distraction would also hinder her once she was out of the room. If Blair brought their lunch, she decided, halfway would suffice. But Elvis would require initiating a full distraction plan. Elvis always called out to them to move back from the door, but Blair didn't. This would give her maybe ten seconds to change from one course of action to the other as the door was unbolted. Would it be enough? A new refinement came into her mind. It would remove the hindrance, but it would require a speedy adjustment between full and half.

Knowing there was only one way to be certain, Samantha went to the bathroom and practised switching from maximum distraction to half, counting the seconds in her head as she practised. Once she had got the changeover time down to the count of nine she rejoined Kyle and finalised her plans.

Which way to go once they were outside?

Judging by the lack of traffic sounds, the farm they were held in was somewhere remote, so there would be no cars to save them. Roads were out as the men would just drive after them and they'd be caught in no time. Running across fields would be hard going and they would soon tire. However, the men would too. Samantha bet that both she and Kyle would be faster over fields than their out-of-shape kidnappers. Fences and hedges would provide greater obstacles for Kyle than they would for the men. They would have to be avoided at all costs until they had got far enough away. As long as the men didn't have a tractor or one of those four-wheeled bikes outside, they'd stand a better chance going across fields. A small river or stream would be a godsend, as it would prevent the men following them on any kind of vehicle. If only there was a wood or forest nearby. Then they could lose the men in the trees or find a hiding place.

Samantha decided to wait and see. Everything depended on which direction looked best once they were free of the house.

Chapter 37

Campbell was tying his laces when an insistent knock at the door announced Evans's arrival. He wasn't looking forward to tonight as he'd rather have been with his wife and new son. His kidneys ached in anticipation of a drinking session with Evans, but he had to show willing with his new team.

When he'd discussed it with Sarah, she'd told him that he should go and enjoy himself as she would be home the next day and he'd be back to work on Friday.

Opening the door, he found Evans shifting his weight from foot to foot. In his hands was a large parcel wrapped up with a cornflower blue ribbon.

'I got you a few bits for the lad, like.'

As Campbell thanked Evans for the gift, he could sense the older man's discomfort. He was used to kicking doors in and arresting people, not delivering gifts for babies. Remembering Evans had told him he was childless, the penny dropped. Evans was envious of him, but rather than being the type to be bitter he was generous enough to not only to hide his jealousy but to come bearing gifts.

'C'mon then, lad. That drink'll not sup itself.'

Smiling at Evans's false gruffness, Campbell followed him out to the car.

They met up with the other team members at a pub in the heart of the city. Campbell had never seen the team away from work and was delighted to see they'd all made it along.

Lauren was deep in conversation with a couple of guys he recognised as detectives based in Carlisle. Her expressive mouth conveyed her thoughts to anyone who cared to look. Chisholm nursed an orange juice and fiddled with his phone, looking ill at ease. Bhaki raised a questioning eyebrow from his position at the bar, tipping his hand to his mouth to complete the enquiry.

The team gathered around him with congratulations and enquiries after the health of mother and baby.

He knew he was being a stereotypical new parent, but he didn't care, as he showed them the pictures of Alan on his phone and soaked up their comments. The euphoria of last night still undiminished.

Soon the conversation drifted away from Alan to more usual topics.

'There's plenty of folk out tonight, eh?'

'Yes, sir.'

'Knock it off with the, sir, Neil. We're off duty tonight.'

'Does that mean I can call you John then?'

Unable to stop himself, Campbell made a comment he knew was inappropriate. 'In that dress you can call me owt you like.'

Lauren was wearing a tight cerise dress, which clung to every curve of her body. From hem to underarm on each side was a sheer black panel an inch wide.

Campbell knew he shouldn't be looking tonight of all nights, but he couldn't stop his eyes from checking out the flesh on display through the sheer panels. The absence of underwear caused a pang of desire to tug at his conscience, testing for a vulnerable spot. Her perfume was Issey Miyake, the same as Sarah wore. Looking was all he planned to do though.

You can still read the menu when you're on a diet.

They were all in good spirits as they laughed and joked their way around the city centre hotspots. Evans appeared to know at least half of the people they bumped into regardless of the fact that most were at least half his age. Bhaki and Chisholm were trying to get close to Lauren, who was getting sent endless drinks from guys wherever she went. She seemed to be almost as well known as Evans, a fact Evans commented on. 'She must be anti-religious, in one night she's gonna make a good Hindu boy forsake all others and have half the male population of Carlisle bashing the bishop.'

'The sight of her in that dress is enough to make a bulldog break its chain.'

'What was that?' Lauren joined them.

'I was just suggesting that we go to the George next.' Evans covered for Campbell without batting an eyelid.

Campbell was content to let Evans choose the venues. 'Lead on, Harry. You know Carlisle much better than me.'

'C'mon then, drink up.' Evans turned to the younger members of the team and informed them of their next destination.

'This I've got to see. You're taking DI Campbell to the King George?'

A needle of trepidation pricked at Campbell when he heard Chisholm's words.

'At least he'll be safe tonight.'

The team made their way out of the bar, with Evans leading them down Botchergate at a brisk walk. The air had turned cooler and the first spits of a cloudburst fell sideways from the leaden skies, propelled by an ever-present breeze that blew down from the Crescent which had once been the city's south gate.

Chisholm waddled in the rear, his girth preventing him from matching the pace set by Evans.

There was a queue outside the King George. A pair of doormen was only allowing people in when other customers left. As was his wont, Evans ignored the queue and went straight up to the first doorman who was a hulking figure of six and a half feet plus.

'Are you gonna let us in or do I have to ask you to turn out your pockets?' Evans demanded of the doorman who towered over him.

'Alreet, Harry.' The hulking doorman smiled and proceeded to turn out his pockets anyway. 'I'm as clean as ever and you know my stance on drugs.'

'That a do. How's the wife and kids?'

'She's grand, thanks. Did you hear she's pregnant with number five? I think she's trying to trap me.'

Laughing at the man's joke, Evans led the team into the bar and turned to watch Campbell's expression as he gazed around the bar. The whole team doubled over as Campbell's gaze circled the crowded room. His eyes flitted from one poster to another, first Beckham, then Shearer, Bobby Moore, Bryan Robson, Bobby Charlton and assorted other English footballing legends.

'You bastards! You shower of utter bastards.' Despite his words, his smile showed he could see the funny side of a

Scotsman being taken into a staunch English bar a mere four hours after England had won a vital World Cup qualifier.

Campbell waited until the laughter subsided and then delivered the best rejoinder he had on the subject. 'Next time any of you buggers cross the border, I'll take you to a certain pub in Glasgow so you can see the centre circle we claimed in 'seventy-seven.' He pointed at the picture of Geoff Hurst, which held pride of place above the bar. 'It's a damn site more impressive than a picture of the only man in history to score a two-goal hat-trick.'

Evans went off to the bar to get a round in leaving Campbell to explain to the others the infamous pitch invasion after Scotland beat England all those years ago.

As the drinks went down, Campbell kept a close eye on the behaviour of his team. Bhaki draped an arm around a girl who'd sidled up to him and was hanging on every slurred word that left his lips. As long as he didn't have too much more to drink his luck would be in. More concerning to him was the way Lauren was rebuffing her various suitors. He didn't want to flatter himself, but it appeared to him, she'd decided he was the man she wanted to take home. A keen people-watcher who could observe the little details most overlooked, Campbell could hear Lauren's body language screaming, 'I'm available. All you have to do is ask.' Her laughs at his jokes were just that little bit too loud. She made contact where none was needed. She underlined comments with suggestive twists of her mouth.

Returning from the toilets, Campbell could tell that the something had been said between Evans and Lauren. Her mouth was crinkled into a defiant pout. He guessed it was about her blatant flirting with him. As he approached them, she made her excuses and left their company to talk with a bunch of guys eager to receive her attention.

While grateful for the concern shown, he was a big boy and had no intentions of doing anything more than a bit of harmless flirting with Lauren. Although a part of him felt the prick of desire, Sarah and Alan were far too important to him. Even a night with the beautiful and sexy Lauren wasn't enough for him to risk losing them.

God, it'd be bloody good though!

Midnight came and went, but Evans showed no sign of slowing. Campbell was struggling to maintain a clear head. The edges of his peripheral vision were blurry and he'd taken a drunken lurch the last time he'd visited the toilets.

Bhaki was the first to leave. He went arm in arm with the girl he'd met earlier. Then Lauren departed with one of the men she'd been talking to.

After another round of drinks Campbell, Evans and Chisholm left the bar and set off in opposite directions. Evans and Chisholm went looking for a taxi while Campbell found a take-away that was still serving and ordered a pizza.

Eating his pizza as he searched for a taxi, Campbell felt a hand on his arm and heard a soft voice whisper in his ear. A familiar scent filling his nostrils.

'Your place or mine, John?'

Chapter 38

Thursday

'What does our sainted oracle have to tell us today?'

Chisholm looked up from his computer screen and told Evans the contents of his emails. There had been two more break-ins to licensed premises, a tractor had been stolen from a farm near Barrow, along with a quad bike and the usual variety of hand-held power tools.

'Who got robbed this time?'

'It was the King George down Botch' and the Dog and Duck in Keswick, sir.'

'Fuck's sake, we spent half of last night in the George. If that gets out we'll be a laughing stock.' Evans did not want to end his career as the copper who'd spent all night drinking in a pub that got robbed the same evening. He wiped his face with a hand as if the action would remove his hangover and transform the robbery into a figment of his imagination.

'How much was taken in total?'

'Five six from the George and over five grand from the Dog and Duck.'

Bhaki let out a muted whistle as Evans shot a dirty look at Lauren as she entered the office. 'I need a word with you later, young lady. Although I use the term lady with the same looseness you reserve for the term chastity.'

Chisholm carried on with his report, breaking the tension and rescuing Lauren for a short while. 'According to the attending officers' reports, there was no damage, no obvious sign of entry and everything appeared normal until someone looked in the safes. In both cases, it was the owners who had totted up at the end of the night and had put the money into the safes. Both insisted they were the only ones with keys.'

'This is getting serious now. That's eight robberies from licensed premises in five days and we haven't got a clue who's behind it.'

'Thank you very much, Lauren. I'm so glad you pointed that out.' Evans was irritable because the nagging suspicion in the back of his mind would not show a clear picture. He knew he could identify the thieves if his brain would just allow the picture to uncloud itself.

It was only a matter of time before DCI Grantham or someone higher up the ladder got onto his case. The local news last night had been critical of the police and he could see why. They'd even come up with the moniker 'Licensed Premise Pinchers' for the elusive thieves. He needed a result and fast, if he was to have any chance of salvaging a role in the force after his retirement.

Bhaki spoke for the first time. He looked terrible to Evans. If he'd had less of a caseload, he'd have sent the lad on a pointless errand to hide him until he sobered up. 'I hate to ask. But is there anything else?'

'Nothing else has come through. But my algorithm has homed in on half a dozen properties which are using far more electric than they should be.'

'We'll be lucky if more than one of them is what we're looking for.' Evans was being realistic as he reached across for the list of addresses Chisholm was handing him.

'What do you want us to do then, guv?'

'You can arrange for a tracker to be put onto a quad bike which is due to be delivered. I was speaking to a mate who works for West Cumberland Farmers last night. He told me that to prevent delivery wagons being followed from their depots, they now make all quad bike deliveries direct from their supplier in Manchester. The tracking devices will have to be fitted to the bikes there and will have to have a range of at least ten miles. Speak to Terry Mannion, he's in charge of their Carlisle depot. He'll put you in touch with their suppliers. Then you'll need to arrange for a techie from the Manchester area to fit the bloody things.'

'What've I to do, sir?' Lauren looked fresh and gave the impression she'd had an early night followed by twelve hours of deep slumber, instead of a few short hours of drunken unconsciousness.

'You go over the statements from last night's robberies and make sure they've got everything buttoned down tight. When you've done that take a drive by on the addresses on Jabba's list. See if anything looks out of place like all the curtains drawn at midday.'

Evans looked across at Chisholm, who for once was not peering at his monitor. 'Jabba. I want you to cross-reference all the data from these robberies again. I've a hunch there's a connection. We've just got to find it. Also find out who investigated the thefts from the farm near Barrow. I can't be arsed going all the way there to learn nowt fresh if someone competent has already been. Besides, Bhaji Boy is in no fit state to drive.'

Before Chisholm could answer, his computer announced to the room 'Message from control' in a computerised approximation of John Cleese.

'What the hell is that?'

'It's just something I wrote when I got home last night. It's more fun than a simple beep.'

'Never mind that. What does the message bloody well say?'

Chisholm's face was grave as he gave them the gist of the message. 'There's been another robbery, sir. The Lakeland Hotel has had nearly three grand stolen. Penrith CID have someone en route.' Chisholm scrolled back to the email regarding the latest farm theft and reported that a DS Murray was responding.

'Let them know we'll follow up at the Lakeland. Murray is a good lad and there's no point going if he's been there. I want a progress report from all of you, every two hours.'

Eager to get out of the building before any of his superiors decided to waste everyone's time shouting at him, Evans grabbed his jacket and slunk through the corridors until he was outside.

He was relieved to get to his car unnoticed. Things were going from bad to worse. The robberies were piling up and the more he tried to dig out the connection he knew was in his brain the deeper it buried itself.

The King George looked different on a bright sunny morning than it had on a drunken night out. The unforgiving sunlight illuminated every cracked mirror, every piece of chewing gum trodden into the threadbare carpet. The unshaven owner fared little better. Hell, even the legends looking down from behind the dirty frames looked hung over to Evans.

The owner looked as if he should be standing on the eighties terraces, knuckles scraping the boots of the guy standing next to him. He was wearing a stained England shirt, circa 1985; his square features and shaven head sporting a five o'clock shadow reminded Evans of a deformed bulldog.

'If I get my hands on the bastard who did this, I'll kill 'im.'

'Now then, Fred. Don't do anything stupid or I'll end up having to nick you.'

'C'mon, Harry, play the game. I've seen you deliver many a slap instead of nicking someone.'

'Aye, but I know where to draw the line. You'd get carried away and end up with a long stay at Her Majesty's pleasure.'

Evans took a good look around the King George and asked questions of Fred until they encountered the safe. It was the largest electronic model that Phoenix made. Evans walked over, keyed in four digits and pressed the 'Enter' button. Gripping the handle, he twisted it to the right opening the safe.

'What the fuck?'

'Fred, you imbecile. The code was fucking obvious.'

Fred's shoulders went back and his bloated chest puffed out. 'England's finest footballing moment. It was an honour to type that code in.'

'I can't believe that you were stupid enough to use it. For God's sake man, 1966 is the first number any idiot would try considering the theme of your pub. Please tell me your alarm code is different.'

A shake of the head gave Evans his answer.

He left Fred posturing and headed back to his car, wondering how the hell he was supposed to protect people when they were so damn stupid.

Chapter 39

Kyle looked terrified when Samantha told him of her plan to escape. She filled her voice with as much positivity as she could muster, but he was unconvinced. He sat on the mattress with his knees pulled up to support his forehead.

'What if it doesn't work?'

'It will.' She lifted his chin to look in his tear filled eyes. 'Trust me, Kyle. It'll work.'

Samantha's own doubts plagued her, but when she had tried to question Elvis earlier, he'd told her that they wouldn't know if the ransom had been paid until midnight tomorrow.

Not knowing how much her father owed, Samantha assumed it was more than their parents could pay, otherwise they would have paid it by now. Following that logic, there was no way her parents could raise the amount of money needed before the kidnapper's deadline. Therefore when the deadline passed, they would be mutilated with the gas torch.

It was up to her to save them. Although her plan was flimsy and had at best a fifty-fifty chance of success, it was the only plan she had and there wasn't time to wait for another opportunity to arise like the one with the police car.

'What do you think the men will do to us if it doesn't work?'

Samantha struggled to answer the question. As she um'ed and ah'ed, Kyle watched her and then offered her his worst-case scenario.

'Do you think they'll take the PlayStation away?'

If only. I would try right away if I knew that was the punishment they would dish out.

'It'll be something like that.' Samantha was filled with self-loathing for lying to her brother.

There was no way that she could tell him the truth about what the men might do to them. He wouldn't dare follow her and she needed him to go as fast as possible. Without his full commitment, their bid for freedom would fail before it even started.

'Don't you want to see Mum an' Dad?' Samantha despised herself for manipulating his emotions, but she could feel the weight of desperation growing with each passing hour.

''Course I do.' Kyle's head snapped up at the implied rebuke. 'I want to see them right now.'

'If you do as I ask, we can get away from here and go home.'

'Do you mean we can see Mum and Dad today?'

'We will, if we can get out of here and away from the men.' Giving him false hope was the last thing she wanted to do, but she'd do anything to convince him.

'It will work, won't it?'

Samantha held out a fist, her little finger sticking out. 'Pinkie promise.'

Accepting her assurances Kyle wound his pinkie around hers and they shook on it.

'OK. Here's what we have to do.'

Samantha spent the next hour drilling him on her escape plan. She showed him where she wanted him to stand. What to do once they got outside. How she wanted him to follow her in the house and then run in front of her when they left the building.

She drummed into him the importance of running as fast as he could for as long as possible.

The next part of the process was one she'd agonised over for hours. Her final reasoning was that as Kyle would be watching her at all times, he must be immune to her distraction.

'What do we do when we get out?' Samantha took her trainers off.

'Run as fast as we can.'

'What do you do?'

'Exactly what you say?'

'Where do you go?' Samantha's top landed on her trainers.

'Where you tell me to.'

'Well done. Now look at me a minute, Kyle.'

This was the hard part, the part that Samantha dreaded as much as the men seeing her naked body. Summoning her resolve she slipped her bra off and then started unbuttoning her jeans.

'Your boobies are bigger than Mummy's.' Kyle's analytical comment almost brought a smile to her lips, although it felt weird to be compared to her mother. She watched his face as she pulled down her jeans and her thong in one combined movement.

His eyes wandered over her body with a total lack of interest. He'd made his point about the size of her breasts and that was it for him.

Thank God he's not a bit older. He'd be fixated then.

Pleased that he wouldn't be distracted by her nudity, she got him to his feet and led him through a series of stretching exercises. It was important they were both as supple as possible. A pulled muscle would spell disaster.

Taking one of the games discs, she took it into the bathroom, slipped it halfway between the seat and the lid and then pushed down on the protruding part until the disc snapped. Choosing a jagged piece she scrubbed the smoothest edge against the grout between two bathroom tiles, until it could be held without cutting into her palm. This weapon she planned to give to Kyle. If one of the men grabbed him he could slash at them and perhaps get free. She would carry the stiletto heel as her primary weapon.

Samantha's next task was to make sure the laces on Kyle's trainers were tied tight with no long loops or tails for his feet to catch. She had tied her own trainers for security. Next, she again rehearsed pulling her jeans on, until she could go from naked and empty-handed, to topless with the stiletto heel in her hand inside the ten seconds she'd allowed herself. She would have to forego her trainers to pull her jeans on but she'd rather be barefoot and topless than naked and shod.

Once again she took Kyle through a series of stretches until she guessed that lunchtime was approaching.

'We need to be quiet now, Kyle. I have to be able to listen for the men bringing our lunch up.'

'Yeah, OK.'

Time dragged for Samantha as she waited and listened. Her nerves jangled with tension. More than once she had to stop herself drumming her fingers on the wall.

Soon they would either be free or facing some unimaginable torture.

The bang of a door preceded heavy thuds on the staircase.

In a blur of movement, Samantha had her jeans on and her weapon cocked ready to strike. Flashing a look at Kyle, she could see he was nervous but determined to be brave.

This is it. This is the moment of truth.

There was so much that could go wrong at this moment. If Blair swung the door open and didn't enter the room as normal, she'd have to move forward to attack him and the advantage would shift back to him. He could block her, duck back or a dozen other things to stop her. She had to make sure her distraction worked.

The rattle of the bolts being shot open caused her body to surge with adrenaline. She had chosen fight over flight, but every instinct she possessed compelled her to just run. First though, she had to get past the locked door.

Blair burst through the door with a tray in his hands.

Samantha jiggled her shoulders to make her breasts wobble. His gaze fixed on her chest and he never saw the shoe coming. Samantha scored a bull's-eye, hitting his temple with the point of the stiletto heel. When he dropped to his knees in front of her, she repeated the blow. The impact jarring the shoe from her hand as Blair fell to the floor.

'Quick.'

Grabbing her top from the floor she padded along the landing with Kyle at her heels. Wary of creating too much noise, Samantha went down the stairs as quietly as she could. They were so close to freedom. She reached the front door and paused, uncertain what to do if the door was locked.

'You might need this.' Elvis dangled a key from one finger.

Samantha was distraught. She'd tried to escape and had only made matters worse. Blair was upstairs unconscious, when he came too he'd be furious and would have murder in his veins.

'I'm sorry, Kyle.'

He didn't answer her. Following Elvis's outstretched finger, he trooped back up the stairs, Samantha behind him. Blair was lying on the floor at the top of the stairs, soft groans emerging from his mask as they stepped over him.

'Elvis pointed to the bathroom. 'Wait in there. I'll deal with youse in a moment.'

Kyle ignored all Samantha's apologies and turned his back, leaving her in a world of solitary torment. They had failed and would now have to face the wrath of Blair and Elvis. She could only hope the punishment wouldn't involve rape or the gas torch.

Crashing sounds from the bedroom began, punctuated by loud groans and swearing from Blair as he came to. Hearing him ranting about what he was going to do to her chilled Samantha to the bone. His threats oscillated between violence and lurid descriptions of how he'd rape her. Realising her top was still in her hand, she pulled it on and tried to shut out Blair's vivid threats. At last, the shouting stopped and she could hear footsteps stomping out of the room and down the stairs. Elvis opened the door, and told them to come out. Samantha tried and failed to judge his anger level by his voice. To her ears there was nothing other than the usual dominant force of personality.

The bedroom had been stripped bare. The PlayStation and TV were gone, as was the mattress and everything else in the room. There was only the threadbare carpet and the walls left. Even the underwear Samantha had left behind was absent.

A finger pointed at Samantha. 'You. Come with me. The boy stays here.'

Terror filled Samantha, but she did as she was told, pausing to reassure a sobbing Kyle that she would be back soon. She knew he was petrified she wouldn't return. Her legs struggled to support her as her own thoughts echoed his worries.

Elvis took her into the sitting room where Blair was nursing his head. When he saw her he let out a stream of invective and threw himself forward, fists bunching ready to strike. Elvis stepped between them, pushing Blair back into the chair he'd been occupying.

As he turned to face her, Samantha could feel his eyes burning out from behind the mask.

'What did I tell you about not trying to escape?'

Samantha hung her head and mumbled her answer. 'Not to do it.'

'That's right. I told you not to do it. And what did I say would happen?'

'That you'd punish me.'

'No, I didn't. I said I would burn off one of the boy's limbs.'

Samantha had been hoping against hope the threat was merely bluster to make her behave, but now it seemed as if Elvis was serious about his threat to maim Kyle.

'Please. Don't do that to him. I'll do anything you want, but don't do that to him. Do it to me if you must punish anyone.'

'Give me an' her an hour alone. I'll show her.' Blair's voice filled with lecherous intent as he spoke.

'No chance. You're the clown who fell for her little ruse. Here's what we're gonna do.' Elvis pointed at Samantha. 'You are going to strip naked. So he can make another video for your parents. Then I'll take you back to your room. Make another attempt to get away and you're all his.' Elvis gave a sharp nod to Blair. 'Get your video camera.'

While they were waiting for Blair to retrieve his camera, Elvis warned Samantha that once she returned to the room the next time the door opened would be when the deadline had passed. There would be no more food or water, no more games to entertain them.

Blair returned with his video camera and Elvis told her to strip.

With tears running down her face she awaited his next command. Her relief this was the extent of the punishment was diluted by the odious notion of having to strip for the perverted Blair.

Samantha turned her back on Blair as she went to take her top off, but Elvis told her to face the camera.

'Get yer fuckin' tits out, or I'll come and undress you meself.'

Samantha whipped her top off and stepped out of her jeans. Standing up straight again she used her hands to protect her modesty.

'Hands by your sides, lass.' Elvis pointed at Blair. 'You've got one minute to get any close-ups you want provided your arse doesn't leave that seat.'

That minute was the longest of Samantha's life, as she stood to attention while Blair filmed her naked body. The desire to run, to flee, was unbearable for her, but she stood resolute. As punishments went, this was the absolute best she could have hoped for.

Telling Blair to put his video camera down, Elvis walked across the room and stood in front of Samantha, his body shaking with contained fury. Without any warning, his right hand shot out slapping her cheek. Her head snapped back at the blow and was met by a hard-knuckled backhand, splitting her lips and loosening teeth.

'Don't even think of trying to escape again. Right?'

Samantha was marched back to the bedroom with her clothes left where she'd dropped them.

Kyle was laying in the corner. Curled in a ball, his shoulders heaved as he wept away his disappointment. Nothing Samantha said or did could make him turn round and face her. Samantha took the opposite corner and, mimicking her younger brother, allowed herself to become lost in her own private misery. The release of her pent-up despair caused Samantha physical pain. Her body wracked itself with the tidal force of each new wave of emotion. Tears mingled with the blood from her shattered lips as she howled in fear and grief.

There would be no escape for them. Their one chance had failed. Only their parents could save them now. They now had to wait to discover their fate.

Chapter 40

Andy Charters was behind the bar of the Dog and Duck when Evans walked in. There was the usual smattering of drunkards seated around the room, each trying to find escape through inebriation. The decor was seventies at best and not in a positive way. The only thing that looked clean were the packets of crisps stacked at the back of the bar.

'Thank God it's you, Harry.' Charters laid down the dirty cloth he was holding. 'You'll catch the buggers what robbed me. There would be about five grand in the safe last night when I locked up. When I came in this morning the safe was empty and the door was standing wide open.'

Evans looked around the dingy room and ordered a bottle of beer, not trusting the glasses to be clean or the draught beers or spirits to be undiluted.

'That's a lot of money to take in a bar this size. Don't you bank on a daily basis?' Evans knew from experience the Dog and Duck was not one of the busier watering holes in the little town. Located halfway along St Johns Street, it never attracted the younger crowd. Instead it attracted seasoned drinkers searching for oblivion. Patrons left here in a wobbling mess of unsteady limbs powered by memory rather than purpose. Tourists were wont to take little more than a step or two inside the door before turning around.

'I've been busy for a couple of days and haven't managed to get to the bank since Monday morning.' Charters had a belligerent attitude which rankled Evans.

'Even so, that's only three days' takings. That means you've been averaging over fifteen hundred quid a day. That seems bloody good to me for a place like this.'

'And what exactly do you mean by that like?'

'Fuck off, Andy. You can't make money like that in shithole like this.'

'Just catch the buggers who did this and get me my money back will you. I'll also need a crime number for insurance purposes, like.'

Evans eyed a jar of pickled eggs as he took a slug from his bottle. It sported a green tinge he didn't like the look of.

'I bet it was those buggers who've been targeting all the other pubs an' hotels around the area like. They've been all over the news and your lot haven't been able to catch them.'

Evans ignored Charters's rebuke. Instead he strode behind the bar. Opening the till he lifted out a handful of notes, scowling as he flicked through them. He replaced the notes, grabbed Charters by the collar and hauled the bigger man through the door that led through to a stockroom-cum-office.

'What are you doing, Harry, like?'

'Where are your till readouts for the last week, Andy?' Evans's voice raised to a near shout, enjoying the fact the larger man was visibly quaking.

'The... the... the till roll ran out. I just got a new one this morning.'

'Where's the receipt for it?'

'I threw it in the bin.'

'Bollocks, man. You are too greedy to do that. You'd have kept it for your accounts, suspect as they most probably are.'

Evans stormed back to the bar and after a quick investigation of the till held a depleted till roll an inch from Charters's nose.

'So you've had a busy morning have you, Andy?'

'Aye, that's right like.'

'Bigger bollocks. You have only got about a hundred quid in that till when you discount the float; you've done bugger all trade this morning. There are seven customers in that bar and none of them looks as if they can afford more than a few drinks. You're trying to pull a fly one, Andy, and I can tell you now that it just won't work.'

'What do you mean, trying to pull a fly one?'

'The bullshit you're trying to peddle. Five grand in three days is unbelievable for a shithole like this. You'll be lucky if you do that a quarter.'

'I was robbed by those bastards who've been doing over pubs an' hotels all over Cumbria. There ain't no way you can prove otherwise.'

The defiance and resistance shown by Charters made Evans change tack. 'In the absence of till readouts, we'll take a look at delivery notes for the last month, your accounts and we'll start interviewing every customer out there to see just how busy you have been this last week. I'll call Jennings brewery and speak to Walter Wiley. He'll know exactly what kind of turnover a place like this should be doing. If he says five grand in three days is the norm, I'll believe him.' Seeing the colour drain from Charters's face he added one final damning threat. 'Mind you, I could inform Customs and Excise, Environmental Health and the tax office this place needs a thorough inspection instead.'

'There's no need for that, Harry.'

'There's every need, you stupid bugger. Attempting to defraud an insurance company is a serious crime. There's no way you did that kind of turnover. By rights I should be arresting you right now.'

'Please, Harry. You don't know what it's like trying to run a business these days.' There were tears in Charters's eyes, desperation etched onto his downcast face.

'This is what you're gonna do: on Saturday night every drink you sell will be a pound. Whether it's regulars like that lot out there or folk you've never seen before, every drink they buy will be a pound.'

'I'll barely cover my costs at that—' Charters tried to protest, but Evans held a finger to his lips to silence him.

'I wasn't finished. Every pound coin that is collected will be given to the old folks' home on Meadow Road. If you only run out of one drink, then I'll be back on Sunday morning with a warrant for your arrest. You are not allowed you refuse to serve anybody for any reason other than they are too intoxicated to stand or they are trying to start a fight.'

'That'll ruin me.'

'It's that or jail. Your choice.'

Resignation and defeat filled Charters's face. 'I'll do it.'

'Good man. I'll call the old folks' home and have them drum up some publicity for your very generous offer. It would be such a shame if the only people turned up were your regulars. Oh, and you better call the brewery to make sure you have plenty of stock in.' Taking pity on the man, Evans threw him a crumb of comfort: 'If you clean this place up then you may just win a few more regulars from Saturday night. Might help you out long term.'

Evans turned his back on Charters, smiling as he overheard him grumbling under his breath about bastard police taking the law into their own hands.

As Evans walked along St John's Street towards his car, he took a call from Bhaki, who informed him that he'd arranged for a tracker to be put onto a quad bike due to be delivered later that day.

'Good lad.'

'What's the score with the surveillance of it?'

'DCI Grantham said one of us must join a uniformed officer every night. I've contacted a farmer close to the quad's new home, who's agreed to let us hide in one of his sheds. That way we'll be close at hand.'

'Right then. Inform Totty Tits that she has drawn tonight's straw. You and her can do alternate nights until we catch the buggers.'

'OK, guv.' Bhaki paused for a moment before asking what Evans wanted him to do next.

'Organise a minibus from Carlisle to Keswick for Saturday night and fill it with off-duty coppers. I know of a very special offer from a kind publican. No brass, mind. I want to be the highest-ranking officer there.' Evans then gave Bhaki the details he'd learned from the George, and told him to scratch the Dog and Duck from their enquiries.

'Anything else, guv?'

'Aye. I want you to get a second tracker organised as well. Just don't tell DCI Grantham. Keep it between us, I'll find a way to get it through the budget.'

Next on Evan's list was a visit to the Lakeland Hotel. He wanted to drop in there before heading back to the station. The drive of nineteen miles took him twenty-five minutes as he was held up by a procession of tractors leading cattle trailers towards Penrith Market. Try as he might there was no safe way he could get past them on the busy A66. As he drove, his mind wandered back to the familiar ground of the impending trial. It was never far below the surface. He'd stood in court many times over the years. The victims and their families always conformed to one of three stereotypes. Some would sit in silence, their faces a stony mask. Others would weep throughout, inconsolable in their sadness as painful memories were re-visited in the courtroom.

It was the third group he expected to belong to. They looked at the accused with open hatred, cheering every point scored by the prosecution, jeering when a sentence was pronounced. It was these people he felt sorriest for. They had no way to contain or manage their grief and anger. They would be chastised by the judge, removed from the court if their behaviour went too far. Upon returning home, the memory of their outbursts would shame them.

Yates's trial would be a formality. Grantham and his team had built a solid case against him. Janet had identified him before she died. A CCTV camera had footage of Yates entering the building which housed their flat. Twenty minutes later the same camera had caught him coming out, scratches from Janet's long nails distinct on his face.

In Evans's mind she hadn't committed suicide. She had died. A broken heart had killed her. Taking the pills and vodka was a symptom, nothing more. As a husband he'd failed her. He'd been unable to mend her broken heart. To salve her wounds with love. His own grief and rage distracting him from her needs.

The fact his last case was escalating annoyed him. He didn't want his last case to be a failure, even if it was a soft case. What he wanted was to go out with a bang, to catch a killer or rapist, not some common robbers. He wanted to walk into that court with a conviction as his last act as a policeman.

To distract himself, he put in a call to control and had them patch him through to DS Murray. He spoke to Murray for a few minutes to see what he had discovered about the robbery. Dismayed to find out that it fit the pattern of the gang he was after, he cut the call and resumed his vehement condemnation of every driver who slowed him down.

When Evans at last entered the Lakeland Hotel reception, he flashed the girl behind the desk his warrant card and asked for the manager. While the girl went off to find the manager Evans paced the reception floor, ignorant of the neutral decor that populated all such conference hotels. The striped wallpaper in earth tones and fleur-de-lis-patterned carpets of the Lakeland would have assaulted his eyes had he not been so wrapped up in his thoughts. A mechanical whirr followed by a whoosh got his attention when an automated air freshener shot a cloud of sandalwood at him.

'Sergeant Evans? I'm Dean Lennox.'

Evans fixed the man wearing a pinstripe business suit with a glare. 'It's Detective Inspector Evans.'

'Sorry.' The word was automatic. 'One of your colleagues just left here about twenty minutes ago. Why are you here exactly?'

'Because he's a DC and I'm a DI. I've come to check he hasn't missed anything. Also I'm the lead officer on all the thefts involving licensed premises.'

'Oh, right then. So you're the person responsible for catching these burglars? Or not, as the case seems to be.'

'Just show me round and stop with the attitude,' Evans made sure his expression knocked the insolence from the manager.

Lennox said little as he showed Evans his office and the safe.

'What about the alarm? Where's the control panel?'

'Unfortunately, the alarm isn't working. Head office won't let me employ a local firm to fix it and the company they use have been fobbing me off for a fortnight.'

'I bet they will now.' Evans laughed at the distressed look on Lennox's face before spotting something hanging on a wall.

Images flashed through his mind as he recalled all the other venues that had been turned over. It fit. This was the connection he had been trying to make. Reaching out he took the calendar from the wall. Emblazoned across the top was the logo for Stockcheck UK. In smaller print was the name

Victoria Foulkes, accompanied by a mobile number and an email address.

'When was the stocktaker last here?'

'Yesterday. You surely don't think it's her, do you? I've never heard anything so preposterous. Victoria is the last person I'd suspect.'

'And that, Mr Lennox, is why I'm a detective inspector and you are a jumped-up fuckwit.'

Lennox was speechless as he stormed away from Evans.

A quick conversation with the receptionist got Evans the information he was after. Whistling to himself, Evans climbed into the BMW and set off towards Carlisle in a more positive frame of mind. Exulted at having a firm lead, he followed the wagon in front without commenting on the driver's skill or making any attempt to get past. He pulled off the M6 at junction 43, then drove along Warwick Road, turning onto Victoria Place, past Cumbria College. He crossed the river and went up Stanwix Bank onto Scotland Road. Turning into the car park behind the Cumberland Park Hotel, he parked the M3 and went inside.

The hotel was created from a row of terraced houses that had been knocked through into one long building. There were lots of different levels separated by two and three steps apiece as the hotel followed the contours of the hill. The brick exterior was clad in decades-old ivy.

As he went into the main building, Evans spied Victoria Foulkes typing figures in an office behind the reception. Across the desk from her a receptionist-cum-clerk was talking on the telephone.

'Victoria. Can I have a word?' The way her face dropped when she recognised the speaker told Evans he'd just apprehended one of the thieves.

Before she could answer him, his mobile rang. Keeping a close eye on Victoria, Evans thumbed his keypad lock across and answered the call.

Lauren's voice was breathless with excitement. 'Guv. We've got a hit on the DNA from the blood found at the Drover's Inn.'

'Whose is it?'

'A Jonathan Green. Last known address was a cottage on the outskirts of Alston. He's nineteen years old...'

'And his parents are called Eric and Jennifer.' Evans kicked the reception counter. Eric and Jennifer Green were decent people; their lives would be torn apart if their son went down for murder.

'Penrith CID are on their way to bring him in and they've asked me to do the interview.'

'Thanks for letting me know. Keep me posted.'

Evans hung up the call and asked Victoria if there was somewhere where they could talk in private.

Chapter 41

Jonny's hands stung from the various cleaning fluids, a spot on his cheek burned where a splash of bleach had landed. Since returning from their expedition yesterday, he and Steve had spent hours cleaning the cottage in case any evidence had found its way into their home.

All he could focus on was the fact the police may well be coming for him. At best, he was an accessory to manslaughter, if such a charge even existed. At worst, he would face a murder charge. Time and again he'd cast a glance out of the window expecting to see police cars and a dozen burly coppers charging up the path. His nerves were shredded to the point of disintegration. Gone was his calm demeanour from the day before. All he could do now was smoke and worry.

When a knock on the door sounded, he jumped out of his chair. Answering the door Jonny found himself face to face with a man in a well-cut suit. In his hand was a wallet of some kind.

'Good morning, sir. I'm DC Thompson. Are you Jonathan Green?'

'Yes.' All the previous day's planning for this event washed from Jonny's mind like driftwood being carried away by a high tide.

'I have a few questions I'd like to ask you, Mr Green. Are you able to come down to Penrith Station with me?'

'Can't you ask me them here?' Sweat formed on Jonny's forehead but he resisted the urge to wipe it off, afraid the gesture would bring it to Thompson's attention.

'The fact you haven't asked me what questions tells me that you know what I'm going to be asking.' Licking his lips in a reflexive action, Thompson began to caution Jonny. 'You do not have to say anything but it may harm your defence if you do not mention when questioned—'

'You've got it wrong. I didn't do anything.'

Thompson finished the caution as he retrieved a pair of handcuffs from the holster on his belt.

Jonny continued protesting his innocence as Thompson led him to the waiting car. His brain was working on a different plane as he tried to figure out what was going to happen next.

His private queries were interrupted by Thompson asking where Steve was.

'He's in the shower.'

Thompson lifted a radio to his lips and relayed this information to what Jonny supposed was his backup.

Stay calm and remember the plan. Stay calm and remember the plan.

Jonny kept repeating the mantra over and over all the way to Penrith. He'd been kept waiting until Steve had been rounded up and deposited in the car behind him. Just before driving off he'd seen some people dressed in white all-in-one suits entering the cottage. He guessed they were whatever the British equivalent of CSI was called. The stinging blotch on his cheek reassured him they'd find nothing.

Arriving at Penrith police station was an unnerving experience for Jonny. He was asked to identify himself by a sergeant behind a desk, his fingerprints were taken using some kind of scanner and he was readied for a cell. His watch, belt and shoelaces were collected along with his wallet and the contents of his pockets. His cigarettes and lighter joined the collection. What he wouldn't have given to have a smoke to calm his nerves.

Settling himself down on the gym-mat-thin mattress on the concrete bed, Jonny prepared for a long wait. He'd watched enough police dramas on TV to know what was happening. The police would need time to build a case against him. Locking him in a cell was a tactic of theirs. They'd want him to panic. Become stressed out, so he incriminated himself. He would use the time to control his nerves and recall the plan. But the time spent in the cell was endless and boring. There was nothing to do but think about the trouble he was in and stare at the graffiti covering every wall, which on closer inspection revealed a roll call of names and dates of those who had preceded him.

Chapter 42

The journey to get to Alston had been a marriage of controlled aggression and driving skill. Travelling via Brampton he'd thrashed the BMW as hard as he dared. The A689 curled and twisted its way up hill and down dale as it crossed the moors. On three occasions he'd missed oncoming traffic by inches as his overtaking manoeuvres became ever more desperate.

Entering the town, he had to fight to control the BMW when its rear-wheel drive came into contact with the wet cobbles on Front Street. Snaking up the hill, like an automotive sidewinder he found the street he was looking for.

This was not a task he was looking forward to, as his intentions were both honourable and dishonourable. He walked up the garden path of number twelve and knocked on the blue door. The colourful spring flowers brought a happiness to the surroundings that he was about destroy.

The door opened and Jennifer Green appeared. 'DI Evans, what a lovely surprise. Come on in, I'll get the kettle on.' With that she disappeared into the house leaving Evans to find his own way in.

With a knot tightening in his stomach, Evans followed the rotund frame of the ardent churchgoer into the kitchen. Despite having time to arrange the words in his mind, he still hadn't formulated a nice way of telling Jennifer her only son was facing a lengthy spell behind bars. He delayed the moment, until she had made tea for them both. She would need the restorative powers of Britain's national drink.

As she made the tea, she twittered about how sorry Eric would be to have missed him, but he was in a meeting with their accountant, and filled him in on all the gossip of life in Alston.

'I'm afraid it's not a social visit today.'

'What's wrong? It's not Eric is it? I keep telling him he drives too fast.'

'It's not Eric. It's Jonny.' Raising a hand he silenced her questions. 'He's gone and got himself into some real trouble this time, I'm afraid.'

'There must be some mistake. My Jonny is a good lad. We brought him up to be a good person.

'I'm sorry but there's no mistake.'

'Why what's he done?' As she spoke she walked across the kitchen and tore off a sheet of kitchen roll to dab at the tears beginning to form in the corners of each eye.

Evans eased himself into one of the chairs around the table and gestured for her to do the same.

'A blood sample at a crime scene was collected and when we ran the sample against the database it turned out to be a positive match for Jonny.'

'I'm sure that there must be some explanation.' Jennifer wiped her eyes a second time. 'So what's he accused of, then? And where was the crime scene?'

With as much tenderness as he could muster, Evans informed her that the crime scene was the Drover's Inn and the crime was murder.

'No!' The shouted word full of disbelief. 'I don't believe you. It can't be. He wouldn't kill anyone. He lifts spiders up using toilet paper and puts them outside instead of killing them. You're wrong! How can you come into my house and tell me such lies?'

Twice her right hand went from forehead to navel and then across her chest. Jennifer no longer made any effort to wipe her tears. Instead she let them flow. Her head shook from side to side as she disputed the preposterous idea which Evans had planted into her brain.

'I came to tell you because I didn't want you to get a call from the station. Because I would rather tell you myself than let you hear it from some desk jockey at Penrith or from Jonny himself. He is going to need you to be at your best, to be strong for him.'

And because I want you to under my influence, so that Lauren can get the confession signed and sealed before your husband gets one of his high-powered lawyer friends sat beside Jonny.

He didn't like what he was doing to prevent Eric Green riding to his son's rescue. However, he knew that without the confession, a man in Eric's position would be able to find a way to keep his errant son out of jail.

Her eyes scanned the room and she whirled around searching for a phone. 'I have to call Eric. He'll get a lawyer and get this all sorted out. You'll see. You're wrong.'

'Come on, Jennifer. I'll take you to see him at Penrith nick, you can find out for yourself what he has to say and then you can call Eric.'

As they travelled back to Penrith, Evans questioned Jennifer about Steve. He'd heard of Steve's family. They'd had lived in Alston for many years, but he'd never met them. Steve's father had been lifted a few times for drunken fights and petty misdemeanours.

'It looks like he has got into the wrong crowd with this Steve.'

'On the contrary. The apple fell a long way from that particular tree. Steve has been in and out of our house for years now and he is like a brother to Jonny.' As with all mothers, Jennifer could not believe the baby she had nursed into manhood could be guilty of a heinous crime. In the short period she'd had to digest Evans's news, she had gone from disbelief to denial in record time.

Evans escorted her into the station and took her straight to the custody suite. 'Mark, can you give Mrs Green here a minute or two with Jonny.'

As the duty sergeant escorted Jennifer to Jonny's cell, Steve Collinge was brought out of a cell, protesting his innocence, 'It was all Jonny's doing. I only went along to be a lookout.'

Regardless of all the police around her, Jennifer stepped forward and delivered a hard slap to Steve's left cheek. 'You liar. You've dragged my little boy into trouble and now you're blaming him. He treated you like a brother and now you're blaming him. You... you... shit!'

Despite his own foul tongue, Evans's jaw dropped when he heard Jennifer Green lapse into profanity.

His phone started to ring. It was Grantham. Wisely Evans moved the phone away from his ear before Grantham deafened him. Gradually he moved the mobile closer to his ear as the tirade subsided.

'Wait a minute, sir. Are you saying that DCI Tyler would like to meet for a coffee?' Evans scratched his chin. 'I take it he isn't going to nominate me for a knighthood.'

Chapter 43

The cell door creaked as it opened. When Jonny saw his mother his heart fell. She was distraught. He'd been so wrapped up in his own worries he'd never once considered the effect this would have on her. Her face was stained mascara smudged by tears.

'I didn't do it, Mam. I didn't.'

'Don't worry, Jonny. I'll call Dad and he'll get one of his friends to help you. The Lord will not let you suffer injustice.'

Keeping his head down so that his mother couldn't see the shame in his eyes, Jonny listened to her reassurances and put his palms together while she prayed for him. All too soon it was time for Jennifer to leave. The desk sergeant opened the cell door, a finger crooked in Jonny's direction. 'C'mon, you. They're ready to interview you now.'

'But what about his lawyer?'

'There's a duty solicitor who'll sit in with him until his own lawyer arrives.'

Deciding that the best course of action was to go to the interview room and keep mute until one of his father's lawyer friends arrived, Jonny followed the sergeant to an interview suite. Inside was a cheap Formica table and four plastic chairs. A series of switches decorated the wall beside the table.

A rumpled man in his fifties rose from one of the chairs, extending a hand. 'Henry Oakes, the duty solicitor.'

Jonny took the proffered hand and shook it. Nothing about Oakes inspired confidence in him. His hair was overdue a cut, an egg stain decorated his creased tie and he'd knocked his briefcase off the table when he'd stood up to greet Jonny.

The door opened as he sat watching Oakes retrieve the contents of his briefcase. The arresting copper walked into the room followed by a stunning blonde. She wore a pencil skirt with a slit running up her right thigh. As she strode across to the chair, the slit opened to give a glimpse of stocking top. The crisp white blouse she wore was unbuttoned just enough to show a generous amount of cleavage without being indecent.

Jonny looked at Oakes. The man was entranced. He nudged his arm.

Fat lot of use this clown's gonna be. I'll just keep saying no comment until I have a decent solicitor beside me.

The blonde unwrapped two cassettes and fed them into the tape recorders fixed to the wall, pressed record and then named everyone in the room and gave the date and time.

Jonny felt the full force of her gaze as she turned to face him. 'So then, Mr Green, can you explain why your blood was found on a window at a murder scene?'

'My client has nothing to say on the matter.' Since the blonde had entered the room Oakes had been unable to remove his eyes from her chest, he almost gave himself a squint trying to make eye contact with her.

'Mr Green?'

'No comment.'

The blonde tried asking the same question in different ways, but Jonny stuck to his guns and kept repeating his two-word answer.

'Perhaps we can start from the beginning. Can you account for your whereabouts the night before last?' Her eyes were soft and the way she looked at him made Jonny confident enough to answer this harmless question.

'I went out with me mate.'

'That's fair enough. What's his name so we can verify your story?'

'Steve Collinge. He lives with me.'

'We've already spoken to him.' The blonde established direct eye contact with Jonny as she asked her next question. 'Do you live together as a couple then or just as flatmates?'

'I can hardly see the relevance of the question. Mr Green's sexuality has no bearing on the case whatsoever.'

'I apologise. You're right. It has no connection whatsoever. I'm just a girl who likes to keep her options open.'

Jonny noticed the obviously insincere statement from the blonde had a profound effect on Oakes. He could see the lust in the duty solicitor's eyes. He himself regarded her with a mixture of hope and fear.

'So then, Mr Green, or may I call you Jonny?' At his nod of assent, she resumed her questions. 'Do you frequent the Drover's Inn, Jonny?'

'I've been once or twice in the past. A girl I was seeing from Penrith liked to go there for the odd drink and a bite to eat.'

'So when was the last time you were there?'

Tiring of the charade, Jonny decided to go with the story he and Steve had agreed to stick to. The longer they held out the less chance they had of being believed. The blonde wasn't a hardass. She was his best chance of having the lie believed. By the time his father rustled up a solicitor to represent him, he could be facing someone much less understanding.

'We went a couple of nights ago. Steve fancied the barmaid, so we went down so he could try and chat her up.'

'What time did you leave?'

'About half ten. The manager threw us out because Steve kept bothering her.'

'Her?'

'The barmaid. The manager is an old guy. Used to be in the army I think.' Aware he was starting to babble, Jonny fell silent.'

'What was the barmaid's name? If she can verify your version of events then it'll help us to put you in the clear.'

'Not so fast, DC Thompson. I think that the manager throwing them out gives us a motive for his murder.'

Damn. The blonde wasn't letting anything go.

'I didn't murder no one.'

'I didn't murder no one.' The blonde repeated the phrase and then leaned back as if about to pounce. '"I didn't murder no one" is a statement containing two negatives. Therefore you must have murdered someone. Who was it, Jonny? Colin Armstrong? Were you pissed off 'cause he threw you out?'

'Mr Green, I'd advise you to give the name of the barmaid so you can have your story verified.'

'What was her name, Jonny?'

'It was…' Jonny couldn't think of a name. The blonde was leaning further back in her chair while Thompson rested his folded arms on the table and hunched over them.

'I'm sorry, Jonny, but I think you're lying to me. There was no barmaid, was there?'

'No comment.'

'Why was your blood on the window, Jonny?'

'No. Comment.'

Why wouldn't she shut up using his name? They weren't friends, so why did she keep calling him Jonny?

'Why, Jonny? Why?'

Jonny had held out for this moment so his lies would carry more weight. 'The manager called me some names as I went back to the car. I'd had a few pints so I threw a punch at a window. That must be how my blood got there.'

'A punch you say Jonny? With a closed fist?'

'That's right.' As soon as he answered her, she looked at his hands face down on the table.

The blonde smiled a cold grimace at him as she exchanged a look with the other copper. 'For the benefit of the tape, Mr Green has no wounds on the back of either hand, yet the duty sergeant who admitted him recorded, a recent two inch cut on the palm of Mr Green's right hand.'

The blonde used her fingertips to turn Jonny's right hand over. Her mouth twisted into a knot far more damning than words.

There in the centre of his palm was an angry laceration.

'That looks like a recent injury, Jonny. You're not going to try and tell me you didn't do it on the window we found your blood on, are you? Because a forensic examination of your hand would almost certainly prove the glass in the window made that cut.'

Jonny said nothing. There was too much evidence against him for the lie he and Steve had agreed on to work.

'Why don't you save the taxpayers a small fortune and tell us the truth? We'll find out anyway.'

Thompson took over from the blonde. 'I would say that a cut on the palm of a hand is more synonymous with someone climbing through an already broken window, rather than someone punching one.'

'I agree. Admit it, Jonny. You were one of the people who were there when Mr Armstrong was killed.'

'No, I wasn't. I've told you the truth about it and that's all I have to say.'

The blonde reached down and lifted up the briefcase she had carried into the room. Removing an envelope she put the briefcase back on the floor and stood up.

Jonny hated to think what was in the envelope. Whatever it was would have to be bad otherwise the blonde wouldn't have kept it in reserve.

She stood up. Bending at the waist she leaned forward, giving him a close up of her cleavage. She had retained her position over the desk and seemed oblivious to the way Oakes's eyes were locked on the contents of her bra. One by one she pulled pictures of blood droplets from the envelope.

'These pictures were all taken at the Drover's Inn. Forensic tests have proven each of these drops contain your DNA.'

Even as he fought to cope with the implications the pictures carried, Jonny found he could not tear his eyes from the view down the blonde's blouse. The realisation her exhibitionism was a deliberate act to nullify the duty solicitor and distract him angered Jonny, but he had enough wits left to realise that if he got mad he'd end up doing something very stupid.

He and Steve had never considered the idea that he'd cut his hand on the way into the building. His blood in there was damning evidence. To think how clever he'd thought himself when they were burning their clothes to hide their tracks.

'Go on, Jonny. Tell us what happened and we'll try an' help you. The early opinion from our head of Forensics is that you were there when Armstrong was murdered. He doesn't believe you killed him though.'

Thompson's jaw was set firm as he shook his head. 'Don't waste your time expecting a confession. Jonny boy hasn't got the sense to tell us what really happened. He'll deny everything, try and fob us off with a pack of lies. We've got plenty of evidence against him. Let's just build our case and let him take his chances with a judge. If he's lucky he'll get less than ten years.'

'So what's it gonna be, Jonny? A confession and a reduced stretch, or a fight to the end and the longest sentence the judge can pass?'

Seeing nothing but a dead end, with a side road leading to a long time in prison broke Jonny. He accepted that the game was up and the police had too much on him. All his father's solicitor friends would be able to do was get him a reduced sentence when he went to court.

'OK. OK. Me and Steve did it. We went there on the rob. Old Man Armstrong went for us with a cricket bat. Steve whacked him with his crowbar and when he went down we took off. We never meant to kill him. Steve was just trying to stop him so we could get away.'

'By Steve, do you mean Steve Collinge, your flatmate?'

Jonny nodded. 'It was his idea to rob the place. We'd seen Border Crack and Deeks Aboot and heard about the pub robberies. Steve said it would be a piece of piss to turn one over and we'd get plenty drink and a good few quid.'

'Mr Collinge has tried to lay all the blame on your door, but he didn't know the forensic evidence didn't support his claim that you were the one who killed Mr Armstrong.'

'The bastard. It was him that hit Armstrong. Not me.'

Jonny watched as the blonde removed the tapes, dated them and pushed them across for him to sign.

Oakes rose to leave. 'I wish you good luck at court, young man.'

'Fuck off, you useless tosser. You're a fucking disgrace. You spent more time looking at her tits than you did helping me.' Spittle flew from Jonny's mouth. 'Believe me, I'm gonna make a complaint about you, you useless pervy arsehole.'

Oakes shrugged with seasoned indifference and left the room.

Jonny's fingers shook the way his grandad's did. His stomach had knotted itself into a ball causing his bowels to roil and twitch. The prospect of soiling himself was a realistic worry.

He knew his outburst at the duty solicitor had been unfair. While Oates had been guilty of the accusations levelled at him, the viciousness with which Jonny had spat the words shamed him. The man was doing a job and in his eyes, Jonny would just be the latest in an endless queue of losers to require his services.

The blonde and Thompson took him back to the custody area where, in the presence of the duty sergeant, the blonde charged him with breaking and entering and accessory to murder.

Chapter 44

Victoria was pacing back and forth across the cell. Since Harry Evans had walked into the Cumberland Park Hotel, her worst fears were being realised one by one. She wasn't concerned for herself – she would face any music she had to, as long as her kids came back unharmed. All her worries were for Kyle and Samantha.

Denial would be her only course of action. Deny everything until they released her and just hope and pray it happened in time for her to get the rest of the money. She had refused to answer any of the questions Evans had thrown at her. All her focus was on getting released and raising the last £2,500 needed for the ransom. She had already worked out and tested the alarm code for the Cumberland Park Hotel. When she'd keyed the number into the alarm panel, the siren had sounded after about thirty seconds – more than enough time for her to get back to her desk and arrange a puzzled look on her face.

Try as she might, Victoria was struggling to fight back the feeling of despair. With all her belongings confiscated, she had no way of contacting Nicholas to let him know of her capture. She could not escape the feeling that she had failed her children, that they would be killed or mutilated because she hadn't been able to raise the money. Her mind raced through a dozen different scenarios with each new one worse than the last.

What if the police find out about the kidnapping and the kidnappers find out the police know? What if the police search the home and find the money we've stolen? They'll take it as evidence and then we won't be able to pay the ransom. What if they have conclusive proof Nicholas and I are behind the robberies and bring him in too? Who will save Samantha and Kyle then? What if the police search my laptop? It has details of everything: all the robberies and the link to the kidnapper's website.

She'd considered telling Harry Evans everything when he'd taken her to the police station. She'd known him for years and the tales of his rule-breaking were legendary. Doubting that even a renegade like Evans would be able to keep the kidnapping quiet, she had kept quiet.

The cell door swung open and Evans slumped himself against the door frame.

'C'mon, Victoria, it's time for your interview.'

Chapter 45

Samantha was all cried out. Her body ached from the sobs that had engulfed her body, her eyes were raw. Her lips still stung from the cuts inflicted by Elvis's knuckles and her probing tongue had identified two loose teeth.

Looking across the room she saw Kyle's back. The hand scratching his ear told her he was awake.

'Kyle?'

No answer. He was still rejecting her.

She tried again. 'Kyle, I'm sorry we didn't get away.'

Silence. But she could tell he was listening. That gave her a glimmer of hope. Being cooped up was bad enough, but knowing he was mad at her made it ten time worse.

'The bad men had locked the front door. I'm so sorry, Kyle. I never expected them to do that.'

'You pinkie promised.' There it was. The worst let-down of his short life had involved a pinkie promise. Promises made upon the shaking of interlocked pinkies were legally binding as far as he was concerned. Samantha had known the risk of a broken pinkie promise would be terrible for Kyle, however she had been so keen to escape she had offered the promise without hesitation.

'I know I did. I honestly thought we'd get away.' For the first time in hours he looked at her. The fear and hurt in his face was terrible for her to see. She felt a deep responsibility for his pain, as it was she who had raised his expectations by offering false hope.

She moved across the room and wrapped him in her arms. After a minute or two he turned and returned her embrace. The hug from her brother felt like redemption. For the first time since being captured Samantha felt a natural grin caress her mouth, until she remembered were they were and what awaited them. They were one day away from a horrible fate if their parents failed them.

Releasing Kyle she got to her feet and went to the bathroom. There on the floor was a large piece of the games disc she had broken earlier to give Kyle as a weapon. A new plan came into her head. Sure it was risky and there was every chance that they'd be caught again. Yet if they had not been released by tomorrow night, there would be nothing left to lose. Samantha didn't believe her parents could raise the ransom. All she and Kyle had left to look forward to was a long wait followed by an uncertain ending. Taking the piece of disc in her hand she started to gouge at the wall behind the bedroom door. If the men came in again, the signs of her latest escape bid would be hidden behind the open door.

Chapter 46

Evans drove back to Carlisle thinking about his encounter with Victoria. He'd tried to catch her out with a few well-chosen questions, but she hadn't told him anything. All she was interested in was being interviewed and getting away. Her behaviour was unusual for people in her situation and while he had nothing solid to tie her to the various robberies, there was an awful lot of circumstantial evidence. He'd had Bhaki call round all the premises. Each one had told the young Asian that Victoria was their regular stocktaker.

Something about Victoria's demeanour was off kilter and he couldn't put his finger on it. She should be shouting to be freed, protesting her innocence, demanding a lawyer even. Instead, once he'd arrested her she'd remained mute, only speaking to request that she be interviewed as soon as possible. In his experience the people who were the guiltiest and had the most to hide behaved the way Victoria did. Yet he couldn't work out what she would have to hide, other than her involvement in the thefts. They had been on polite speaking terms for years. He knew that she was a stereotypical hard worker with a loving family and a respectable life. She was the type who would give to charity, bake cakes for birthdays and help out at community events. The thought of her sneaking through dark rooms and emptying safes didn't add up.

However, she was the one person who had a common link with all the premises. Even more damning was the fact her husband owned an ironmonger's shop. One of the facets to his business was key cutting. Evans could recall times when the police had engaged Nicholas Foulkes to pick locks, so they could enter certain places without causing damage. When you added that to the look of horror on her face when he turned up at Cumberland Park Hotel, Evans was convinced she was guilty. But not as guilty as her behaviour indicated. With a clean record like hers, she would be unlucky to get more than a couple of years suspended sentence should the money be recovered. Yet she was acting as if she was up on a charge of mass murder or treason.

He wanted Chisholm to have a root around her laptop before he started the interview. He'd forgotten to hand it over when he'd brought her in earlier, so he'd have to wait until the computer genius had done his search. Evans was quite happy to delay the interview until he got Chisholm's report. Not only would it agitate Victoria to be delayed but it would also give Lauren time to return after she'd finished at Penrith. Depositing the laptop with Chisholm, he spent a few minutes learning Bhaki's progress. While he was talking with Bhaki, Lauren called to tell him of Jonny Green's confession and the duty sergeant from the front desk rang to tell him that Nicholas Foulkes had been delivered by a couple of Workington PCs.

Getting to his feet, Evans made for the door. His team had enjoyed a successful day and he wanted to deliver the news to Grantham before he was summoned.

'Sir, I've some good news for you.' Evans entered the DCI's office without knocking, as was his wont.

'What is it, Quasi?'

'We've now got a confession for the murder of Colin Armstrong and we've made two arrests for the licensed premises case.'

Grantham raised an eyebrow. 'Who is it? Any of the usual toerags?'

Evans paced the room restlessly as he filled his boss in on the day's news. A murder solved and a spate of thefts about to be cracked. He felt better than he had for weeks.

Grantham picked at the obvious hole in the investigation. 'Why wasn't this Victoria Foulkes listed in the lists of suppliers for all of the locations?'

'Because her husband is a steward at Maryport Golf Club and because two of the places robbed seemed to think she was above suspicion. They'd accuse dray and bar staff like a shot, but not Victoria's professional type.'

'It's the usual bloody thing, isn't it? The public give us half a story and then act surprised when we can't solve the crimes.'

Evans could have grumbled on with Grantham about the inadequacies of the public's information giving skills, but he had work to do. 'I'm off to interview Victoria Foulkes now. I'll let you know how I get on.'

Tempting as the idea was, Evans decided against sharing his triumph with Greg Hadley. He didn't want to make the younger man feel pressured. News would filter up the chain of command soon enough and Hadley possessed enough nous to work out who had solved the crimes.

I'll get Chisholm to type up my reports as soon as he's done with that laptop. Won't hurt to get them in early for once!

Returning to their office via the canteen for a coffee and a bacon roll, Evans walked in to find Bhaki and Chisholm hunched over the laptop with mouths hanging open.

'What you got, lads? Dirty pictures of the lady downstairs?'

Chisholm's face was paler than usual when he looked up. 'No, guv. It's a lot worse than that.'

Chapter 47

Annoyed by the delay in being interviewed, Victoria was relieved to see Evans when he opened her cell door. Standing behind him was a young woman.

'Are you going to interview me now?'

'No.' The word was delivered with a soft shake of the head.

'Why not? I need to get home. My kids'll be worried.' The last sentence tore at Victoria's heart, but she was determined to keep up the pretence.

Evans's answer wasn't forthcoming so Victoria tried asking him again. Saying nothing, he motioned for her to exit the cell.

Puzzled, Victoria left the cell and followed him, aware of the young woman falling in behind her.

Evans led her into an interview suite.

'I thought you weren't going to inter…' Victoria fell silent when she saw her laptop on the table.

Oh my God, no. Please God, tell me they haven't found out about Samantha and Kyle.

Fighting to give her legs enough strength to support her, Victoria managed to get herself into a seat before she collapsed. She took a breath and lifted her chin with a determination she did not feel. She needed to know how much the police knew. Her eyes searched the faces of Evans and his colleague but reported only bad news. While both wore poker faces, their eyes radiated compassion and empathy. The temptation to dissolve into tears and beg for Evans's help was overwhelming, but the memory of Elvis's warnings trumped her despair. Elvis's source in the police may not exist, but the possibility that someone in the police force was in his pocket was too great a risk to take.

'Victoria, this is DC Lauren Phillips. We've been through your laptop as a routine part of our investigation. We found more than enough evidence to link you to all the burglaries you've done.'

'Then charge me and let me go.'

Is that all they've found? Please God, let it be all they've found.

'I paused that investigation because we also found a link to a website with three videos of Samantha.'

'Three?'

Have they sent another video? Are Samantha and Kyle OK?

'Yes three. And from the way you said three I'm guessing that you only knew of one or two.'

'It's a project that she and her friends are doing for school.'

'Really?' Evans's eyebrows arched in disbelief.

'Yes, absolutely. Now will you please either charge me or let me go.' Victoria stuck to her lie, hoping the bluff would work.

It was the young DC who spoke next. 'A school project? Are you sure? Because when I was at school we didn't make nude videos.'

'Nude? Is she OK?' The question fell from Victoria's mouth before she could stop it.

Damn.

There was no way that the police would believe her story about a school project, if Samantha was now being filmed naked.

'Can I see the last one?'

The DC fiddled with the laptop and then turned it around so Victoria could see the screen.

Watching the short clip sickened Victoria. She imagined the men behind the camera, leering and leching over her little girl as they made their threats. The only positive that she could take from the experience was that she'd seen only one sign of bruises or mistreatment on Samantha's body. The only blemish on her skin was a blackened eye. Under the circumstances, the damage to Samantha's face was of small worry. If she'd been raped her body would show the signs of a struggle, bruises and reddened areas at wrists and ankles where she'd been held or tied up.

'They've been kidnapped, haven't they?'

Victoria couldn't answer the question. Her mouth was immovable. Her tongue was a dry lump that wouldn't move. She gave a small nod.

'Don't worry. We'll do everything we can to get them back safe and sound. I've got someone tracing the website's origin. We've already brought Nicholas in.'

Victoria let the tears flow as she begged Evans not to tell anyone else in the police. The next hour was spent going over all the details she knew about the kidnapping.

Chapter 48

Evans was struggling to contain his feeling of excitement. At last, a decent case had come his way. If his career was going to end, then he wanted it to end on a high, and rescuing kidnapped children would be the highest of highs. Solving Armstrong's murder had been good, but most of the credit would and should go to the lab technicians who had analysed all the samples.

It wouldn't be easy though, he and the team had just thirty hours before the deadline. While he didn't believe the kidnappers' claim they had a police informant, he was experienced enough to know that it could and did happen. Naive fools took a few quid to share information or look the other way. After they had done it once, the second and third times became easier. Savvier criminals took pictures of the exchanges and used blackmail to turn the screw ever deeper into the bent coppers.

As he entered the office, he noticed that Lauren's mobile was ringing, the screen registering Campbell's name. Wondering what the man wanted, he answered the call.

'What do you want, Jock?... We've got the pub thieves, but it's more complicated than you think... They were doing it to raise a kidnap ransom... What about your wife and bairn?... Well, if you're sure, an extra pair of hands won't go amiss. Be here in fifteen minutes as we have to go search the house.'

After disconnecting, Evans looked at the phone. There were five missed calls from Campbell.

Bhaki entered the office as Evans was instructing Chisholm to keep the news of the kidnapping off the system and within the team.

Evans fished his car keys from a pocket and passed them to Bhaki. 'Go and fill it up for me will you. I have a feeling I'm gonna cover a lot of miles in the next few hours.'

Heading downstairs again he met Lauren.

'Go home and get changed into something more appropriate, lass. It's one thing flashing yourself to criminals but I'm not having you dressed like that when talking to folk who've had to watch their daughter in those videos.'

'I've only got short skirts, guv.'

'You must have a pair of trousers or jeans even.'

'No. Only skirts and dresses. And they are all above the knee.'

Evans raised a questioning eyebrow, unable to believe that she only ever wore short skirts or dresses. Thinking about it, he realised he'd never seen her wear anything else.

'I've got nice legs and if I show them off then there's a better chance of getting someone between them.'

'You're a right little slapper, aren't you?'

'I prefer the term sexually liberated, guv, but I'm not gonna split hairs.'

'Here.' Evans held out a twenty-pound note. 'Nip to Asda and get a pair of trousers and a blouse that hides your tits. If you can't do that, go home. I'll have you transferred off my team in the morning.'

Leaving Lauren standing mouth agape, Evans consulted the admissions file and went to Nicholas's cell.

'Where did you run up the gambling debt, Nicholas?' Evans was struggling not to punch the stricken man.

The contempt he felt towards Nicholas bubbled through his veins. He was self-aware enough to keep his distance from the man, in case the wrong answer fell on his ears and caused him to lash out.

'I asked where you ran up the gambling debt, Nicholas. I want an answer and I want it fast. Your children's lives may depend on it.'

'Blackpool.'

'Where in Blackpool?'

'Aces High Casino.'

'Whereabouts is that located then?'

'Opposite the Pleasure Beach.'

'You got a membership card or something?'

Nicholas handed over a piece of plastic with his name and the casino's logo embossed on the front.

218

'Is it the casino you owe the money, too?'

He nodded and then hung his head, overcome with more tears and protestations of how sorry he was.

Evans returned to the office and spent ten minutes in conversation with Chisholm and Bhaki until Campbell arrived.

Satisfied Chisholm could and would do his bidding, he instructed Bhaki to take Lauren's place on the stakeout that night and report for work at lunchtime the next day.

'Are you sure, sir? Isn't the kidnapping more important?'

''Course it is, lad, but the brass'll want to know why, if we don't show face. Then we'd have to tell them about the kidnapping and maybe put those kids at risk.'

And we'll be forced to hand over the last good case I'm likely to be involved in.

'What have you learned about the website, Jabba?'

'Nothing good, I'm afraid. The site was built using free online software that could be accessed from any laptop or computer. The IP address of the source material belongs to a laptop registered as stolen.'

'You must be able to track it back.'

'I could. But not in time. I'm sorry, guv.'

Evans felt a pang of sympathy for Chisholm. He knew the computer geek would hate being unable to give him the answers he needed.

'What about the contact form?'

'Another dead end. The message goes to a Gmail address. The account was set up from the laptop a week ago and hasn't been accessed since. I reckon they've linked the Gmail address to a smartphone, but I don't have a way of tracing it.'

Evans scowled, before grunting at Chisholm to trace the number plate of the van the kidnappers had used. He doubted they had used one they owned themselves, but if he'd learned anything about criminals during his years of policing, it was that the majority of them were stupid.

'Put the word out that I need to speak to Tommy and Terry. Mebbe they can shed some light on things.'

Chapter 49

With aching fingers, Samantha kept drawing the broken piece of disc along the plaster. This groove was the harder to do than the first two, as she had to stretch above her head to reach it. She closed her eyes to the falling plaster dust, working by feel alone. Time and again she gouged a track into the soft plaster until her makeshift tool broke through and found the supporting lath. By sliding the sliver between the plaster and lath, she managed to pry loose a section above the groove.

Now she had a makeshift ladder of grooves carved out of the bedroom wall, which would now allow her to start work on the ceiling. When she had first broken through the lattice framework, she'd hoped she would be able to cut her way straight through the wall into another room. Praying for a possible easier method of escape, her probing fingers had found only the thick stone walls of the old farmhouse.

The door into the room was recessed back into the wall so she knew that she'd be unable to get through that way either. The bathroom was tiled floor to ceiling with ancient ceramic tiles and offered no soft surface to exploit. With a tender care Samantha climbed up the grooves she'd cut. Her bare feet and soft hands were scratched from the rough timber and coarse plaster of the wall. At any moment she expected the door to swing open and hit her back or the fragile supports she'd created to give way. Reaching up, Samantha began to attack the ceiling. Luck was on her side: the ceiling plaster was much softer than the wall's. After five minutes scratching she had created a hole large enough for her to feed a hand through.

Hearing movement outside the room, she returned to ground level, scooped up the towels she'd been using as dustsheets and threw them into the bathroom.

Footsteps thudded around but the door never opened.

The stairs creaking as someone descended. Samantha retrieved the towels from the bathroom and prepared for another assault on the ceiling. She wanted to wrap the towels around her feet as they were bloody from the rough steps she created, but the need to leave no trace if they were surprised was more important than her own comfort. Gritting her teeth against the pain she resumed her attack on the ceiling. Slipping her hand through, she groped around, trying to determine where the ceiling supports were, so she didn't waste time making a hole beneath them. She located a joist with her fingertips, then used the disc shard to mark out the area she needed to work on. Samantha pulled down on the laths supporting the ceiling, which helped to speed up her progress.

After ten minutes of pulling and gouging, she had created a gap large enough for her body to pass through. The cold air blowing down caused her to shiver, but she paid no heed to the change in temperature or the musty smell accompanying the draft. Her hands were scratched and bloody and they itched from contact with the loft insulation she'd had to keep pulling free. Reaching as high as possible, Samantha tried to grasp the top of a joist. Her fingertips found one, but she couldn't get a firm grip. She was too low.

Instead of despairing, she folded the towels over and deposited the detritus from the ceiling into the bathroom. Then, summoning her strength, she went back to the wall and started to cut out an extra step to allow her to climber higher.

Chapter 50

Campbell was back with the team, leaving Sarah at the hospital to recover from the effects of the caesarean section. The midwifes and nurses had sent him home, telling him to get some rest as he would be needed to look after both mother and baby when they returned from hospital. However, upon hearing of the kidnapping he'd offered his services without hesitation. He disagreed with Evans's insistence that only the team should be in the know and had listened aghast when Evans outlined his plan. The idea he was pitching was preposterous. It flouted dozens of protocols and if the brass got a sniff of it then it could end all their careers.

'No way am I getting mixed up in that. It's madness.'

Evan's had sneered at his protestations. 'Just listen to me, will you? You know what'll happen if we report this. A SOCA team will be sent from Manchester. They'll bring a dozen officers and will be as subtle as a terrorist attack. Within an hour of their arrival, the kidnappers will know they're involved. What do you think will happen then?'

It was a good point. Campbell would give him that. SOCA would turn up with their Enterprise vehicle. A 'red centre' would be established and they'd be sidelined from the investigation.

'It's too risky. Even if your plan works, which I doubt it will, there'll be hell to pay when the brass find out. We'll be lucky to stay out of jail, let alone keep our jobs. It's all right for you. You're retiring after tomorrow. I have a long career in front of me.'

'I don't give a shit about your career. All I care about is saving those kids. I'll take any rap going and tell the brass it was my idea.' Evans's voice was unexpectedly pleading. 'We're the only chance those kids have. Without us, they're doomed. If SOCA waltz in with their hostage negotiators, they'll just frighten the kidnappers off. The kids will be killed and their bodies dumped. I don't want that on my conscience. Do you?'

'It's illegal, immoral and a long shot at best.'

'True. But it's the only shot we've got. You're a father now. How far would you go to save Alan?'

Campbell winced at Evans's use of his son as a bargaining tool. The simple answer was that he'd do anything for his son. Take any risk to protect him.

'That's a low blow.'

'Well?'

'Are you sure Chisholm won't get caught?'

'Positive. He can get into places you can't begin to imagine. Raising the ransom will be a walk in the park for him.'

Weighing up the options and hearing Evans's repeated insistence that he'd bear the brunt of any fallout, Campbell made his decision. If Evans managed to save the kids, then he'd get some of the glory. If not, they'd at least have given it their best shot and he could lay all the blame on Evans.

'I'm in, provided that no shit sticks to me. I've got Alan and Sarah to think about.'

*   *   *

When they reached the Foulkes's home on Park End Road, Evans took Victoria's keys from his pocket and unlocked the door. The house was neat and tidy as Evans had instructed the search team to make as little mess as possible. This wasn't some drug dealer's house where they were ripping everything apart. This was a middle-class home, thus both the house and its owners were treated with more respect. The house was a large semi, with a steep roof cut around gabled dormer windows. The outer walls were rough-cut white sandstone, with keystone, lintels and sills of pink sandstone.

The lack of electrical goods in the house amazed Campbell. The house didn't have a TV, DVD player or a stereo in any room. Empty spaces and indented carpets spoke of recent furniture removal. Remarking on it to Evans, he learned that the Foulkes's had sold everything of saleable value in an attempt to raise money.

Checking the attic, he saw an area where the dust had been disturbed. He lifted the loft insulation. There was nothing but the plasterboard of the ceiling below.

'Is it there?' Evans's voice carried up from below.

'No. They must have found it.'

'I'll give them a call. Buggers should have been in touch wi' me though. What's the point of searching a property if you don't report what you've found?'

'You better phone Chisholm as well. Call him off.'

'The fuck you talking about? I'm not gonna call him off. I'm gonna tell him to adjust the amount he needs to collect. The numbers are irrelevant as far as I'm concerned.'

* * *

Evans piloted the BMW along the A66 and down the M6 above his usual excessive rate of knots. Taking the M55 towards the seaside town of Blackpool, they discussed their planned approach. Evans was to cause a distraction so Campbell could install a remote programme on one of their computers. Once the software was uploaded, Chisholm would be able to access the casino's network. Campbell knew that he'd have to guide Evans safely between his own renegade methods and correct procedure. He didn't fancy his chances of success though.

Parking at the South Shore car park, they walked across to the casino. The salty tang of sea air was carried by the evening breeze which threw tiny droplets of rain at them. They paid the admission fee, entered the casino floor and looked around. The casino was similar to the ones Campbell had been in, in Glasgow. There was a main floor with roulette tables, blackjack tables and various other small-stakes games. There were the ubiquitous slot machines lining every available inch of wall space. Two bouncers flanked a doorway below a flickering neon sign advertising a VIP suite where higher-stakes games would take place. The atmosphere was charged with nervous excitement tinged with desperation. The patrons all seemed intent on their gambling. The odd glance was thrown towards the waitresses dressed in showgirl costumes cut to show a lot of leg and generous amounts of cleavage.

Painting a smile of wonderment on his face, he looked up and spun through 360 degrees. He counted twenty obvious cameras and knew that there would be at least as many again. Evans nudged his arm and nodded towards a door marked private. There was a keypad to the left hand side of the door. Pretending to be choosing between the various gaming tables, Campbell waited until a waitress went through the door and memorised the access code she typed in.

When she returned, he gave Evans a wink and watched as the older man sat down at a blackjack table at the opposite side of the room. After a few minutes of gaming, he saw Evans summon a waitress. When the girl approached him with a smile, Evans leapt to his feet. Even from across the room, Campbell could hear Evans's words as he pretended to recognise the waitress as his daughter. Bouncers moved in towards Evans as he tried to haul the girl along by her wrist. Evans was demanding that the manager be called to explain why the girl he *knew* was his daughter was there.

One of the bouncers pulled a walkie-talkie from his pocket and put it to his mouth. Seconds later a well-dressed woman emerged from the door marked private. That was his cue. Campbell hit send on his mobile to alert Chisholm and typed the number into the keypad. He walked through the door, expecting to be stopped at any moment. Following a bland corridor, which held none of the cheap furnishings the public areas sported, Campbell found an open door. He slipped inside. In front of him was a desk with a PC and all the usual desk accoutrements; beyond them, the walls were lined with file laden shelves.

Campbell jiggled the mouse to see if the computer was active. When the screen came to life he sent a blank email to Chisholm who replied within seconds. There was an attachment with his reply. Campbell opened the attachment and watched as the screen went black for a microsecond before returning to the mail service. Closing the mail service down, Campbell exited the room and returned to the main room without incident. He couldn't believe the ease with which he'd breached the casino's security.

Campbell scanned the room for Evans and not finding him, he checked his phone and saw that there was a text from the older man.

Thrown out. In pub across road. If safe stay put. Keep me posted.

Ordering a bottle of beer from a waitress, Campbell took up station at a blackjack table which allowed him to keep an eye on the door he'd been through. He had been playing the game with minimum bets for less than ten minutes when he saw Evans approaching the entrance. As the bouncers moved to eject him a second time, he flashed his warrant card and walked across to join Campbell.

'That fucking bastard lied to us. According to Jabba, he's nearly a grand in credit with the casino.'

'Why would he do that?'

'Fuck knows. But I'm gonna use his guts as a washing line for wasting our time and endangering his kids like this.'

'Now what do we do?'

'We go and talk to the manager. See what he has to say about the lying prick.'

Campbell approached one of the bouncers, asking to speak to the manager. Again a walkie-talkie was used to summon the well-dressed woman. She was frowning to see Evans again and the expression did nothing to improve her looks.

'You again.' The woman's thick Liverpudlian accent grated on Campbell's ears and he struggled to make out what she was saying.

'DI Evans and DI Campbell. We've a few questions for you, Miss…'

'Hughes. And it's Mrs.' She brandished her left hand to emphasise the point. 'Will I need my lawyer present?'

'Not at all. We just need some help with our enquiries.' Campbell took the lead as Mrs Hughes watched Evans with evident suspicion.

'OK then. Come with me.'

They followed her to a quiet spot at the bar. Taking up station on a stool, Evans reached for a handful of the salt-coated nibbles on offer, while Campbell began the questioning.

'Do you have many VIP members?'

'I'm not at liberty to give specifics. All I can tell you is that we currently have between two and three hundred members. We cap membership at three fifty so the casino doesn't become overcrowded. If customers want to bet on sport, they can do it via our secure website.'

'How much is it to join?'

'It is two thousand pounds to join and one thousand pounds a year after that.'

'How often does Nicholas Foulkes come here?'

'I will handle that question, thank you, Rachel.' Unnoticed a suave man in his mid-fifties had arrived behind them. Dressed in an expensive three-piece suit, he looked every inch the successful businessman. Campbell guessed he was the real power behind the casino, and that Mrs Hughes was his daughter, employed so he could maintain control over her. He walked towards the two detectives, right hand extended and introduced himself. 'Gerry Potter. If you would like to come through to my office, I will help you in any way I can.'

Potter's office was both grandiose and functional. There was an ego wall featuring pictures of him with various Liverpool footballing legends. There were two different mayors, along with people Campbell supposed were local dignitaries.

Gesturing at the two seats on the opposite side of his desk, Potter settled into his own chair. 'I am afraid my daughter can be very protective of our little empire. Our customers are often influential people and we pride ourselves on our discretion. However, we understand that there are occasions when we are required to be more forthcoming. I feel it would be a dereliction of duty to not help you wherever possible. To summarise, tell me what you want to know and I'll answer any questions you have to the best of my ability.'

'You have a member called Nicholas Foulkes.' Campbell ignored the man's evident love of his own voice. 'We want to know everything you can tell me about his gambling and specifically how much money he owes you.'

Potter consulted his computer for a couple of minutes, before a printer click-clacked into life and spat forth five pages of headed paper. 'I am breeching client confidentiality by giving this information to you, detectives. However in consideration of the circumstances, I am of the opinion that I would be guilty of neglecting of my morality code were I not to facilitate your request with the utmost expediency.'

He sounds like the love child of a thesaurus and a dictionary.

'You what?'

'He said he'll help us, you imbecile. D'you not understand the Queen's English?' Evans took the offered sheets and moved his arm back and forth until the top sheet was in focus.

'That is correct, detective. If you look at his account history you will see that he is very lucky when selecting horses, but whenever he comes in to play cards he loses all the money he has amassed.'

'That's fishier than a North Sea trawler. No way can he win on the horses and lose at cards. There's got to be a con somewhere.'

'Detective, I resent the insinuation that my establishment would engage in confidence tricks with our customers. We merely provide comfortable amenities where our clients may fulfil their desire to take a financial risk. The very suggestion that either I or my staff are obtaining money from customers by unfair means is abhorrent to me.'

'It's transparently obvious to the appreciative observer that there is a serious anomaly in the finances displayed here.' Campbell bit his lip as Evans played Potter at his own linguistic game. Looking up from Foulkes's account statements Evans locked eyes with the man. 'Pursuant to our investigations, Mr Potter, our mandate is crystalline in its opacity. We have authorisation to procure a warrant to impound the previous and incumbent year's accounts for your organisation. Our intention is not to cause unnecessary disruption to your business. However, we will be consulting with all of your customers, to seek illumination upon our enquiries. I should imagine those conversations will have a detrimental effect on customer perception of your confidentiality practices. Now will you please tell us what the *fucking* score is, before I have Blackpool's finest rip your business apart!'

'There is no need to resort to foul language or threats, detective. I have offered unresisting cooperation and will continue to do so. Some of our clients win and others lose. That is a simple fact of gambling.'

Campbell could see the first signs of serious resistance in Potter. To prevent Evans from alienating the man altogether, he tried another tack, 'Say we believe you, Mr Potter. He named this as the place where he ran up the gambling debts, which led to the case we are now investigating. If you owe him money, why didn't he cash it in to pay his debts?'

'Our policy is that a client can only draw money out of the casino when they have more than five thousand pounds amassed. It's in our terms and conditions.'

Evans opened his mouth to speak, but Campbell shot him a look then turned back to Potter. 'So where do you think his debts are from then? Did he meet with other clients to play elsewhere? Or is he a member of another such club?'

'I cannot possibly comment on his membership at other establishments. If you are prepared to wait, I'll look at our records and see if there is a pattern to his visits.'

'Would you also be able to ascertain if specific individuals frequent your establishment in conjunction with his visits?' Evans's request was well-mannered but there was no mistaking the anger in his tone.

'Yes, I can do that for you.'

Evans took up station behind Potter, watching everything that happened on the computer screen.

After fiddling with system reports, Potter leaned back in his chair and reached across to the printer, which had spat out several more pages. Sorting them he found the report that detailed the clients whose visits had matched those of Nicholas Foulkes. There were fourteen names on the list.

Campbell looked at the list before asking, 'Is there a way you can bring up the number of visits each of these people made without Foulkes being present.' He pointed at the names of some minor celebrities. 'You can discount these guys as they're not likely to be mixed up in anything.'

Potter turned back to his screen to fulfil Evans's request. Another sheet of paper exited the printer. Five of the remaining eleven were regular visitors who were at the casino most weeks, another three were also more regular visitors than Foulkes, which left the last two. One of whom matched the visits of Foulkes with a perfect accuracy. The other had just three visits to his name.

'I do believe that Mr Teller is from the Cumbria area as well and that they travel here together.'

'Teller? Not Frankie Teller?'

Campbell ran his finger down the list. 'That's the name on here, Harry. Who is he?'

'He owns the largest building firm in Cumbria. Now then Potter, what can you tell me about the other guy on here. Keith Morgan?'

'I am afraid that I do not know him well. He has always conducted himself well at Aces High, but there are some rumours about him being connected with... um... organised crime. I've tried to find out more so I could exclude him, but nobody would confirm any of the rumours. When I think of it, he and Mr Foulkes enjoyed a game of poker at the same table.' Potter interpreted Campbell's sceptical look. 'Because Mr Morgan was a person of interest, I spent no small amount of time and resources observing him in close detail.'

'I want to speak to him. What's his address? What information do you have on him?'

Potter aimed a finger at the printer, which started to whirr.

Evans snatched its latest missive and held it at arms length, squinting at the information. 'Do you have his personal details as well?'

'I am not sure I should disclose such private information unless you can prove its pertinence to your investigation.'

'You've got ten seconds before I leave and come back with Willy the Warrant.'

Potter sighed, turned back to his computer and sent the required information to the printer.

Campbell got the sheet containing Morgan's details and strode towards the door with Evans in tow. As Evans reached the door he turned to deliver a parting shot. 'D'you understand what'll happen if I find out you've been holding out on me? To quote a well-known actor – I'll be back!'

Campbell managed to keep his laughter inside until they reached the car, then he doubled over, tears streaming from his eyes. 'I can't believe you just said that. And your attempt at the accent was terrible.'

'Bastard deserved it. Did you hear him speak? It was like listening to some bugger reading a legal document. If he'd used the word aforementioned, I was gonna punch him. Now pull yourself together and call Chisholm with that info. I want him on the trail of this guy's money.'

Evans punched Morgan's postcode into his satnav before gunning the engine and setting off towards Liverpool.

Chapter 51

Frances was a light sleeper. The barn door creaking open was enough to rouse her. She awoke with a suddenness only an unfamiliar noise can produce. Swinging her arthritic legs out of the bed, she padded across to the window.

As she drew back the curtain, she could see human shapes moving around in the moonlight. A small cattle wagon was parked by the barn, its rear door formed a ramp. Two of the figures were pushing her quad bike towards the ramp.

Moving back to the bed, she dialled her son, the number recalled by practiced fingers rather than memory. Since her husband's death last year, he now ran the farm despite living in a two-up two-down in Ambleside. Frances had suggested they swap homes but the offer had been declined. She knew that once her day had gone, her daughter-in-law would gut the house, throwing out the things she'd amassed over a lifetime and adding her own minimalist touches.

His mobile went straight to answering service. Presuming, once again, he'd let the battery go flat, she dialled treble nine and recounted her story to the bored sounding operator who told her someone would be there within an hour.

'That's no bloody good. They're robbing me now.'

'I'm sorry, but that's the soonest we can have someone with you. Make sure that you stay inside with the doors locked. Don't switch on any lights. If they are the gang we've been chasing, they are not believed to be dangerous. All the same, we don't want you taking any unnecessary risks. Hello... Hello... Mrs Elliott?... Are you still there Mrs Elliott?'

Frances lost patience with the call handler and dropped the receiver onto the bed. If the police weren't going to be here for an hour, she'd have to stop the thieves herself.

The farm had been in her family for generations. Over the centuries, they had battled sheep rustlers, encroaching neighbours and herd-destroying epidemics like foot and mouth. She'd be damned if she was going to allow anyone to rob her now.

Pulling on her quilted dressing gown, she crept downstairs and went to the cupboard where the shotgun was kept. According to the letter of the law, the shotgun ought to have been in a locked gun cabinet but the idea was ridiculous to her. There had always been guns on the farm and they'd never been locked away, even when Andrew and Elaine were children. She broke open a twelve bore and inserted two cartridges with experienced hands, despite not having fired a shot for twenty plus years. Removing the security chain from her front door, she eased it open and flicked the hall light on so she was backlit. Lifting the shotgun to her shoulder, Frances took a deep breath and raised her voice to a yell. 'Bugger off. I've called the police and they're on their way.'

She squeezed the trigger of the shotgun and fired a blast of pellets high into the air. Frances had forgotten the power of a shotgun's kick and failed to pull it tight against her shoulder. The stock smashed into her collarbone and rocked her off balance. As she fell backwards her head slammed against the dresser. She was unconscious before her frail body hit the floor.

Chapter 52

Campbell was perturbed. There was a distinct lack of residential property in the area. They were on the outskirts of the city centre, and all he had seen for the last couple of hundred metres were shops, various bars and restaurants and a stream of takeaways.

Evans interrupted his train of thought with a complaint. 'This isn't bloody Penneigh Lane. It's Matthew Street!' He drove along the narrow street until bollards halted his progress. The satnav announcing they'd reached their destination.

'Look.' Evans cast his gaze to where Campbell was pointing, and saw the world-famous Cavern Club – the place where the Beatles started on the road to fame.

'Fucking satnav must be wrong.'

'This must be wrong too.' Campbell showed him the app on his phone.

'The fly bastard! I'm gonna go back there and rip that Potter a new arsehole.'

'It's not him. Morgan is the one we're after. You heard what Chisholm said: he's run both of them and Morgan is definitely a person of interest to Merseyside Police. Potter checks out.'

Evans's temper wasn't appeased. He turned the air blue with a rant that lasted until they left Liverpool and were on the motorway back to Cumbria. Ignoring the older man's invective, Campbell attacked the puzzle from as many angles as he could. Whichever way he looked at it, he could not get past the thought that while Morgan was the likely candidate to be behind the kidnapping, there was no easy way to find him. He hadn't attended the casino since the children were taken. The information Chisholm had unearthed on Morgan supported the name and address he'd registered at the club. That the address was a dead end pointed to the whole identity being false. With no real name, address or other information to go on there was nothing they could pursue, unless Potter had retained CCTV footage of his last visit. The chances of that were low. With so many cameras in the casino, the amount of footage would be immense. Plus, he suspected the cameras would automatically over-write the previous day's footage unless there was a specific incident.

The Merseyside police neglecting to tell Chisholm that address was false didn't surprise him. There was supposed to be full cooperation between different forces. In reality, each force was territorial: when one encroached on their patch, the other offered the minimum help possible. However, Campbell was surprised Chisholm hadn't spotted the address was false. Campbell expected that the computer geek to have used Google StreetView to check out the site. He knew he would have. Five minutes on a computer would have saved them a wasted hour travelling to Liverpool, not counting the hour it would take to get back. He would have to take it up with Chisholm in private the next day.

Rather than draw Evans's attention to the mistake, Campbell asked him what he thought they could do next.

'Fuck all tonight. It's gonna be after two by the time we get back to Carlisle. We'll grab a couple of hours' kip. Tomorrow will be a bloody long day.'

Evans put a call through to Chisholm, told him of the false address and gave him a set of new instructions.

Chapter 53

The attic was pitch black. She used touch alone as a way of navigation. A sliver of light seeped through the hole she'd made and what did, gave her no help whatsoever. She was on edge with each movement she made. There was so much that could go wrong. A careless foot could go through a ceiling. If the TV aerial was in the loft, knocking it could bring the men into the roof space to realign it. The scratchy glass-fibre insulation against her bare skin made her body shiver involuntarily. Though she couldn't see it, every move she made kicked up a plume of dust which swirled up her nose. The only way she prevented a sneezing fit was by sacrificing one exploring hand to keep her nostrils pinched together. Cobwebs adhered themselves to her groping fingers and tangled into her unkempt hair, their fine threads caressing her face.

Samantha lowered herself through the hole in the ceiling and groped with her toes. Finding one of her improvised steps, she clambered back down into the bedroom. Reaching floor level, she related to Kyle what she'd found up there and then took a quick shower to try and ease the discomfort caused by the loft insulation.

Clumping footsteps sent panic through her. It would be terrible to be caught again, when she was so close to fashioning another escape route. She didn't fear Elvis's threat of dismemberment anymore. She had resigned herself to the fact it would be her fate at midnight tomorrow unless her latest escape attempt worked. She breathed a sigh of relief when the door didn't open, and then concentrated on finessing the details of her plan for tomorrow.

She'd found the access hatch into the loft. There was no loft ladder, but she was confident she could hang down and drop the last couple of feet both quietly and without injury. If Kyle lowered himself down, she could take his weight and lower him to the floor. It was too risky to try now with the men settling down into their bedtime routine. She would have wait to try until tomorrow. With the decision made, she prepared herself for a long night of sleepless anticipation.

Chapter 54

Victoria lay curled up on Samantha's bed. Clutched in her arms was Kyle's beloved soft Super Mario toy. Everything had unravelled. Her plan to raise the money had been so close to completion when she and Nicholas had been arrested. Now the only chance she had of getting her children back unhurt was in the hands of a semi-alcoholic detective whose best days were behind him.

The first thing she had checked, upon returning home, was the attic but just as the police had told her, the money had been confiscated. She hadn't had chance to speak to Nicholas at the police station. Not that she had anything she wanted to say to him. But the chance to shout at him, to berate him once more for the trouble he'd caused would have given her a small crumb of comfort. The rage at Nicholas's stupidity was a growing fist within her gut. It held her intestines in a vice grip which twisted and pulled without mercy.

Overpowered by a spike of anger, Victoria sprang from the bed and went into her own bedroom. Throwing open the wardrobe doors she grabbed Nicholas's clothes, tearing and ripping them as she launched them across the room. Always a natty dresser, Nicholas took great pride in his appearance. She knew he would feel actual pain at seeing his expensive clothes ruined.

It wasn't enough to loosen the fist in her gut. Swinging the window open, Victoria ejected his torn clothing. Shoes followed shirts. Suits fluttered out of the window to join the growing heap. She grabbed her lighter and an old newspaper on her way through the kitchen, and stalked outside into the garden. Moving the pile of clothes away from the house, she scrunched the pages of the newspaper into balls and thumbed her lighter.

As the newspaper caught fire she added Nicholas's clothes one by one, until they were all smouldering. Watching the flames take hold loosened the fist's iron grip on her stomach.

Now released, her anger turned to despair. Victoria felt a wave of emotion smother her body. Falling to the ground she wept until she could weep no more. The dying embers of the fire cast flickering shadows across her face as she lay on the wet grass, oblivious to the falling drizzle.

Chapter 55

Friday

Finishing his call with Sarah, Campbell walked into the office to find the team assembled. Chisholm's desk was littered with empty Red Bull cans, his bin overflowed with the plastic cups dispensed by the vending machine in the hall and an empty pizza box lay on the floor beside his chair. If this was not indication enough he'd never left his desk, the unshaven chin and bloodshot eyes would have told of his nightshift.

'Any news?'

It was Evans who answered him. 'Nowt on the kidnappings. An elderly woman was found unconscious in a farmhouse near Windermere. A shotgun was lying beside her. She came round when she was taken to Westmorland General.'

'Who found her?'

'Her son when he arrived for work at half five. When she came round she told the attending officer that she'd fired a warning shot at some thieves. She also said she'd seen shadowy figures loading things into a small cattle wagon.'

'Sounds like our thieves, but we've got to prioritise the kidnappings surely?' Campbell was pleased his theory had paid off but was more concerned about the two children. They had only sixteen hours left before the deadline and no leads whatsoever.

'Of course we have to prioritise the bloody kidnappings. Do you think I'm fucking stupid?'

'So what do you propose then?' Campbell squared up to Evans, unafraid to challenge him.

'I want to see what that lying fucker Nicholas Foulkes has to say about Keith Morgan. If I don't learn owt helpful, you and me are gonna go see Frankie Teller and drop in on the old dear who saw the burglars.'

'At what point do you inform the brass?'

'I don't. If we can't find them by midnight, then we'll pay the ransom and deal with tracing them afterwards.'

Even after a night's sleep, Campbell still wasn't convinced about Evans's plan, so he argued the points that troubled him most. 'How the hell are you gonna pay the ransom? Isn't it against all police and government principles to be extorted?'

'Chisholm will sort the ransom, and for all intents and purposes it will be the Foulkes's who make the payment.'

Campbell bit back a response. Evans was risking everyone's career and Campbell had no idea if it was worth it. Should he turn a blind eye and help Evans, or should he be a good little boy and trot off to the DCI to whisper tales into his ear? Too much was at stake to make the wrong decision. Not least for his own career. This was a great chance for him to make his mark on the force and perhaps overturn the limit that had been put on his prospects for promotion.

Turning to Chisholm he asked for details on how the money would be acquired.

'You sure you want to know, guv?' Chisholm flicked a glance at Evans asking for permission to inform Campbell of their plan.

'No, I'm not sure. But if I'm involved, then I need to know everything.' Campbell gestured for Chisholm to speak.

'Basically we're gonna transfer a penny from lots of different accounts into the Foulkes's account.'

'That's theft.' Campbell shook his head. 'There's no way I can be a party to anything like that. You'll get caught in no time. Besides, how are you gonna make that happen?'

'We won't get caught, guv.' Chisholm's voice was soft. 'I'm writing a programme which will transfer one penny into and out of millions of bank accounts. When the programme is finished, enough of those pennies will have found their way into the Foulkes's account to pay the ransom.'

'What about bank security systems, firewalls, all the measures in place to stop people doing exactly what you're planning to do?'

Chisholm smiled. 'Don't worry about that, sir. I've never yet met a system I can't get into. The sheer volume of transactions I'm planning will take a hundred analysts a lifetime to trace.

And when they've finally checked the millions of transactions for every account, they will find a very small percentage of them out by just one penny. Trust me, it's not worth anybody's time chasing after us when all they'll find is the odd missing penny.'

'It's still theft.' Campbell jerked his head forward as he spat the words.

'Technically it is borrowing, sir. The money will be returned to the accounts as soon as the children have been rescued. I'm gonna insert a retrieval code which will follow the money and identify the kidnappers account.'

'That won't be admissible in any court.'

Evans stepped in. 'No, it won't. But it'll save two children from a terrible fate. Now stop wasting his time and get cracking. Paying the ransom is a last resort.'

Campbell shuffled papers across his desk trying to find anything that might give them a breakthrough. The mother had given them a registration number for the kidnappers' van. It had been a dead end. The number plate belonged to a Ford Mondeo, registered in Aberdeenshire. He turned to the CCTV footage supplied by Potter, which showed Keith Morgan to be a short, barrel-shaped man in his mid-fifties. Well-dressed, with salt-and-pepper hair, Morgan cast an intimidating presence on-screen. In person, he'd be able to dominate people, bending them to his will through sheer power of personality.

Looking up, he saw Evans in conversation with Lauren. Evans pulled out his wallet and handed a sheaf of notes to her. Campbell noticed that the young woman wasn't wearing her usual attire of short skirt and revealing top. Today's clothes were unflattering black trousers and a loose pink top.

Turning his focus back to the case, he got Evans's attention. 'Harry, I want to question Nicholas Foulkes. Let's get him to tell us everything.'

'Me and Lauren are gonna speak with him just as soon as she comes back. We're gonna break that lying bastard.'

Chapter 56

Evans was desperate to get Nicholas Foulkes to talk, but reason told him the man was holding out on him out of fear for his children's safety. He knew that to get truth from Foulkes he'd need to break his resistance. He'd tried interrogating him when he'd arrived at the station. Rousing him from his sleep, Evans had tried to break Foulkes without success. Foulkes had stuck to the same lie despite all the insults and threats he had thrown at him. More drastic measures were called for, and that's what he'd conspired with Lauren for. She had been agreeable to his plan.

He couldn't understand the DC's propensity for exhibitionism. She delighted in flaunting herself, making herself desired by every man who came into her orbit. His Janet had been different. She had been shy and reserved, possessed of a grace far more entrancing than the slutty behaviour Lauren displayed. Janet knew her looks attracted men's attention, but she never set out to capitalise on it, whereas Lauren was brazen in her choice of clothing and open about her busy sex life.

'I'm ready, guv.' Lauren's head poking around the office door interrupted his reverie.

'You sure about this?'

''Course I am. If it wasn't so serious then it'd be fun.'

That little slapper is getting off on this.

Evans despised himself for what he and Lauren were about to do, but there was no way he was not going to do it. The thought of those two children alone and afraid was too much for him to bear.

'C'mon then, lass, let's get it over with.'

As they walked past, Campbell stood and confronted Evans, his hand extended towards Lauren. 'Harry, whatever you're planning is a serious no-no. Getting Lauren clothes like this and making her wear them in the office is a step too far. I think DCI Tyler should hear about this.'

'Excuse me, DI Campbell, but if I have a problem with DI Evans's conduct then I'll deal with it myself. I know you've noticed that I always wear revealing clothes. DI Evans is the one man in this room who looks at my face when he's talking to me.' Lauren smirked as Campbell, Bhaki and Chisholm all started examining their shoes or vague spots around the ceiling. The back of Chisholm's neck was fire engine red as he hunched over his keyboard. Her mocking tone wrapped in pure venom 'I dress the way I do because I enjoy the attention. If it was warm enough and PSD would let me, I'd wear a bloody bikini. If DI Evans is asking me to wear this, then he's got a reason that's sod all to do with getting his jollies.'

Evans had watched the exchange with as near to wry amusement as his escalating temper would let him. 'Turn that radiator back down, Jabba.' Chisholm stopped fumbling about at the side of his desk. 'She won't ever be wearing a bikini in this office. Lauren, put your coat on and come with me. The rest of you can work out our next move. See if you can think up a way to find those poor bloody kids.'

Taking a deep breath and putting on a polite mask, Evans entered the interview suite and spoke with a false bonhomie. 'Me again, Nicholas. DC Phillips here has a few questions for you.'

Evans could see wary suspicion in Foulkes's eyes as he answered. 'I don't see how I can help you, I've told you everything.'

'You can start by telling us the truth. This is off the record and whatever you say stays between us.' Evans held a hand up to stall Foulkes's protest. He gestured at the controls for the suite's various recording devices. 'None of what we discuss in here will be recorded. The only people who'll be told will be members of my team.'

He took a seat opposite the man and took in his haggard face. 'What can you tell us about Keith Morgan and your real gambling debts to him?'

'Nothing. I've told you everything.'

Evans could tell that Foulkes was lying. He could also see fear in the man. 'Let me show you something, Nicholas. I want you to understand exactly what they are doing to your daughter.'

He nodded at Lauren, who stood up and peeled off her coat revealing a French Maid costume.

'This is what they made your daughter wear, Nicholas. Young Samantha, aged seventeen made to parade around in a sex costume. We've watched the videos, Nicholas. Watch DC Phillips as she moves around the room. Every eyeful you get of her is the same eyeful those bastards are getting of your daughter. We've been through her wardrobe, looked at her Facebook pictures. She doesn't wear clothes half as revealing as her friends do. She keeps herself covered up.'

'I know, I know.' Foulkes was sobbing and hiding his eyes with one hand.

'Tell us what you know so we can catch these bastards and save your kids.'

'I can't, he'll kill us all. He threatened me after the second card school I attended.'

'Tell us.' The two words were a command and entreaty in equal measure. When Nicholas's head shook, Evans gave a resigned nod to Lauren who moved behind Foulkes and removed the maid's outfit.

Underneath the costume she was wearing a red lacy dress identical to the one Samantha had worn in the second video.

Lauren moved until she was stood right in front of Foulkes and spoke for the first time since entering the room. 'Nicholas.' He lifted his head and focused his eyes on hers. 'Look at me. Can you see my nipples through the sheer material? Do you remember Samantha being filmed wearing a dress like this one?'

'Please. Stop this.'

'That's probably what Samantha said. She didn't have a choice. You do.'

'I don't.'

'You have to think how she felt, dressed like this against her will. She'd be expecting to be raped any minute. I know I'd be expecting it.'

Nicholas's gaze moved from Lauren to Evans. 'Please. Stop her behaving like this. Please stop her.'

'She's right, Nicholas.' Evans kept his voice soft. 'Samantha will have been terrified of being raped from the moment they were taken. I'll bet that being forced to dress like that will have made her expect it even more.'

'I'll tell you something, Nicholas, I'm a bit of a slapper. I think I've got a lovely body and I love showing it off with short skirts, sheer tops and so on. I love the attention my clothes get me. By wearing the clothes I do, I can pull almost any man want to. I can feel their eyes drinking me in. I can sense their lust and desire. By dressing the way I do, I'm the one in control. Do you think Samantha is in control? Do you think she can manipulate men the way I can?' Lauren's voice was filled with scorn as she fired the questions at Nicholas.

'No.' His head was in his hands. He could hardly speak for the sobs emanating from deep inside his body.

Before Evans could stop her, she grabbed Nicholas by the hair and lifted his head so it was level with her chest, and slapped him hard across the face.

'Do I have to go on, or are you gonna grow a pair of balls and tell us what we need to know so we can rescue your daughter? Or are you gonna leave her to be tormented and raped by the men who have her and Kyle at their mercy?'

'OK, OK, I'll tell you.' There was defeat and self-pity written all over Nicholas's face, his voice cracked like ice cubes in a cold drink.

Not bothering to cover herself up, Lauren sat down in front of Nicholas and asked in a gentler tone. 'Who is he and how did you meet?'

'We met by chance at Aces High, the casino I told you about yesterday.'

'Who introduced you?'

'Nobody really. We were at the same poker table and got talking.'

'And then what?'

'He asked me if I fancied a high-stakes game with no limits.'

'And you said yes,' Evans's words a statement rather than a question. 'Fuck's sakes, Nicholas. Hadn't losing money at Aces High taught you that you're shit at cards?'

'I thought that I could have a big win and make all my losses back. Once I was into him for over fifty grand, I kept chasing a big win to clear my debts. It never happened, though.'

'You dickhead. You even wasted our time yesterday with your lies about owing the money to Aces High. I've seen your account. You're in credit with them for God's sake. That time wasted meant another day for your kids to stay in the pervert's hands.'

Lauren asked the next question, cutting Evans off. 'Where and when did these card schools take place?'

'They were at different hotels every time. Usually a county house hotel, in or near the lakes. Keith Morgan would hire a suite and we'd all go, have dinner and then a game of cards. They were held on the last Friday of every month.'

'Did Frankie Teller join you for these games?'

'God, no. He hated Keith and told me to stay away from him.'

'You should've bloody listened to him. You'd have saved that lad and lass of yours a shedload of grief.'

Lauren waved Evans down to keep him quiet. 'Nicholas, can you tell me how these games were arranged? And can you remember which hotels you went to and on what dates?'

'I'd get a text two days before each game. It told me the name of the hotel, the postcode and a time. The games were always on the second Friday of the month.'

'Have you still got his texts in your phone?'

'Yes, but the texts came from a different number each time. I tried calling once to say I couldn't make it but there was just a message saying the number was not in circulation.'

Evans lifted his mobile from the desk and called Chisholm. 'Run a trace on the father's mobile for every text he got on the second Wednesday of every month.'

'So where did they take place?'.

Nicholas recited the locations. He described Keith Morgan as being short and stocky, around fifty-four or fifty-five years old. He described Morgan as being initially charming until he was in debt. He'd turned nasty and Nicholas was intimidated by him and daren't refuse him anything. Then the threats had come: 'Pay up or else. If you don't pay up, then you'll be sorry. We know where you live, where you kids go to school.' He'd remortgaged the house and his shop without telling his wife, but still hadn't been able to clear his debt.

Nicholas only knew the first names of the other players, in two cases he could only remember a nickname. Each of the men had sported either a Lancastrian, Cumbrian or Scouse accent which muddied the waters further. Some of the players were shady like Morgan, most others had been enticed into the card school the same way as him. He knew that two of the latter group were also members of Aces High.

Feeling they had got the truth from him, Evans dismissed him with a warning that if he found out Nicholas had kept anything back, he wouldn't be responsible for his actions. Evans was pleased to have got the information he needed, but disturbed by the methods he'd had to use. Even for him, dressing someone up like that to force a confession was low. Also troubling him were the urges the sight of Lauren's body had awoken. He was disgusted at himself, but he knew that he'd soon have to have his itch scratched.

Chapter 57

Campbell was rereading statements when Lauren and Evans returned to the office. Lauren's face was shining with triumph while Evans wore a mixed expression of self-loathing and smugness.

They've got the result they were after. Brilliant. Now we've got a lead, we can maybe crack this before Chisholm steals the money.

Something wasn't right though. The disgust on Evans's face indicated not all the news was good. Before he could ask, Lauren started to tell him of the interview. Evans was scratching his backside with a miner's attention to depth, while Chisholm was busy writing a programme to collect the ransom money. When Lauren had finished, Campbell turned to Chisholm. 'What's the score with the father's mobile?'

'Those numbers were from pay-as-you-go phones, sir. Bought for cash at various places in the Liverpool area.'

'Shit.' Buying pay-as-you-go phones was step number one for criminal gangs who didn't want to be traced. If by some miracle they could identify the buyer and track them down, he knew they'd only be told that the phone had been sold to a stranger in a pub, and no, they couldn't remember the pub or what the stranger's name was.

'That speaks of organised crime to me.'

'Well, duh.' Campbell regretted using the slang term as soon as it left his lips. It was both immature and insulting to Bhaki.

Evans glared but cut off his apology with a waved hand. 'Of course it's organised crime. It's a kidnapping, for fuck's sakes. However, it does tell us they are properly organised, not some bunch of amateurs. Those phones were bought at different places on different days. Half-arsed chancers would have bought a bunch of them from one shop on the same day.'

'Can we ask Merseyside police to take a look and see if they can trace the sales from CCTV footage? Maybe they'll at least be able to identify someone who is known to them and then we can trace the gang that way.' Campbell knew it was a long shot but they had to do everything they could.

'I doubt it'll work but it's worth a try.' Evans thumbed his mobile, scrolling in search of a number. 'Chisholm, put all the dates and locations into an email. I'll give you the address in a minute.'

'Mike? Harry Evans here...'

While Evans was on the phone, Campbell gave Bhaki a quick apology and listened to Lauren recount the rest of the interview. Then he detailed Bhaki to speak to all the venues for the card games, while Lauren took a call from control.

He didn't fancy Bhaki's chances of success. He'd bet good money the venues lacked CCTV and had been paid for in cash. False names would have been given, but still they had to try. It was usually silly mistakes by criminals that gave them their best leads.

'Guv, Tommy and Terry have been spotted.'

Evans finished his call and turned to Lauren. 'Where? When?'

'Heading towards the Railway Inn, about twenty minutes ago.'

'Get whoever spotted them to keep an eye out until I get there. Jock! C'mon.' Evans's jacket swirled in his wake as he strode to the door.

'Who're Tommy and Terry?' Campbell looked around the room waiting for an answer.

'You'll see,' Bhaki gave a cryptic grin as Campbell ran after Evans.

* * *

'So who are Tommy and Terry then?'

Evans gave a tight smile. 'My best snouts. But whatever you do leave the talking to me as they hate Jocks.'

Looking at his watch as Evans navigated his way along Eastern Way onto Warwick Road. 'It's too early for the Railway Inn to be open. Where will they be going?'

'The Railway Inn. The landlord opens the back door at eight, for railway shift workers.'

'Why haven't they been closed down then?'

Evans took his eyes off the road long enough to throw Campbell a knowing glance. 'Because half the cops on nightshift go there for a pint after work. Anyone stupid enough to close the Railway down would be treated like a leper.'

Upon entering the Railway Inn via the back door, Campbell could see the pub's name was redolent throughout. Everywhere he looked was railway memorabilia, from the pictures of trains to the signal lamps that provided the lighting and framed timetables mounted on the central supporting column.

Evans told Campbell to get the drinks in as he made his way over to a corner table occupied by a wiry little man in his mid-forties. Opposite him were a full pint of Guinness and a half-drunk pint of Jennings bitter. Their conversation could be overheard from the bar, but the few patrons were too consumed with their own tired thoughts to listen.

'What do you want, pig? I thought you'd've been busy fitting up some bugger for a crime they didn't commit.' The Cumbrian accent was broad and harsh.

'Fuck off, Terry.' The man in front of Evans drained the Jennings, eyeing him with suspicion. 'It's Tommy I want to talk to.'

'Aye, well, he's not here, and if he was, I don't know why he'd want to talk to the likes ov you.' Abruptly, the man's voice changed into a Geordie burr and he addressed Evans with a smile. 'Howway, Harry, how you doing?' Any trace of hostility was eradicated from the booming voice. Tommy's politics were very different from Terry's.

'I'm fine, Tommy. Is your mother still in her flat or did she get moved to the secure housing I told you about?'

'The old girl is doing grand now she's moved. Thought she was gonna end up in a home though. I expect you'll be wanting to pick my brain about summat that's gan doon.' He took a mouthful of Guinness, leaving an off-white moustache on his face.

Campbell took a tray bearing three pints across and sat down beside Evans after handing a pint across to Tommy and Terry.

'Is this yan ov your copper mates, Evans? If it is, he can stick his pint up his bacon-flavoured arse.'

Without reacting to either the tone or Terry's words, Evans introduced the two men and again asked for Tommy.

'Who's he, Harry?'

'This is DI John Campbell. He's part of my new team.'

Tommy stood up and proffered his hand for Campbell to shake. 'Alreet?'

A bemused Campbell struggled to keep his face inscrutable as he shook the hand of the man before him. He was amazed at the man before him. Both Tommy and Terry appeared at random and seemed to co-exist inside one body with awareness and acceptance of each other's presence. Although he was aware of multiple personality disorder, he couldn't shake from his mind thoughts of Dr Jekyll and Mr Hyde.

'Diven't worry about Terry. He's all talk and no trousers.' He turned to Evans. 'So, Harry, what d'you want to know?'

'We want to know about a kidnapping in the area. Two kids have been taken and their parents have been told to pay up or else.' Evans let that sink in before showing Tommy a photo of Kyle and Samantha. 'Apparently the father has run up huge gambling debts and the kidnappers want them settled in full.'

'Poor buggers'll have no chance if you are investigating it. Ah reckon you pigs'll just nick the parents for illegal gambling.'

Campbell saw Evans's neck flushed red as his temper flared at Terry's jibe, but his voice was more or less even when he pressed for more information. 'What have you heard, Tommy? Are any of the local boys in on this or is it someone new coming onto the manor?'

'I diven't know owt about any kidnappings, but I do know that the Leightons are on the warpath. They diven't like the fact that there's been all them pubs and hotels robbed on their patch without them getting a cut. There's also all the stuff gan missing from the farms. They aren't in on that either. If they find out who's responsible before you do, there'll be bodies to bury for some poor sod.'

Campbell digested this information for a few seconds before Evans tried a different question. 'I take it the Leightons are looking into it themselves?'

'Aye, they are. And if they diven't know who's behind it, then it's nobody local.'

Evans drained his pint and stood up indicating the conversation was at an end. 'Thanks, Tommy. I'll leave a few pints behind the bar for you.'

'Cheers, Harry. I hope you get them bairns back safe and sound.'

Chapter 58

Evans had bullied the secretary of Teller Construction into giving him Frankie Teller's mobile number. A quick conversation with Teller saw the heavens align for once, as Evans found out Teller was visiting a construction site half a mile from the Westmorland General Hospital. He arranged a time to meet and powered south.

Arriving at Westmorland General, Evans parked in the staff car park and entered via the door beside the cafeteria. Although the kidnapping was his priority, he also wanted to check in on the woman in the faint hope he could point that investigation at a specific target. Approaching a nurse's station on the orthopaedic ward, he made enquiries as to Frances's location and health.

The duty nurse appraised him with a tired expression. 'She is not too badly hurt, but you can only speak to her for a couple of minutes. She has a mild concussion and is on a lot of medication for the pain in her shoulder. She'll be going down to theatre soon to have it rebuilt.'

'Hello, Mrs Elliott. I'm DI Evans. Do you think you can answer a few questions for me?'

The old woman on the bed fixed her rheumy eyes on Evans. 'Of course I can. It's my shoulder that's buggered not my brain.'

Knocked off-balance by the fierce life force emanating from her, Evans tried to justify himself. 'I just wanted to make sure you are up to it. That's all.'

'I'll be fine so long as you're quick. They're taking me down for an operation soon and they'll need to dope me up first.'

'Can you tell us what you saw?'

A scowl of concentration furrowed across Frances's brow. 'I didn't see owt much worth the mentioning. A few bodies running about helping themsel's to my stuff.'

'Did you manage to count how many there were?'

'I was just about to tell you when you interrupted me. I counted seven of the buggers.'

'Would you be able to identify any of them?'

A gentle shake of the head. 'It was dark and they were at the other end of my yard. All I could see were shapes.'

'What about a vehicle? Where were they putting the stuff they stole?'

'They had a cattle wagon. I could see them taking stuff into the back of it. I couldn't tell you what colour it was though. It was too dark.' A wave of disappointment washed over Frances's face.

Recognising there was nothing else she could tell him about the robbers, Evans sought to give her what comfort he could. 'Thank you for your help, Mrs Elliott. Your answers have confirmed our suspicions about the methods used.'

A wan smile touched Frances's lips. 'Don't flannel me, young man. I know that my answers have been next to useless. Just catch them will you? Farming is hard enough these days without being robbed.'

The nurse came in asking them to leave as they were bidding her goodbye. Evans left his card in case she remembered anything else and set off back to the car.

* * *

Campbell and Evans pulled up beside the Portakabins that housed bait rooms and offices on building sites the length and breadth of the country. All around, men bustled back and forth: joiners carrying timber, electricians with rolls of wire and foremen with sheaves of plans. Every person they could see was dressed in the uniform of the site worker: hard hats, checked shirts beneath hi-vis vests, jeans and steel toe-capped boots. Noise assaulted their ears from various generators and power tools. Every vehicle was reversing, if the cacophony of beeps was any indicator.

Evans led the way into the site office and asked for Teller.

'He's just out inspecting the site. Can I get you a cuppa?' Even the receptionist-cum-secretary was wearing jeans and boots, although hers were more stylish and much better fitting than any others they had seen.

'Now that what I call a builder's bum.' Evans frowned, but ignored the whispered comment from Campbell and instead studied the various plans and working regulations, taped or pinned to the walls of the office. He didn't like the way Campbell was turning out. Now that he was settling in a little, he seemed to be sex obsessed. The younger man had everything he'd lost. Evans was aware it was his own jealousy that was starting to turn him against the younger man. It was not a trait he was proud of.

As they were finishing their teas, a party of what must be architects and engineers came into the office engaged in a debate about fitting two pieces of roof together and the necessary cranage required. Recognising Teller, Evans levered himself from the chair he'd slumped in, waiting until the man caught his eye.

'Hi, Harry. Shall we go through here?' Teller pointed to the next office.

Evans introduced Campbell and asked Teller about Aces High and Nicholas Foulkes's gambling habits. Teller didn't pull any punches. 'Nicholas is a decent man but a terrible gambler. I never liked Morgan, though. I couldn't understand how Nicholas could be taken in by him when he was so clearly dodgy.'

'Do you know where Morgan lives?'

'No idea, I'm afraid. The less I know about him the better. I can spot a wrong'un a mile off and when I do, I steer clear.'

'What about the card games with Morgan?'

'What card games?'

'High-stakes poker games. Organised by Morgan.'

Teller looked bewildered. 'I don't know anything about any high-stakes poker games. Sorry, I can't help you about that.' A frown crossed Teller's face. 'Is there something wrong? Is Nicholas in trouble?'

'Not at all. He's helping us with our enquiries, that's all.'

Evans bade Teller goodbye, leaving him a card and instructions to call if he thought of anything else. Another dead end. It did not sit well with Evans. Never one for clockwatching, he found he was now constantly checking the time. Every minute was now precious and the ticking clock in his head was getting louder with each passing second. If only he'd made the connection sooner, the team would have had more time to find those children.

Chapter 59

Kyle clambered up Samantha's makeshift ladder with ease. Her arms were out, ready to catch him should he fall. His natural athleticism made her caution redundant. He was out of her reach in seconds and made his way into the attic without mishap.

'Urgh. It's dark and smelly up here.

'Shush. Remember what I told you. Have a look about and find the way I told you about.'

There was silence as Kyle peered into the gloom, picking out the route Samantha had told him to follow.

Keeping her voice to a whisper, Samantha checked his progress. 'Can you find it?'

'Yeah.'

'Good. Now go along it nice and quietly and then come back to the hole.'

''Kay.'

Samantha wanted Kyle to familiarise himself with the attic, so that when they made their final attempt to escape, he would be able to follow her in the dark attic. Tempting as it was to try now, she planned to wait for darkness. At what she hoped were regular intervals, she had gone into the bathroom and switched off the light. When the thin streams of light stopped coming through the ventilator fan, she would put her plan into action, provided she could hear no sounds of movement outside the bedroom door.

'Sam.' Kyle's head poked out of the hole in the ceiling.

'What?'

'Let's just go now.'

'No. Come down.' Seeing Kyle about to refuse, she added a little steel to her voice. 'Now.'

With a stony face, he clambered down.

'Why don't we try now? It was easy to get to.' His confidence buoyed her, but she wanted to stick to her plan.

'I want to wait until it's dark, that way we'll be harder to find if they start looking for us.'

'I guess.' His eyes locked onto her bare feet. 'How you gonna run with no shoes?'

'We'll go across the fields.'

'Fields?'

Realising she hadn't said anything about what she'd seen when she'd been taken downstairs, Samantha explained they were being held on a farm.

'Why don't we steal a tractor when we get out? They'll never be able to stop us then.'

Samantha smiled. In Kyle's world, tractors were all powerful vehicles that could do anything. Stealing a car or some other vehicle had crossed her mind before she discounted the idea. She'd only ever had a few driving lessons. It was one thing driving her instructor's car, with him sitting beside her offering advice and encouragement. It would be a different story altogether by herself and she didn't want to run the risk of being caught before getting out of the farmyard. Besides, if their captors had a second vehicle they would give chase. Samantha knew she wasn't a competent enough driver to win any kind of race. Either the kidnappers would catch her and force her to stop or she would crash in her attempts to get away.

'I don't know how to drive a tractor, and anyway, I bet there'll be no keys in them.'

'Oh.' Kyle's face dropped. 'Boohoo for no keys.'

'As soon as it's dark we'll go. OK?'

''Kay.'

Samantha didn't dare think what would happen if they failed this time. The same questions burned their way through her mind.

Would Elvis let Blair rape her if the ransom wasn't paid?

Would the men really use that torch on them?

Would they survive the threatened amputations?

How many limbs would the men cut off?

How could she protect Kyle?

Could she bring herself to ask for Kyle to be spared if she took his punishment?

Chapter 60

Evans treated a law-abiding driver to a stream of abuse accompanied by a series of hand gestures, which didn't require an expert in sign language to translate. Campbell had spent half the journey back to Carlisle talking to his wife. While Evans was pleased for the man, he still felt the tightness in his chest that belied his well wishes. The pride and love in Campbell's voice made his own loss even more acute.

Updates from Bhaki soured his mood further as every possible lead turned into a dead end. This case was like a darkened maze. Every time he thought the investigation had turned a corner he was faced with an identical blank wall. Nothing was going for them and he was wracked with doubts as to what to do. Never in his thirty years on the force had he been faced with such a situation.

He'd instructed Bhaki and Lauren to run interference for Chisholm, as he wanted his entire focus on obtaining the ransom through his bank-swindling programme. There was so much that could go wrong, he didn't dare believe Chisholm could get the money into the Foulkes's bank account undetected. A bank safety measure could derail Chisholm's efforts, as could a failure to break security codes or the ever-tightening noose of the deadline could prove too close for Chisholm's programmes to assemble the necessary funds.

He couldn't bear the idea that he may fail those kids. That they may suffer because of his own failings. Irrespective of what anyone told him, he believed he'd failed his own unborn child. Saving Samantha and Kyle was his chance for redemption. The days of sitting in court for Yates's trial would be torturous enough, without the added burden of a second major failure weighing on his shoulders.

The sound of his mobile going off jerked his mind away from his melancholy thoughts.

'Harry. It's Greg. I need to talk to you.'

'I'm with DI Campbell, sir, and you're on speaker.' If Greg was going to drop the hammer on him, he didn't want Campbell's commiserations before he'd had time to accept the news himself.

A pause as ACC Hadley chose his words with care. 'Come and see me as soon as you get back to the station.'

For the last few miles Evans was puzzling over Greg Hadley's request to see him. ACCs didn't summon DIs to their office themselves. A DCI or even a chief inspector usually ran such errands for them. As a rule of thumb, 'shit rolled downhill', each rank bollocked by the one above.

Without this chain of command, Evans figured Hadley wanted to see him regarding his future. The urgency of the meeting was not a good omen. However, there could be another reason his old friend had summoned him. Perhaps he'd found out about the kidnapping and how Evans had been keeping it secret from his superiors. If that was the case then he'd lose his job, pension and all entitlements on the spot. He needed information. To go into Hadley's office without any idea of the reason for the meeting could have disastrous consequences. If Hadley already knew about the kidnapping and his handling of it, the shit would have already hit the fan for his team. Evans put a call into the office and waited to see who answered.

'DC Philips.'

Lauren. Thank fuck. If she's still in the office answering the phone then the powers that be can't know about the kidnapping. Or could they?

'Lauren, it's me. Have you an update?' An innocuous question in case anyone was listening at her end.

''Fraid not, guv. DS Chisholm is still battering away at his keyboard. He only speaks to us when he wants another coffee.'

'I'll be back shortly. Tell Bhaki to go home and get a couple hours kip as he's on stakeout duty again tonight.'

Evans wasn't concerned about Bhaki's well-being or state of alertness. He wanted him out of the building, so he could speak to him before entering the police station. Something had been off in the conversation he'd just had with Lauren. A

261

missing element nagged at his mind, an observation as yet unprocessed but somehow vital.

Driving into the car park of the station he parked next to Bhaki's Golf. As the DC walked across to his car, realisation struck Evans. Hard. Chisholm hadn't been in the office. That's what was missing – the sound of a keyboard being pounded within an inch of its digital life. Whenever Chisholm was doing any kind of programming, he battered the keys making his keyboards rattle and clack as his hands tried to keep up with his brain.

Climbing out of the car, he called Bhaki over. 'They know, don't they?'

Incomprehension spread across Bhaki's face. 'Who knows, guv? And what do they know?'

'The brass. They know about the kidnapping. When I called in just now, Chisholm wasn't there. Just Lauren. They got her to act normal, didn't they?'

Sympathy edged its way into Bhaki's voice. 'No, guv. Nothing like that happened. DS Chisholm was in the toilet when you called. He's been gulping down energy drinks and coffee all day. It's the only time he's left his seat all day.'

Feeling stupid for his mistake, Evans made sure that he didn't meet Campbell's gaze. 'Fine. Get back to work. You can sleep later. There'll be a wooden top to wake you if anything happens.'

Chapter 61

The two men approached their boss, nervous about what they were about to say but neither prepared to let the matter drop.

'What do you want?' Marshall glared at his cohorts. He'd been watching them over the last few days and knew they were uneasy with their new role as kidnappers. There had been glances he wasn't supposed to see. Conversations had stopped when he'd walked into a room. He wondered whether they were about to walk out on him now that push was coming to shove.

Williams was their elected speaker. 'The ransom's due to be paid tonight. What happens if it isn't paid?'

'We'll do as we're told.'

'You've gotta be kidding.' Williams shook his head. 'That boy's only about eight or nine. Surely you're not gonna let that sick fucker Billy use his acetylene torch on a kid that young. Hell, the lassie isn't that much older.'

Marshall sighed. 'Like I said. We do as we're told.'

'And what exactly have we been told?' Pete Johnstone spoke for the first time, supporting his friend.

'You know what we've been told. Take a limb off each of them and then upload the video to the site along with directions to wherever we dump them.'

Williams screwed his face in revulsion. 'If that's what you're gonna do then we're leaving now. If we get caught doing this, we'll do a lot of very hard time. We didn't sign up to maim and torture kids. A bit of stealing here and there, you said. Helping to kidnap them was bad enough, but this is way too heavy for us.'

'So. You're walking out on us then?'

'I ain't staying round here to get involved in that shit. Are you, Pete?'

'No chance. I want nowt to do with cutting limbs off kids.'

'I'd think long and hard before you did anything like that. You don't know the boss as well as I do. When he learns you abandoned us, he'll come after you.' Marshall lit a cigarette and leaned back in his chair. 'It won't be anything personal. It'll be business. He makes it his business to make sure his men do as they're told.'

'So now you've resorted to threatening us?'

'Me? I'm not threatening you. I'm warning you that the man you're planning on crossing will not take it lightly.'

'So that's it then? Fucked if we stay, fucked if we leave?'

'That's one way of putting it, but you can think yourselves lucky: you'll be out on the rob tonight while I'll be here with Billy.'

The two men left and Marshall smoked his cigarette and contemplated their role as kidnappers. He wouldn't admit it to anyone, but he felt the same as Johnstone and Williams. Mutilating kids was a terrible thing to contemplate. His boss had no qualms about such methods and he knew from painful experience that any sign of disobedience incurred brutal retribution.

Billy Alker was his boss's private torturer. The man derived a perverse satisfaction from inflicting pain on others. He would be happy to take his acetylene torch to the kids, although in all probability he'd try to rape the girl first. It had taken all of Marshall's efforts to make sure it hadn't already happened. This kidnapping hadn't turned out the way he'd expected. He'd thought the father would have found the money by now and paid up. As the deadline was nearing with no sign of payment, there was every possibility he'd have to deliver those poor kids into Alker's hands.

Johnstone and Williams might complain, but by his reckoning they had it easy. They'd be meeting up with the boys from Liverpool to burgle two of the farms he'd pinpointed. Two more wagonloads of stolen goods would come in tonight. Once they'd been stripped of all identifying plates and serial numbers they would be moved out and sold on at various points around the country. After that there would be one more week here, before they packed up and moved on. In the meantime, it was left to him to prevent Billy Alker raping the girl.

Thank God this job is nearly finished.

Chapter 62

Evans took a deep breath then gave a single rap on the door of Hadley's office. The next five minutes would either end his police career or give him the lifeline he'd been praying for. The only solace he could find was the kidnapping remained unknown to his superiors.

'Come.'

Opening the door he walked into Hadley's office and obeying the waved hand sat in the ergonomic seat opposite Hadley.

Without asking Evans if he wanted a drink, Hadley retrieved his bottle of whisky and poured two generous measures.

The sight of the whisky intimated both good and bad news to Evans. Good, because there was no way he'd be getting whisky if Hadley knew he'd covered up a kidnapping. Bad, because of the size of the measures: Hadley wasn't a big drinker, yet his glass held three fingers of whisky, neat. His face was set in an inscrutable mask.

'What's the score then, Greg? Do I get to keep my job or not?'

'Not.' A pause as Hadley took a drink to give Evans time to process the news. 'I'm sorry, Harry, but the chief constable himself has stepped in on this one.'

'That sneaky bastard.' Evans's tone was full of resentment. 'He's spent more time climbing the greasy pole than he has policing. What the fuck does he know about anything?'

'He knows all about policies, targets and budgets. Sadly those are more important than ever before. He plays things strictly by the book and has no room for individual thinkers and free spirits like you.'

'That tosser will ruin policing. What about hunches? Local knowledge? Intuition? I've been a copper for thirty years and have the best arrest record in the county. I know every bugger and every bugger knows me and what I stand for.'

'I know, Harry, I know. But it's all about due process and public image these days.' Wiping a hand across his face, Hadley chose his next words with care and softened his tone even further. 'You also have the highest number of complaints against you. In fact, there have been more complaints against you every year for the last ten years than there have been against any other two officers combined.'

'So? I filled the fucking cells, didn't I?' Evans raised his hands in apology. He hadn't meant to attack Hadley.

'You did, but that's not enough nowadays.'

'So what happens now then?' Evans was resigned to his fate. He'd done everything he could to retain his job and failed.

'You'll be on compassionate leave for the duration of the trial and then you'll be given the usual send off.'

'What? A few drinks with folk I've worked with over the years. A speech from you or the chief constable. A pat on the back followed by my arse hitting the pavement.'

'It's tradition.'

'Fuck tradition. I don't want any of that shite. Once Yates's trial is over, I'll clear my desk and just slip away.'

'Fair enough, Harry. If that's what you want.'

Evans rose from his chair, the whisky untouched. 'Thanks for trying to help, it didn't work but at least you tried.'

*   *   *

Striding through the police station, Evans swallowed his disappointment and refocused on the task at hand.

Bursting into the office he ignored everyone else and went straight to Chisholm. 'How you getting on?'

'Nearly there, guv. In about half an hour, I'll be ready to set my programmes into action. I have them all set up and ready to go.' Chisholm's eyes stayed on the screen and his hands never stopped typing as he answered.

Evans didn't understand why the programmes weren't already starting to raise the ransom. 'Then why don't you start now? We need that money in the Foulkes's account by eleven at the latest.'

'I know, guv, but this computer doesn't have the all the processing power I need to run my programmes. I need a more powerful computer.' Chisholm gave tight grin. 'Don't worry though, I'll soon have two of the UK's biggest computers at my disposal.'

'What do you mean?'

'I'm taking over management of Google's and Amazon's server farms. With their power I'll be able to run all my programmes at once and leave the trail so muddy that nobody will ever trace it back to us.'

Evans knew Chisholm was worried about being digitally traced. If that happened, the computer genius would face prison time. Realisation of what he was asking Chisholm to risk washed over him. He rested a hand on Chisholm's shoulder and took in his sweat-covered face. 'If you want to walk away from this now, I won't blame you. I'll go upstairs, tell them about the kidnapping and take all the fallout.'

Chisholm's face was grim. 'And what'll happen to those kids? It's too late for that, guv. We're the only chance they've got now.'

Chisholm's words echoed around Evans's brain as he looked round the team. Perhaps the chief constable had a point, he was a renegade in charge of a team consisting of a rookie, a slapper and a geek.

Straight-laced by-the-book coppers like Campbell were the future of policing. All investigations would be conducted by the latest set of rules. Nobody would need local knowledge any more. Instead they'd sit in an office using computers, forensics and statistics to catch criminals. Gone would be the days of shaking down suspects, or using real detective work to make an arrest. Everything would be all touchy-feely and politically correct. Maybe he was better off out of it.

He looked at his watch. It was just after seven thirty. 'Will three hours be long enough to get the money?'

'Guv.' Chisholm's tone was laced with a patronising disapproval. 'Three seconds will be long enough. The rest of the time is me making sure that we aren't traced. When I'm finished doing this, everyone who holds a UK bank account will have a statement that'll show over a million transactions.

Nobody will be able to unravel it all. Now would you please bugger off and leave me to it.'

Chapter 63

Victoria was sat at her kitchen table. An empty coffee cup and overflowing ashtray sat in front of her. Pushed to one side was a plate of uneaten sandwiches.

'You need to eat something. The kids need you fit and strong. I need you.' Nicholas had been released, but was due to appear in court on Tuesday morning.

Ignoring him, Victoria stubbed out the last of her cigarette and lit another.

'I said you need to eat something. Harry Evans will get the kids back tonight and they'll need you at your best. I'll need you.'

This time his words cut through her dark thoughts, driving her to give voice to the bitterness that was threatening her sanity.

'You need me? *You* fucking need *me*? What about our kids? They needed a father who wouldn't risk their lives, not some lying scumbag whose selfish actions would put them in danger.'

Nicholas stood in from of the table and let her shout and scream at him until she was spent.

'Eat up, Victoria. You need something to keep you going. Whatever happens tonight, it's going to be a long night.'

Knowing that Nicholas was right, Victoria forced herself to eat the sandwiches. She was aware there was ham and cheese on the sandwiches only because she'd looked. The bread was like cardboard against the inside of her mouth but she knew she'd need the energy.

The roiling in her stomach was calmed for a few moments as the food settled. Before she'd finished the last sandwich, it started up again as nightmare scenarios flickered across the movie screen that was her mind's eye.

A knock on the front door caused her head to spin. Pushing Nicholas out of the way, she made sure that she got there first.

Stood outside was the young DC who'd questioned her with Harry Evans. In her hand was a sheaf of leaflets.

The DC trailed Victoria into the kitchen, dumping the leaflets into a pedal bin. 'I've been posing as a Jehovah's Witness in case the kidnappers are watching your house.'

'Never mind that. Have you any news? Are my babies OK?'

'There's no news, I'm afraid. DI Evans sent me here so we can keep you updated at all times. My name's Lauren.'

'Standard policy isn't it? Put someone with the family to dole out tea and comfort.'

Ignoring the barbed tone, Lauren nodded. 'Normally it's a family liaison officer, but as we're keeping the... ah... situation within our team, the guv sent me instead.'

'Thanks for coming, but I don't want tea, and the only comfort you can give me will be my children back safe and sound.' Victoria was grateful for the young woman's presence, but was too busy steeling herself for what the night may bring to worry about niceties.

'That's what we all want.'

For ten minutes Victoria listened with incredulity, then hope, as Lauren explained how the team were raising the ransom money.

'Do you think it'll work? Do you think my children will come back safe?'

'I do hope so. All our careers are riding on this.' Lauren's hand flew to her mouth as she realised how tactless she'd been. 'I'm so, so sorry. I didn't mean it like that.'

'It's OK. I appreciate you taking such a risk to help save my kids.'

'Still, I'm sorry.'

'Forget it. It's not your doing.' Victoria patted Lauren's hand and threw a disgusted look at her husband. 'Put the kettle on and make the lass a cup of coffee. Looks like she's gonna have a long night with us.'

Chapter 64

Campbell put his mobile down and sighed. Sarah was doing fine in the hospital and baby Alan was being well looked after by the nurses. She'd understood about his having to work, but they were coming home tomorrow and she expected his undivided attention for the full week's paternity leave he'd booked.

Campbell hadn't had the heart to tell her his future career was at risk thanks to a wild scheme cooked up by a man she'd yet to meet. He knew she'd be furious at the gamble and wouldn't see anything but the financial jeopardy he was placing them in. Whichever way the case went, there was no way it could be kept covered up. Whether they saved those two children or not, come tomorrow morning the brass would be demanding answers. An inquiry would follow. Blame would be allocated as fingers pointed. He was the new man on the team and may end up as the scapegoat.

Is that why Harry Evans had been so persuasive when he asked to be allowed to handle things his way?

He knew he shouldn't have listened to Evans. He should have reported the kidnapping straightaway and let SOCA deal with it. Now it was too late to do anything but wait and see which way the dice rolled.

Chisholm was silent as he watched his screens. The only sign of movement from him was the flickering of his eyes, shifting focus from one monitor to the other. Bhaki had gone to join a PC on the stakeout and Evans had disappeared in search of food.

'Grub's up.' Evan's entered the office with three pizza boxes. 'Got youse a pepperoni each.'

Campbell took his pizza and started to eat while Evans spread liberal amounts of Tabasco sauce onto his own pizza.

'Just so you know, Jock, I've got firearms teams on standby at Carlisle and Kendal.'

Campbell swallowed before speaking 'How did you swing that with the brass?'

'Simple. I reminded them about the three shotguns taken from farms, suggesting it would be wise to have firearms teams ready around the county, as we had surveillance in place.'

Campbell found himself marvelling at Evans's manipulation skills. One way or the other, he always seemed to get what he wanted. Perhaps that was the secret behind his team's loyalty.

Chapter 65

Disappointed at being sidelined from the more urgent kidnapping case, Bhaki sat with PC Robert Malcolm in an unmarked car, hidden in a barn neighbouring South Fell farm on the southern reaches of Broom Fell. They were watching the screen of a tracker, waiting to see if the quad bike would move. Neither man expected there to be any movement until at least midnight but were professional enough to remain alert.

'Bloody hell, this is boring.'

'It's not so bad. What would you have been doing of you weren't doing this?' Bhaki looked across the car at the man who had been detailed to join him on a night's surveillance.

Robert Malcolm was a long-serving officer who'd never risen above the rank of constable. The bulging belly and constant grousing from his lopsided mouth would ensure he retired at the same rank he'd always held.

'Paperwork, rounding up drunks or dealing with domestic violence probably.'

'Paperwork is always boring and the other two just generate paperwork.'

'You're not wrong there.'

The two men chatted about football to alleviate the boredom, although Bhaki soon tired of Malcolm's obvious bias towards Manchester United. He could handle fair debate, but Malcolm couldn't admit the slightest fault in his team, even though no impartial football fan would say it was their finest team.

'Gonna have me some soup. Want some?'

'No thanks. I've got some of my own but I'm saving it for later.' Bhaki reached for his bottle of water.

Malcolm had eaten almost non-stop since he'd joined him at nine. So Bhaki planned to treat the ever-hungry Malcolm to a cup of his mother's mulligatawny. It was spicy enough to boil itself and perhaps a burnt mouth would prevent the older man from distributing crumbs all over his car.

'Suit yourself.'

A call came through to Bhaki's mobile. When he hung up his eyes showed both disappointment and concern.

A slurp came from Malcolm. 'What's up?'

'Another case the team has been working on, that's all.' Bhaki had to stop himself adding, 'and I'm sat hear with a moronic suckling pig, while the rest of the team are tracking down kidnappers'. However, he knew he had several more hours in the man's company and, as bad as it was now, it would be much worse if he antagonised the slob.

'So what's he like then, your guv? I've heard lots of stories but have only met him a couple of times and he's been fine wi' me.'

'What did you expect him to be like? He's a good copper who's just a bit stuck in the past with his attitude to policing.' Bhaki paused to take a slug of water from his bottle. 'He can be a bastard at times, but he's basically fair. If you do your job, he leaves you alone.'

'Oh right.' There was disappointment in Malcolm's voice.

'Tell the truth I was delighted but nervous when he took me out of uniform to join his team.'

'Head-hunted, eh? It's all right for some. Still, I s'pose having you on the team'll help with the quotas.'

Knowing what the elder man was getting at filled Bhaki with more sadness than anger. He'd thought that such attitudes were in the past. Filling his voice with innocence he repeated Malcolm's last word back to him as a question. 'Quotas?'

'Oh, come off it. You know fine well what I mean. He's got that slag Lauren Phillips on the team and now he's got someone from a minority as well. No offence, like.'

'It's just a shame that neither of us is a black one-eyed lesbian dwarf. That way he'd only need one of us.' Rather than rise to the man's insensitivity, Bhaki had decided to goad him as far as possible. The fact that he was a DC, while Malcolm was still a PC at his age, meant that he was already on a better wage than the elder man. Plus, Malcolm's obvious prejudices meant he was never going to progress his career.

Malcolm chuckled. 'Aye well, lad. I don't think that's possible but a few of them on the books would leave more spaces for coppers who cared about the job. Bound to be better than a load of people shown favouritism because they fit a demographic.'

'That's a very good point you have made. I'll ask my DI if I've been promoted on ability or the colour of my skin the next time I see him. I'll also tell him that you were the one who enlightened me regarding quotas.'

'Now wait up a minute.' Worry showed on Malcolm's bean shaped face. 'There's no need to discuss it with your DI.'

'Sorry, but there's no way I can let this rest. You've raised a very valid point.' Bhaki kept a straight face as the older man protested his innocence and tried to extricate himself from the hole he'd just dug.

Bhaki saw Malcolm's unthinking comments as ignorance rather than outright racism. After all, the aged PC hadn't been nasty, just outdated in his thinking. For all his guv was old school, he didn't give a hoot about colour, sex or creed. All he cared about was ability, which is why Bhaki was so pleased to be on his team.

Chapter 66

After she was certain light no longer penetrated the bathroom fan, Samantha pressed her ear against the door of their prison. She strained her ears, listening for sounds of movement within the house. Taking shallow breaths, she kept her ear to the door until she was convinced none of the men were upstairs or near the bottom of the stairway. Throughout the day she'd heard bangs as the front door slammed, but there was no way of identifying whether the men were coming or going.

Now, she could hear loud music but no signs of life.

They would try now. With luck, the loud music would cover any noise they might make. The sooner they got away the longer their escape would remain undetected. Pushing doubts aside she turned to her brother. 'C'mon, Kyle, we're gonna go now.'

'Will it work this time?' His earlier jubilation at exploring the attic had been replaced by worry they would again fail to escape.

'Dunno. But it's worth a try isn't it?' Before he could answer she flashed him a smile of encouragement. 'If it works, we'll see Mum and Dad again.'

'Cool.'

Kyle started up the makeshift ladder, tutting at Samantha's reminders to be as quiet as possible. 'I'm eight now, Sam. I can remember to be quiet.'

'Shush then.'

Seeing his legs disappear into the roof space, Samantha clambered after him, the makeshift steps biting into her bare feet. At the top, Samantha moved in front of her brother and crawled forward on the narrow boards that ran the length of the attic, until she reached the hatch. She fumbled as she tried to lift it, but it remained stuck fast. Her fingers weren't strong enough to haul the piece of plywood from the opening.

She needed some kind of tool or lever. She groped around, looking for any kind of implement or tool to aid her efforts.

Every careful sweep of her arm disturbed more of the glass-wool insulation, which scratched at her bare skin until it was almost unbearable. Gritting her teeth against the itches, she searched around her using touch alone. Her eyes were useless in the pitch-black attic, though her ears were alert for sounds of discovery. She concentrated on the messages sent by her fingertips.

'What's up?' whispered Kyle from across the attic.

'The hatch won't open. I'm looking for something to help me open it.'

'I'll help.'

'No, you stay still. I don't want you falling through the ceiling.'

She again tried to haul the plywood hatch cover free with her bare hands. Carefully, she reached down through the insulation. Her fingertips brushed against a series of screw-tips poking out from opposite sides of the hatch. Cursing whoever had sealed the hatch, Samantha returned to sit beside her brother and tried to think of another way out of the roof space.

Set in the roof were two ancient roof lights. A foot wide by two long, they consisted of a single pane of glass held within a cast iron frame. Samantha examined them with care before discounting them. The roof was too steep for them to exit that way and the rain battering against the glass would only make the roof slippy. They'd end up sliding down the roof and crashing to the ground. Clambering across the roof would see them killed or crippled.

A new wave of despair was starting to flood over her, when an idea began to blossom. Leading Kyle to the end of the attic, she positioned herself over what she reckoned was the men's bedroom. Her mental map of the house told her it was the furthest point from the lounge, where the men would be. Folding back a section of the prickly insulation, she exposed the ceiling below. As her fingertips found the lath and plaster framework, she whispered to Kyle her new plan. It would call for more urgency than stealth, but with the deadline looming ever closer she was running out of options.

Setting herself in position, she raised her already painful right foot and clenched her jaw. Then she slammed her foot into the plaster. Pain shot up her leg and she had to swallow the scream lest it escape her lips. Her teeth clamped together as her foot stomped on the ceiling for a second time. The ceiling started to give way. Encouraged by her success she stamped again and again until she had created a narrow hole.

Light poured upwards from the bedroom, but no shouts or running footsteps accompanied it. For once luck was on their side. The hole was above a bed.

They haven't heard us!

Samantha fed her legs through the gap and dropped onto the bed. When she was certain she hadn't been heard, Samantha helped Kyle make his descent from the attic. His jubilation at getting free of the attic could barely be contained. She had to throw a hand over his mouth before he shouted out in glee. 'Quiet, remember?'

Wriggling free from her, Kyle crossed to chest of drawers and lifted an iPhone connected to a charger. 'Look Sam.'

Oh, my God. We can call the police and be rescued.

'Quick, pass it here.' Samantha took the phone and pressed the button to bring it to life. Wiping her finger left to right she activated the phone's menu, only for the display to show a numerical screen.

Damn, damn and double damn. I don't know the security code.

She tried a few combinations unsuccessfully, then handed it to Kyle. 'Put this in your pocket.'

Grabbing a grubby sweater from the floor, Samantha pulled it on, ignoring the smell of nicotine and sweat. Leading Kyle, she crept down the stairs expecting to see Elvis at any second. Using as much stealth as possible, Samantha turned the handle to the front door only to find it locked as before.

Bugger.

She turned and peered along the corridor. The door to the lounge was closed, so she went the opposite way and entered a room that appeared to have once been an office. Old desks were pushed into a corner and the walls were adorned with rows of empty shelves. The wall opposite the door was blank, the other two walls sported identical windows. Samantha thought about what she knew of the house: the window on the left probably faced away from the road, so it would let them out to the rear of the property. Samantha tried it. It was stuck fast. Years of being painted without being opened had glued the sash in position, never again would it slide upwards. She crossed to the other side and tried the front window. It opened with ease. The counter-weights rumbled as the sash went higher.

Poking her head out, Samantha checked the farmyard for signs of life. It was silent. She clambered out and had turned to help her brother when a shout rang out.

'Hey!'

Samantha grabbed Kyle's hand and took off, not daring to look back and see who was pursuing them.

Chapter 67

Andrew Woods swung his feet round and lifted them onto his desk, crossing his legs at the ankle he reached for the Tupperware box. He retrieved one of the bland salad butties his wife was forever supplying him with. Using the fork she'd provided, he ladled a scoop of low fat coleslaw onto the nest of rabbit food. Thank goodness she didn't know about the stash of chocolate bars kept in the bottom drawer of his desk. This was his ten o'clock snack. At two he would have a bigger meal followed by another snack at six. He hated the night shift; there was nothing to do but routine maintenance jobs after midnight. Before midnight there would be spikes in activity as people came home from work and logged on to the Internet.

Certain events would see a spike in activity on Twitter or Facebook as the public applauded or condemned some minor celebrity, politician or sportsman. His desk was festooned with monitors displaying reports from the banks of servers on the main floor. Row after row of servers were connected, forming a supercomputer to handle the millions of queries typed daily into his employers' search engine. He'd thought working for Google would have been more energising, romantic or at least exciting, but it transpired he was little more than the night-watchman for the digital security systems protecting the server farm.

An alert sounded from his computer. Pushing the last of the sandwich into his mouth, he turned to see what the problem was. It was the daddy of all problems. The entire server farm was showing an overload. Normally the server ran at seventy per cent capacity with spiked peaks up to ninety – during the Olympics it had hit an all time high of ninety-seven point two three per cent as people used social media to discuss the opening and closing ceremonies – but never before had he seen it hit one hundred per cent.

Woods set off his system of searchbots to determine what was causing the increase in searches. As he waited for the results, he scanned the Internet news channels to see if there were any breaking stories driving people online. Nothing he found seemed important enough to cause such a sudden upturn in traffic. Within minutes the searchbot delivered its report. Ignoring all the irrelevant data such as dates and times, Woods focused on the important parts.

System Check:	Compromise Found
Source:	Unidentified IP: 00.000.000.000
Details:	System Check – Code: brainpeg
Status:	Ongoing

'System check?' His voice was a confused mutter. He scanned the report again. The IP address rang false: a full row of zeros. Someone was cloaking their identity. He was savvy enough to work out the code brainpeg was an anagram of the surnames of Sergei Brin and Larry Page, Google's founders.

Woods deliberated a second. This was a new situation as far as he was concerned. The system had never been compromised before. Then he put in a call to Google's UK head office on Buckingham Palace Road, London. He adjusted the settings on the server farm to a maximum of eighty per cent capacity while he was being routed to the head of Digital Security. It was a protocol that allowed them to replace or maintain individual servers without the remaining servers risking an overload.

When he was finally put through, Woods explained the effects of the compromise, watching in disbelief as his monitor showed the rogue programme commandeer more and more server space, while pushing out all other search queries. Where once it had occupied thirty per cent of the server's full capacity it now occupied forty per cent of the new limit.

Relaying the information to the man on the other end of the line he was given an immediate answer.

As instructed he cut the servers back to twenty-five per cent until the man had contacted Google's head office in Los Angeles to see if they knew anything about the compromise to the server farm.

Chapter 68

Bhaki and Malcolm had fallen silent. Malcolm was reading a horror novel, using the interior light to illuminate the pages. Bhaki fiddled with his phone, texting back and forth with the girl he'd met on Wednesday night.

A beep from the tracker console alerted them the quad had been moved.

'Bloody hell. They're early.'

Bhaki ignored Malcolm as he watched the light blinking on the console map. When it reached the road, he twisted the ignition key and called Evans. The phone went straight to voicemail, so he called Campbell, who instructed him to keep following and to call in every ten minutes or once the bike stopped moving. Bhaki drove the Astra diesel hard until he was within a half mile of the vehicle carrying the quad, then hung back, thankful for the driving rain which would help to hide his presence.

'What'd your guv say?'

'Just told me to follow them as per the plan. They can't join us because of the other business. Once we've located their base we're to call in the locals.'

'Typical bloody bosses. Leave us out in the cold all frigging night, then swoop in for the raid where all the glory and excitement is. Bastards.'

'What do you expect? You're a PC and I'm a newly promoted DC. You don't get chief inspector's doing stakeouts. Just keep your eyes on that tracker and let me know which way they go. They'll be at the '66 any minute now.' Bhaki's exasperation at the man was starting to show, but he didn't care. The sooner they knew where the quad bike would end up the sooner he would be back in his own team, away from the bigoted slob. He just hoped they'd be wrapped up in time for him to get in on the kidnapping case, although he was doubtful.

'My money's on east. It'll be some bunch from Liverpool or Manchester. Tenner says I'm right.'

'No chance. We've spent half the night guessing that's where they'll be from.'

A little way along the A66, the cattle wagon flashed its indicator. Putting his Blackberry on speaker, he got Campbell. 'Sir, it's Amir. They've turned off the '66 and are now travelling north towards Caldbeck.' Bhaki listened to Campbell's reply, nodding his head as he listened. Before Malcolm could open his mouth to ask, Bhaki told him that Campbell had instructed him to keep reporting back. When they had a location for the robbers' base he would despatch some help to make the collar.

'We may get the glory after all.'

Bhaki ignored him and kept his eyes on the north-bound road. Driving conditions were deteriorating as the wind picked up. Small branches were being swept from trees bordering the road. The narrow two-lane highway was pitted with tight corners, bumpy straights and myriad potholes. Hanging well back to prevent being spotted, Bhaki trailed the cattle wagon by tracker alone. After about fifteen minutes, as it passed through Hesket Newmarket, the light on the console map pinged off the B road. Bhaki navigated his way along a series of single-lane back roads until he was near where the wagon had stopped.

Bhaki continued along the road until they were out of sight behind a small wood and turned the car round in a gateway. He opened the door and gave his radio to Malcolm. 'I'm going up there for a look-see. I'll call your mobile to let you know what I find.'

'You're a bloody fool going out there on a night like this. Why don't you just call it in?'

'Because I want to make sure.' Bhaki wanted to get a lay of the land in case there was any other route in or out. The last thing he wanted to do was end up in a high-speed pursuit or precipitate a manhunt. This surveillance job gave him a chance to repay Evan's faith in him. Despite brushing off Malcolm's earlier comments, he was starting to wonder if there may be any truth in the accusation he was only there to fill quotas.

Chapter 69

Evans drained his hip flask and scowled across the room at Chisholm. 'Is the money in their account yet?'

'Not yet. Like I told you earlier, the programme has to finish its cycle before we can make the transfer.'

'I thought it was supposed to be done by now. It's ten past eleven for fuck's sake.'

Chisholm grimaced, unwilling to make the admission. 'Google somehow caught onto my programme. They shut down three-quarters of their server farm. I've put in a patch to the programme and taken exclusive control of the remaining servers.'

'I don't give a shit about that. When will the algorithm be finished?'

'If they don't pull the plug on the other servers it'll be done in five minutes.'

Campbell gave voice to what they were all thinking. 'And if they do pull the plug?'

'Then we'll fail.'

'No way, Jabba. That's not an option. Do whatever you've got to do but get that money into the Foulkes account in the next minute.' Standing up Evans took a deep breath. 'On my head be it. If the shit hits the fan, I'll make sure that I'm the one holding the fan.'

This latest setback was grating on Evans's nerves. His career was over, but all he could think about was those two children. If Chisholm's programme failed and those kids were hurt, the guilt would rival the pain of failing Janet. If he'd followed procedure to any degree, Grantham or Hadley would have called in SOCA. Their team would have specialist knowledge of what to do. Instead he'd been his usual self and had eschewed sharing the case. Now it looked as if his quest for one last piece of glory may charge a price he was unwilling to pay.

'That's it done, guv. The money is in the Foulkes's account.'

'Right then, Jabba. Pay the ransom.' Evans wiped his forehead. To think it had come to this. Paying a ransom without proof of life went against all the rules and basic common sense. Yet they were left with no option. 'And don't forget to make sure you trace where the money goes.'

'Will do. I'll send confirmation the money has been transferred via the contact form.'

Evan's mobile sounded. 'What?' Cocking his head to one side he listened to the caller as he paced the office.

'Thanks for keeping me informed. Let me know what the outcome is.'

His colleagues looked at him expectantly. 'Bhaki's scouting out the farm where the rural thieves are based and is again requesting backup.'

He felt none of the usual elation at this success. Judging by the silence from Campbell and Chisholm they felt the same way.

'That's it done, guv. The ransom's paid and the message sent.'

'Thank you. Well done.' Evans was hit with a level of fatigue he'd never experienced before. All they could do now was wait for the kidnappers to get in touch and hope they would release the two kids.

Campbell reached for his phone. 'I'll call Lauren and give her the news. Hopefully it'll ease a bit of stress for the parents.'

Chapter 70

Marshall kicked the chair across the lounge. As soon as he'd seen the girl helping the boy out of the window, he'd known events had turned against him. What had promised to be an easy job had turned into a nightmare. Two hours had passed since he'd re-caught them, but his rage had grown as realisations of the consequences of their bid for freedom had wormed their way into his brain.

Big though he was, he'd managed to catch the boy as he was dragged along by his sister. Soaked to the skin, he'd hauled them into a shed and bound them to a tractor with cable ties. As an early punishment, he'd stripped the girl of the sweater was wearing.

What was worst wasn't that they'd tried to escape. He could understand that. Hell, he could even forgive the knee she'd planted in his balls. In her position, he'd have done the same. What galled him was the fact that they'd seen his face. He hadn't had time to cover up and had needed to switch a light on when he was securing them to the old tractor. The hooked scar on his left cheek would be enough to identify him, just as it had always been. A ten-minute search on a computer would have police looking for him.

'Fucking little bitch.' Another chair flew across the room. 'What the bloody hell we gonna do now?'

Alker didn't answer him. Marshall knew what he would suggest. What he would want to do. Like most predators, Alker was a coward at heart. Marshall wasn't often this angry, but when he was, he was prone to lashing out at anyone who offered an opinion he didn't like. No way would he get an honest answer from Alker until he calmed down.

'We're gonna have to do them, aren't we?'

Alker kept his silence.

'Seriously, Billy. What the fuck are we gonna do?'

'I reckon you should ask the boss that question. It's his decision. Not ours.'

This was the last piece of advice Marshall wanted to hear. The boss would be most displeased to learn just how close the kids had been to escaping. He'd want to have Alker punish them. The boss would want him punished, too. He was supposed to be in charge. But for a stroke of good luck on his part, the kids would have got away.

Now he was caught between a rock and a hard place. On one hand, there was the boss, a no-nonsense man who wouldn't hesitate to use whatever force necessary to punish failure. On the other were two children who could identify him to the police.

Logic dictated that he kill the kids so that they couldn't identify him. Alker would probably be happy to do it for him. Yet the kids didn't deserve that. They'd done nothing wrong. It was wrong for them to suffer at the hands of Alker for his mistakes. At the same time, his boss wouldn't want the kids dead if the ransom was paid. If that happened, the parents would have nothing to lose by going to the police. It would only be a matter of time before the police were knocking on his boss's door, and he didn't want to be the man responsible for that. Another thought flashed across in his mind and it was the most worrying of all. The easiest way for the boss to solve the problem of identification was to have him killed.

He had no choice but to make the call. He went upstairs to get his phone. Seeing the charger lead without a phone attached re-ignited his rage. He had to force deep breaths into his lungs to stop himself from losing the plot completely. With a massive effort, he managed to control his temper and look about the room. He took in the plaster on the floor from the ceiling. There was a white trail towards where his phone had been charging.

The kids must have found the phone. *It has a security lock, but what if they cracked the code?*

There were only two people who could answer his questions. He scampered downstairs, grabbed his mask and ordered Alker to follow him.

Entering the shed, he marched over to the two kids, roaring questions as he walked. 'Where's my phone? Did you call the old bill?' When he didn't get an answer, he leaned in close to the girl who shrank back against the tractor. 'If you don't answer my questions by the count of three I'm gonna hand you over to him.' His thumb jerked in the direction of Alker who was wearing his Tony Blair mask.

'One... Two—'

'It's in Kyle's pocket. We tried to call, but didn't know the code... I'm sorry... please don't hurt us.'

Dragging his phone from the boy's sodden jeans, Marshall tried to switch it on without success. Water dripped from the casing and the screen was cracked. He remembered the struggle he'd had when he'd caught them. The boy had fallen arse first into a puddle.

Marshall didn't dare trust her. He needed definite proof, so he gave a terse command to Alker.

'Nooo, Please, I'm telling the truth. I didn't call the police. I couldn't unlock it.'

Alker laid his meaty fingers on the girl's left hand and gave a sudden jerk. The resulting snap was accompanied by a scream.

Marshall took hold of the broken pinkie. 'Did you call the cops?'

'No. I swear it. I didn't call anyone.' Tears streamed down her face, shaming him for his bullying of a defenceless girl.

He believed her now. There was no way she was tough enough to lie when he was twisting her already broken finger. Sickened at what he had just done, Marshall's temper softened as frustration replaced his anger. Without his phone he couldn't contact the boss. The boss's latest mobile number was stored in his phone and was not shared with anyone else who was here. Now the only way he could get in touch with his employer was to call the boss's club and ask the manager to have the boss call Alker's mobile. The boss would know something had gone wrong and would be furious, before he even heard Marshall's news. Still, he needed the boss to let him know if the ransom had been paid or not. He might have set up the system preventing anyone from tracing where the money went, but he wasn't privy to the log-in details for the account where the money would end up.

Looking at the naked girl and sodden boy, shivering in the cold night air, he suddenly wished they'd managed to escape. Whatever happened, tonight would not go well for them. 'Go and tell the boys to put their masks on. Then get this pair across to the other shed where we can keep an eye on them.' He held his hand out to Alker. 'Give me your phone. I need to call the boss.'

Marshall made the call as Alker walked to the other shed where Williams and Johnstone were unloading the stuff they'd stolen on the night's first run.

Marshall sighed, thankful the rest of the gang of petty thieves who helped steal from the farms were waiting in a van near their next target. The last thing he needed was a bunch of coked-up idiots bouncing about causing mayhem.

Chapter 71

It was much further than Bhaki though it would be. He'd been slogging along the track for more than twenty minutes. Any thoughts at stealth had been abandoned in favour of making the best time possible. He would have ran, had the going not been so uneven, but he'd be no use to anyone with a twisted ankle. He had to convince himself not to turn back. The line from *Mastermind* ran like a mantra through his head: 'I've started so I'll finish.' Every inch of his skin was soaked, his fleece offered no protection against the driving rain. His vision acclimatised enough to allow him to see a farm a couple of hundred metres in front of him. There were a couple of large sheds and a farmhouse connected to some outbuildings. All was in darkness except for the largest shed, which had shards of light seeping through plastic roof-lights.

Bhaki slowed, crouched-over, using a stone dyke for cover. Top of his list was finding out if there was a secondary entrance. He didn't think that there would be, but having come this far he had to make sure. He ducked left, following the dyke around the perimeter of the farm. At the field gate, he took a careful look to make sure he wasn't spotted, before dashing across to the other side.

At the third gateway, he eased up and poked his head over the dyke to take a look. Less than a hundred metres away, a man was leading a young child across the yard. He had grasped the child by the upper arm and didn't seem to notice him stumble over potholes as he yanked him behind him.

Uncertainty flooded Bhaki's mind. Were the farm thieves the kidnappers as well? He needed to get closer. The last thing he wanted to do was cry wolf and disrupt the real kidnapping case. If it was the kidnapping though, he could perhaps save them. He glanced at his watch. There were only fifteen minutes to the midnight deadline the kidnappers had set.

Creeping alongside a barn, he watched as the man led the child into the shed that was lit up. Engine sounds rumbled from the shed as the men unloaded their haul. As Bhaki neared the illuminated shed, the man exited and bending his head against the driving rain, trotted to the unlit shed. Shrinking into the shadows, Bhaki watched the man re-emerge. This time he was marching what appeared to be a naked figure in front of him. The contours of the silhouette left him in no doubt it was a female who was being taken to join the child.

They must be the kids who've been kidnapped.

Torn between making the call for backup and checking to see if the kids were OK, Bhaki opted to do both at once.

Chapter 72

The tension was eating at Evans's nerves. There had been no contact from the kidnappers. Campbell had kept an open line to Lauren so they would know as soon as possible if the parents were contacted, but so far there had been nothing from the Scot.

That his career was ending in disgrace wasn't bothering him as much as he'd thought it would. The thought of failing those two children was uppermost in his mind. He leafed through the pictures of them on his desk, willing the kidnappers to free them unharmed. Not a religious man, he offered mental prayers to whoever was listening. God. Allah. Buddha. It didn't matter who saved them, just as long as they were saved. He planned to wait until one o'clock. If he'd heard nothing by then, he'd contact Greg Hadley and bring him up to speed on the whole operation.

Picking up his mobile, he answered Bhaki's call with little grace. 'What do you want, Bhaji Boy?... What?... You're fucking joking. Where are you?... I know the area. Stay on hand and keep watch. Hang on a second...'

Evans grabbed his jacket, jubilation all over his face. 'Bhaki's found the kids. Jabba, mobilise all available coppers to the lane end of Fellside Farm near Hesket Newmarket. Jock, you're wi' me.'

'Bhaki, you're in charge until I get there. Call the guy you're doing the surveillance with and get him to park across the lane until the backup arrives. Get everyone into place and wait for me. I'll be there in ten minutes. If the kids look to be in any danger, go in and go in hard. Otherwise wait for me.'

Evans sprinted to his car. Campbell hadn't managed to get his door shut when the wheels started turning. Evans struggled to keep control of the car as they hurtled through the streets. Every turn he took saw the car drift sideways until he made the necessary corrections. The powerful rear wheel drive was fine in a straight line on a dry road but a nightmare on rain-soaked corners. His mind raced as fast as the engine, plotting the quickest route to Fellside Farm. Whenever he reached a straight section of road he allowed his eyes to drop to the clock on the dashboard.

Deciding on a course of action he spat instructions at Campbell. 'Call Lauren and tell her to put the parents in a car and take them to Caldbeck. I want to re-unite the kids with them as soon as possible. Then call the hospital and tell them we'll need an ambulance on standby with a trauma psychologist in it.' He hadn't accepted any counselling when Janet died, but he knew it helped a lot of people. God knows what those poor kids had been through.

Five to twelve.

Beside him, Campbell was relaying his instructions to Lauren. Half listening, he pressed down that little bit harder on the accelerator. Evans stood on the brake pedal as a sharp corner appeared in the glare of the headlights, forcing the ABS to kick back rhythmically at the sole of his boot. Concentrating on driving, he almost missed what Campbell said to Lauren.

You're fucking joking, he thought in disbelief. *Can't be.*

Then he remembered the five missed calls on her phone from Campbell.

Evans waited until Campbell ended the call before accusing him: 'You're shagging her, aren't you?'

'What the hell are you on about?'

'You and Lauren. You just called her hon then. Short for honey. Hardly the way a senior officer should address his staff. And all those missed calls yesterday. You said you were trying to find out about the case. You could have called me when she didn't answer. You didn't though, did you? You kept calling her instead.'

'You're talking shite, Harry. I called her hen. In case you didn't know, it's a Glasgow term which equates to dear, love or sweetheart.'

'Don't give me that bollocks. There's a big difference between hon and hen.'

Despite everything else that was happening, Evans was shocked at discovering this affair. He'd done his fair share of sleeping around before he'd met Janet, but he'd never cheated on anyone. Let alone cheated on his wife.

'So what if I am shagging her? We're both adults.'

'So what? So fucking what?' Evans corrected a slide as the car hurtled round a corner. 'You've got a wife and a son. That's fucking *what*.'

Evans couldn't believe his ears. Here was a man who had everything – everything that had been snatched away from him – and he was jeopardising it for a fling with a junior officer whose reputation would shame an alley cat. His wife, son and career were all at risk because he couldn't keep his trousers on.

'Look, there's the road end.' Campbell seized the opportunity to change the subject.

'Don't for one minute think this discussion is finished.' Evans had plenty more to say to Campbell about his infidelity, but he needed to concentrate on rescuing the two kids first.

Evans looked at the clock. Eleven fifty-nine. Having heard nothing from Bhaki he could only assume that the children were still unharmed. He didn't dare him in case his phone wasn't on silent. He waited until a PC moved the car blocking the lane, put the BMW into first gear, switched off the lights and let the car haul itself along the rutted lane.

Chapter 73

Samantha's teeth rattled a staccato beat as she waited for their fate to be revealed. Her broken finger throbbed a separate rhythm, out of step with her chattering teeth. She and Kyle were tied to wooden chairs which Blair had dragged out of a corner. The other two men in the shed wore their masks as they unloaded a cattle wagon. Not once did they look their way.

Kyle was shivering and complaining of the cold, but being cold was the least of her worries. As soon as they were secured to the chairs, Blair had wheeled across a sack barrow which carried two gas bottles. The smaller of the bottles was red with 'propane' stencilled on the side in white paint. The second bottle was taller but thinner, the legend 'oxygen' ran along its length. Connecting the bottles were hoses, leading to a lance identical to the one she'd seen in the video.

Faced with the failure of all her plans, she tried to summon the last of her courage. The task would have been beyond her had Kyle not been by her side. Whatever happened, she must try to protect him. She daren't give way to the tears that pricked her eyes or the gorge threatening to rise up her throat. That would spell defeat. Once she started to cry she wouldn't be able to stop, wouldn't have the strength to plead for her brother to be spared punishment.

Before the men started on her, she had to secure Kyle's safety. Elvis was the only one she trusted to do that. Blair was an evil lech who would enjoy making her suffer. When the men came to punish her, she would either be mutilated or killed. Oblivion would take her one way or the other. Death would stop everything, but if she was mutilated, she could only hope that she passed out like the man in the video.

The fact that Elvis's phone was ruined puzzled her. Using the mystery as a distraction she bent her mind to the problem. *What was so important about the phone? Who did he need to speak to at this time of night?* The obvious answers were that he needed the phone to see if the ransom had been paid. That didn't add up though as she knew they had a laptop. So he must need to speak to someone. *But who?* Judging by Elvis's behaviour – demanding of answers, the sadistic treatment – it must be someone who scared him. *But who would scare the boss of a bunch of kidnappers?* she wondered. Then it struck her: Elvis wasn't the real boss. He was just the boss of these men. They must be working for someone else. Someone scary.

Blair walked over to them. Rainwater slick on his coat, running down his mask. He stood before her, eyeing her cold and naked body.

'My Grandma, what big nips you have.' Adopting a higher tone, Blair answered himself, 'All the better to hang your coat on.'

'If you let him go. Then I'll let you shag me.'

'Come again?' Blair's head cocked to one side. His eyes sparkling with desire.

Screwing her nerves, Samantha repeated the words she'd never expected to say. The very thought filled her with revulsion, but it might save Kyle's life.

Blair's head tilted back as he roared with laughter. 'You'll let me shag you. That's fucking priceless. You'll *let* me.'

Bending in close to Samantha, he cupped a breast with his hand. His foul breath polluted her nose as he moved his mouth close.

'I can shag you anytime I want, missy. In case you're forgetting, *you're* the one tied to the chair.'

'Please.' Samantha hated pleading with the dirty lecherous oaf, but it was her only hope. 'Let him go and I'll shag you any way you want. You do want to shag me, don't you?'

'You're right, I do. But if I do as you suggest, then I'll end up occupying the boy's chair. Be much easier to just turn you over, tie you down and help meself.'

She thought quickly. 'But surely shagging me with my consent will be more pleasurable than raping me?'

His head cocked to one side as if considering her question. 'Dunno about that. What about the boys? Can they join in?'

Samantha's mouth opened and closed but no words came out.

'No matter. We'll just help ourselves.' A firm squeeze of her breast caused her to gasp as dirty fingernails dug into tender skin. 'According to statistics, nine out of ten people enjoy gang rape... let's see which side you're on.'

'No... please don't do that.' In spite of her terror, she held her gaze high, looking at Blair's piggy eyes behind the mask.

A hand grasped Blair's collar and hauled him away from Samantha.

'You'll get your time with her soon enough.' Marshall jerked his thumb. 'Go get your video camera.'

Elvis stood before her, a mobile phone in his hand. 'I've just found out that your parents have paid the ransom.'

Samantha felt her shoulders droop as the tension flooded out of her. They were going to be set free. Somehow Mum and Dad had got the money needed to free them.

'What did you mean by telling him he'd get his time with me? Are you really going to let him rape me?' Every instinct Samantha possessed told her that Elvis was a dangerous man. Yet there was reluctance in his eyes, as if he was following a course he didn't fully believe in. Beneath Elvis's mask, she saw his throat bulge as he swallowed before answering her.

'No, he's not going to rape you. I won't let that happen.'

'Thank you. Thank you so mu—'

Samantha fell silent at his raised hand.

'My boss is concerned that you saw my face. He wants to send you back with a message you'll never forget.'

'What message? I'll take any message back you want me to.' Words gushed out of Samantha's mouth until she saw Elvis's throat bulge again. Following his gaze to the gas bottles, she pushed back against the chair.

'No. Please no. Not that. Please don't do that to us. You've got your money. There's no need to do that to us.'

'It's your own fault. If you hadn't tried to escape then you wouldn't have seen my face.'

'I'll never tell. I won't tell a soul. Ever. I promise.' Tears rolled down her face as she fought for control of her voice. 'There's no need to do that to us.'

Thoughts of her brother leaped into her mind. She must protect Kyle. It was her turn to swallow now.

'I want you to leave my brother alone. Whatever you were going to do to him I want you to do to me instead.'

'Really?' Surprise and admiration laced Elvis's voice.

'Yes.'

Samantha nearly faltered when she saw Blair return with the video camera. Turning her head she looked at her brother. His eyes were full of fear, his cheeks stained by the tears that had flowed non-stop since they'd been caught trying to escape.

Elvis turned at the scuff of Blair's boots.

'The boss says we have to take one of her feet off and video it. You get your torch ready and I'll do the rest.'

Samantha pleaded for all she was worth but to no avail.

Elvis bound her left ankle to the chair leg. Removing his belt and doubling it over he held it in front of her mouth. 'Put this between your teeth, it'll stop you from biting your tongue or crushing your teeth.'

'Please no. Don't do this to me.'

Seeing her final plea ignored, Samantha opened her mouth and allowed Elvis to place the belt between her teeth. Its foul leathery taste made her gag, but she endured it, recognising the warped kindness which had compelled him to put it in her mouth.

Her eyes fixed on Blair. He picked up the lance, which was connected via hoses to the two gas bottles. He twiddled with one of the knobs on the lance until Samantha could hear the hiss of gas escaping. Producing a lighter from his pocket, Blair ignited the gas. A yellow flame enveloped the end of the lance. He adjusted the twin knobs, allowing more gas and air to pour through the nozzle.

Samantha could hear whooshes and crackles as the flame became a long, focused jet.

As Blair fiddled with the knobs, the jet shortened and turned from orangey yellow to blue tinged white. The cone-shaped flame shrank in length as oxygen mixed into the gas feed. He pressed on a lever and the lance emitted a loud hiss. The flame shrank in length but grew in intensity as pure oxygen was forced through the nozzle, until it was four inches long and the ice blue of an arctic sky.

Blair turned to Elvis. 'Ready when you are.'

Chapter 74

Evans crept the car along the lane without headlights, using the ruts to guide him. He had an open line to Bhaki, which he put onto speaker, who gave him a full layout of the shed, from the locations of the kids to the exit points. Beside him, Campbell was updating the armed response units and keeping in touch with Chisholm, who was tracing the money as it moved from one account to another. The armed response units would be on-site in less than five minutes. Five minutes could be at least four minutes too late. The dashboard clock stood at midnight. If anything developed in the next few minutes it was up to him, Campbell, Bhaki and a few woodentops to go in and save the kids. That might not be enough bodies to catch everyone and they had no firearms with them.

The BMW grouched along the track, pitching as it found every hole, scraping its underbelly on ridges. Rain battered against the windscreen forcing him to concentrate on not driving into the ditch running alongside the track. A van filled with PCs followed a hundred yards behind him.

'Anything happening, Amir?'

'Nothing to report, guv.'

In spite of all that could go wrong, these were the moments Evans lived for as a policeman. The arrests, takedowns and interrogations, gave him a buzz nothing else could replace. Cresting a hill, he could see a dark outline of the farm ahead. Shards of light emanating from a large shed drew him in like a homing signal.

Suddenly Bhaki's panic stricken voice came through the speaker. 'Guv. They've just lit the blowtorch and it looks like they're getting ready to use it on the girl. Should I go in and stop them?'

Fuck.

Evans switched on his headlights and stamped his right foot onto the accelerator. 'I'll be there in a second. On my signal, follow me in.'

'What signal, guv?

'You'll know.' He slammed into third gear.

Shadows flitted around the BMW as the following van threw beams of light their way, its driver sensing the sudden urgency. There was no time for finesse. This takedown would have to be done with brute force and the element of surprise used to its maximum capacity.

'Hold on.' His warning was unnecessary; Campbell had already braced himself against the violent jolts the car was sustaining from the rough track. Slaloming his way through the gate to the farmyard, Evans executed a controlled slide then pointed the nose of the car at the illuminated shed's massive wooden doors. As the car raced towards the doors, he gripped the wheel tight, prepared himself for the impact.

The air reverberated with the splintering sound of the twin wooden doors buckling inwards, followed by the tinkling of glass and crunch of metal as the BMW's speed carried it through the doors and into a cattle wagon with a vicious thump. Evans batted down the airbag, choking on the talcum powder used to prevent it from sticking together. Throwing his shoulder against the car door he fought his way from the wreckage of his beloved car.

'Police. Everyone down on the ground now.'

Two men ran out from the back of the cattle wagon and made for a side door, where they were met by Bhaki holding a fence post in front of him as if it was a sword. At the far end of the room, the other two had dropped the blowtorch and video camera and were looking for better weapons. Evans sprinted across the floor and threw himself at the nearest one. Rugby tackling the man to the ground, he got on top of him and smashed his fist into the grinning Tony Blair mask that covered his face until he felt the man go limp beneath him.

He looked up to see the remaining man wrestling with Campbell and winning. Campbell took a knee to the groin, which left him rolling on the floor gasping for air. The man scrambled to his feet and, straightening his Elvis mask, made to run to the door. Before the man could escape, Evans grabbed his jacket, spinning the man round to face him.

He was a big bugger, Evans would give him that. But there was no way he would allow the man to escape. Elvis jabbed with his left hand, then sent a right cross at Evans that would have beheaded him if he hadn't ducked below it. Getting inside the man's reach, Evans drove lefts and rights into Elvis's gut. His blows had little effect on the man mountain in front of him so he switched his aim and pummelled Elvis's kidneys.

Elvis only grunted and wound his arms around Evans, and squeezed the older man in a brutal bear hug.

With both arms trapped, Evans had only his head and feet as a weapon. He hadn't enough purchase to get a decent kick in, so he arched his back and delivered a crushing headbutt. The vice-like grip loosened. He repeated the blow a second and third time until he could break free. Picking his spot with care he swung a roundhouse that felled the already dazed Elvis.

Evans directed the PCs arriving from the van towards Elvis and Blair as he ran across to free the two children. Noticing the girl's nakedness for the first time, he removed his jacket and draped it over her to cover her exposed body.

'It's OK, lass. You're safe now.' Evans ran his eyes over the boy and then looked back at the girl. 'Have they hurt you?'

'No. But they were going to cut my foot off with that thing.' Samantha nodded at the still flaming blowtorch.

Evans pulled a Leatherman multi-tool from his pocket and cut Samantha free before doing the same for Kyle. Campbell groaned as he dragged himself to his feet but Evans had no sympathy for him. 'Hey, Jock. Call your bloody girlfriend and tell her to bring the parents.'

As Samantha and Kyle hugged each other, sobbing with relief. Evans walked across to the gas bottles and twisted the outlet valves on the bottles to stop the flow of gas.

With the swoosh of the blowtorch silenced, Evans could hear the kidnappers protesting their innocence, accusing them all of police brutality and demanding their lawyers, but none of it mattered to him.

He'd saved the two kids. Job done.

He'd attend the interviews with Lauren later, and spend the next day helping Campbell build the case against the four men, but as far as he was concerned this was his last real act as a policeman.

He expected to be hauled into someone's office for a bollocking when the full details came out, but he didn't care. They couldn't sack him and they daren't take his pension away after this result.

Turning back to the kids he bent his knees until he was face to face with Kyle. 'Your Mum and Dad are on their way, lad. They've missed you very much and can't wait to see you again.'

Kyle shrank tighter against his sister, his mouth widening as he started crying again.

Standing up, Evans told Samantha that an ambulance was coming and that they'd have to be checked out by a doctor before they could go home.

'Don't worry, though. Your folks'll be here any second.

Chapter 75

Victoria was beside herself. Lauren did her best to offer distraction, but all she wanted was for the girl's phone to ring and someone to tell her that her babies were safe. They'd been parked beside a street light in the little village of Hesket Newmarket, for what seemed like hours. Although Lauren had told them the police had located their children and were working on a plan to rescue them safely, Victoria couldn't bring herself to believe it.

The silent phone nestled in a compartment between the seats of the standard issue Astra diesel. Lauren had made sure the phone had a decent charge and was showing four bars' worth of signal reception. Victoria's eyes hadn't left the phone since they'd parked. Nicholas's head peered between the seats from his position folded into the back of the car. Between Victoria's fingers was a picture of her children.

A shrill ring startled them all from their individual reveries. Lauren's hand shot out to grab the phone.

'Yes?' She listened for a moment. 'We're on our way.'

'What did they say?' Victoria searched Lauren's face in the half-light.

'They've got them. They've rescued your children and have arrested the kidnappers. Both Samantha and Kyle are shaken up but largely unhurt.'

'Thank God. Thank God my babies are OK.' Victoria's words gushed out as Lauren started the car.

At the farm, Lauren showed her warrant card to the PC standing guard at the gate. The PC directed her to the shed where the children were waiting. Victoria ran as fast as her legs would carry her. She burst inside and looked around wildly until she saw Samantha wrapped in a blanket with a man's jacket over her shoulders and Kyle cuddled against her side.

Harry Evans stood beside them in the role of protector.

'Sam! Kyle!' Victoria raced across to her children and swept them in her arms. Tears flowed down her face as she let go of the pent up tension she'd contained all week. 'Are you OK? Did they hurt you?'

Nicholas approached them and joined in with the group hug. Kyle detached himself from his mother and sister to wrap his arms and legs around the father he idolised.

'We're fine, Mum.' Samantha raised her left hand and showed her mother the broken pinkie. 'Well, a couple of bumps and scrapes but nothing that won't heal.'

Victoria's eyes ran over Samantha's face, taking in the black eye, the cut and swollen lips. 'Are you sure? Oh, my poor babies.'

'We're fine Mum.' Samantha nodded towards Evans. 'If it wasn't for him we wouldn't be.'

Evans gave a self-conscious shrug. 'Just doing my job.'

'You saved my children. Thank you. Thank you so much.' Victoria strode across and hugged Evans, laughing at his embarrassment when Samantha came to join her.

Victoria watched as Nicholas unwound Kyle and passed him back to her. He reached for Samantha, who pulled her father close, before holding him at arms length and fixing him with a fierce glare.

'It's your fault we were kidnapped, isn't it?'

Unable to answer, Nicholas just nodded.

'Bastard.' Samantha drove her knee deep into her father's crotch.

Victoria left her husband lying in the filth and held her children. Samantha apologised for hitting her father, but Victoria waved it away. A knee in the bollocks from his daughter was the least he deserved.

Victoria felt the heat of Samantha's breath at her ear. 'Kyle's loose tooth fell out. I didn't have any money on me so I told him the Tooth Fairy would have put it under his pillow at home.'

The whispered words threatened to melt Victoria's heart. Despite everything they'd been through, Samantha had done everything possible to protect her brother and to avoid shattering childhood illusions. When Samantha told her just how close she'd been to facing the blowtorch, Victoria's lips went thin.

Ushering her children towards the arriving paramedics she returned to where Nicholas lay by the gas bottles. Picking up the blowtorch she walked towards her prone husband. Hoisting the lance over her shoulder like a baseball bat, Victoria tensed her muscles, ready to swing, but the sight of Nicholas cowering at her feet brought her to her senses. Her children were safe. They were alive and intact. Punishing Nicholas didn't matter any more. Samantha's knee had done far more damage than she ever could. The pain of the contact would heal in a few short minutes. The disgust that had fuelled her action would prey upon his mind for years. It would eat into the depths of his psyche.

Victoria threw the lance down, feeling nothing but contempt for the man she'd once loved.

'Get up, you worthless piece of shit. They've suffered enough because of you. The least you can do is stand up and face them.'

Chapter 76

Evans uncrossed his feet and took a sip of the fifteen year-old Balvenie he kept in his drawer for celebrating results. The whole team were gathered around him and each had a glass of the delicate Speyside malt.

Standing up, he raised his glass high. 'Lady and gentlemen. I'd like you to join me in raising a toast to Samantha Foulkes, one of the gutsiest young women I've ever met. You've all heard her story and I have to say her bravery astounds me.' He raised his glass above his head. 'Samantha Foulkes.'

Every member of the team joined in with the toast and echoed Evans's sentiments with toasts of their own.

The family liaison officer had called from the hospital to say that Samantha and Kyle had undergone a full examination. Apart from Samantha's broken finger and a few minor scrapes and bruises, they were nothing more than a little undernourished. Kyle would see a child psychologist for a few months, but the report indicated he was coping remarkably well.

Evans, for once, felt satisfied. Lauren had made short work of extracting a full confession from the lecherous fool who'd been wearing the Tony Blair mask. The other three had refused to speak without a lawyer, but the evidence they had against them would ensure none of them would escape a lengthy jail sentence.

Chisholm had documented proof the money had ended up in the account of a Stephen Harper from Lancaster. The Home Office Large Major Enquiry System had identified Harper as a dubious businessman. The accompanying surveillance pictures of Harper matched those of the man calling himself Keith Morgan. After talking over some options with Chisholm, Evans decided to leave the money in Harper's account. To remove it would weaken the case against him. Armed with a name and address, Chisholm had run some traces on Harper, and found another bank account in his name. He used this account as the source for the £95,000 that would be returned to all the contributing bank accounts. Learning from his earlier mistake, he set the programme in motion and once the money was taken from Harper's second account reduced the usage figures so that there would be no red flags raised at the server farms.

Tempted as he was to go down to Lancaster and arrest Harper himself, Evans knew doing so would cause friction with Lancashire police. Instead he'd agreed with Campbell and had asked the Lancashire CID to make the arrest. They had been delighted to have the opportunity.

'Right then. You buggers listening?' Evans stood and four sets of baggy eyes looked his way.

'I'm gonna call in the brass and lay the whole thing out to them. As far as the money's concerned I'll tell them it's from an anonymous benefactor. All you need to say if you're asked is that *I* arranged it. I'll deal with any questions after that. Understood?' There was a murmur of acknowledgements. 'And thanks for trusting me with your careers. It wasn't an easy decision for any of you, but it paid off.'

Evans knew he wouldn't be popular for calling Greg Hadley at three in the morning, but still he picked up the phone.

A sleep filled voice answered him. 'Hadley. Who is it?'

'Greg, it's He-Man. You're never gonna believe what I've got to tell you.'

A Novella from Graham Smith
featuring DI Harry Evans

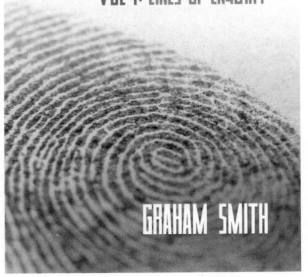

ISBN: 978-1-910720-28-8

£4.99